CW01099979

IT SHOULD HAVE BEEN YOU

www.penguin.co.uk

IT SHOULD HAVE BEEN YOU

Andrea Mara

bantam

TRANSWORLD PUBLISHERS
Penguin Random House, One Embassy Gardens,
8 Viaduct Gardens, London SW11 7BW
www.penguin.co.uk

Transworld is part of the Penguin Random House group of companies
whose addresses can be found at global.penguinrandomhouse.com

First published in Great Britain in 2025 by Bantam
an imprint of Transworld Publishers

A CIP catalogue record for this book
is available from the British Library.

ISBNs
9780857505873 (cased)
9780857505880 (tpb)

Typeset in 11.5/15.5 pt ITC Giovanni Std by Jouve (UK), Milton Keynes
Printed and bound in Great Britain by Clays Ltd, Elcograf S.p.A.

The authorized representative in the EEA is Penguin Random House Ireland,
Morrison Chambers, 32 Nassau Street, Dublin D02 YH68.

For Elissa, with love

Prologue

I HAVE TO KILL my sister.

I can't. I can't do this.

I glance across the kitchen.

I have to. I have no choice.

My face is wet, my throat is bone dry. There's a buzzing inside my head, the sound of abject terror.

'Do it,' my sister says in a croaky whisper, as if it's that simple, as if killing her is something I can do.

She's my family, my blood, one of the three people I love most in the world.

Tears slide down her face. Greta never cries. She's the strong one, the practical one. And now I have to do something unforgiveable.

From outside comes the sound of fireworks. The Oakpark summer party. Our neighbours eating and drinking on the green, oblivious to what's happening in my kitchen.

'I love you so much.' My voice is hoarse, my limbs are loose. 'I'm so sorry.'

The sky lights up with fireworks as she rolls up her sleeve.

My throat contracts with grief.

I lean towards her, Death come to take her. A sob lurches through me.

The syringe feels like nothing. It should feel cold or hot or heavy, something to signify the power it holds, but it doesn't. It's light and nothingy. I glance around the kitchen one more time. How is this happening? Everything looks just as it always does. The scratched wooden table of our childhood, the blue-painted cupboards, the knotty hardwood floors.

My hand shakes as I inch the tip of the needle towards my sister's vein. She closes her eyes.

'I'm sorry,' I say again, and push the syringe, flooding her blood with poison.

To my horror, it's instantaneous. As the dusky sky lights pink and gold to the pop of fireworks, Greta slips sideways and slides off the chair. Her prone figure on my kitchen floor. In seconds, it's over.

Ten days is all it took for my world to implode. Ten days, four deaths, one teen in hospital, one in police custody, my family destroyed.

And all because of a text.

1

Susan

Tuesday, nine days earlier

HAVE YOU EVER DONE something stupid – something unintentional, acting without thinking? You have, I'm sure; we all have. And then afterwards, you pull at your hair and wonder why you didn't slow down and think first? Of course, by then, it's too late. The damage is done.

This is about my mistake.

And it starts with a screenshot. Well, a screenshot accompanied by an uncharacteristically mean message. At least, I like to *think* it was uncharacteristic. Maybe that's just something I tell myself, because I got caught. But when it all kicks off, I'm not thinking at all. I'm cranky and sleep-deprived and ready to do battle with anyone crossing my path. That's a metaphorical path – I'm at home on my couch, under my four-month-old baby, staring at a just-out-of-reach cooling cup of tea. The walls have been closing in over the last few weeks and I'm irritable. Missing my pre-baby structure, the outside world, the old me. And every time that thought bobs to the surface, the guilt sets in. My beautiful Bella. I adore her, of course I do, but still. I miss . . . me. And I'm tired. Have I mentioned the tired? The up-six-times-a-night tired? *Nothing* prepares you. And last night was a bad one. And then of course Jon is at work all day (which is fair, he has to go to work) and I'm trying to get Bella to nap, and she won't and it's hard. And I'm a little scared too in the last few weeks, just a little, that things will go back to how they were when Bella was born. Back when I didn't cope very well at all.

So yeah, I'm cross and sleep-deprived and ready to do battle, and that's when I see the message in the Oakpark WhatsApp group. Oakpark – where we live – is a huge housing estate built in the sixties, with criss-crossing roads and cul-de-sacs and about three hundred members in the neighbourhood messaging group. It's very useful for passing on furniture and borrowing hedge trimmers. It also has occasional open-the-popcorn dramas when something kicks off. I secretly like those moments.

I never planned to cause one.

The message is from Celeste Geary, mistress of pointy comments. Badly parked cars and barking dogs are her pet peeves, but this evening, it's about WhatsApp group etiquette. Another resident has shared information about a local business loaning glasses for next week's Oakpark summer party, someone else has thanked them, and I've chimed in with my thanks too. (I'm trapped under a baby, so responding to people on Whats-App is one of my top three hobbies.) Celeste's missive comes moments later:

General note: there's no need for multiple people to thank everyone who posts, the group has 300 members, and we all lead busy lives. I appreciate that some are busier than others, but please think before you type.

She's not even the admin of the group, she just takes it upon herself to write posts like this. I read her message again and my cheeks flame. As the second and only other responder, I'm clearly the target. The 'busier than others' part, a dig, no doubt, at my maternity leave, or maybe even my job. I'm a teacher. And nothing annoys people more than the supposedly short hours teachers work. Celeste, something big in a bank, with her frequent travel and airtight schedule, hadn't taken more than a minute's maternity leave when her kids were born. That's according to my sister Greta, who's lived in Oakpark her whole life. And it's Greta and my other sister, Leesa, I text, with a screenshot of Celeste's message, my cheeks still hot:

omg she's such a smug wagon. I'd love to send her the pics of her husband wrapped around the PR girl at the opening party for Bar Four. Or tell her that her bratty daughter bunks off school to see her boyfriend. And that everyone knows she covered up what her son did to the Fitzpatrick toddler. That would wipe the pass-agg smile off her face. Urgh. I know. I'm awful. I just needed to get that out of my system.

I throw the phone beside me on the couch and let out an irritated sigh. Everything is annoying me. This room, where I now spend most of my time. The deep-blue walls that looked so good when we first painted them. The velvet ochre couch that cost a small fortune. The cooling cup of tea on the coffee table, mocking me. At this point, the South Dublin water pipes are mostly filled with my cold tea. In the crook of my left arm, Bella nuzzles in, her tiny eyelashes fluttering in sleep. Seven o'clock. Sleep this late is a terrible idea, but god, I can't bring myself to wake her.

Beside me, my phone buzzes and, at the same time, I hear the sound of the front door. *Oh, thank god.* Now Jon can take the baby and I can get a shower or do laundry or any one of the myriad things I've dreamt of doing all day. Imagine dreaming of doing laundry.

My phone buzzes again as Jon comes through to the living

room. His eyes crinkle into a smile and he bends to kiss the top of my head, sweat glistening on his forehead from his post-work run. Running is new. He started about six weeks ago and has become completely obsessed. He's already lean and wiry, so I don't think it's a fitness concern, despite what he claims – I have a sneaking suspicion it's a response to Bella's birth. A kind of early midlife crisis, a sense that he's suddenly adult and old. If you could see him, you'd laugh at that – he's thirty-eight, but with boyish looks and a bouncy energy that make him seem much younger. I get it though. Having Bella has changed both of us.

'How're my girls?'

'OK.' I wriggle forward on the couch until I can stand, trying not to disturb Bella, then pass her into Jon's arms.

'Oh, I was going to shower first and—'

I cut him off. 'No chance. I've been waiting for a shower since this morning.'

He knows better than to argue. That's when my phone begins to ring. Nobody ever rings. Greta, Leesa and I text all day, my friends text, my mother-and-baby group send voice notes, because nobody has time to type. I turn over the phone. Greta's name flashes onscreen.

'Hey, what's up?'

'Your message. Delete. *Delete!*'

Greta is the calm one, so to hear her shrieking down the phone unnerves me.

'What? Why?'

'Your message about Celeste. You sent it to the whole Oak-park group. I've been texting you. Delete!'

Fuck. Fumbling, I click into WhatsApp. Oh god. In the pit of my stomach, everything flips. Greta is right. My blood runs cold. I've sent the screenshot and my bitchy message about

Celeste to the entire group. *No, no, no . . . please say I'm wrong.* My words stare back at me. I'm not wrong. I've sent it to all three hundred members. Including Celeste.

'Susan, make sure you click "Delete for Everyone", not just "Delete for Me", or it'll be there for ever!' Greta is shouting down the line.

All fingers and thumbs, I hit delete. How many people have seen it? Has Celeste seen it? *Shit. Shit. Shit.*

Greta is still on the line, her voice distant, barely audible through the blood pounding in my ears. Jon is asking what's wrong and Bella is awake and beginning to cry. Before I can process or explain what I've done, I manage to knock my full cup of cold tea all across the living-room floor. *Oh, for god's sake, can things get any worse?*

As it happens, things are about to get much, much worse.

2

Susan
Tuesday

MY MESSAGE SPREADS LIKE wildfire. In the ten minutes between sending it and deleting it, dozens and dozens of Oakpark residents have seen it, and many, it turns out, have taken screenshots and sent those on to friends. On a slow-news Tuesday in July, this is the quintessential open-the-popcorn moment. Updates on the screenshot-spread reach me via Greta, who has seen it in her hockey coach group, and Leesa, who has seen it in her school mum group. Replies and follow-up posts appear in the Oakpark group and I give silent thanks for my relative anonymity – my display name is 'SO'D' and my profile picture is a daisy. But still, as I read them, I'm absolutely mortified and sick with guilt:

Uh oh, wrong group, I think?

I think he or she meant this for someone else . . .

Who is SO'D? Apt initials ☺

opens popcorn

Guys, this isn't funny, it's not fair on Celeste. I've seen screenshots shared in other groups now, people need to think before they post.

Yeah, especially SO'D

Anyone know who SO'D is? Bad form, whoever it is.

And from Celeste: nothing.

I put my face in my hands. How the hell had I sent it to the whole group instead of to my sisters?

'I've done it – we've all done it,' Jon says, reading my mind and rubbing my back. Bella is on his shoulder now, whimpering sporadically. We're both ignoring the spilt tea. 'Remember when I was moaning about the cost of the trip to Spain and sent it to the lads' group instead of you?'

I love him for trying, but it's not the same. Jon's gang have been friends for ever and the banter is a daily ritual. That's not *this*. Jesus Christ, I mentioned Celeste's kids. Teenagers. And I'm their teacher. A grown woman, a secondary-school teacher, bitching about teenagers. What had I called Nika? Bratty. *Oh god.*

'Would it make sense to call Celeste?' Jon suggests, laying Bella gently in her Moses basket, soother in her mouth. 'To apologize?'

'Oh god, I can't bear the thought of that. Maybe it'll all blow over. She might not even know it's me.'

Jon takes a bottle of Glenmorangie from the cupboard under the TV. 'If she has your number saved in her contacts, she'll know it's you. And realistically, you're her kids' teacher and you live in the same estate . . . I'm guessing she has your number saved.'

He pours whiskey into two tumblers. 'Or someone will tell her. She's good pals with Juliette next door, isn't she? And obviously since Juliette has your phone number, she'll have seen that it was you . . .'

I want to cry. 'This is going to make parent–teacher meetings horrendous.'

'Well, that's why it might be worth calling her now, get it over with.' He hands me a whiskey. 'Medicinal.'

Bella starts to whimper and Jon gets up to put the soother back in her mouth.

'Why can't you be the kind of husband who tells me to put my head in the sand and doesn't make me do hard things?' I smile to stop myself crying and he kisses the top of my head as he sits back down, Bella now settled again with her beloved soother.

The drink is welcome, the strong taste a distraction. Jon is right: I need to bite the bullet and apologize. Deep breath. I take another sip of whiskey and pick up my phone. Taking responsibility must surely count for something . . .

Celeste isn't in my contacts so I go back to the Oakpark group to get her number. The replies are still streaming in, including calls for people to stop replying and move on. Mostly, though, they are posts about me – asking who 'SO'D' is, asking me to apologize, asking for me to be expelled from the group. I feel hot and sick. This is the last thing I want. I'm not confrontational; I hate arguments. With shaking hands, I save Celeste's number and before I can chicken out I hit call.

No answer.

She must know it's me. I try once more anyway, out of a sense of duty more than any real hope that she'll pick up. And of course, in all honesty, the coward in me doesn't want her to answer. What am I going to say? Sorry for telling the truth? No, the best course of action is to leave the group and never speak of this again.

Unfortunately, leaving the group doesn't stop the replies – direct messages now, coming straight to me. People who don't know who SO'D is but take the time to reply privately. People telling me I'm a disgrace, Celeste is hurt, her children are upset. I've dropped a bomb, and everyone, faux moralizing notwithstanding, is loving the drama.

'What am I going to do if they find out that SO'D in the group is Susan O'Donnell, local teacher?' I ask Jon, once Bella's settled upstairs and we're back on the couch.

A grimace. 'I'd say it's more of a when than an if . . .'

As capital cities go, Dublin isn't exactly anonymous. And South Dublin is no different to any other area – through a network of schools and sports clubs and housing estates, everyone knows everyone.

I google my own name. Nothing much comes up – there are multiple Susan O'Donnells on Facebook and LinkedIn, but I'm not on social media under my own name, and you have to scroll a good bit before you find anything. I'm listed as a teacher on the Rathwood Park website, and there's a mention in an online magazine about a charity dinner I went to with Jon, though I'm not pictured – it's just Jon looking cute in a tux, presenting a cheque to the charity organizer. There are also, I remember, with a curl of anxiety, the posts on the parenting forum back when things were bad. I don't want to think about what I wrote there. But they're not under my own name, so nobody could know it's me.

'Set up a Google Alert,' Jon says, offering me the Glenmorangie bottle. 'That way, if your name gets out online, you'll see it.'

I'm not sure Google Alerts can pick up gossip from social media, but there's nothing to lose so I do as he suggests, waving away the whiskey – the last thing I need is a fuzzy head and a phone in my hand. He pours one for himself and, just as he settles back on the couch, my phone beeps with a text:

You should be ashamed of yourself. A teacher bitching about children. Someone should pass this to your principal.

So at least one person knows 'SO'D' is a teacher. Brilliant. And I have only myself to blame.

*

Just after midnight, I go to bed, with Jon following a few minutes later. We don't speak or turn on lamps, not with Bella in the crib in our room, but Jon is still on his phone half an hour later, its glow irritating me as I lie here trying to sleep. It's not really the phone keeping me awake, of course, it's the guilt and the worry. I keep thinking and hoping it will all blow over by morning, that people will find some other drama to entertain them. But what if it doesn't? What if word reaches the school? Could I be in trouble? Possibly . . . If I wasn't a teacher, it would be easier. But rightly or wrongly, we're held to a higher standard. And quite apart from the worry, I feel horribly guilty. Nika, Celeste's daughter, is not my favourite kid in the class, and Cody, the son, is hard work – however *nothing* justifies what I said in the text.

Exhaustion eventually takes over, and I close my eyes.

Then comes the crash.

3

Susan

Tuesday night

BLOOD POUNDING IN MY ears, I bolt upright. *Jesus Christ.* It takes a second to process, but the noise, the crash – somehow, it came from inside the room. Adrenaline floods my body. I shout Jon's name and jump out of bed, rushing to a wailing Bella, and it's only when I have her safely in my arms that I start to understand what's happened. Something's hit the window. Something's *smashed* the window.

Jon is up now too and yanking back the blind as Bella soothes in my arms, her crying dropping to a whimper. A spider's web of cracks radiates from a hole at the centre of the window. Jon waves me back, shouting about broken glass. *Oh my god, did any of it hit Bella?* Back by the bed, I switch on the lamp and check her over, then check again. She seems unharmed. But the glass could have landed anywhere. The stone or brick or whatever was thrown could have hit her. The whole window could have caved in. *God.* My throat is tight with what-might-have-beens and I pull her close. All the old feelings flare up. The fear that she's in danger, that I'm a bad mother, that I'm the one who'll hurt her. Tears threaten as Jon pulls the blind back further, trying to look out without getting too close to the glass. We both hear it then – the sound of a car somewhere nearby. There's nothing to see though. Maybe it's gone from Oakpark already? Out to the main road?

Jon carefully lowers the base of the blind and neither of us speaks as he backs away from the window and bends to pick something up. A brick. Someone's thrown a brick through our window. Making his way over to me, Jon checks the Ring doorbell app on his phone, but whoever smashed the window was too far back to pick up on the camera. Onscreen, it looks like a normal night in suburbia – dark, but with streetlights and security lights, never quite pitch black. Quiet. Safe. Until now.

I take Bella to the smaller guest room, a room that looks out on the back garden, and keep her in the bed with me while Jon calls Blackrock garda station to report what's happened. His words filter in from the landing, low and urgent.

It was probably kids, he says in a whisper when he climbs into bed – teens from the school, friends of Nika or Cody, maybe. The guard he spoke with had given him an email address, in case we had any more trouble. More trouble – the idea makes me feel sick . . . I close my eyes, but all hope of sleep is gone.

On Wednesday morning, Jon calls a glazier and suggests he stay home to let me catch up on sleep. This catch-up-on-sleep offer is new, and very sweet, and also straight out of our last counselling session. Nobody else knows about the marriage counselling, and it's not a big deal, not really, but there's been a little distance between us since Bella came along. Distance is normal, my friends say; the baby is everything for a while. But coupled with my own problems when she was born, I got worried. So six weeks ago, I booked us in for marriage counselling. More of a multivitamin to help than a medicine to cure – that's how I explained it to Jon. We tell my sisters it's physio any time we need a babysitter. Physio for post-partum something or other – they glaze over and don't ask. And to be honest, I wasn't sure the counselling was really helping, but this offer to stay home today is definitely a step in the right direction.

Anyway, I tell him to go to work – Greta is calling around to keep me company while I wait for the glazier, and I wouldn't sleep anyway, even if he did stay home. I can never sleep during the day – the whole 'nap when baby naps' thing is wasted on me – and it's particularly unlikely today after everything that's happened. So Jon leaves, frowning at something on his phone, lost in the world of work already, just as Greta arrives.

Greta conveniently lives right next door in number 28 Oakpark, our childhood home. Our two houses couldn't be more different though – Greta has fully modernized number 28, a world away from the pine-and-lino house in which we grew up. Now it's all light-tiled floors, marble worktops, and bright white walls. Minimalist, practical, no frills – just like Greta. She lives alone and has turned my old room into a home gym and Leesa's old room into an office. There's still a guest room too, in case I ever need a break from Jon's snoring, she sometimes says, with a grin. Jon has some flaws – putting butter-encrusted knives directly on the counter, leaving coffee cups lying around – but snoring, thankfully, is not one of them.

Our house, meanwhile, is a little shabbier around the edges than Greta's. Good shabby, I think. Jon and I bought it from my old neighbours four years ago, and I was delighted to return to Oakpark. When we moved in, we stripped the carpets and sanded down the original floorboards, so throughout the house the floors are a yellowy, knotty oak that's not in style but feels warm and homely. The walls are mostly dark blues and greens, with prints and tapestries from pre-baby trips to Bali and Thailand and Cape Town. The kitchen is teal-painted wood, with a row of battered copper pots hanging from the ceiling. The kitchen table is the one from my childhood, passed on to me by Greta when she replaced it a few years ago, the scratched wooden surface engraved by our childhood pens. That's where we sit now, waiting for the glazier.

Greta is in her usual tracksuit bottoms and trainers, and a plain navy T-shirt with 'Coach' in white letters across the back, her curly red hair tied in a high ponytail. Her cross-body bag clinks as she slings it over the back of a chair, bottles of supplements and tablets jostling inside. She reaches to take Bella from my arms and I brave switching on my phone.

Six new messages, all from people saying I shouldn't be allowed to teach. People *love* a bit of outrage, even when they've no skin in the game. I'm half tempted to delete WhatsApp, but then I'd be cut off from Jon and my sisters and friends too, so I block the senders and close my phone just as the doorbell rings.

I get up to answer, but it isn't the expected glazier, it's Juliette Sullivan, who lives next-door on the other side. My heart sinks. Juliette, who also happens to be BFFs with Celeste Geary.

'Susan!' she says. 'Just checking you're OK after' – gleaming white teeth dent her plump lower lip in performative hesitation – 'well, after your message last night?'

I force a smile. 'Absolutely fine, thanks for checking.'

'Good! And look, I'm sure loads of people don't even know it was you.' She beams benevolently. 'I mean, obviously, *I* have your number, so I knew. "Poor Susan," I thought, and poor Celeste, of course.' A headshake. 'And I suppose most people on this road would know it's you, and people whose kids you teach might save down your number over the years, so *they'll* know. But honestly, I'm sure literally half or maybe a third of the people in the Oakpark group don't know it was you. You'll be fine!'

Oh god, she's loving this. All I want to do is close the door in her face, but I'm in enough trouble already.

'Can I do anything?' she adds, tilting her head in faux sympathy.

'Unless you have a time machine, probably not . . .' Something strikes me then. 'Actually, I don't suppose you saw anything last night – someone smashed our window around half twelve?' I crane my neck and point at the wall that divides Juliette's driveway from ours. 'I reckon they took a loose brick from the top there, where it's damaged.'

'Oh my goodness!' Her eyes gleam. 'I *did* hear a noise late last night – looked out and saw someone getting into a car.' She tucks a long, glossy strand of dark hair behind her ear. 'I couldn't make out any details though, too dark, and I didn't think anything of it. Goodness. Someone broke your window? Do you think it was because of your message?'

'Probably kids messing.' I take a step back. 'Right, I'd better get back to Bella.'

She puts her hand on the door jamb. 'I'll be seeing Celeste for dinner at hers on Sunday, I'll be sure to check she's OK and let her know how awful you feel. But don't beat yourself up. It could happen to *anyone*.'

Her face says it absolutely could *not* happen to anyone, only an idiot like Susan O'Donnell. I nod and smile and shut the door.

When I return to the kitchen, Greta is staring at her phone, a worried look on her face.

'What is it?' I ask, sitting down again.

She slides her phone across the grainy tabletop, her hand on Bella's head to shield her from the surface as she leans forward.

'I think you should see this.'

4

Susan
Wednesday

I SWIVEL HER PHONE to look. Facebook. *It's made it to Facebook?*
'I don't think I want to . . .'
'I think you should. Someone in a local buy-and-sell group
doxed you. They've shared the screenshot, your phone number,
your postal address, and suggested people might like to email
your principal.'
My stomach drops. 'How could they have got that information?'
'Well, everyone in the Oakpark WhatsApp group can see
your phone number, and any of them who know you in real
life know who "SO'D" is and which house you live in . . .' She
trails off, biting her lip. 'It's shit, I know. People with too much
time on their hands. Look, it'll be old news by tomorrow.' Even
Greta, ever practical Greta, doesn't sound convinced.
How is this happening? Why do people care so much? If I
was in *any* other job, this would have blown over by now. But
people – some people, anyway – like to get a dig in at teachers
when they can. To get up on high horses, to get all 'won't someone think of the children'. A little voice inside my head reminds
me that, this time, maybe they have a point.

*

When the doorbell chimes again, I check the Ring app. A familiar red uniform fills the screen – a delivery. My heart lifts just the tiniest bit. Packages cheer me up. I know that sounds shallow, but the anticipation of a delivery has got me through many a fraught day in the last four months and I'm waiting for some skincare stuff I ordered last week. By the time I get to the door, the courier has gone, but the package is waiting for me, tucked behind a pot of pink hydrangeas on the porch. A brown box, a familiar logo. My briefly lifted mood dips. Sighing, I carry the box through to the kitchen counter.

'Anything nice?' Greta asks, looking up from her phone, Bella still cradled in her arms.

'Undoubtedly, but sadly not for me.'

She squints at the logo. 'Sézane. What's that? Something for Jon?'

'Nope, worse.' I sit back down at the table. 'It's for my alter ego, the beautiful Savannah Holmes.'

Greta tilts her head. 'OK, you have an alter ego now? Have you been on the wine?'

'It's a long story.'

It's not a long story, but it *will* earn me an eyeroll.

'Go on, I have loads of time. I don't have to be at hockey camp until this afternoon.'

She's trying to distract me from the text drama, and I love her for it.

'Here though' – she adds, passing Bella carefully into my arms – 'take this one for a sec.' She rummages in her bag and pulls out two lots of pills – one brown bottle, one cheerful orange-and-purple container. She pops a supplement into her mouth, then a tablet. She takes a *lot* of supplements and chastises me regularly for taking none.

'Right, go on?'

'So, you know the other Oakpark, down the N11 towards Loughlinstown?'

Greta rolls her eyes. 'You know I wrote to the council about that?'

In the midst of all that's going on, this makes me smile. Greta is generally calm and largely unruffled by the kind of minor frustrations that get to me – very much a don't-sweat-the-small-stuff kind of person. So it's surprising to hear she'd taken the time to write to the council over something like this. Then again, she has a history with the council . . . a memory that makes me deeply uncomfortable. I push it away.

'Did they reply?' I ask.

'No!'

I *adore* that this surprised her. 'It probably isn't the biggest issue on their agenda.'

She folds her arms. 'Who on earth thinks giving two housing estates the same name is a good idea? I mean—'

I decide to cut her off before the rant escalates. 'Anyway, the woman who lives at the same address as ours – 26 Oakpark – is called Savannah Holmes. I get her packages sometimes and she gets mine.'

Greta's eyebrows arch. 'Eh, how often is this happening? I've had maybe two packages that went to the other Oakpark in the last three years.'

'Yeah, I'd say Savannah and I have similar online shopping hobbies . . .'

Greta tsks. As the anti-fast-fashion member of the family, she has never understood my weakness for shopping.

'It's mostly stuff for Bella,' I say, faux defensiveness masking actual defensiveness. 'Babygros and bibs.'

'And what does Savannah buy?' She nods towards the package.

'ME+EM, Sézane, Reiss, and one time I opened a parcel by

accident and it was a Marc Jacobs tote bag. I googled it and they're, like, €300. Imagine.'

Greta, who's had the same black leather bag for twenty years, shakes her head.

'So yeah, Savannah lives quite a different life to me.' I look down at my outfit. Ancient denim shorts, a tank top I got in Oasis before the shops closed down, and a muslin cloth over my shoulder.

'Maybe she's sitting in the other Oakpark right now with a baby on her knee, as her Marc Jacobs bag gathers dust.' Greta is nothing if not loyal.

'Nope. Here, look.' I tap into Instagram and type Savannah's name. This is definitely more appealing than worrying about my screenshot drama. 'See? She's roughly the same age as me, but no kids. She works in banking and lives on her own. She spends a lot of time at the gym, takes luxury all-inclusive holidays, loves clothes, eats out a lot, and has an allergy she posts about to raise awareness.'

A thoughtful expression settles across Greta's face. 'You got all that from Instagram?'

'Yep. There aren't many Savannahs around, even in South Dublin. And she *looks* like a Savannah.' I turn my phone again to show her. Like me, Savannah has dark, shoulder-length hair, but where mine is usually shoved in a ponytail, hers is glossy, highlighted and well maintained. And while I stick on some CC cream before facing the world, Savannah has the skills of a professional make-up artist – contouring and dotting like she's Charlotte Tilbury herself. Yes, I know far too much about this person.

'She's very pretty,' Greta says. 'Why is she doing her make-up on Instagram?'

'She just does the occasional get-ready-with-me post.'

'And you're watching all of this?' She's shaking her head, but she's also searching for Savannah's account on her phone.

'Eh, pot, kettle?' I point at her screen. 'And speaking of kettles . . . tea?'

'Yeah, go on, thanks.'

I make green tea for her and a coffee for me, all one-handed with Bella on my shoulder.

Greta is still scrolling Savannah's page. She stops on a make-up reel.

I lean in to see. 'It's a great account to follow for product recs.'

Greta looks up at me.

'I tried the retinol she recommends in this,' I add, 'but weirdly, it's disappeared. I'm waiting for a new one.'

Greta shakes her head.

'Stop judging!' I punch her shoulder lightly. 'Anyway, following Savannah is genuinely educational – she posts a lot about her tree-nut allergy and one of the girls in my tutor class has a tree-nut allergy. So I'm not just here for the make-up.'

Greta looks unconvinced.

'I'm *serious*! You wouldn't believe how many things contain nuts – Oh.' I go cold as it hits me. 'Actually, it's Nika Geary who has the allergy. Celeste's daughter.' *'Bratty' daughter.* 'God, that bloody message. I'm such an idiot.'

Greta puts her phone down. 'Yeah, there's something else about Nika Geary you should know . . .'

'Oh no, what now?'

She fiddles with the lid of her pill bottle. Is she avoiding eye contact?

'Actually, it's not important, I'll fill you in another time.' She pushes back her chair. 'I'd better go, I've to do paperwork before I go down to hockey camp.' She gives me a quick half-hug.

Greta is not tactile, and this takes me by surprise. 'Turn off your phone,' she adds as she leaves.

I watch from the sitting-room window as she walks down our driveway, phone clamped to her ear, and I do as she suggests and switch off mine.

Just before 10 a.m., the drama escalates. I'd switched back on my phone in case Jon was trying to reach me, and it almost jumped off the table, buzzing and chirping with notifications, including a text from a number I don't know:

You got away lightly last night. You deserve to die for that message and what it's done.

And even though it's the kind of keyboard-warrior empty threat I've heard about on social media, there's something about seeing it here on my own phone – directed at me – that sends a sick feeling snaking through me.

I blink back tears. Why would I deserve to die? Someone having a bad day and taking it out on me? Or has my message triggered something I don't know about? And what does 'you got away lightly last night' mean? The broken window? Maybe the text is from kids at the school, assuming that's who threw the brick? God, imagine the glee in some quarters of the pupil cohort, getting their hands on a teacher's phone number. They already do whatever they can to find us on social media, which is exactly why I use a made-up name online. Now that they have my phone number, all bets are off. A small part of me feels stung, hurt. I've always prided myself on being firm-but-fair. I genuinely thought I was reasonably well liked. Nobody is liked by everyone, I suppose, and never has that been clearer than now.

I send a screenshot to the email address the guard gave

Jon last night and try calling Jon, but it goes to voicemail. Just then, a calendar notification reminds me that I've overlooked an appointment, one I'd been dreading, yet completely forgotten. Maybe this is my out? On autopilot, I snooze the notification and sit in my kitchen, trying to order my thoughts. My eyes keep going back to my phone, to the text. If this happened to anyone else, I'd tell them to ignore it, but it's different when it happens to you. It's weird and uncomfortable and upsetting and kind of scary. I'm lost in a spiral of confused thoughts when my calendar reminder pops up again. I really don't want to leave the house. I don't want to go anywhere or do anything. But that's what happened the last time, back when Bella was new and I was failing. And that's why I need to go.

5

Susan
Wednesday

I TEXT GRETA, but she's out and can't babysit. I rarely ask her –
she has Long Covid, which means good days and bad days, so
I keep requests to a minimum. Her text is brief – 'sorry, can't,
am out' – which isn't odd in itself, Greta can be terse, but it's
strange that she didn't mention anything when she was leaving my house earlier – I'm nearly sure she'd said she was going
home to do paperwork? Maybe the call she got when she was
leaving pulled her away to something.

I figure I'll ask Leesa instead. Unlike Greta and me, Leesa
doesn't live in Oakpark. She lives *all* the way across in Rowanpark, a ten-minute walk away. Meaning the three of us are back
living where we grew up. Our twenty-year-old selves would
have baulked at the term 'home birds', yet here we are. Leesa's
not starting work till two today, I think, as I text. She has the
best work–life balance of anyone I've ever known. Made redun-
dant from her IT job three years ago, she now contracts for the
same company that let her go (with a very good pay-out) doing
however many or few hours she likes, for an eyewatering hourly
rate, and always from home. With all this post-pandemic
work from home going on, I'm starting to regret my career in

25

teaching. Leesa replies 'of course' to my babysitting request, so at eleven, I drop Bella into her and go to see my counsellor.

Two hours later, emotionally drained, I collect Bella from Leesa's and walk home along a route that takes me past Celeste Geary's house. I'm not sure why. Maybe the likes-to-be-liked side of me is hoping for forgiveness. That Celeste might pop her head out the door, tell me it's all a fuss over nothing, and wave absolution. *If only.* Hers is one of the bigger homes in Oakpark – a five-bedroom double-fronted house with room for three or four cars in the driveway, though right now there are none. Twin camellia trees bookend granite porch steps that lead up to a heavy sage-green front door. The blinds on each window are drawn three-quarters way down and I get the sense nobody's home. Celeste will be at work, of course, and Warren too. My mind goes back to the last time I saw him. His secret dalliance at the opening of Bar Four. Not so secret now, thanks to me. My cheeks heat up and I push the pram towards home.

As I reach our driveway, I have the sudden sensation that someone is watching me. My head swivels side to side. I'm still the hot topic of the neighbourhood, so maybe someone *is* looking out their window right now, judging me. That's not it though . . . it's more than that. I pick up my pace to get Bella's pram up the driveway. The broken upstairs window gleams in the sun and I wonder now if that's what's causing it. Because, last night, somebody *was* actually watching, right here, in our driveway. As I fumble in my bag for my key, unnerved and eager to get inside, a shadow falls over me. I jump, and spin around, heart racing.

Right behind me, there's a man; tall, bearded, with a cap pulled low over his forehead. He nods a greeting.

'Jon Mullane live here? Called looking for a glazier?'

I nod, give a shaky smile, and let out a breath.

When the glazier leaves, I tip my half-eaten lunch into the bin and settle on the couch to feed Bella, thinking back over all of it. One thing jumps out now: Greta's comment just before she left this morning.

There's something else about Nika Geary.

What did she mean? I know Nika; I've taught her over the years. She's confident, glossy, popular, polite. Polite with a hint of . . . fake. A sense that behind the beaming smile, she's quietly laughing at you. I text Greta to ask her, but she doesn't reply. It's three, though; she'll be out on the pitch at the camp she runs. I send a second text, asking her to call in on her way home.

On Google now, my face heating up as I imagine anyone seeing me, I type Nika Geary's name. All her socials are private, and part of me is glad – snooping on a pupil's Snapchat or TikTok feels like a step too far. She comes up on our school website, for Student of the Year in first year, Spirit of the School in second year, and Sportsperson of the Year in third year. No prizes in fourth year or fifth year; maybe her halo slipped. Other mentions for hockey wins, but nothing that tells me what Greta meant.

The next search result is from Hollypark, her primary school, the same one my nieces, Aoife and Maeve, used to go to. I click into a sixth class graduation photo and spot Nika in the front row, and something snags at my memory – something familiar about her in that uniform . . . It hits me now: not often, but occasionally, in Leesa's house, Nika was there. Of course. She was friends with Maeve. Not any more though, I don't think I've ever seen them together in secondary. Does that mean something? Greta will fill me in later, I'm sure.

*

Just after five, Leesa calls in to see how I'm doing, followed soon by Greta. Leesa chatters while she makes tea, wondering about the mood in the Geary household, reassuring me that it will all blow over, raving about a film she saw, then speculating that Samir, her husband, might divorce her for watching it without him. Samir travels a lot for work and sometimes Leesa goes to the same film twice rather than confessing that she's already seen it. Greta is unusually quiet through all of this. I ask her if she's OK and she grimaces, shaking a bottle of pills. Code for bad day.

'Greta, what did you mean earlier when you said, "There's something else about Nika Geary"?'

Greta and Leesa exchange a glance so fleeting I almost miss it.

I look from one to the other. 'Come on, spill.'

Greta's eyes meet mine. 'Nika is part of the group that was bullying Maeve at school.'

'Oh.' I wonder briefly how Greta knows more than I do about who was bullying our niece, but she's always been extra close to Leesa's elder daughter. The first grandchild, though there were no grandparents to meet her, so Greta took that mantle. Aunt, godmother, stand-in grandparent, all in one.

Leesa nods. 'I didn't tell you because I knew Nika was in your form class and, no offence, but I didn't think you'd manage to stay neutral.'

'Too right, I'd have given her detention every time she so much as *moved* in class.'

'That's *exactly* why I didn't tell you.'

This makes no sense. 'Why are you protecting Nika Geary?'

'I was protecting *you*. You wouldn't have been able to stay impartial and then you'd have ended up in trouble.' She bites her lip. 'Hopefully nobody will think your message last night was a deliberate attempt to target Nika . . . because of Maeve, I mean . . .'

'Most people won't know Maeve is my niece or about the bullying. It's fine.'

It probably isn't fine. Then again, if Nika was involved in targeting Maeve, I don't feel so bad about calling her 'bratty'.

'Maeve's doing OK now, right?' I ask.

'I don't know. I don't think she'd tell me if she wasn't.'

'Aoife would tell you,' I reassure her. 'Like last time?'

My niece Aoife, Leesa's younger daughter, is thirteen going on thirty. She's no nonsense in a way you don't always see with thirteen-year-olds, which doesn't necessarily win her friends, but she doesn't seem to care. Long may it last, I always think, wishing I could have been more like that at her age. It was Aoife who realized what was happening to her older sister and told Leesa about it.

'Yeah,' Leesa says without any conviction at all.

I hit the kettle to make more tea and that's when it happens – a Google Alert pops up in my email:

Google Alert – 'Susan O'Donnell'

Murder in Oakpark, Susan O'Donnell dead

Blood rushes to my ears and the room sways. I reach for the counter to steady myself. *What the hell is this?* The words swim as I try to focus on the next line:

The woman found dead in Oakpark this morning is a second-ary school teacher who sent a defamatory message last night that went viral. Her name is Susan O'Donnell.

6

Susan
Wednesday

'OH MY GOD.'

'What is it?' Leesa asks, standing. Greta stands too.

I turn the phone to show them. Greta frowns and Leesa's eyes widen.

'It's not true, right, I *am* here in front of you?' My attempted laugh is shaky. There's something very chilling about reading of your own death even when you're clearly very much alive.

'You're here.' Leesa puts a hand on my arm. 'But how the hell did something like that end up online? Is someone trying to troll you?'

'I . . . I don't know.'

'It's real.'

Both of us turn towards Greta, who's holding up her phone. Leesa frowns. 'What?'

'There's . . . a real murder.' Greta's voice is hoarse. My usually unruffled sister is anxious and this compounds my unease.

Greta passes her phone and, together, Leesa and I read what's onscreen:

Gardaí are investigating the discovery of three bodies in two locations in South Dublin. A man and a woman were found dead

early this morning in a house in Waterview, Cherrywood, and in a separate incident, in nearby Oakpark, Loughlinstown, the body of a woman has been found. Names have not yet been released, and gardaí cannot say if there is a link between the discoveries.

Leesa's eyes widen. 'Oh my god, a murder here in Oakpark?'

'It's . . . it's the other Oakpark – the one in Loughlinstown.' It comes out in a whisper.

Leesa is clicking and scrolling. 'My god, I wonder what happened? I don't know why death always seems worse if it's nearby, but it does.'

Greta nods. 'Of course. It's scary when it's close to home. Like it could happen to us.'

'And that's . . . that's obviously it.' The pieces fall into place. 'Someone thinks this happened to me.'

I try to focus on the Google Alert, to make sense of it. *Deep breaths. Slow down.* I sit at the table and click into the message to read it properly. I can see now that the headline and the extract are from a post on MessageBoards.ie. It's a chat site a bit like Reddit, but resolutely Irish. The posters there are regular people, not journalists. *OK. OK.* I let out a breath. So, this is probably erroneous speculation rather than a deliberate attempt to troll me. Someone genuinely thinks I'm dead. But why? It seems like quite a leap to assume that the woman who sent the viral message is the murder victim, just because we both live in Oakpark.

Leesa and Greta are leaning in on either side of me, reading my phone.

'So it's a misunderstanding,' Leesa says, flopping into a chair. 'Probably not deliberate, right?'

I nod. Greta is quiet, wincing slightly as she lowers herself into her seat. 'I'll text Jon,' she says. 'In case he sees it and gets a shock.'

He doesn't use MessageBoards, but she's right, it's safer to let him know. And maybe when he told me to set up a Google Alert, he set one up too.

It's just six o'clock now, and I switch on the radio so we can listen to the news. The three murders make up the first headline. The two victims in Cherrywood are not yet named, but the victim in Oakpark is. And when I hear the newscaster identify her, my skin goes cold.

7

Susan
Wednesday

'THE BODY DISCOVERED EARLIER *today at 26 Oakpark Loughlinstown has been named as Savannah Holmes, a thirty-five-year-old woman who had been living in the area for two years. Gardaí say . . .'*

The news report continues, but I don't hear it. I'm stuck on her name.

Savannah Holmes.

'Oh my god.' My hand flies to my mouth.

'What is it?' Leesa startles. 'Are you OK?'

'Savannah Holmes . . .'

'What – do you know her?' Leesa asks.

I'm shaking my head. I don't know her. Not really. But still.

'Susan, what's going on?'

Greta, visibly pale, fills her in – the packages, the address, the alter ego conversation – which now seems silly and trite.

I slide down in my chair, sagging against the back.

'So you *did* kind of know her,' Leesa says, eyes wide.

'We'd texted about misdelivered packages, arranging for them to be picked up and re-delivered. I dropped them off myself at her porch a couple of times. And . . . I suppose I liked living her life vicariously, through her purchases and her Instagram. A kind of one-sided bond that was all in my head.'

Leesa nods. 'You connected with her. I get it.'

Greta purses her lips. Clearly, she does not get it.

'I guess she had the life I might have, if I wasn't walking around with a muslin cloth on my shoulder,' I explain. 'If I was that kind of person – beautiful and poised and glamorous.'

Beautiful and poised and glamorous and dead. I google the story, and her photo comes up now, a familiar one from Instagram, and suddenly, I feel like crying.

Grim-faced, Greta rubs my shoulder. Leesa takes over making tea.

More details begin to emerge – on Facebook mostly, not on official news channels. Savannah's body was found by a courier, it seems. A man there to collect a package. He'd peered through a crack in the blind and had seen something that made him call the Gardaí.

'Oh my god,' Leesa says as we read this update, heads bent together over the phone. 'Maybe it was your package. Are you missing any deliveries?'

I nod slowly, thinking of the skincare order that hasn't arrived.

'So maybe he was there to pick up yours and found her dead? Jesus.'

Silence as the three of us take this in.

'Wait.' Leesa again. 'What about the death threat you got? The doxing. Like, your address was put online. And she looks like you. It's almost as if . . .'

'Oh, come on, that's a leap,' Greta says.

But Leesa is adamant. 'No, wait, listen. Savannah Holmes, a dark-haired, medium-build woman living at 26 Oakpark, the same address as yours. You got a death threat and she is dead. Jesus Christ, Susan, is Savannah Holmes dead because someone mixed you up? Because . . . because it should have been you?'

8

Savannah
Thirty-six hours earlier

ON HER LAST DAY ON EARTH, Savannah Holmes woke at 6 a.m., just as she always did. Her morning began with a workout in her home gym, followed by a protein shake and 600ml of filtered water. The home gym was Savannah's pride and joy. A simple room, really; the room most of her neighbours used as a second living room or a playroom for their kids. Wooden floors, ceiling-height windows and the vast array of mats and weights she'd accumulated over the years. Savannah liked to get out to XSGym in Dún Laoghaire three or four times a week to use the machines, but on mornings like this, with the sun streaming in through slatted blinds, home was idyllic. Plus, it meant she could be showered and logged into her laptop by seven, getting a head start on her day.

'You're a machine!' her colleagues liked to say, when, bleary-eyed, they logged on at nine to find a slew of emails from Savannah. But she didn't see it that way. She was efficient and disciplined. That's all. She worked hard, and had the lifestyle to show for it. She played hard too, no doubt about that. Otherwise, what was the point?

At nine, two packages arrived. She already knew what was

inside one – silver ballet flats – and recorded herself opening them. Her Instagram followers liked pretty much anything she put up, but shopping hauls and make-up reels always got the biggest response. The other package was from Cult Beauty, containing the retinol she regularly used, but, she realized, looking at the invoice inside, it wasn't actually for her. As she taped it back up, a ping on her email announced that the Sézane jumpsuit she'd ordered had been delivered too, only it hadn't. The 'proof of delivery' photo showed her package sitting behind a pot of pink hydrangeas. Savannah had two faux bay trees on her porch and no pink flowers of any kind. She let out a sigh. The package had gone to the other Oakpark. Again. She shot off an email to the courier company, reminding them for the umpteenth time that if they just used the Eircode, none of this would happen.

The jumpsuit, cream and flowy, was for a barbecue at her mother's next weekend. Her mother would say cream was impractical and that she looked like a runaway bride. Savannah would drink too much white wine and seethe inwardly then feign a headache and leave early. Her mother particularly loved a wedding barb. The only time she had ever been happy with her daughter was on Savannah's wedding day. And she had never forgiven the divorce. Savannah glanced at her wedding photo on the kitchen shelf. Her ex was getting married again, according to his sister. Not that they were in direct contact, Savannah and her sister-in-law, but they *did* still follow each other on Instagram. Maybe, eventually, Savannah would marry again too. And, just to annoy her mother, next time she'd elope.

At one, she put together a prawn salad. The dressing she wanted to use – a substitute in her online grocery shopping – contained traces of nuts. *For god's sake.* She sighed and left it unopened. Why could these people never read her notes about substitutions? She decided to eat lunch in the garden, stopping at the back door to pluck sunglasses from the shelf. Only they weren't her sunglasses. She frowned, confused at first, then realization dawned. Popping them on, she checked how they looked in her reverse camera. Cute. Too big for her face, but cute. She took a selfie, sent it with a text that read 'might keep these!' and got on with her lunch.

By three, she was contemplating a crisp glass of white wine. She was trying not to drink during the day, but in weather like this . . . normal rules didn't apply. She went inside for a small glass of wine, glancing at her wedding photo as she passed the kitchen shelf. It stopped her for a moment, thinking. About her ex, about the past and about the future. About moving on.

By half three, she'd poured herself one more small glass of white. Who knew how long the sun would shine? She imagined sitting indoors next week, staring out at rain, wishing she'd had the wine. Of course, she didn't know then there wouldn't be a next week. This time tomorrow, Savannah Holmes would be in a morgue.

9

Susan
Wednesday

THE GARDA WHO TAKES my details – a fair-haired woman in her twenties – looks sceptical, and I'm not surprised. It smacks of self-absorption, making their murder inquiry all about me.

Leesa is beside me, pitched forward in her chair, in a dimly lit office inside Blackrock garda station.

'Do you know why Savannah Holmes was killed?' she asks the garda, though surely she's aware it's pointless. The guard can hardly give away confidential information.

'We're investigating.'

'Look, maybe it was a random attack or a break-in,' I say, 'but even if there's the smallest chance someone thought she was me, I figured it was worth passing on the information.'

A nod, and she shuffles on her seat, squaring her notebook on the desk. I get the feeling now that it's not so much that she thinks it's impossible, more that she doesn't know what to do with the information.

'How did the courier spot her?' I try.

'He could see the package through a crack in the blind and he peered in to get a better look.' A small hesitation. 'She was in the hall.' A grimace.

39

'As far as we've read online, the courier was collecting a package from her, which I guess might have been delivered in error, and was possibly meant for me. Do you know where the package was?'

'Just inside the front door.'

'OK, so a parcel that may have had my name on it was sitting just inside her front door. She lives at 26 Oakpark, as do I, albeit five kilometres away. We're similar age, same colouring, same build, I got a death threat earlier today, and my address was posted publicly online. Do you see why I'm anxious?'

A short nod. 'I do, and I know you're worried that if this hypothetical person realizes they got the wrong house, they're going to come after you, but—'

'Oh god.' Leesa's eyes widen. 'I hadn't even thought of that.'
Neither had I.

'But look,' the garda continues, 'it's more than likely not a case of mistaken identity. I don't think you need to worry.'

This statement does the exact opposite of making me not worry.

'Could you look into it though?' Leesa asks. 'Treat it as a serious line of inquiry?'

'Of course we will,' she says, closing her notebook and pushing back her chair. The notebook remains on the desk, and we are clearly dismissed.

At home, I flop on the couch, exhausted from all of it. Bella's asleep, Jon tells me, ashen-faced, snapping the cap off a beer and sitting down to hear the full story. I can see Bella on the baby-monitor screen, eerily greeny-grey, her little chest rising and falling. The video monitor is a new addition to our array of baby goods, courtesy of Leesa. I'm still not sure we need a camera in Bella's cot, but Leesa says having video as well as audio is reassuring, and her old one was gathering dust.

Greta had stayed with Bella while Leesa and I went to the garda station, handing over to Jon when he arrived in from work, so this is the first time I've seen him since this morning. I fill him in now on all of it – the links with Savannah Holmes, the worry that someone thought she was me – and wait for him to tell me I'm losing it. That's how our marriage works. I catastrophize and he placates. His role has always been easy-going charmer, while I'm a tiny bit neurotic. I worry, he reassures. But not this time. His complexion greys as I go through the story and, by the time I get to the end, he's up and pacing, wearing a track in our faded oriental rug.

'It's probably all coincidence,' I say, working to play it down. 'Leesa was more worried about it than I was, and Greta doesn't believe it's a mistaken-identity thing,' I add, to reassure him. Jon tends to gravitate towards my older sister when we need advice. She's the rock, the one who's always looked out for us, taking on a pseudo-parent role when our mother died.

'Yeah, she said that when I got home.' He sits beside me again, his familiar smell grounding me, soothing me. 'And I'd trust her judgement. It's just . . . a lot. A *murder*.'

'I know. Poor Savannah . . .' It hits me as the words come out that I'm speaking as though I knew her.

'Are *you* OK?' he asks, and I realize he looks truly shaken, which makes me worry even more. I really wanted him to brush this off, but he's doing the opposite. I force a smile and nod yes, then stare at my phone, my mind running over everything that's happened in the last twenty-four hours. Was it really only last night that I sent the text to the Oakpark group? And I still haven't managed to apologize to Celeste. I curl my legs under me and hit the call button. Still no answer. Texting is less than ideal but better than nothing, so I start to type.

Celeste, it's Susan O'Donnell. I can't begin to put into words how sorry I am for what I did. It was inexcusable. I apologize to you, your husband and your children. I wanted to say it on the phone instead of by text, but I completely understand why you wouldn't want to answer. I'm also trying to reach you because of the murder of a woman in Oakpark (the Loughlinstown Oak-park) – I've been to the police already but wanted to tell you too. It sounds crazy, but a couple of people suggested there's a tiny chance she may have been killed by someone who thought she was me. And that it may be linked to the message I sent about you. I don't suppose you could shed any light?

I consider the last few lines. Does it sound like I'm trying to say one of her vehement defenders has committed murder on her behalf? But if there's even a small chance that there's someone unhinged in her life who might be involved, it's worth asking the question. I send the message and wait.

10

Celeste
Wednesday

CELESTE GEARY TUCKS HER hair behind her ear, examining her skin in the bathroom mirror. Still porcelain smooth at fifty. Not bad. Of course, nobody knows she's fifty. She's been five years younger than her passport says for the last decade and a half. Warren knows, but he's the only one. And only because he needed her passport for their life assurance policy. The children don't know. It's a little silly now, she thinks, but somewhat difficult to backtrack. And anyway, it's no one's business but hers. She plucks her phone from the vanity and reads Susan's text again. The absolute gall. First she sends a vile message, then tries to insinuate – what? – that Celeste has gone and killed someone because of it? Or one of Celeste's friends? Or Warren? She grimaces. Warren probably would kill Susan O'Donnell if he could get away with it. She grits her teeth and goes downstairs. Evening sunlight filters through the huge hall window, casting an amber glow on the polished walnut floor, illuminating a smudge on the gilt-edged mirror that hangs above the console table. Celeste tsks and uses the cuff of her sleeve to clear the mark, and moves into the kitchen.

Warren is at the table, staring at his phone, as always.

He looks up. 'Hey!' The faux cheer is not fooling anyone – he's squirming and doing a dreadful job of hiding it. Presumably, his impromptu post-work drinks yesterday evening had nothing to do with a last-minute invitation and everything to do with Susan's message. Celeste can imagine him peering into their bedroom late last night, making sure she was asleep before sneaking in. And feigning sleep when she left this morning. She looks at him, sets her expression to disdain and walks over to the sink.

'Can we talk?' he tries.

'There's nothing to say.'

Celeste plucks a Marni dinner plate from the display shelf above the granite sink and turns to look at him.

His forehead glistens with sweat in the glare of the evening sun.

'I'm so, so sorry.' His voice cracks over the awkwardness, the unfamiliarity of the words, and he clears his throat.

Celeste opens her fingers, letting the plate slip to the tiled floor.

Warren's jaw drops.

'Oh my god, Celeste. Did you . . .' Then, resolutely: 'It was an accident, I'll get a dust pan.'

'Don't get a dust pan. Say sorry to the plate.'

'Wait, what?'

'Say. Sorry. To. The. Plate.'

Eyes wide, he's silent for another moment before seeming to realize she's serious.

'Sorry,' he mutters, his face colouring.

'Now, did the plate go back to the way it was before, when you said sorry?'

His face is beet red now, right to the roots of his dyed hair. He thinks she doesn't know he dyes his hair. Everyone knows he dyes his hair.

'No.'

'Well then.'

A whisper. 'I get it. If there was anything I could do to turn back time, I would . . . but it's no diff—'

He stops. She knows what he wants to say: *It's no different to other times I've strayed.* Only it is, because this time it's public. And Celeste can handle *anything* as long as it's not public.

'So where do we go from here?' he says instead.

'When I decide, I'll let you know.'

'The Sullivans are supposed to be coming for dinner Sunday night . . .' He trails off, his questions unasked – will they be talking by then? Will she forgive him by then? Will he be living here by then?

'You and I are nothing if not good actors, Warren.'

He bows his head.

She re-reads Susan's text, debates for a moment, then presses call.

11

Susan
Wednesday

'Oh shit. She's phoning me. What do I do?'

'Answer it,' Jon says after a pause. He's taking all this more seriously than I'd hoped.

My thumb hovers over the green button. *Oh god*. Here goes.

'Celeste. Hi. Thanks for calling back. I am so, so sorry.'

Silence.

'If there's anything I can do . . . I could meet with your kids? Apologize in person? And . . . and your husband?'

'I don't think my children or my husband want to be anywhere near you, to be quite frank.' Her tone is ice-cold. I've met her over the years at parent–teacher meetings and Oakpark street parties, and she's never seemed particularly warm, but this is a whole other level. Understandably.

'Of course. But truly, if there's anything I can do . . .'

'You can make a public apology, explain you made it all up.'

This chills me. 'I'm sorry?'

'Yes, that. But with more detail, and publicly.'

'It's just I didn't make it . . .' I stop. That's only going to make it worse. 'You're right. I will.'

She means in the WhatsApp group, right? Not like, a letter to the Irish Times?

'Good. I'll look forward to it.' She disconnects.

I pull a cushion over my face, screaming into it, but soundlessly, since we have a sleeping baby upstairs.

'OK, what did she say?' Jon asks.

'I have to make a "public apology".'

He takes my hand. The contact, his skin on mine, stills me, reassures me. Even after all these years, he has that magical power to fix me with just one touch. 'Don't mind her. It'll all blow over, and she can't make you do a public apology. Who does she think she is, the queen of Dublin? It was one mistake.'

I squeeze his fingers. 'Thank you for being lovely. Why am I such an idiot? How have I ended up here?'

'Because you're human. We're all human. Remember what your counsellor said.'

He gently untangles his hand and gets up to grab another beer from the kitchen. I sit, unmoving, on the couch.

Remember what your counsellor said.

Remember that I'm human, remember to go easy on myself. Remember that intrusive thoughts are just that – thoughts. And that worrying I'm going to hurt my baby doesn't mean I'm actually going to hurt my baby. God, it was so hard though, in the early weeks. The non-stop crying. The thoughts of rocking her and rocking her to make her stop. Or leaving her for good . . .

From the kitchen comes the sound of the fridge, the suck of the door opening and closing. On the lamp table beside the couch sits the baby-monitor screen. I can see Bella, asleep in her cot, her soother on the mattress beside her. The image is grainy, and sometimes it's hard to see her clearly. Sometimes when I worry that she's not breathing, it's quicker to run upstairs than to sit staring at the screen trying to work out if her movement is real or a flicker in the feed. There's nothing wrong with her breathing, I've just turned into a worrier. Maybe I'd worry less if I didn't have this screen to watch. I haul myself off the couch and go upstairs to check on her properly.

Bella is fast asleep, arms flung above her head. I watch her for a moment then my eyes go to the window, and the plywood that boards it up. It will take a week at least, we've been told, for new glass to be fitted. And suddenly there's something very unnerving about it – about not being able to see out. Imagining someone out there, watching and waiting . . . A shiver runs through me. I shake myself and turn away.

12

Maeve
Wednesday

MAEVE KHOURY STARES AT the screenshot, feeling hot and cold and sick. What was her Aunt Susan thinking? It's bad enough that Susan teaches at her school, but sending messages about people in her class . . . *shit*. So this is what her mum was on about last night, with her *what the hell?* shout, followed by a much quieter call in her home office. Maeve's sister, Aoife, had tried to find out more, but their mum wouldn't say. Now Maeve knows. Not because her mum gave in or Aoife sneaked on to her phone (though, no doubt, she did) but because it's doing the rounds on Snapchat. God, her family are mortifying.

To be fair, not that many people know that Susan is Maeve's aunt. They both keep it quiet at school and Susan treats her the same as she does everyone else. And Susan is actually quite well liked for a teacher, which makes things easier. But *this*. And of all people, her aunt had picked on Nika Geary. Nika, who'd made Maeve's life hell all through Transition Year and on into fifth year. And over something so *stupid*. Her mind goes back to that day, as it has done many times since, no matter how hard she tries to move on.

It happened on Junior Cert results day. Transition Year

students were told to gather in the canteen at noon. Envelopes would be handed out at twelve thirty, and then students were free to go home and open their results in private. Of course, nobody was going home, they were going into Dublin city centre to drink.

And it was for this reason that one of Nika Geary's friends brought a bottle of Smirnoff into school, stolen from her parents' drinks cabinet. But as she was smuggling it from her school bag into her locker, it slipped from her hand and broke on the corridor floor.

Moments later, Maeve came running around the corner, late for class, skidded, slipped and fell flat on her back on what she assumed was a huge puddle of water. Stunned and embarrassed, she lay there for a moment, catching her breath.

Then a voice from somewhere above boomed: 'Maeve Khoury! *What* are you doing on the floor?'

Ms Costello, the vice-principal. This was *not* good.

She ran over to help Maeve, annoyed for sure, but probably worried too – it's never good for a school if a student gets hurt on the premises. Then, right at that moment, Nika, Ariana and the rest of their friends arrived on the scene with wads of toilet roll, clearly about to clean up the spill, and the one shard of glass they'd missed.

Ms Costello was helping Maeve, sniffing as she did. Once Maeve was on her feet, she stepped back to look at her dripping uniform skirt and the cluster of girls with their clumps of toilet roll.

'Right, down to my office, immediately.' This was to Nika, Ariana and the rest of them. Maeve was ordered to go to the bathroom and dry herself off as the girls, chins high, trying to look both unbothered and disgusted at once, sauntered to Ms Costello's office.

Bit by bit, word went around about what happened next: the girls claimed they had nothing to do with the smashed vodka. They said they'd noticed a spill and were rushing to mop up before someone slipped. Maeve almost sprained an eyeball when she heard that part.

And according to the grapevine, it was this claim more than anything that got them in trouble – nobody, least of all Ms Costello, believed they had any interest in keeping the school clean and safe.

Of course, their parents stuck up for their kids, denied their daughters would bring alcohol into the school. They pointed out that there was no proof, and Maeve heard that one of the mums who was a lawyer or solicitor or something had started to talk about legal action. Even at seventeen, Maeve is fairly certain you can't sue a school for trying to discipline students, but obviously, the board or whoever is in charge of these things decided it wasn't worth the drama. The school eventually let it go.

But the girls didn't.

It was all Maeve's fault, they said. If she hadn't slipped and caused a fuss, Ms Costello would never have noticed. And despite the fact that nothing had come of it, they tormented Maeve for the rest of the year. Spreading rumours that she'd ratted them out, turning their backs when she walked into a room, posting about her on social media. It wasn't just about the slip, of course. Maeve was quiet and a little bit nerdy. Her hair was curly, in a world of glossy waves. Her trainers were last season. She hadn't quite figured out foundation and concealer. She was an easy target and the vodka incident gave them an excuse to set their sights on her.

Maeve tried to keep her head up. She had her own small group of friends – one best pal at school, plus her GAA team – she didn't need Nika Geary's approval. But some days, it was hard. Lots of days, it was hard, not least because she and Nika had once been close friends.

Then in fifth year, Maeve's best pal moved to Spain, and she was on her own. Facing Nika and her gang every day got tougher and, some days, Maeve couldn't bring herself to go in. She faked sickness, ate little, stayed in her room. Her mother worried, but Maeve didn't feel like talking. It was Aoife who told in the end, and then things escalated, because Leesa went to the school. Parents always think going to the school is the answer, and maybe sometimes it is. But for Maeve, everything got worse. It was only when school broke up for summer of fifth year that Nika and her group stopped – distracted by holidays in the Algarve and shopping trips to New York. But now, *this*.

Maeve scrolls and clicks and scrolls and clicks. The screenshot is everywhere, now that she knows where to look. People from her year, sharing it all over social media, surprised and gleeful to see a teacher mess up. Maeve groans, lies back on her bed, and keeps scrolling.

It takes another ten minutes to realize that the focus on Susan's faux pas is already fading. Overshadowed by something else – the question of Nika's 'boyfriend', the one mentioned in Susan's message. Because, as it happens, Nika Geary doesn't have a boyfriend.

Maeve sits up. *Drama.*

13

As soon as Jon leaves for his pre-work run on Thursday morning, Greta arrives with takeout coffees, and Leesa soon after with almond croissants, and in spite of everything that's going on, this makes me feel warm and glowy. I *love* that my house is where we gather now. For the longest time, Greta's was where we congregated – understandably, because it was our childhood home. Even after we moved out – Leesa to work in the Middle East for an engineering firm, me a little closer to home at a school in Drumcondra – we always gravitated to what became Greta's house after Mum died. It went to all three of us, of course, but once Greta knew we were definitely moving on, she bought us out. She'd had a settlement from the county council after an accident left her with a limp, and I suspect she paid over the odds for our portions of the house. That's Greta though, always quietly looking after us. When Leesa had kids, *her* house became the central point, to save her gathering changing bags and buggies and snacks. And now, for the same reason, everyone comes here. I don't know how much Jon likes it – Leesa and Greta here every other day, mostly arriving unannounced – but I adore it.

'Anything new in the news?' Leesa asks, shaking the croissants on to a plate.

There is nothing new, I tell her. Half the headlines are taken up with Savannah's murder and the other half with the couple found dead in Cherrywood, but every article is just a rehash of the one before.

My phone rings, and 'Garda Station' flashes onscreen. For some reason, I feel nervous. I stand and pace as I answer.

'Ms O'Donnell?'

'Speaking.'

'This is Detective Kellerman, about the report you made yesterday. We'd like to call in to you with some further questions – does tomorrow morning at ten suit?'

'Yes, but is there news? Do you think I'm right, it was someone trying to . . . to hurt me?'

A pause that makes me even more nervous.

'We can't say anything for now. But we appreciate your help. We'll see you in the morning.'

She disconnects. Greta and Leesa wait, eyebrows raised, and I fill them in.

Leesa bites her lip. 'So we can assume Savannah's murder is connected to your message?'

I start to protest and she holds up a hand. 'I know, I know. But if the police are coming to talk to you tomorrow, they're obviously considering it.'

'But what in my message would prompt murder?'

'Well, I imagine Warren Geary is furious, for a start.' She settles back on her chair. 'I know you told us about it at the time, but give me a refresher – talk to me about the husband and the PR girl?'

The husband and the PR girl. It sounds like such a cliché, but for what it's worth, this is what happened.

It was a Friday night in June and I was at the opening of a new pub called Bar Four. I was invited by a teacher friend who then texted to say she was running late, making me half wish I'd said no. But I'd hardly been out since Bella was born and it seemed like it might be good for my brain to go for an hour.

The bar was cool when I walked in out of the evening warmth – the aircon turned too high maybe – and I immediately regretted my short-sleeved wrap dress. I recognized half a dozen faces but nobody I knew well enough to chat to, and was just contemplating hiding in a corner with my phone when I spotted Warren Geary, Celeste's husband, standing by the bar, Guinness in hand. I knew him from Oakpark – not well, we didn't socialize, but I'd seen him out walking his dachshund. They always struck me as an incongruous pair – the tiny dog and the oversized man. Warren is about six foot four, an ex-rugby player who hasn't yet gone to seed, though his thick hair is starting to thin ever so slightly and his thick neck doesn't suit his fifty-five-year-old body quite as well as it did when he was a forward for Leinster. He saw me come in and waved me over, gesturing for the bartender to pour me a glass of Prosecco.

'Great to see you, thanks for coming.' He passed me the drink, and perhaps seeing confusion in my expression, he elaborated. 'I'm a shareholder in the bar. Silent partner.'

'Ah, congratulations.' I clinked my Prosecco against his pint. 'Lovely spot.' Actually, it looked the same as every other bar that's opened in Dublin over the last ten years, but who was I to judge? I looked around. 'Is Celeste here too?'

'No, she's away on a work trip.'

'And how are the kids?'

'Nika's great.' A proud smile broke across his face. 'She's a real all-rounder. But sure of course you know that. I worry sometimes that she's pushing herself too hard between study and hockey, but look, she's managing brilliantly. She's got her sights set on doing law and I'd say she'll get the points no bother.' He seemed to realize then that he'd broken one of Ireland's cardinal rules: No Showing Off. 'Of course, Cody's a different story.' An eyeroll.

'Not as into the books?'

'Not into anything except shutting himself in his room with his Xbox. I wish we could find something to get him out of the house.'

'Maybe he'll get a part-time job for the summer? I know he's too young to work, but even a bit of gardening or babysitting?'

Warren's mouth tightened and, too late, I remembered why Cody might not get work babysitting. Greta had told me what happened with Cody and the Fitzpatrick child he was minding, and I made a mental note to ask her to remind me of the details while working to camouflage the thoughts that were spinning across my face.

'Of course, they're only young for such a short time,' I added hurriedly, 'and maybe they need those summers in front of the Xbox.'

'True. And he has work experience coming up with a Big Four accountancy firm in August. I had to go through *many* hoops to set that up for him, but it'll be worth it for the contacts he'll make.'

I smiled inwardly at the idea of a fifteen-year-old making contacts in an accounting firm as Warren turned and called to the bartender.

'Venetia? Pint, please, and for Susan' – he turned to me – 'another Prosecco?'

I smiled at the bartender. 'That would be lovely, thanks.'

Venetia, a tall woman with dark choppy waves and a full

fringe sweeping low over her eyes, nodded somewhat tersely. With her retro hair, black T-shirt and skin-tight jeans, she looked like she'd walked straight out of a sound check with an eighties rock band. She didn't return my smile. One of my fatal flaws is a need to be liked, and it bothered me slightly that she seemed immune to my admittedly moderate charms. I couldn't help wishing Jon was with me. He's good at social situations. He's good company, full stop, and this is something we've been missing since Bella was born – getting out together, just the two of us.

A woman sidled over then, looking strikingly similar to Venetia but with a twenty-first-century blow-dry and a well-cut silver blazer. She kissed Warren on both cheeks and held out a hand to shake mine.

Warren introduced us. 'Susan, this is Aimee from Jordan-Birch PR – she's the one who's going to get us into the papers, isn't that right, Aimee?'

'Well, it's a fabulous turnout,' Aimee said, 'and we're very grateful to you for joining us, Susan.'

I warmed to her immediately. As an underdressed, under-made-up completely uninfluential randomer drinking free Prosecco, I was of zero use to their opening but Aimee made me feel like I was single-handedly launching the pub.

She touched my arm, perhaps noticing the goosebumps. 'Are you cold? We could turn off the aircon?'

In true Irish fashion, I lied enthusiastically rather than put someone out. 'God no, it's a perfect temperature. But thanks.'

'Great. Now, I hope this guy is looking after you.' She nudged Warren playfully then turned and called the bartender. 'Venetia, any chance of a sparkling water for your parched sis?'

Now the similarities made sense. 'Oh, you're sisters!' I said, appraising them. Beyond the hairstyles and clothing, their faces were almost identical. 'I have two sisters; we're all like chalk and cheese. One blonde, one red, and I'm the brunette. Are you two close?'

'We are.' Aimee's face clouded as she glanced towards her sister. 'It's just the two of us. So yeah, we look out for each other.' She tucked her hair behind her ear and smiled, but I couldn't help thinking there was suddenly something desperately sad in her expression.

After some more small talk, I left them to find my friend, but about an hour later, on my way out of the Bar Four bathroom, I took a wrong turn and pushed through a door into a storeroom. And there, at the far end in a darkened corner, were the husband and the PR girl. They were leaning against a stack of crates, and although Warren's broad back obscured my view somewhat and although he could have been, I don't know, checking her teeth, I could fairly happily swear on a bible that they were kissing – her silver jacket already on the floor beside them, his once neat shirt untucked. Backing slowly and quietly out through the door, I left without being noticed and hurried away, my eyes burning. *Jesus!* That was not what I was expecting. A big part of me felt sorry for Celeste. A small part of me couldn't wait to tell Greta and Leesa.

14

Susan
Thursday

'So, was it an affair, do you reckon,' Leesa asks when I finish retelling the story, 'or a one-night stand?'

I shrug. 'Who knows, but it's not my business and, honestly, I'd never have wanted Celeste to find out.'

'Except for the bit where you're the one who told her . . .'

I'm mortified all over again, thinking about the message, and how Celeste must feel to discover so publicly that her husband is cheating.

'Does that mean Celeste sent you the threatening text?' Greta muses, fishing in her bag for one of her tablets. I don't know how she remembers what to take when, but Greta is a machine. She researches, listens to medical advice, sees her GP regularly and takes anything and everything that will help. I'm the kind of person who buys a pack of multivitamins, takes them twice, then forgets again till they're out of date.

'I don't know if she'd resort to anonymous texts.'

'OK, what about the other person in the love triangle – Aimee?'

'She seemed very nice . . .'

'You think everyone is nice,' Greta mutters. Her tolerance for other people isn't quite as high as mine.

'What if it's Aimee's husband,' Leesa says. 'What if she's married, and now her husband knows something happened at the bar opening and he's the one sending death threats?'

'I didn't use her name in the message . . .'

'But you said' – Leesa scrolls on her phone – '"wrapped around the PR girl at the opening party for Bar Four".' She looks up at me. 'There's enough there to identify her. Assuming there was just one PR there?'

She's right, and I feel sick. My throwaway bitchy comment could be affecting two marriages.

Greta squeezes my arm. 'It's worded as though it was all Warren. You didn't actually say what you saw in the storeroom. So it could be explained as just a bit of one-sided flirting, couldn't it?'

I hope she's right.

'Should we talk to the PR – Aimee?' Leesa asks. 'Sound her out, see if there's any chance she's the one who sent you the threatening text?'

Greta purses her lips. 'Shouldn't we leave all this to the guards?'

'We could just get a vibe,' Leesa says. 'We'll know from talking to her if it was her or not.' She turns to me. 'Do you know her surname?'

'Nope.'

'We could try her sister, who works in Bar Four.' Leesa's on her feet, looking at her watch. 'It's just after half ten, the bar will be opening, we'll get coffee.'

'Hang on.' I wave for her to sit. 'I'm in enough trouble already – this doesn't sound like a good idea.'

'I'll do the talking. I'll say a friend of mine needs PR and remembers the bartender's sister from the opening. Come on.' She's off her seat again.

I contemplate that for a moment. If we don't say anything about the message or why we're really there, it probably can't do any harm . . . I look down at Bella in my arms.

'What do we do with Bella, and don't you have to work?'

'Bring Bella. It's a gorgeous day. And I'm not working till two.'

Greta will leave us to it, she says; she's heading down to the hockey camp. So Leesa and I, with Bella in a sling, set off for Bar Four.

Inside, the bar is dark, with scant sunlight slipping in through the half-open door. A man in a white shirt is polishing glasses behind the bar and he looks up at us.

'What can I get you, ladies? Coffee machine's just warming up.'

'Lovely,' Leesa says chirpily. 'Two cappuccinos, please, and is Venetia in this morning?'

His face falls. 'Ah. Venetia's not in. She won't be in this week at all. There's been a . . . a bereavement in the family.'

'I'm so sorry to hear that. Will she be back on Monday, do you think?'

'Honestly, I don't know.' He hesitates. 'It's her sister who died. You know the story in the news – the couple who were murdered?'

We are both frozen into silence. The barman continues when we don't respond: 'It was Venetia's sister and the sister's husband.'

'Aimee?' Leesa manages. 'Was that her name?'

'That's the one. Dreadful thing. Not far from here – down the N11, one of those new developments in Cherrywood. Just shows, even when it's somewhere nice and safe . . .' He shakes his head.

I need to sit down.

The barman looks alarmed. 'Sorry, love – you've gone a bit

pale. Did you know Venetia's sister? Maybe I shouldn't have said anything . . .' He starts filling a glass of water.

'I didn't know her, not really.' I lower myself on to a chair, cradling Bella in the sling. 'I . . . I just met her at the opening of the bar.' An image flashes through my mind, Aimee and Warren in the stock room. The husband and the PR girl. And now one of them is dead.

15

Susan
Thursday

FROM A CORNER TABLE in the empty pub, I phone the garda station and ask to speak to Detective Kellerman. Going back over the whole story – my message about Celeste, the broken window, the threatening text, the two Oakparks, Savannah's death and now the connection between Warren and murder victim Aimee, it sounds incontrovertible. At least to me – the person caught in the middle – it does. But Detective Kellerman is reticent.

'Thanks for passing this on, Ms O'Donnell. I've taken note, and we'll see you tomorrow, as planned, unless we need something sooner.'

I suppose gardaí aren't going to give much away, but I come off the phone sick and deflated and worried.

The barman brings us two coffees and apologizes again for passing on the shocking news.

'I didn't realize you knew poor Aimee, god rest her.'

'Don't worry at all,' Leesa says, 'but could you give us Venetia's address, so we can send a condolence card? I don't want to intrude with a call.'

'Sure, of course. I don't know the postal address, but she's down the road there, the cottages in Coal Place.' He points to his left. 'The first one in the row is hers. Lives there with her husband. Foreign fella. You could walk past and check the address for your card?'

We finish our coffees and do as he suggests – walk towards the row of pretty terraced cottages in Coal Place, stopping for a moment outside the first one. It looks a little shabby beside its pristine neighbour, in need of a fresh coat of paint, but otherwise, just a normal house on a normal road, and it's hard to believe that inside is a woman whose sister has just been murdered.

'Should we knock in?' Leesa whispers.

I shake my head. 'God, no. We don't know her; it would be insensitive. And I . . . I need to stay out of it, not draw more attention to myself.'

That evening, Greta calls in at ours just after Jon gets home from work. They chat in the hall for a bit, voices hushed. I'm in the sitting room, cross-legged on the couch, still numb. When they join me, Greta beside me, Jon on the other couch, I fill them in on the day's events. The long version. I'd texted both of them earlier with the news that Aimee – PR girl of my message – is a murder victim.

'I'm really worried now that there's a link with me.' I pull a cushion on to my lap and briefly bury my head in it. 'That Savannah and Aimee and Aimee's husband – Rory was his name – were somehow, bizarrely, killed because of my message. I need to understand how all of this is connected if *not* by me.'

They both nod, indicating listening rather than agreement, I think, but I'd really rather they tell me I'm wrong.

I play devil's advocate to my own argument. 'Of course, it

might all be coincidence. Because it doesn't really make sense – why would someone kill Aimee and Rory just because she was mentioned in a message?'

Jon speaks gently now. 'Could it have been murder-suicide? Like . . .' He swallows. 'Could it be that Rory saw a screenshot of your message, thought Aimee was cheating, lost it, killed her, then killed himself?'

I let out a slow, controlled breath. 'It wasn't suicide, from what I've read online. It's not mentioned in the news reports, but people are saying Rory and Aimee were hit with the same weapon. So it can't be self-inflicted. I guess it could be speculation or maybe a leak, or even the person who found the bodies, but if it's true, both of them were murdered.'

'That's . . . better, I think?' Jon says, and though it sounds awful, I know what he means. Because the idea that Rory killed his wife, as a direct result of my message, is too hideous to contemplate.

16

Nika
Thursday

NIKA GEARY IS FURIOUS. Ms O'Donnell's message is all over the place now, and Nika has many, many thoughts and feelings about this. She flops back on her bed, staring at the pink chandelier on her ceiling. First and foremost, the absolute *cheek* of a teacher, talking about a pupil like that. *Unreal.* She hopes Ms O'Donnell gets fired, and if someone else doesn't send the message to the principal, Nika will do it herself. Or at least, she'll get her mum to do it. She's still a bit in the bad books at school after the vodka situation, though clearly that was Jessica's fault for dropping the bottle and Maeve's fault for being so clumsy.

Ms O'Donnell's message is embarrassing though: 'bratty'. It's obviously rude, but also kind of . . . infantilizing? Is that the word? She might have preferred it if Ms O'Donnell had called her 'entitled' or 'spoilt', something more . . . princessy. Even if she'd said 'brat', that would actually be quite good. But not 'bratty'. That makes her sound like a toddler.

And the stuff Ms O'Donnell said about the rest of her family too. *God.* Nika hopes her dad will sue. He said he would. Then again, that's the kind of thing her dad says about everything. *We should sue. We should take them to court.* He never actually does it. And he's walking around like a sad dog with his tail down at the moment, not surprisingly. How unbelievably mortifying to have that message doing the rounds, claiming he was with some other woman. *Gross.* He should definitely sue for slander or libel or whatever. That would show Ms O'Donnell. And anyone else who might think the message is true.

Meanwhile, her mum is smiling her way through it, but quietly fit to kill Susan O'Donnell.

And Cody? Well, Cody's the same lump he always is – hiding in his room, glued to his stupid Xbox, curtains closed all day like he's some kind of vampire. Why can't she just have a normal, not embarrassing family? She turns over on her stomach and picks up her phone again. From downstairs, the click of the kitchen door signals her mother may be on her way upstairs. On autopilot, Nika slides her vape from her bedside table into the drawer and lights a scented candle. No footsteps on the stairs after all. Celeste is probably hunting for Warren so she can hammer home that she's not talking to him; the silent treatment only works if you're in the same room.

Nika clicks into Ms O'Donnell's message again.

None of it is good, but the worst part, the bit that's making her nervous, is the mention of her 'boyfriend'. How is she going to get out of this one? Nobody's put two and two together just yet, as far as she can tell, but it's only a matter of time. She's meeting Zach tonight and they'll talk about it then, get their stories straight.

She checks her watch and hauls herself off her bed. At her vanity, she starts with concealer, eyeing herself in the mirror. She might wear her new Urban Outfitters dress; Zach likes her in dresses. He'll be waiting for her in *their* spot – the hidden grassy patch behind the football clubhouse, where nobody can see them. Her stomach knots. What if people find out about

Zach? She'll be dead. Literally dead. Her English teacher would tell her that's not a correct use of the word 'literally', but to be quite honest, if people realize she's seeing Zach, it could end up being true. She pushes the thought away. If she's careful, nobody will find out.

Her mind goes again to the message. The bunking-off school part is less worrying than the rest. Her mother believes everything Nika tells her. If she asks, Nika will say they had a free class and they were allowed out. Celeste hasn't actually asked her yet, though it's a full forty-eight hours now since Ms O'Donnell sent the message. Then again, that's not unusual. Nika is lucky that way. Her mother mostly leaves her in peace. And Nika does exactly what she wants.

17

Susan
Friday

SOMETHING JOLTS ME AWAKE. A dream? Bella? I sit up in bed, listening. There's only the sound of Jon's slow, even breaths and a passing car outside. The bedroom is pitch dark, but the plywood on the window keeps it that way day and night. I check my phone: 3.11 a.m. There's a text. A number that's not in my contacts, but, I see now, the same one that sent the death threat Wednesday morning. Ignoring common sense, I read the new message.

Lock your doors, Susan. I told you, if you tell anyone, I'll be back. Remember, I know exactly who you are and where you are, and you know nothing about me. I'm the monster who comes in the night. I'm the monster who'll make you pay. I'm the monster outside right now. Watching.

My hand flies to my mouth and, for a moment, I'm frozen, staring at my phone, then at the boarded-up window. Is someone out there?

'Jon. Jon.' I shake him awake, holding my phone out to show him the text.

He rubs his eyes, squints to read.

'Jesus.' He's hoarse, groggy.

'We need to look outside – out the window, I mean, and we need to phone the guards,' I whisper.

I check on Bella, then together, Jon and I slip across the landing to the nursery that will be Bella's bedroom. The blind is up. Jon is heading straight for the window, but I hold him back.

'Don't, they'll see you,' I whisper. 'We should try to look without being spotted.'

He nods. We hang back in the darkness and crane our necks. My heart pounds in my chest. A movement outside startles us. But it's just a fox, darting across the street. Nothing else stirs. Streetlights illuminate darkened lawns and cars and driveways. There's nobody out there, not that I can see. But someone could be hiding out of sight, watching us. My skin prickles.

Jon squeezes my hand. 'There's nobody there, but I'll call the guards anyway. You go back to Bella.'

The guards, to their credit, send a car, and phone Jon half an hour later to confirm there's nobody outside the house. They ask us to send a screenshot of the text, and we do. Bella wakes for a feed, and there's comfort in it, comfort in holding her close.

Jon kisses me, and turns over, telling me he's not going to be able to sleep, but is somehow out within thirty seconds. I lie awake, feeding Bella, thinking. Going back over the text, word by word. Something snags. Something that doesn't fit.

I told you, if you tell anyone, I'll be back.

What does that mean? *Who* told me? I rack my brain, but it doesn't make sense.

And if I 'tell anyone' *what*? Somehow, this feels like the key to everything, if only I knew what it meant.

18

Susan
Friday

ON FRIDAY MORNING, I'M a crumpled heap from lack of sleep
and worry. Jon, somewhat fresher, says he'll stay home with me,
even though I know he's got a big meeting with his French bosses
this morning. I remind him that the guards are calling at ten to
ask questions about the report I made on Wednesday night. I
couldn't be in safer hands, I tell him, and if I'm really worried, I'll
give him a call to come home. He kisses me and wraps me in a
bear hug, promising he'll be here within twenty minutes if I need
him. I inhale him, the clean smell of shaving foam and cologne,
and give silent thanks I'm not dealing with this on my own.

Soon after he leaves, my phone flashes up with a call from
the garda station.

'Ms O'Donnell? It's Detective Kellerman.'

'Hi, yes, good morning, how are you?' People-pleaser Susan
is back.

'Change of plans: we'd like you to come down to the station.
Would that be OK?'

What? Why am I being asked to go in? A flurry of thoughts
rushes through my head. Maybe it's a manpower issue? It feels
more than that, though. It feels like I'm being summoned.

'Eh, sure. I'll have to see if my sister can mind the baby . . .'

'Great, thank you, we'll see you at ten.'

She disconnects, and the low-level unease I've been battling all morning nudges higher now, morphing into full-blown anxiety.

Detective Kellerman meets me in the foyer and brings me through to a dark, surprisingly untidy meeting room. She sits at an ancient-looking chipped desk and gestures for me to take a seat opposite, then opens a notebook and appraises me for a moment. It's hard to read her and difficult to know where to look, and I can't help feeling on edge. But maybe everyone feels on edge in a garda station?

I ask if she knows anything about who's been sending the texts, and she tells me they came from a pay-as-you-go phone bought seven years ago, and can't be traced back to anyone. Of course. Nobody is going to send threats from a traceable phone, but still, I'd hoped.

Detective Kellerman turns over what looks like a copy of the report that the other garda had taken from me on Wednesday and begins to go through all of it again. I repeat my story, doing everything I can to show her I'm keen to help, like a schoolchild desperate to please a teacher. She asks me if I'd ever met Savannah (no), Aimee (just that one time) or Rory (no) and asks me if I've ever used Aimee's PR firm or if I'm a member of Rory Quinlan's gym. I crack a joke about newborns and not having time to shower let alone go to a gym, but Kellerman doesn't smile.

There's a pause and I venture a question.

'I saw online that people were speculating that Savannah's murder was a burglary gone wrong. That someone pushed her and accidentally killed her. Do you think that's what it was?'

Grey eyes bore into mine.

'We don't believe it was a burglary,' she says eventually. 'Only her car keys are missing, nothing else.' She gazes at me, as though waiting for me to speak. Like I'm supposed to know something about car keys?

From Savannah's Instagram alone, I know she has an iMac, an iPhone 16 Pro and some very lovely Stonechat jewellery and I wonder how anyone would know what's been taken or not, if the only resident of the house is dead? Kellerman must read the unspoken question in my expression.

'Ms Holmes's ex-husband was able to help us establish what was or wasn't missing. Are you acquainted with her ex-husband?'

'What? No! I don't know Savannah at all. I've explained that.' I can literally feel my face heating up, even though I'm telling the truth. God. This must be how they get people. Fluster them into confessing. I clear my throat.

'So was it a car thief then?' In a way, this wouldn't surprise me. Savannah's car, a sleek silver Audi A8, features regularly on her Insta and I googled once to see how much it cost. I can see why a thief would take a car worth over a hundred grand.

Then Kellerman says something surprising.

'Her car wasn't taken, just the keys.' She continues to gaze at me. Part of me wonders why she's telling me this. Don't police usually keep these kinds of details to themselves? Maybe she's trying to get me to admit something. There's nothing to admit. I'm not hiding anything. And yet, I'm squirming.

When I don't respond, Kellerman moves on, straightening the pages of the report as she speaks.

'Are you acquainted with anyone called Sam?'

'Eh . . . I don't think so – is that her ex-husband?'

'So,' she says, ignoring my question, 'we'll need to take fingerprints and a DNA sample from you.'

A lurch of anxiety blooms, propelling me forward in the chair.

'It's for exclusionary purposes. There are fingerprints at both crime scenes that don't belong to the victims. And some other forensic evidence.'

She doesn't elaborate on this 'other forensic evidence'. Blood, maybe? Hairs? Everything I know about crime scenes comes from the Patricia Cornwell books I read in my twenties and episodes of *CSI*.

'I mean, of course,' I say, while at the same time wondering if I should be saying no, or if I *can* say no, or if I'm supposed to have a lawyer?

'Great, thank you.'

'It's just . . . can I ask why you need it when I didn't know the victims?'

She stares at me for a moment. Assessing me? Trying to freak me out? It's working.

'It's just procedure, to exclude you.' She picks up a flat paper bag from the desk and tears it carefully open, extracting a plastic bag with what looks like an oversized cotton bud inside. 'It's very simple; you administer it yourself. Both cheeks, roof of mouth, under tongue. Painless.'

'Yes, of course, and I'm happy to help, but . . . just to understand, you need this even though I have no link to the victims?'

'But you *are* linked to them, as you told us yourself, with your packages going to Savannah Holmes, and your WhatsApp to your neighbourhood group about Aimee Quinlan.' Her tone contains more than a fragment of disdain for neighbourhood WhatsApp groups, and my *god* she's preaching to the converted.

'So you *do* think the murders are linked?'

'Obviously nothing is conclusive, but we have to seriously consider that they are, yes. And you're the common denominator.'

'Right. God.' A thought hits me then. 'Wait, do you mean the *only* common denominator?'

She nods. 'Exactly. I can't give you too many details.' She hands me the package with the swab. 'But in terms of understanding if there's a connection between the Cherrywood and Oakpark murders, so far, it's you.'

Back home, having collected Bella from Greta, I let myself into my house and turn the deadbolt on the front door, then check the patio door. It's locked: I knew it would be, though we sometimes forget. A false sense of security that comes with living in a big, built-up suburb with mostly nice neighbours and a very active Neighbourhood Watch group. But that's so foolish, I realize now. If someone wants to get into our house, or anyone's house, they'll do it. They can barge in or break a window or pick a lock. If they've got a weapon – and anything is a weapon when you think about it: a golf club, a hurl, a wrench, a kitchen knife – people can do whatever they want.

And I can't stop thinking: if Savannah is dead because someone thought she was me, they might try again. Suddenly, I don't want to be on my own. I message Jon, knowing he's at work and can't be here but needing the small comfort a text brings. I message my sister chat group, asking Greta and Leesa if they could come over. Both are working, but they'll call over this evening – a Friday-night glass of wine, maybe a takeaway. I nod at my phone, unexpected tears brimming. *God, what is wrong with me?*

I need sleep, that's what's wrong. Bella is out for the count after a feed, and there are a hundred things I should be doing, but maybe I'll give this sleep-when-baby-sleeps thing one more go.

Half an hour later, I'm curled under my duvet, still awake. The room is almost pitch dark with the plywood blocking the window, but it's no good. That's when I remember Jon's melatonin – the pack he picked up in New York to help him sleep on the plane home. I text him to ask where they are and he sends a quick reply: 'Bedside drawer.'

The top drawer has his passport, tangled wired earbuds, random receipts, a Yorkie, but no melatonin.

The lower drawer is stuck at first and, when I manage to yank it open, the entire night-stand pulls away from the wall and something drops to the carpet. Something that was wedged between the night-stand and the wall, I reckon, as I rummage through the drawer contents. Paracetamol, throat lozenges, more receipts and, finally, the melatonin. I push the drawer in and feel around on the carpet to see what dropped. My fingers close around something metal, something round. I pull it out to look. It's a bangle. A rose-gold bracelet. Is it mine? It's not mine. It's beautiful. I'd remember if I owned this. Whose then? That's when the words catch my eye. An inscription on the inside:

'Happy one-month anniversary, all my love, Jon.'

19

Susan
Friday

HEAT FLOODS MY BODY as the implication hits. *But wait. Wait.* Maybe it's for me? A present? It doesn't feel like a present. It feels like something lost. Something lost by someone else. And 'happy one-month anniversary' is not what you say to your wife of six years. No box, no bag, no bow. It's not a present, and it's not mine. I sit for the longest time on the side of the bed, staring at the bangle, wondering what to do. Confront him? Get peace of mind? But what if I don't like the answer or the outcome . . .? What if he's been building up to tell me something? What if this – me confronting him – is the impetus he needs to break away, to leave us?

In a daze, I move to my side of the bed and put the bracelet in my top drawer, underneath my copy of *Daisy Jones and the Six*. The melatonin is back in his night-stand – there's no hope of sleep now. I'm numb. I want to shut it all out, to un-know it, and I want to know everything, immediately. On my phone, I click into my banking app and scan our joint credit-card bill. We each have our own credit cards and bank accounts, but it's worth a try. I scroll back and back, through groceries and petrol, and then there's something – a charge for €24 at the

Marker Hotel in Dublin city centre. The cost of two drinks? He'd know not to put a hotel room on our joint account – that thought makes me physically ill – but if he tapped with his phone, his Google Pay app could default to the shared credit card and he might not think to change it. Was that what had happened here?

I sit, thinking. He's working late more than he used to, and there have been overnight trips, like the one to New York. And he's taken up running . . . which, when you think about it, is the perfect cover. A solo activity you can do any time – late in the evening after work, weekend afternoons, early mornings. It's a much better alibi than saying you've joined a book club or a football team, because those involve other people, and your partner might bump into someone who blows your cover. Not so running. You arrive home sweaty and tired and get straight in the shower. And Jon, who has never run for a bus in his life, has taken to it with gusto.

But surely he wouldn't do this to me? Jon loves me; I know he loves me. There has to be some other reason. Some explanation. My brain scrambles, trying desperately to find it. But I keep coming back to the bangle. The inscription. The running. The late nights. The distance between us. *Oh Jon.*

I feel like I might cave in, collapse. I want to turn back the clock, I want my only worries to be stupid embarrassing messages and broken windows. Jesus. What do I do? Do I tell Greta and Leesa?

Leesa would tell me to leave him immediately. She loves Jon, but she loves me more. Greta would be more circumspect. I can already hear her in my head. *Think about Bella. Think about the cost of divorce. Think about the house; you'd have to move.* She's not wrong. Jon is the big earner – head of legal in GS Bank. My teacher salary doesn't come close.

My phone beeps with a text from Leesa to say her daughters, Maeve and Aoife, will be over this evening too. There it is, normal life going on. My fingers hover over a reply. But I can't. There is no world in which I can imagine telling her what I've just found. If I tell them, I can't untell them. And I'd have to deal with it, confront him. No. I need time to process without noise from my well-meaning sisters. I text a reply: **Sure, looking forward to it**, and hot tears roll down my face.

I don't know how long I sit there. A babble from the crib pulls me back to reality. God, Bella's facing being raised by separated parents . . . then again, she's so young, it would always feel normal to her, like it did to me. My dad left when I was a newborn; I don't remember him at all. And it's fine, I don't miss him, my mother was more than enough, but I never wanted this for Bella . . . Wait. I sit up straighter. Would Jon want custody? Knowing what he knows, would he want Bella with him? He's fully aware it was never real; I was never actually going to hurt her. But once you admit something like that – the fear that you might hurt your child – you can't unsay it. The only people who know are Jon, my GP, my counsellor and the other anonymous members of the parenting forum – the ones who gave me the support and advice I needed when I couldn't admit any of it to people I knew in real life. They're the ones who sent me to my GP, who in turn got me medication, counselling, and encouraged me to tell Jon. I couldn't bring myself to tell Greta and Leesa, and three months on, with the intrusive thoughts mostly gone, there's no need. But Jon knows. And up until this morning, I trusted Jon with my life. Only in the very far recesses of my mind did I ever think, 'He could really use this against me if we ever broke up.' The merest whisper of a half-thought. Until now.

20

Susan
Friday

GRETA AND LEESA ARE already here when Jon arrives in from work this evening, which means I don't have to face him on my own. I honestly don't know if I could have found a way to act normal. But they're here, they're noisy and it's easy to hide. They greet Jon and I notice that he and Greta exchange a look. The paranoid part of me wonders for a moment if she knows he's seeing someone. Surely she'd tell me, though? And it's a leap to think a small, possibly imagined glance means something so huge.

Leesa makes room for Jon at the table, telling him about some restaurant he must try, and he hides his irritation. I know he doesn't love to find a houseful of people waiting for him when he gets in from work. Well, tough, I think, with a visceral flash of anger, inching my chair a little away from him. *You absolute fucker.* Just as quickly, the anger gives way to immense sadness and I have to fake a bathroom trip to hide my tears.

Calm and dry-eyed again, I come downstairs and pop my head around the living-room door. Leesa's kids, Maeve and Aoife, are on the couch, ostensibly minding Bella but mostly looking at their phones and wondering, I imagine, how long until we order the takeaway. In the kitchen, Greta asks me about my trip to the garda station. I'd all but forgotten it over the last few hours, and telling them is a good, if small, distraction.

'It's not that they think I had something to do with it, obviously,' I add, 'but I'm connected to both cases so they needed DNA to exclude me. Which it will, because I wasn't there.' I force a watery smile.

Jon gets up to put on the kettle. There are shadows under his eyes, but otherwise he looks pretty much the same as he has for the fifteen years I've known him. And yet, he's a completely different person, a stranger. How could he do this? *You know how* says a little voice in my head. *It's not the first time.* It's not. But the last time we hadn't been together very long. This time we're married. We have a baby, for god's sake.

Leesa touches my hand. 'Are you OK?'

'Yep. Just the DNA thing rattled me.' I rearrange my face and glance over at Jon again.

He's staring at the boiling kettle, but now reaches for a bottle of Malbec and four glasses. Something draws my attention to Greta, and I realize she's watching Jon too. Again I wonder, does she know something about his affair? Of course not. I've only just found out myself. And she's my sister; she'd tell me.

Jon places a wine glass in front of Greta and starts to pour but stops and points at a bottle of pills she's left on the table. 'Are they the ones you can't drink on? I can make you a green tea?'

This breaks my heart. He is always kind to my sisters, even when I know he'd prefer a quiet house. But what does any of it matter when the manners and politeness are hiding lying and cheating?

'Nope.' Greta looks up at him. 'These ones actually reduce the effect of alcohol, so make it an extra large.'

'Oh really?' He picks up the bottle to read the label. 'Naltrexone. Are they prescription?'

She nods. He's still scrutinizing the bottle.

'Wow, I didn't know things like this existed. I wonder why they don't make it available over the counter, let people go out for a few drinks but get less drunk? Fewer fights, less aggro?'

Greta shrugs. 'I'm guessing lots of people who drink actually want to feel the effects . . .'

'But say in a work situation – drinks with clients. I'm always trying to pace myself, not make an eejit of myself.' A smile. *God, that smile. I loved that smile.* 'Maybe I'll take one of these the next time.'

'I mean, you could just not drink,' Greta says dryly. 'That would have an even more sobering effect.'

Jon is still reading the naltrexone bottle. 'I could even drive home after . . .'

I frown a warning. Greta's lingering limp is the result of a car accident and, although nobody was drunk, joking about drink driving is insensitive. Plus, Jon's not without blame for what happened that night.

Leesa shakes her head in admonishment. 'Jon.'

He grins. 'I'm kidding.' He fills Greta's glass. 'Still, be handy, wouldn't they, for client drinks.'

I stare down at the table. *Client drinks.* The charge from the Marker Hotel. My eyes bloom again and I blink back tears.

Oblivious, Jon pours a glass for me, and one for Leesa.

He still has Greta's tablets in his hand. 'Could I try just one?' He does a wide-eyed puppy look that pretty much everyone except Greta finds cute. I wonder if he's like this with his . . . this person, this *girlfriend*, and the thought cuts like a knife.

Greta gives him a withering look. 'Do you have Long Covid?'

'Nope.' Still grinning, he puts the naltrexone back on the table. His phone beeps. 'Takeaway en route. Fifteen minutes.'

I push back my chair. 'I'll let the girls know.' I need a breather.

In the living room, Aoife and Maeve are huddled over Maeve's phone, and spring apart when I appear in the doorway. Aoife glances furtively at me then flicks her gaze away. Maeve avoids eye contact entirely.

'Everything OK, girls?'

Silence.

'OK, spill, what's going on?' This comes out in my teacher voice, instead of my nice Aunt Susan voice.

Still nothing. Maeve starts to slide her phone under a cushion. I hold out my hand for it. Maeve's eyes widen in horror. This is not the Susan she's used to.

'Let me see.' Again in teacher mode.

With a small sigh Maeve hands it over, and I find myself looking at Snapchat, open in a group called 'Did You Hear'. The screen is full of comments from different users. I scroll through, confused at first.

> hahahahahha, like ariana is supposed to be her friend
> I can't wait to see what she says when Ariana says it to her
> Is it definitely him? do we know its zach? omg shes such a bitch
> Has anyone seen her? bet shes hiding. I would RUN

It hits me now. Nika.

Aoife looks at me. 'It's about the message.'

Maeve bites her lip.

'About Nika bunking off with her boyfriend?' I ask, though it's hardly anything else.

Aoife nods. 'Except he's not her boyfriend.'

'What do you mean?'

'He's another girl's boyfriend. Everyone's going mad.' She nods towards her sister. 'Maeve knows.'

I look at Maeve, waiting. *Christ, what a mess.* I have no love for Nika, but this is too much. And now I'll have to text Celeste to alert her about the pile-on, to keep an eye on Nika . . .

Maeve sighs. 'Yeah. Everyone in our year knows who's going out with who, and Nika isn't going out with anyone. So when your message went around, people from school were wondering who the guy was. And they did some digging and worked out it was Zach, Ariana's boyfriend. Ariana is this other girl in our year, who's also Nika's friend. And *that*,' Maeve says, 'did *not* go down well at all.'

21

Susan
Friday

AN HOUR LATER, WE'RE at the kitchen table, halfway through the takeaway and all the way through the wine. I'm holding it together, smiling and nodding while, inside, I'm dying. Jon goes out to the utility room to get another bottle of Malbec and some Cokes for the girls. Leesa's telling us that she and Maeve are going shopping in Kildare Village tomorrow and Greta's rolling her eyes. I'm barely listening.

'Oh, guess who I bumped into when I was there last week,' Leesa says to Greta. 'Your new friend Phoebe. She says hi.'

Something in Leesa's tone makes me tune in properly to the conversation.

Greta is nodding but doesn't respond, wondering, perhaps, if this is just a ploy to stop her fast-fashion lecture.

'Who's Phoebe?' I ask.

Leesa's answer comes with a conspiratorial nod. 'Greta's friend she met in her hiking club, who also happens to be' – she lowers her voice and glances left to right with exaggerated care – 'Albie Byrne's sister.'

Ah. Inwardly, I squirm, and glance towards the utility room.

For Jon and for me, Albie Byrne – or, more to the point, the story behind how we know his name – is an awkward topic.

Albie Byrne was the driver of the other car in Greta's accident. Not his fault, not hers, just bad luck and ice on the road – made worse by potholes and a failure on the council's part to salt the route. Greta got a good settlement from the council; Albie didn't look for anything out of it, but then again, all he suffered was a broken ankle. He's a local councillor now; his big, round head beams down at us from lamp-posts around Blackrock, but ten years ago, when the accident happened, he was just plain old Albie Byrne.

Out in the utility room, Jon is still clinking around getting ice for the Cokes, and I'm quietly glad he's not here for this conversation. Greta's accident is a difficult subject, one we avoid. She shouldn't have been out driving that night, and it's down to Jon and me that she was. I was giving a maths lesson to a Leaving Cert student in Carrickmines, and Jon was supposed to collect me afterwards. We only had one car – still do – officially, because we're trying to do better for the environment; unofficially, because I hate driving and will walk or bus anywhere to avoid it. But that night ten years ago, Jon forgot he was picking me up and went for drinks after work. When he saw my text to say I was ready to be collected, he rang Greta to ask her to do it instead. And that's when she had her crash. She never blamed Jon, never blamed me, but whenever the topic comes up, it still makes me sick inside. As for Jon – well, I guess I always assumed he felt just as bad, and that's why we don't discuss it. Through the filter of my discovery today, I wonder . . . Maybe he's just coasting through life, not giving his part in Greta's accident a second thought.

Leesa is still waiting for a reaction, nodding meaningfully, as though this connection between Phoebe and Albie is serious gossip. It's not though. Everyone knows everyone around here: Albie Byrne is a former team-mate of Warren Geary's, and Celeste went to the same school as Leesa and Greta, and Leesa's husband, Samir, works for the same engineering firm as Warren. So Greta becoming friends with Albie Byrne's sister is not the big deal Leesa would like to infer. She loves gossip though, and I can't blame the girl for trying to drum something out of nothing.

'Phoebe was saying she's just booked a ski trip with Albie and his fiancée in January,' Leesa adds. 'Verbier. They go every year, apparently. I googled the resort. It looks *amazing*. Then I googled how much.' Her eyes widen. 'Greta, you should cosy up to Phoebe and wrangle an invite.' She grins, then stops. 'But seriously, is it not weird being friends with her when her brother basically crippled you?'

I wince.

Greta shakes her head. 'The accident wasn't Albie's fault, you know that.'

My cheeks heat up. *It wasn't Albie's fault, but it* was, *to a degree, mine and Jon's.* A seemingly small action with huge repercussions.

Jon arrives back with the drinks and I quickly change the subject.

'How's the summer going, Maeve? Big year from September with the Leaving Cert ahead?'

'Ugh. Don't remind me of school,' she says, forking more rice on to her plate.

'Oh, wait,' Jon says. 'Isn't the Geary daughter in your class, Maeve?'

Maeve nods.

'The bratty daughter,' Aoife pipes up, grinning delightedly. 'She *is* a brat. You're not wrong.'

I throw her what is supposed to be an admonishing look, though my heart's not in it, then glance at Maeve, who is beside her, still engrossed in her food. They're like twins with their long dark hair and deep brown eyes and White Fox hoodies. Maeve's purple beanie and Aoife's glasses make up the only discernible differences and I'm reminded again of another pair of sisters, Aimee and Venetia. *God. Imagine losing your sister.*

'So what's the story with the boyfriend and the bunking-off?' Jon asks me. 'I'm guessing not a motive for threatening texts or smashing windows?'

Everyone looks at me, though Greta and Leesa already know the story.

'OK, basically, I was out for a walk with Bella one day in May, down by the football pitches, and I saw her there with a guy.' I glance around at my audience. 'In her uniform, during school hours, I mean. She didn't see me, so she wouldn't have known until the message this week that she'd been spotted.' I turn to Maeve and Aoife. We probably shouldn't be discussing Nika in front of them. 'Do *not* repeat those details though. I'm only saying it because I trust you and you're here with the grown-ups.'

Two heads nod vigorously.

'Did you not say something to her?' Greta fails to keep the disapproval from her voice. She'd never have let it slide.

Leesa squeezes my arm. 'She's on mat leave; she doesn't have to care what they do. And come on, we all did it back in the day.'

Greta's only reply is a firm headshake, and I'd well believe it – this isn't just for show in front of Maeve and Aoife. Greta was the good girl, the one who followed the rules. Leesa was the troublemaker, though no worse than half the kids her age. As usual, I was somewhere in the middle – experimenting with a bit of everything without going too far.

I shrug. 'I might have said something if I'd walked right past her, but she was at the other side of the pitch, and by the time I got around there, she and her boyfriend had gone. Well' – I glance at my nieces – 'not her boyfriend, as it turns out.'

I fill the others in on the Zach–Nika–Ariana love triangle and the comments from the other kids in their year.

'Serves her right,' Aoife says, and Maeve raises her eyebrows in a gesture that means, I think, she agrees with her sister but isn't going to say so out loud.

'But . . . does this pile-on give Nika a reason to break our window and text you, and so on?' Jon asks.

'The first two, maybe,' I concede. 'It's the "and so on" bit I can't imagine.'

Silence then. I guess none of us are comfortable discussing murder hypotheses in front of Maeve and Aoife.

'Well, I'm not sorry Nika's getting a taste of her own medicine,' Greta says, with uncharacteristic malice. I don't think she means it, really. I don't think she'd wish bullying on any teen, but she's still angry on our niece's behalf.

'A taste of her own medicine . . .' Maeve repeats thoughtfully. 'Wouldn't it be good if there was a medicine you could give to fix people like that.' She looks up. 'Fix them or get rid of them.'

22

Celeste
Saturday

CELESTE SIPS HER MOROCCAN mint tea, watching Warren over the rim of her cup. He's psyching himself up to tell her something. She knows the signs. Jittery, keys jangling, pacing. Offers of tea, although she's clearly already got one. The Saturday-morning papers sit unread on the island. Warren has them delivered every weekend but only ever reads sports news, and only ever on his phone. The front page of the *Irish Times* has a photo of the Cherrywood murder victims. Aimee smiles up from the page, white teeth gleaming, dimples buttoned in her young skin. Thirty-three to Warren's fifty-five. The husband – Rory – is handsome. *Was* handsome. Dark hair, even features, a cheeky glint in his deep blue eyes. Warren's gaze follows hers to the newspaper and his face colours.

'Right, I'd better go, I'm golfing at ten. And . . . well, the police want me to go down this afternoon to give a statement about the girl. The Bar Four thing.'

She looks at him, doesn't respond.

'Have you . . . have you heard any more from Susan O'Donnell? Did she say anything else?'

'About what, Warren?'

He opens his mouth but can't seem to bring himself to say more. Celeste takes another sip of tea. She doesn't need to hear about Warren and this Aimee. She can imagine very well without further input from Susan O'Donnell. Anyway – though she doesn't tell Warren this – she's blocked Susan's number.

Warren closes his mouth, nods and walks to the doorway. Then he turns, as though something's struck him last minute. 'Ah, I meant to say, Cody's work experience's been pulled.'

Celeste lowers her cup to its saucer and crosses her hands on her lap, eyebrows up, waiting for more.

'Yeah, they said it was something to do with numbers – they'd already accepted more kids than they realized.'

'But?'

Warren looks down. 'I believe they heard about Cody and the Fitzpatrick situation.'

'I see. And what do you have to say about that?'

'Come on, Celeste, that's hardly my fault. You can't blame me for everything.'

I can and I do.

She traces a finger on the rim of the cup. A wedding present, part of a set. Wedgwood Gold Columbia.

'Maybe if you hadn't done what you'd done, Susan O'Donnell would never have sent the message and none of this would have happened.'

'Sorry. You know I—'

'Don't speak.' She says it lightly, calmly. But she wants to hurl the cup at him, watch hot tea drip down his giant, stupid face.

The sound of someone on the stairs halts her. Cody, tousle-headed from sleep, ambles into the kitchen. He's wearing an oversized T-shirt and boxers, though she's told him time and again to dress before he comes downstairs. He stops when he sees his parents, looks from one to the other.

'What?' he says in that insouciant way teenagers do. It drives her mad.

'Your work experience has been cancelled,' she says. 'They know about the Fitzpatrick incident.'

Cody's eyes widen, his cheeks colour. Warren is backing out of the kitchen, still jangling his keys. He makes a 'gotta go' gesture. *Coward.*

Cody turns to the fridge, grabs a carton of juice and pours a glass. His back is tight with tension.

'Don't think you're going to spend your summer in your bedroom,' Celeste says in a low, controlled voice. 'And don't dare sulk. You brought this on yourself.'

Cody slams the fridge and stomps up the stairs without looking at her. Celeste, knuckles white, picks up her tea.

23

Jon
Saturday

JON IS SURPRISED TO hear the TV on when he arrives downstairs on Saturday morning. Susan's still asleep upstairs, Bella
beside her, after a wakeful night. Did they leave the TV on
when they went to bed? It was late when Greta and Leesa
and the girls left, and he'd had a fair bit of wine, but he's
pretty certain he switched it off . . . He slows as he moves
towards the living room, suddenly nervous. He stops, swal-
lowing, listening. It's definitely the TV. It takes him another
moment before he reaches out a hand and, carefully, pushes
the door. Onscreen, he recognizes an old episode of *Stranger
Things*. And in front of the screen, cross-legged on the rug, sits
Aoife.

She turns now to look at him.

'Hi, Jon.'

'Aoife! How are you? I mean . . .'

'My mum let me in with your spare key.' She pushes her
glasses up her nose. 'She said not to wake you or Susan, that
you need your sleep.'

He remains, however, baffled. They're a close family, Susan
and her sisters, cloyingly close at times, and they all keep spare

keys in case someone gets locked out, but they're not in the habit of letting themselves into each other's houses uninvited.

Aoife must read his mind. 'My mum and Susan agreed it. Mum and Maeve are gone down to Kildare Village, shopping. I didn't want to go, so Susan said I could stay here till my friend's mum picks me up in the afternoon.'

'Ah, OK.' Susan should have told him. He scratches his head. Then again, maybe she did and he forgot.

'Uh, coffee?' he asks.

'Yes, please!'

He wonders if thirteen-year-olds drink coffee. He's pretty sure he did at that age, and Aoife's old enough to say if she's not allowed. He raises a hand and heads for the kitchen to put on the coffee machine, rubbing his eyes.

Jon doesn't really like Aoife. Susan admires her confidence, but to him, it's just precociousness. He'd never tell Susan. She'd be horrified. And hurt. Family is everything to her. Jon has no siblings and admits – though only to himself – that he doesn't always get it. This closeness. This living in each other's pockets. Susan claims it's because their dad left when she was a baby and then their mum died when she was in college, and he understands that, he absolutely does. But maybe it shouldn't mean there's a slightly annoying thirteen-year-old invading his Saturday-morning space? Especially with the week they've just had.

He brings a coffee to Aoife, who is now on the couch, looking at her phone.

'I'll head back upstairs,' he says, not sure of the etiquette here but fairly certain he doesn't have to stay and chat.

Aoife nods knowingly. 'You must be tired,' she says, sounding like someone twice her age. 'The message situation,' she adds.

'Um, yeah.'

'The Gearys are still pretty mad.'

'I . . . I'd imagine so.'

'And now Cody's lost some work experience programme he was supposed to be on. Celeste and Warren are fuming.'

'Really?'

'Yeah. My friend's brother is friends with Cody. I hear *everything*. He put it on his Stories just now.'

Jon isn't sure what that means but thinks it might be Snapchat related.

'I guess these things happen,' he says lamely.

Aoife stares at him in that unsettling way she sometimes does. Like she's burrowing right into his brain. 'He lost his place on the programme because of Susan's message. People found out what he did and the company wanted nothing to do with him. That's a direct quote from my friend's brother.' Her eyebrows arch above her glasses.

'OK. That's . . . well, I'd better get Susan's coffee up to her.' He closes the door.

Upstairs, Susan is still asleep. He sets her coffee carefully on her night-stand, without disturbing her or the baby. The coaster that usually sits on the top of the night-stand is missing and he glances around, looking for it. Susan's family can be pretty free and easy about coasters, but he was brought up to take no chances. Her night-stand drawer is ajar, and he slides it open, looking for something to put beneath the hot cup. The drawer is messy. Hair-claws, notebooks, pens, a tube of cream and a paperback copy of *Daisy Jones and the Six*. He pulls out the paperback. That will do as a pseudo-coaster. Something catches his eye beneath the book. Something solid and shiny and sickeningly familiar. His scalp prickles.

He stares, dizzy and hot and cold all at once. The bracelet. *Oh god*. Meaning . . . meaning – he turns it over in his mind, grasping for an alternative conclusion, but there is none, not with that inscription . . . This means only one thing: Susan knows about the affair.

24

Susan
Saturday

ON SATURDAY AFTERNOON, AS soon as Aoife is picked up, I tell Jon I'm heading out for a walk on my own. There isn't anywhere in particular I want to go, I just don't want to be home alone with him. My mind is in a constant whirl, trying to process what he's done. What he's still doing, presumably, and until I decide on my response, I don't want to blurt out anything I can't unsay. As I leave, he mentions something about a run later, but I pretend I don't hear. *A run.* There should be some satisfaction in knowing I'm keeping him from her, but there is only hollow space.

My walk takes me, perhaps intentionally, down past Bar Four and on to Coal Place and the row of cottages where Venetia and her husband live. There's a garda car outside their cottage and, as I watch, two uniformed gardaí emerge from the house and make their way back to the car. Venetia is in the doorway. She's about to pull the door closed when she sees me. Her brow furrows – she's trying to work out if she knows me, I think – and then she lifts a hand, almost on autopilot. There must be a constant stream of people offering condolences, people she half knows, friends of her sister's. The garda car pulls into traffic, and Venetia is still standing in her doorway, holding the door open behind her, still looking at me. She thinks I'm calling in to pay respects, I realize now. Oh god. This is awkward. She waves for me to come in. Shit. I give a small wave back and walk through the narrow gateway and up the front path to her house.

'Hi, Venetia, I'm so sorry for your loss. I . . . we met briefly at the Bar Four opening last month. I met your sister there too. I really am dreadfully sorry to hear the awful news.'

She nods, pulling her black dressing gown tightly around her. She looks dazed and glassy-eyed. Maybe she's been given medication to cope. I know I'd need medication if anything happened to one of my sisters. She steps back into the hallway and gestures for me to follow.

I hesitate. But she's already turned to lead the way, and walking off, leaving this grieving, dazed woman, feels wrong. I step inside.

The hall is dark and narrow, with two doors on either side and one at the end, all closed. Brown carpet and yellowy-cream paintwork give it a dated feel, and there are no pictures on the walls. Venetia pushes open a door to our left and leads the way into the living room.

Inside, a man – her husband, I guess – sits on a cracked black leather couch, staring into space. He startles a little when he sees me, then gives a small smile. He probably thinks I'm a friend of Venetia's or Aimee's. I imagine there are all sorts of people they hardly know dropping by. But then that's something we do well in Ireland – condolences and sympathy and the rituals of death. Venetia sits heavily on an old-fashioned mahogany dining-room chair and I hover by the doorway. This room is similar to the hall – the same dark brown carpet, the same yellowish walls. And again, it's devoid of personal touches – even the mantelpiece is almost entirely bare, with just an old-style gold carriage clock at its centre.

Venetia sighs, readying herself to speak, and her voice, when it comes, is slow and empty of emotion. She's definitely on something. Good, I think: whatever it takes to inoculate her.

'This is Felipe, my husband,' she says, waving in his direction.

To him, dully, she adds: 'She met us at Bar Four.' I can't tell if she really remembers the encounter. I suspect not. Bartenders must meet hundreds of people a night.

Felipe, boyish-looking with deep brown eyes, dark tousled hair and a short beard, stands to shake my hand, a shy smile on his face. Compared to Venetia, he seems sweet and unassuming. I glance over at her again. Even in a dressing gown and medicated state, she's somewhat intimidating.

I gesture towards the door. 'I saw the garda car leaving – did the police have any information about what happened?'

Felipe shakes his head. 'They've been twice now to ask us about Aimee and Rory, to ask if they had been worried about something. Any disputes with anyone.'

'I suppose the guards are speaking to everyone who knew them.' And *people like me, caught in the middle*. 'It's nice that they came here rather than making you go to them.'

'We will go there tomorrow to give DNA and fingerprints,' Felipe says. 'They have to do this for anyone who might have been in the house.' He spreads his hands. 'I don't know what to expect. Maybe it will be like TV or maybe not.' A soft half-smile, a small shrug.

'Yeah, who knows . . .' My face heats up.

'Did you know Aimee well?' he asks, and I get the sense he's uttered the same words to dozens of visitors since Wednesday. He gestures for me to take a seat on the couch and I do. He moves towards the far end, more than polite space between us.

'I didn't know her well, no. I just met her at the bar that one night.'

He looks a little confused now, wondering no doubt what I'm doing here. Venetia has glazed over; I don't think she's listening to what I'm saying. What *am* I doing here? It's time to leave these people in peace.

'I didn't mean to intrude, I just wanted to say I'm sorry. I'll go now.' I stand.

'Of course. Thank you for coming.' Felipe stands too, shakes my hand. 'It was good to meet you – I'm sorry, what was your name?'

'Oh, of course, I'm Susan.'

Venetia sits up straight, focused now.

She stares at me. 'Susan.' The room is deathly quiet. My heart rate speeds up, my throat tightens. 'What's your surname?'

'You know, I really should go. I didn't mean to interrupt.'

'You're Susan O'Donnell.'

Oh god, I should never have come here. I move towards the living-room door, my legs shaking.

'You sent the message about Aimee.'

I turn back to face her, it's the least I can do. She stares at me, speechless now.

'I'm so sorry,' I whisper. 'I never meant to hurt anyone's feelings.'

Her mouth works as though she's trying to find words.

'Feelings?' she says eventually, in a low voice. 'You're worried about her feelings? My sister is *dead*.'

Felipe walks over to her, hunkers down and pulls her into a half-hug, rubbing her back.

Over his shoulder, Venetia stares at me, eyes red-rimmed and disbelieving. Angry. Desperately sad.

'Get out of my house.' She says it so quietly, I almost don't hear her.

Felipe stands to face me, one hand on Venetia's shoulder.

'Venetia is having a very difficult time, she's . . .'

He trails off and closes his eyes briefly, his face washed with pain and something else I can't decode.

'Of course. I'll go. I really am so sorry.' I let myself out.

25

Susan
Saturday

WHEN I GET HOME from Venetia's house, shaky and sick, Greta is in the kitchen with Jon, huddled in close conversation. They spring apart as I arrive, and it's clear from the guilty faces that they're talking about me, the message, the mess I've made. And they don't even know what's just happened . . . I pull up a chair and sink my head into my hands. They listen wordlessly as I tell them about the visit to Venetia and Felipe. At the end, I peer through interlaced fingers.

Jon is shaking his head in what might be disapproval.

Greta, ever practical, is on her phone, poised for action. 'OK, what are Felipe and Venetia's surnames?'

'I don't know. Why?'

'I want to get a sense of them. In case.'

'In case . . . what?'

She looks up. 'In case they're the kind of people to take to social media or turn up at your door.'

Jon chimes in. 'Yeah, it probably wasn't a good idea to call to them.' Although he's right, it irks me. I'm not good with criticism, I hate feeling like a naughty child, and I'm in no mood for taking moral guidance from my husband right now.

Greta is still scrolling and nods agreement without looking up. 'Nothing you can do will bring back Venetia's sister and we don't know if your message had anything to do with her death. It's not a murder-suicide, remember.'

'I know. I should never have gone near their house, it was stupid.' It *was* stupid, and not like me at all. I don't know if it's because of Jon's affair or this stuff with the message or Savannah's murder, but I seem to have lost the ability to think straight and act like a rational person. 'I really do want to get to the bottom of this,' I add. 'I hate how self-centred this sounds, but if someone did kill Aimee because of my message, or kill Savannah thinking she was me, I need to know.'

Greta nods, still thumbing her phone screen. She stops suddenly.

'Oh my god.'

'What?' Jon and I say in unison.

Her eyes widen. 'This is weird.' She holds up her phone, uncharacteristically lost for words. Onscreen, there's an *Irish Independent* article about the murders with a picture that's very familiar, one we've seen on election posters around the area over the last few years.

'What's Albie Byrne's photo doing there?' Jon asks.

'He's Savannah's ex-husband . . .' Greta says, her voice faint. 'Jesus. That's . . . weird.'

Jon's mouth drops open in surprise.

Greta nods slowly, still dazed. 'They're divorced, according to this.' She looks up. 'I didn't know Albie well, so I don't know why I'm finding it strange that he's just lost his ex-wife and that she's a murder victim, but somehow I am.'

I shake my head. 'I get it. I felt the same when I realized it was Savannah who'd been killed, even though I'd never actually met her. It was still a connection. It makes it more real.'

I point at her phone screen, still open on Albie Byrne's photo. 'He's only recently been elected – I wonder if this will be bad for his career. Associated with a murder . . .'

Detective Kellerman's question yesterday morning comes back now – asking about someone called 'Sam'. So not Savannah's ex-husband, after all. I turn that over, but it brings me no closer to clarity.

Jon is quiet, looking down at his hands. He'd missed the whole rehash of Greta's accident last night, but there's no escaping it now, and the memories Albie Byrne's name provokes. And for the first time since that night, I feel something more than guilt and awkwardness. If Jon had just done what he was supposed to do – remembered he was collecting me, left the pub for another time – Greta would have been tucked up on her couch that night. It's everyone's fault and no one's fault, but right now, through the filter of his betrayal, it's mostly Jon's fault.

Greta passes me her phone so I can read the article. Albie was interviewed for the piece, and has lots to say about how much Savannah will be missed by friends and family, how amicable their divorce was, and how making our streets safer will be top of his agenda. 'No woman should have to face what Savannah did,' he's quoted as saying. 'No woman should feel unsafe answering the door in her own home.'

At those words, a shiver runs across my skin. For the first time, I picture it. Savannah, answering her door. Answering to a friend, a neighbour, an acquaintance, a stranger? *Which is worse?* Either way, she opened the door to her killer.

Leesa's words from Wednesday echo in my head: *It should have been you.*

26

Venetia
Saturday

VENETIA CAN'T OPEN HER eyes. It's the sleeping tablets. The chef from Bar Four arranged them when news of Aimee's death broke. Venetia doesn't quite know how. Her colleague isn't a doctor, but it doesn't matter. She got them, and they work.

Felipe was worried at first. What if the sleeping tablets were a gateway back to . . . he didn't finish the sentence. There was no need; they both knew what he meant. But if she went back to her old habits, it wouldn't be because of sleeping tablets, it would be because her sister is dead. And god how she's craved it over the last five days. The fix that would give her oblivion. *Lend* her oblivion, at least. The sleeping tablets, for their part, give her dreamless sleep, six hours of peace. Until she wakes up, as she has just now, groggy and confused, before it all hits again. Aimee is dead. Her only family in the world. The weight of it. The sheer weight of that pain. Like a lead shroud covering every inch of her body. Every fraction of her mind.

A movement beside her tells her Felipe is here. She's on the couch, she realizes, not in her bed. Scraps of something filter into her mind. A visit. A woman.

She turns her head, twists on to her side and curls her knees to her chest.

'The woman. Susan.' Her voice is croaky.

'Yes.'

'She was here?' she asks, though she knows; the memory is clearer now.

'Yes.'

It doesn't add up. 'And she sent the message? The one about Aimee and Warren Geary?'

Her eyes are still closed, but she senses his nod.

She opens her eyes now and looks at Felipe's face. Misery etched all over it.

'I did some googling while you were asleep,' he says. 'And there's something you should know.'

27

Susan
Sunday

A WHEEL WOBBLES ON the trolley and I consider returning to the front of the supermarket to switch it for another, but I don't. It was tricky enough finding one with a seat for babies as young as Bella, and she's snoozing now. Also, this is quite possibly the biggest Dunnes supermarket in Ireland and the walk back to the front might just end me. I throw two bags of pasta into the trolley, then grab a jar of pesto, reaching past a diminutive elderly lady who looks confused. On seeing Bella, she smiles, then goes back to staring at the shelves, immobilized, perhaps, by the mind-numbing boredom of grocery decision-making. *Hard relate*, I think as I push the trolley further along the same aisle towards the condiments section. Jon usually does the groceries because I'm terrible at it and he is a grocery ninja. But while I'm on maternity leave, it makes sense for me to take over. I'm still terrible at it – zigzagging inefficiently up and down the same aisles, taking twice as long as Jon does. And now I realize I forgot to grab tinned tomatoes along with the pasta. Leaving the trolley beside the ketchup, I walk back down the aisle and grab two cans, the ones at eye level that probably cost twice as much as the own-brand ones, but I'm running out of steam and don't have the energy to shop around. The elderly lady catches me yawning and smiles. 'It's hard when they're small,' she says, and I smile back. God, if only it was just Bella keeping me awake, and not the constant ping-pong of worries. That, and the noises from outside I'd never normally notice – front doors and car doors, engines starting and stopping. Even at half three this morning, I could hear the hum of an engine outside. I got up to look, but by the time I made it to the nursery window all I could see was tail lights in the distance. Jon reckons it was a taxi, but still, I sent another email to the gardaí.

My phone beeps now with a message from Leesa, checking in on me, asking me if I want to call in, and I send a quick voicenote to tell her I will but that I'll drop Bella home to Jon first. Then I turn back towards the condiment section. I see ketchup and mayonnaise and rows and rows of dressing. But the aisle itself is empty. Even the elderly lady has gone. I stare at the space where my trolley was only moments ago. *Bella*. Bella's gone. My heart stops. Panic floods my body, making me light-headed. My back was turned for no more than ten seconds. Am I misremembering where I left her? I'm not; I know I'm not. I run to the top of the aisle and look left and right, but there's no sign. In front of me is a row of freezers, perpendicular to the aisles. She's not here. I turn back down the next aisle, parallel to the one we were on, but she's not here either. Where is she? I go back to where I was, back at the condiments, and there are people here, and trolleys, but none of them are mine. I run down the aisle, through to the next one, but she's not here either. She's not anywhere. I'm struggling to catch my breath, from running or panic or both. Ahead is a quiet section for stationery and cards and I can see right through to the line for the tills. No Bella. I'm going to throw up. What do I do? Indecision and panic freeze me momentarily, then common sense takes hold again and I run to a uniformed teenager who's stacking shelves.

'My trolley with my baby, she's' – I'm breathless, struggling to get coherent words out – 'it's gone missing. Can you do an announcement?'

He looks confused.

Deep breaths. 'My daughter is in the trolley, and it's not where I left it. Please.' I grab his arm now. 'Make an announcement. Get help.'

He nods, still unsure. 'I'll ask for them to announce it. Um, what age is the baby? What does she look like?'

'She's tiny, only four months old. In a yellow onesie. I'll keep looking.'

Checking back over my shoulder once, to make sure he's really on his way to get help, I move one aisle over, into a chilled-goods section lined on both sides with fridges. Busy with shoppers and trolleys, but no Bella. Pushing past a man with three small kids, I ignore the 'Careful!' he calls after me and dodge my way back up to the next chilled aisle, my head whipping around, and oh my god, oh my god, there she is. There's the trolley. There's Bella. In three strides, I'm with her, undoing the buckle and lifting her into my arms. She's still asleep. She's still asleep and she's not gone and she's not hurt and she's here. For a moment, I stand there, rocking her, trying to calm my breathing.

'Are you OK?' It's the man I passed in the other aisle.

'Yes. Sorry.' A gulpy breath. I'm close to tears. 'Someone took my baby, but it's OK.'

A puzzled look. 'Someone took your baby?'

'Well, my trolley, I mean.'

'Oh yeah.' He grins. 'I've done that before. Walked off with someone's full trolley and only realized when I spotted dog food in it. We don't have a dog,' he adds, to clarify.

I want to say more, I want to say nobody takes a trolley with a baby in it, but my words won't come, and he's walking off. Maybe someone moved her because she was in the way? But surely not to another aisle?

An announcement comes out over the intercom now, asking customers to look out for a four-month-old baby, and it sounds so ridiculous I want to laugh, but I also want to sit on the floor and cry.

There's no way I can focus on groceries now, and no way I can stay here in this supermarket. With Bella on my shoulder, I push the trolley one-handed to the till to let staff know I found her and to pay for what I have. Out of the corner of my eye, I'm conscious of a figure walking towards the supermarket exit. Someone vaguely familiar. When I look up, the person is gone, and I can't place who it was. But a sense of foreboding seeps into my bones.

28

Susan
Sunday

LEESA'S IN HER FRONT garden with a watering can when I arrive at four on Sunday afternoon, holding back the skirt of her pink sundress so it doesn't get wet as she pours. The weeks of sunshine that have lightened her hair and bronzed her skin have also parched her flowerbeds. She turns when she hears me, pushing her sunglasses to the crown of her head. Her greeting is slightly flustered, accompanied by a sheepish expression.

'What's going on?' I ask.

'Nothing!' Breezy. She's definitely hiding something. She squints, leaning closer. 'Are *you* OK? You look a little . . . wild-eyed?'

I tell her about the supermarket. And horrible though it was, it's much easier talking about this than everything I'm not telling her about Jon's affair and my resurfacing fears of hurting Bella.

'Oh god,' she says. 'I remember the baby-brain days.'

'I don't know if it was baby brain . . . what if someone moved her on purpose?'

'Eh, why?'

'To scare me, maybe, like the broken window and the texts?'

Leesa bites her lip. 'You know me, I'm up for any kind of

conspiracy theory, but that sounds a bit . . .' Her raised palms finish the sentence.

A bit nuts. A bit out there. A bit paranoid. *I know.*

'Look,' she goes on, 'I did stuff like that all the time when Maeve and Aoife were babies.'

I know she's right. But I feel like I'd know if it was me, if I was the one who moved her to the next aisle and then forgot. Wouldn't I? Leesa is looking at me now with a worried expression.

'Yeah. Maybe another customer got confused and wheeled the trolley . . . Anyway, she's safely home with Jon now and I'm free to hang out here for a bit.'

'What did Jon say about it?'

'I didn't tell him.'

'OK, well . . . there *is* something I have to tell you. Now don't kill me, OK?'

I knew there was something. 'What did you do?'

'So . . . I texted Moira Fitzpatrick, the woman whose son got hurt when Cody Geary was minding him.'

'I didn't know you were on texting terms?'

'I'm not, but Maeve babysat her kids a bit when they were smaller, so I have her number. Anyway, I messaged her when we were talking about it, explained that we're worried that the Gearys are sending you threats and—'

'Leesa! You can't say that. We don't know who's sending the threats.'

'I know, but she's not their biggest fan, so I figured it would get her on side. And it did. I'm due to call there shortly. Want to come with? Here, I'll text her to say you're coming too.' She's already on her phone, typing.

I hold up my hand to stop her.

'Just give me a sec to think. I don't know if I should go. It might fan the flames.'

'Oh, sorry.' A grimace. 'I've already pressed send.'

I'm really not sure about this. A huge part of me just wants to know. To figure out who's so upset by my message they've started targeting me. But still.

'Look,' Leesa says, 'we can ask her not to mention to anyone we were there. It's not going to make anything worse, is it?'

I stand there, immobile with indecision, until Leesa looks down at her phone again. 'OK, Moira's already replied, she says she'd love to talk to you – a big uppercase "love" by the way, so come on, there's nothing to lose.'

She's probably right. If Moira doesn't tell anyone, it can't hurt. And if nothing else, it's a distraction from the rose-gold bracelet.

The Fitzpatricks live a few roads over from where we are in Oak-park. Like Celeste's, theirs is one of the five-bedroom homes with larger gardens and longer driveways. Moira Fitzpatrick answers the door and greets us with an easy smile. In her late thirties, she has long blonde hair loose around her shoulders and a tan that looks more tennis court than Marbella. She's wearing white shorts with a coral tank and gold flip-flops and she invites us through the house and out to the back garden. From the living room comes the strain of a TV show, some-thing high-voiced and animated.

'Cannot believe they're indoors on a day like this,' Moira says, gesturing back to the house as we take seats around her garden table. 'I *live* for the sun. Hope it lasts till Thursday now – you'll both be at the Oakpark summer party, won't you? Down on the big green? We have fireworks this year!'

Leesa nods enthusiastically, never one to let a small thing like not actually living in Oakpark get in the way of a night out.

'I don't think I can make it, unfortunately,' I say. I can't think of anything worse than hanging out with neighbours right now.

Moira pouts a little. 'Oh. Well, I'm helping Juliette Sullivan organize it – please do come if you can. We've got a loan of some speakers for the music and heaps of wine. It's going to be *epic*.'

I nod and smile. 'OK, I'll try.' She won't even notice I'm not there on the night.

On a round wicker tray, there's a cafetière, three cups on saucers, and a plate of shortbread fingers.

'Sorry, all I have are biscuits, I meant to pop to the shop before you arrived but my husband didn't make it back in time and no way was I taking the kids.' She does an exaggerated shudder and Leesa and I smile.

'So,' Moira says, pouring coffee for each of us, 'you want to know about Cody Geary?'

Leesa nods. 'Yes. And look, if it's hard for you to talk about—'

Moira cuts her off with a wave. 'I don't mind. And if Cody's done something else, I'll help in any way I can.'

'Right. We're not sure if he's done anything, but I guess the more information we have, the better. To give you some context – you may have seen Susan's message about the Gearys?'

I flush, and Moira nods.

'I did.' She turns to me. 'And everything you said was true, so don't worry one bit.'

I force a small smile.

Leesa continues. 'We're concerned about some threats Susan's been getting, and wondering if it's linked to the message and one of the Gearys. Maybe Cody.' We had agreed on the way over we wouldn't mention Savannah Holmes. 'Would you be able to tell us about what happened with Cody when he babysat for you?'

'Sure.' Moira's lips tighten. 'You obviously know some of it, despite the Gearys' desperate efforts to cover it up. We had asked for Nika to babysit, but she couldn't do that night, so Celeste offered Cody. At first I wasn't sure – he was only fourteen – but we were just popping for pizza down the road and would be two hours max. So I said yes. I'll never forgive myself for that.'

From inside the house, a door slams, and a girl aged about eight or nine comes out.

'Mum, Senan is sitting on the remote and won't let me change the channel.'

'Can you watch what he's watching?'

'No way, it's for babies. Can you tell him to give me the remote?'

Moira grits her teeth. 'In a minute, Tilly. I'm just talking to our neighbours for a sec.'

The little girl sighs and slopes off, cross but resigned, it seems.

'That's Tilly. She told us what happened when we got home that night.' Moira shakes her head. 'God, when I think of it . . . Anyway. Cody arrived and we went out, all fine, but then apparently Senan wouldn't go to bed when Cody told him to, and things got out of hand. Obviously, Cody should have tried reasoning with him and then threatened to call us and then he should have actually called us, but it seems to have escalated way beyond that and, all of a sudden, Cody had locked Senan out in the garden.' Tears glisten. 'Sorry.' She waves a hand in front of her face, composing herself. 'Senan was distraught, as any four-year-old would be, and he decided to try to find us. He walked through the side gate, out to the front, and started along the path' – she points, indicating her neighbour's house – 'and as he passed next door—' She stops and swallows, unable to speak now.

'Take your time,' Leesa says gently.

'God! I honestly thought I could tell this without getting upset any more!' Moira lets out a slow breath and rubs her hands on her lap. 'OK. Next door, Paddy – our neighbour – was reversing out and Senan was hit.' The word 'hit' comes out in a whisper. She clears her throat. 'We got a call from Paddy while he was waiting for the ambulance. Luckily, we were so near, we got home in like, ten minutes, but Jesus Christ, I'll never forget it. Never forget seeing Senan's tiny body crumpled on the ground. I thought he was . . . you know.'

The first time I heard the story, it sounded like hearing a news report or watching something on TV. Removed. This time, it feels all too real.

'But he was OK?' Leesa asks.

'Yes. Bruising, broken rib, concussion. Thank god Paddy was reversing so slowly.'

'And did you talk to Cody?'

'I couldn't bear to. My husband did. I never want to see him again.' Her eyes spark with anger. 'What kind of psychopath does that to a four-year-old child? Locks them out at ten o'clock at night? Because he couldn't get Senan to go to bed? Apparently Cody wanted to watch something on TV and Senan was insisting on watching something else.' She waves towards the house. 'A bit like just now, but even Tilly, who is eight, knows that sometimes you just suck it up. You don't lock a child out.'

'And what did the Gearys say?'

'Oh, they doubled down, protected their child. Said Senan must have provoked their son. I mean, for the love of god, *provoked* him? The child was four. Cody should have known better.'

I clear my throat. 'Do you think Cody has the propensity to be violent?'

Moira nods vehemently. 'Anyone who does what he did?

Absolutely. And like, it's not as though he just politely asked Senan to go out. He pushed him out the door.'

'Did Cody admit that?'

'No. Of course not, he wouldn't admit any of it. But little did he know, we had a nanny cam on. Here, have a look.'

She opens the cover of an iPad and presses play. We lean in. It's hard to see in the sunlight and Leesa is closer than I am, but I can make out what looks like a couch and two figures in the foreground, one tall, one small.

'There's no sound,' Moira says, 'but you can see what's going on.'

The taller figure – Cody – is towering over the smaller figure, presumably Senan. Even without sound, everything signals an argument. Cody is pointing now, to something or somewhere offscreen.

'He's pointing towards those,' Moira says, indicating glass doors behind us. 'They were open on the night.'

Senan grabs something, we can't see what, and runs, disappearing from the frame. Cody follows, striding after him. Moments later, Cody is back onscreen, flopping on the couch, arms folded.

Moira presses pause.

'Basically, Tilly told us what happened, and the camera backed her up, so' – a shrug and a grim smile – 'he was caught.'

I think of the baby monitor camera I have attached to Bella's crib. I've only ever seen it as a way to keep an eye on her, see if she's awake or asleep, but maybe we should have more cameras in the house.

'God, what an awful thing to go through,' I say. 'I suppose they're all just kids – Cody too.'

This was the wrong thing to say. Moira's jaw tightens and her cheeks flush.

'My children are "just kids", but they'd never hurt someone or treat another child the way Cody treated Senan. Would yours?' She directs this at Leesa.

Leesa shakes her head. 'Not at this age. Though they used to batter each other when they were small.'

'That's different though,' Moira says tightly. 'A toddler hitting a big sister is normal behaviour. What Cody did is not normal. He should be locked up.' She looks from me to Leesa, daring us to disagree. We don't risk it.

A door slams from inside, and suddenly a small barrel of energy races out, remote control in hand, his big sister racing after him. Senan. He flings himself on to his mother's knee, clinging to her, the remote control buried somewhere between them.

'Mum!' Tilly is shouting. 'It's my turn now and he still won't give it!'

'No!' Senan turns to shout and nestles his head back into his mother's neck.

Moira is unperturbed. 'Ah Tilly, can't you watch a little bit later? He's only holding on to it because he knows you want it.'

'Then can I have your phone?'

Moira passes her phone and Tilly skips inside.

'Whatever works, right?' Moira arches her brows in a rhetorical question.

Senan twists on his mother's knee and reaches across to grab a handful of shortbread fingers. Moira tells him to stop and manages to get two of the five biscuits out of his hand. He slides off her lap, races to the other side of the garden with the remaining three and crams them into his mouth, watching his mother, pushing it to see how far he can go.

'Sorry, he's a demon for sugar.' She puts the two rescued biscuits back on the plate and eyes them for a moment. 'I was going to say they're safe, his hands are clean, but you know what? I wouldn't risk it.'

'So that was pretty telling,' I whisper to Leesa as we walk down Moira's driveway. 'Did you see how quickly she reacted when we asked if Cody could be violent? No hesitation.'

Leesa shakes her head. 'Doesn't mean a thing.'

'Wait – what?'

We're out on the street now, heading back in the direction of Rowanpark. The late-afternoon sun beams down, dappling the footpath, with only the slightest breeze rustling the treetops.

'Her child was hurt,' Leesa says. 'She's in full Mama-Bear mode. She'd literally grab Cody by the scruff of the neck and throw him out of the house if she found him there again. I promise you, there's nothing in the world like a mother whose child has been hurt. It doesn't mean we can take her word as gospel.'

'I don't know, she seemed pretty rational to me . . .'

A single car rolls past and we step on to the now empty main road that divides Oakpark from Rowanpark. Everyone's either in back gardens or beer gardens, making the most of the hot weather.

'Believe me, when Maeve was being bullied, I had full-blown vigilante fantasies,' Leesa says. 'I imagined going to each girl's house, or waiting till one of them was on her own somewhere and pushing her up against a wall to tell her if she ever went near my child again, I'd fucking kill her.'

My jaw drops. 'Leesa! That's not like you.'

'That's what I mean. When someone hurts your kid, all bets are off. I wouldn't have actually done it, obviously.'

'Yeah. OK. I get you.' We turn into Rowanpark Drive, the tree-lined street on which Leesa lives. The grass verges outside each neat redbrick house are patchworked in sunlight and the only sound is the faint hum of a distant mower.

'So just because Moira Fitzpatrick says Cody is definitely violent, doesn't mean it's true.'

'But to push a child out the door and lock it . . .'

'It's awful,' Leesa agrees. 'Obviously, he shouldn't have done it, even if Senan may have been a bit of a handful.' A grimace.

'I wasn't going to say, but yeah, having just met Senan . . . not the easiest kid for a fourteen-year-old to manage.' We start walking again. I'm too hot now and looking forward to a cool drink at Leesa's.

'Another thing I noticed,' Leesa says, 'Moira mentioned it was ten o'clock at night, though Senan was only four years old. I'd imagine his official bedtime was earlier than ten. I wonder how long Cody had been trying to get him to go to bed?'

29

Celeste
Sunday

CELESTE SMILES AROUND THE dining-room table. Everything is just so. Sleek white candles flickering in heavy gold candlesticks. A centrepiece of fresh flowers from her local florist. Gold-and-white dinnerware from Venetto Design, and gold Georg Jensen cutlery she'd brought back from a business trip to Copenhagen. Her favourite crystal glasses topped up with a 2022 Syrah, her guests almost finished her delicious beef wellington with truffle mashed potatoes.

Of course, good as her food is, the Sullivans are really here for gossip, for something to take home from dinner with the Gearys. And she's giving them *nothing*.

'So you'll come to the summer party on Thursday, won't you?' Juliette Sullivan asks, with a glint in her eye. 'The Oakpark Residents' Association one, on the green. I'm chief organizer, for my sins. As if I didn't have enough to do. But you know what they say, ask a busy person. So, you'll both be there?'

Not on your life, Celeste thinks. She and Warren are *not* parading themselves in front of the entire estate.

'Oh, *such* a pity,' she says. 'I have work calls on Thursday night – it's a terribly busy time of year, especially for my New

York teams. You know how it is. Well . . .' A faux-sheepish shrug finishes the sentence. Juliette does not know how it is. She does not have a New York team or any kind of team because her main function in life, as far as Celeste can see, is running Oakpark summer parties and gossiping about neighbours.

The uncareful slam of the front door tells her Cody's home, and she calls him to the dining room. He slouches in and mumbles a response when she asks him to say hi. Hands in pockets, eyes down, he leaves while Juliette Sullivan is still asking about his summer. *For god's sake.* Celeste will speak to him later. If she has the energy.

'He's exhausted,' she says, smiling benevolently. 'You know how it is with teens – up till all hours then sleeping all morning.'

Juliette Sullivan inclines her head.

'Really? Gosh, mine are asleep by eleven every night. But I don't let them have phones in their rooms.' A light laugh. 'They must hate me. You're probably right to just let them do whatever they want. I'm old-school, I suppose.'

Go you, Celeste says soundlessly, through gritted teeth.

A gentler click of the front door tells her Nika's home. She's a better bet for meeting Juliette Sullivan's high standards. Celeste doesn't need to call Nika in like she did with Cody – Nika comes through herself, perfect smile wide, greeting their neighbours with confident grace. She looks good too (not that that matters, of course) in her denim shorts and black Converse and soft-grey hoodie, her caramel hair lightened by the sun. Celeste can hear Nika's phone buzzing in the back pocket of her shorts, but her daughter ignores it, like the polite girl she is. Thank you for not letting the side down, Celeste thinks. It can't be *all* her fault if one child turned out OK.

Juliette is asking Nika about her summer, about tennis and hockey and her part-time job in an ice-cream shop. Nika smiles, tucks her hair as she chats easily, and Celeste's stress levels slip down a notch. Why can't Cody be more like Nika? Is it a boy/girl thing? Or just a personality thing? She suppresses a small sigh and tops up everyone's wine.

'Will you have half a glass?' Warren asks Nika, nodding towards a spare seat at the end of the table.

Juliette purses her lips, and Celeste can picture it already, Juliette going back to her cronies, with news that the Gearys give their seventeen-year-old wine. That's why she's 'bratty' and bunking off school. Celeste's still not sure how she feels about the bunking-off. Nika has always been a model student. Her teachers love her, she gets top grades, she's on the Senior A hockey team. Celeste hasn't admitted it to anyone, not even to Nika, but she's surprised and disappointed that her daughter was skipping school, and maybe even more so that she hadn't known about it until Susan O'Donnell sent the message. In a perfect world, she'd rather not have everyone in South Dublin finding out at the same time she did, but it was hardly the crime of the century. That Nika was bunking off to meet a boy didn't track well, but again, not something to get too upset about. Celeste hadn't known Nika was seeing anyone, though she doesn't like to admit that either. Nika usually confides in her – she'd told her about the first sip of vodka at her first party, about trying vaping, about her first kiss – not the kind of thing Celeste would ever have told her own mother back when she was a teen. So she was surprised she'd not been told about this boy and, to be honest, a little hurt. But Nika would give her more details in due course, no doubt. So far, since the message went around on Wednesday, Nika hadn't given much away at all, though Celeste had noticed shadows under her eyes and a bid to be on her own a little more than usual. Is Nika worried about the message, or could there be something else wrong?

She'll try to grab a few minutes with her once the Sullivans have left, make sure she's OK. And to find out more about this new boyfriend.

Juliette, too, is trying to find out more about this new boyfriend, Celeste realizes, as she tunes back into the conversation.

'So, any suitors on the scene?' Juliette asks with a tinkly laugh. Like she hasn't pored over Susan O'Donnell's message all week. Like she hasn't discussed it at length with her pals.

Nika smiles. 'My dad always said no dating till I turn thirty, so I'll stick to that.' She winks to show she's joking, but successfully avoids answering. Celeste mentally high-fives her daughter. Celeste would never actually high-five anyone, the idea is hysterical, but in that moment, she's proud of Nika's manners and control. More like her mother than everyone realizes.

Juliette's not going to let it go, though. 'Oh, come on, a pretty girl like you – you must be fighting them off! All the boys – the single ones and the taken ones, I'll bet.'

Nika laughs, but now it sounds forced, if only to Celeste's ears. Celeste glances at Juliette, eyes narrowed. There's something pointed in the way she said it. Celeste has the sense she's missing something, and that, whatever it is, she needs to get ahead of it before Juliette.

'Nika, your grandmother called earlier and missed you. Would you mind giving her a call back before it gets too late?'

Warren glances up, looking surprised, aware that neither grandmother ever calls.

Nika nods. 'Sure thing. Nice to see you,' she says to the Sullivans, and slips out of the room.

'What perfect manners,' Juliette says when the door closes. 'Boys and girls are so different, aren't they?' Celeste feels a flush at the nape of her neck. She can criticize Cody – in her head, to his face, to Warren – but Juliette should know better.

Juliette is still talking. 'Has she been OK, since the you-know-what?'

Celeste goes for feigned ignorance. 'Hm?'

'The airing-of-dirty-laundry situation,' Juliette clarifies, her face full of concern.

Warren gets up to start clearing plates.

'She's fine. It's obviously not a big deal.'

'Well, except to Ariana.' Juliette grimaces.

'Ariana?' Celeste is confused. Ariana is Nika's long-time friend, although 'frenemy' might be a better word. Ariana is the alpha of the group, the ringleader.

Juliette makes a perfect O with her mouth. 'Do you not know?'

The heat at the back of Celeste's neck creeps around to her throat. Warren keeps clearing plates, then disappears through the dining-room door.

'The boy Nika was seeing – Zach – he's Ariana's boyfriend. Gosh, I'm probably telling tales out of school now, I shouldn't really . . .' Juliette touches her lips, miming regret.

Celeste's face burns. 'Oh. You know. Kids. They'll get over it.' She attempts to wave it away.

Warren is back, seated again, reaching for wine.

'I don't know . . .' Juliette's brow crinkles delicately. 'Ariana was with him for a while. You know how important relationships are at that age.' She laughs and waves around the room. 'Well, at any age, of course.'

Warren splutters, choking on his wine. Celeste would like to slap him.

'Anyway,' Juliette continues, 'now that the secret is out, it's jungle law, as you can imagine. All the other pals in the group are rallying around Ariana. Nika's a little out in the cold.' Juliette reaches across and touches Celeste's arm. 'That won't be easy.'

A shiver runs down Celeste's back at that. There's something so ominous about it. As though there's a foregone conclusion, an unstoppable teen-justice train. And this, more than anything, unnerves her.

30

Jon
Sunday

JON WATCHES OUT THE window, Bella in his arms. Susan should be home from Leesa's by now. She hasn't replied to his text asking when she'll be back. That's unusual. She's normally quick – a dashed-off typo-filled reply or a speedy voicenote. It might not be because of the bracelet . . . he shakes himself. *Of course* it's because of the bracelet. He goes upstairs and places sleepy Bella carefully in her crib, then pulls open Susan's drawer again to dig out the bangle. *God*. On so many levels, what a shitshow. What had he been thinking? He moves his fingers over the engraving. The tale-telling inscription. And how on earth is it here in their house – how does Susan have it?

The sound of the front door sends him into a tailspin. He drops the bangle while trying to put it back in the drawer and, for a moment, he can't find it. Terrifying though it is that Susan hasn't said anything, he's also very much not ready to show her he's found it. Her footsteps sound on the stairs now, light on the carpet. On his hands and knees, he swipes around blindly under the bed, trying to find the bracelet. She's at the top of the stairs when he spots it, and he can hear her crossing the landing while he stretches his fingers to reach it. The bedroom door creaks open just as he slides her night-stand drawer shut. He jumps away, ending up at Bella's crib.

'Oh!' Susan startles when she sees him. What does that mean? That she's jumpy in general after all that's gone on this week, or anxious specifically around him?

He puts a finger to his lips and nods towards Bella. Susan tiptoes forward to see their daughter and leans to place a kiss near but not on their baby's head. They've both learned you never disturb a sleeping infant. Together, in silence, they turn to leave the room.

Downstairs, in the kitchen, Jon tries his best to make conversation. 'How was Leesa's?'

'Fine.'

'All good with Maeve and Aoife?'

'I didn't see them.' She's rummaging through a cupboard, looking for chocolate, he thinks.

'Will I start dinner?'

A shrug. 'Whatever. I'm not hungry.'

'I'll do lemon chicken. You can have it if you're hungry later. Any news from Samir – he's still away in Dubai, right?'

Samir is Leesa's husband. Everyone likes Samir. Sometimes Jon hates Samir because of how much everyone else loves him. He's the perfect husband. Perfect dad. Great cook. Good listener. Self-deprecating, funny, fun. Most annoyingly of all, he's genuinely a nice guy, meaning Jon doesn't really hate him – he grudgingly likes him as much as everyone else does.

'Still there.'

God. This is painful. And not at all like Susan, who usually talks non-stop, giving him minute details of every conversation she's had that day. He has perfected a nodding-and-hmming routine over the years, with the occasional question to show he's listening, and right now, he'd love one of her run-downs on the day she's had. But no. Monosyllabic answers followed by a retreating back is what's on offer this evening.

She finds a bar of Lindt, makes herself a tea and goes through to the den, a room they only ever use if they're watching different TV shows. Something that happens for episodes of *And Just Like That* (he can't bear it) or golf (not her thing), but nothing else. Until now.

She closes the door without another word and he finds himself wishing Greta was here; she'd know what to do. He decides to try one more time, and opens the den door, just managing to stop himself from knocking first.

'Want to watch a film later? Or another episode of *Severance*?'

'Not really,' she says, though she adores *Severance*. 'I'm just going to stay in here and catch up on old *Desperate Housewives*.' She smiles thinly. 'Why don't you go for a run?'

He closes the door. She definitely knows. And she has the bracelet. Which means . . . well, his brain can't compute the rest of what this means, because it's far, far worse than just being caught having an affair.

31

Maeve
Sunday

MAEVE IS CROSS-LEGGED ON the couch, laptop open, phone in hand. Aoife is on the other couch, engrossed in her phone, but Maeve's braced to close her laptop if Aoife comes any nearer. Aoife is *incredibly* nosy. On Maeve's phone, the Nika pile-on continues. Mostly Ariana's closest friends, but a handful of other kids from their class too. Thinly disguised Stories on their own accounts – posts about traitors and bitches and cheats. And how 'NG better watch her back'. People love a fight. One post sticks out though, and that's what's made Maeve open Google and do her own search. A boy in their class (someone who's not friends with Nika, Ariana or Zach, so no actual reason to be posting at all really) has just put up a picture of a packet of walnuts, with the caption 'I wonder what happens if you hide these in someone's lunch and that person has a tree-nut allergy?'

Maeve is horrified.

Truly.

She is sure she is horrified.

But OK, part of her is just a little bit . . . thrilled? Not that she'd want anything bad to happen to Nika, despite everything

Nika's done to her. Of course not. But the idea that someone's just posted this . . . That someone could actually do this and . . . what? Well, Google is telling her anaphylactic shock. Which can be fatal. Of course, Nika'd have an epi pen; she always does. And this kid, he's not actually going to act on it. But still. She stares at the search results and clicks into a link. It's . . . interesting.

As she reads, she hears her mum answering the front door, then her Aunt Greta's voice. Her mum is saying something about calling in to Moira Fitzpatrick with Susan. Greta is saying it's making things worse and Leesa should have known better. Her mum and Greta drift into the kitchen and Maeve gets back to Google, adding 'does epi pen always work' to her search.

She clicks into an article from WebMD just as Greta comes through to the living room. Maeve's hand hovers at her track-pad, ready to switch tabs if needed.

Greta asks how they are, though they saw her on Friday night and nothing much has happened since. Maeve doesn't mind. She likes Greta. And she's always been Greta's favourite. It's because she was the first niece and because Greta doesn't have kids and because Greta is her godmother, she supposes, but also because they're alike. Quieter than the others, but practical and smart and good in a crisis. Mostly.

Greta steps closer, reaching for a book on the coffee table, and Maeve panics and closes the laptop. A little too suddenly, it turns out, as Aoife immediately buzzes to attention.

'Ohhh . . . what are you hiding?'

Maeve rolls her eyes. 'Nothing.'

'Show us then,' Aoife says. 'If it's nothing.'

'God, you are so nosy.'

Aoife uncurls her legs, gets up from her couch and comes over to sit on the arm of Maeve's.

'Go on, open it. I dare you. What was it? Something you clearly don't want Greta or me to see.'

Maeve hugs the laptop. 'Maybe I was looking at your TikTok and dying of second-hand embarrassment?'

Aoife sticks out her tongue. 'I've blocked you on TikTok, so you couldn't have seen it.'

'I have my ways,' Maeve says, though she does not have her ways and cannot see Aoife's TikTok account. 'That last video you put up is going to get you bullied for sure.'

As soon as she says it, she sees the open goal. Aoife has ammunition now to get her back ten times over. But they both know she won't. Aoife might slag Maeve off from morning till night but, on pain of death, she'd never taunt her about bullying.

'You're just jealous of how much my followers love me,' Aoife says with a smirk.

Greta is shaking her head, looking baffled.

'You two are exhausting. Would you not go out and kick a ball on a beautiful Sunday evening? I mean—' She stops as her phone starts to ring. Her brow furrows. She mutters something and steps out to the hall, answering as she goes.

'Wonder who that was?' Aoife says. 'She looked kind of stressed.'

Maeve shrugs, reopening her laptop. But she heard his voice when Greta answered, and she's almost certain it was Jon. She flicks a glance at Aoife, but Aoife doesn't seem to have picked up on it. There are many things on which she and Aoife have opposite opinions – Taylor Swift, Percy Pigs, the colour pink – but Jon isn't one of them. They both find him hard work. He's good at making the grown-ups laugh and they all love his company on nights out and nights in, but he's less interested in the teens. He hides it well, he's always reasonably friendly, but there's something not quite genuine about it. Or maybe they're just judging him against their aunts, who are full of warmth and energy at all times, whether you like it or not.

Their mum is calling them, for a late Sunday dinner, and together they walk through the dividing doors into the kitchen. Greta is staying too, Leesa says – could Maeve go out to the hall and see if she's off the phone? Maeve goes through the far kitchen door to check the hall, but Greta's not there any more. She tries the den – maybe Greta went in there for some privacy on her call – but that room is in darkness. Then she pops her head into the living room and startles when she sees her aunt peering at her laptop screen. A sick feeling coils inside Maeve and, for a moment, she freezes, with no idea what to do. She'd left the laptop open, but she'd closed the tab, hadn't she? She hesitates, fear and politeness battling, then steps forward, but Greta has closed the laptop and is moving towards the dividing doors to the kitchen. She hasn't seen Maeve. And she couldn't have seen the search results; Maeve is certain she'd closed the tab. She lets out a breath.

32

Nika
Sunday

NIKA GEARY RUNS UPSTAIRS, taking the steps two at a time. Her parents will leave her in peace now that she's done her daughterly duty, her polite chit-chat with Juliette Sullivan. Her phone is buzzing with notifications. She's been getting messages from Ariana's most loyal supporters on and off since Tuesday night, but this – the avalanche of notifications – feels scarily like things have gone up a notch. On her bed now, she pulls it out and clicks into Snapchat. She's been added to a group chat called xNGx. Her breath stops.

> **@ItsNikaG two faced bitch**
> **@ItsNikaG see u in school in few weeks if ur brave enough bitch**
> **@ItsNikaG u sud just kys now**
> **@ItsNikaG yeah kill urself save us the trouble**

She scrolls, tears threatening. Every single one of their friend group has joined in, and wider friends too. Not Ariana. Ariana doesn't need to. She's got her minions on the job. Ariana who had texted her on Thursday to say she was welcome to Zach, that Ariana was kinda tired of him anyway. It would really help if she would tell everyone else that too . . .

Nika exits the group and throws her phone to the other end of her bed.

Moments later, the buzzing starts up again. She picks up her mobile. They've added her back to the group chat. She leaves again and they add her back. She switches off her phone and buries her head in her pillow. She knows what her mum will say. Delete Snapchat. It's not that simple though. Stupid Ms O'Donnell and her stupid message. How dare she? And it's not surprising that Susan O'Donnell is Maeve Khoury's aunt. Two of a kind.

Nika sits up straight.

Wait.

Could it be deliberate? Would Maeve's aunt stoop that low? For the last few days, as she's waited, feeling sick, for the inevitable pile-on, Nika's been assuming Ms O'Donnell is just a nosy old cow, too stupid to pay attention to where she's sending her bitchy messages. But what if it's more than that? What if Maeve, in some twisted attempt at revenge, fed her aunt the information and got her to send the message? Maeve Khoury is that kind of person. She'd turned a bit of banter into a huge drama last year, claiming they'd been bullying her. She'd sent her mother to school to report them, too much of a coward to handle it herself. They'd all been summoned to the principal, and their parents had been called *again*. Celeste and Warren had believed Nika's side of the story, believed she wasn't involved. And luckily, none of the screenshots Maeve had saved showed Nika's messages. But – Nika acknowledges now – Maeve knew she'd been part of it. And maybe, since she and Maeve used to be best friends, Maeve was angrier with Nika than she was with Ariana and the others. *Is* angrier. Maybe she's not over it. If that's what this is – some kind of revenge – Maeve needs to cop on and get a life.

A knock on the door tells her Celeste is here. Nika really

doesn't want to talk to her mother right now, but Celeste might be suspicious if she doesn't let her in.

'Yes?'

The door opens, and Celeste comes in, hovers near the bed but doesn't sit. Her dark red hair falls in immaculate, precise waves to her shoulders. Her thin eyebrows rise in a question.

'Is everything OK?' She says it in the same business-like tone she uses when taking work calls or talking to the man who cleans their windows.

Nika smiles up. 'Yes, why?'

Celeste clasps and unclasps her hands. 'Well, it's just that Juliette Sullivan is claiming that this boy you're seeing is Ariana's boyfriend?'

'OK. First of all, they were pretty much almost broken up, and second of all, there's nothing serious going on between us. It's all good; Ariana gets it. Wow, was Juliette really talking about us? Like, gossiping about a group of kids?' Nika wrinkles her nose.

'Well, you know how she is. She likes to have her finger on the pulse . . . You're sure everything's OK? You'd tell me if it wasn't?'

'Of course I would, you know that.'

'OK. I'll pop in later to say goodnight.' Celeste hesitates and, for one crazy moment, Nika thinks she's going to hug her. She doesn't. She leaves, pulling the door closed.

Nika switches on her phone. It explodes with notifications. She doesn't exit the group this time. If she does, they'll know she's seen the messages, that they're getting to her, and they'll just add her straight back. What is she going to do? She needs a distraction. A bigger drama.

And then she remembers what's under her bed.

33

Susan
Sunday

JON TOOK UP MY suggestion and went for a Sunday night run. Or a walk, anyway. To *her*, I imagine. I wonder where she lives and if she's married too. I suppose if she's not, they don't need a hotel, they might go to her house. *Happy one-month anniversary.* Who even buys a gift after one month, let alone inscribed jewellery? But Jon loves a big gesture. On our one-month anniversary, he surprised me with tickets to New York. I thought it was romantic. I guess it's just what Jon does. I hate her, whoever she is. Does she know about me? I suppose she might not know he's married. Though if the bracelet was here, then *she* was here, and if the bracelet was stuck behind Jon's nightstand, then that's where she lost it, in my bed. *God* . . . This also makes me wonder *when* she was here – it's not like I'm out much. Apart from one weekend away with Leesa and Bella, I've been here every single night since Bella was born. Could it have started before that, before Bella? Something – the distance between us – tells me it's new. But what do I know? And I guess illicit affairs don't need to happen at night; maybe she was here when I was out during the day. I hate her, I think again. And the feminist in me knows I'm not supposed to blame the other woman, that Jon's the one who's cheating, but I just don't have it in me not to blame her too. I hate her. I fucking *hate* her.

As I move into the living room, I hear a noise outside the window. Is Jon back already? I listen, but there's nothing more. On the baby monitor, I can see Bella, deep in sleep. On TV, there's nothing I want to watch. I flick mindlessly between Netflix and Prime, unable to focus on anything but needing a distraction.

A few minutes later, I hear a noise again, a rustle from outside. I turn down the TV and wait, but again there's no follow-up sound. And although my rational brain knows it was nothing more than a fox or a breeze, and although I can see Bella on the monitor screen, I decide to go upstairs to check on her.

Bella's fast asleep, just like she was onscreen. Her soother's fallen out, but she doesn't need it once she's in a deep sleep. Small, quiet, even breaths through button nose and rosebud lips. I melt on the spot, just as I always do. Pre-baby me would have rolled her eyes. But I can't help it; she turns me to mush. A memory surfaces now, of a less good time. Standing over her Moses basket, sobbing, my hands over my ears. I swat it away and go downstairs.

The house feels ominously quiet. The sounds – the ticking of the living-room clock, the whip of a small breeze outside – are no different to any other night, but now it's eerie. I'm still rattled, I think, about the supermarket. And I still can't make sense of it. Did I move her and forget? Is all this getting to me so much it's affecting my parenting? Or did someone else move her? Neither of these is a good answer. The living room is dark now, as dusk closes in, and shadows of swaying trees pattern the wall opposite the window. We never pull the blinds during summer, but tonight, I feel exposed. I get up to close the living-room one and switch on a lamp. Better. Marginally. Before unpausing whatever I wasn't really watching on TV, I glance at the baby monitor one more time.

And my breath stops.

There's someone in the bedroom. Visible on the screen. A shadowy figure in the grainy feed. There's someone upstairs in our bedroom, standing over Bella's crib.

34

Susan
Sunday

FOR A TINY FRACTION of a second, I freeze. Then I'm running – out of the living room and up the stairs. I don't know what I'm going to do when I get there, only that I'd barrel through anyone to get her, to grab her out of her cot, to keep her safe. I barge into the bedroom, not stopping to turn on the light. It's too dark to see him, to see anything, but it doesn't matter, I just need to get to her. And then she's in my arms and I'm running again, back out of the bedroom, down the stairs and out the front door. Only then, when I'm in the driveway, does it feel safe to stop. If he's inside, we're OK, the outside world has neighbours and streetlights and video doorbells. Out of breath, I lean against the garden wall, confused about what to do next. Someone is trying to hurt me, hurt Bella. Someone is in our house, and maybe the same person was in the supermarket today. My breath starts to slow. Nothing stirs inside the house. From behind me comes the sound of a car pulling into the driveway. Jon. And whatever else is going on, right now I'm just glad to see him.

Worry creases his brow when he gets out of the car and sees me standing there, Bella in my arms. In gulpy breaths, I explain, and now he's pulling me into a hug, Bella sandwiched between us. A delay, he's saying. Something about a delay. It takes me a moment to tune in.

'There's a delay in the feed. You saw *yourself* on the screen.'

'What?'

'I noticed it the other night when I checked on Bella and came back down and looked at the monitor. I could see myself in the video feed. For a second, I thought it was someone else, but then I saw the figure lean in and adjust the camera, which is what I'd just done, and I realized my mistake. Sorry, I meant to say it to you but we've . . . you've . . .'

But you've been avoiding me is what he wants to say.

A shaky laugh. 'I'm such an idiot. Standing in the driveway at half ten at night over a glitchy baby monitor. Why didn't Leesa say it does that? I feel like that's pretty relevant information.'

'She did, on Friday night when they were over. Maybe you didn't hear her.'

Maybe I was distracted by a rose-gold bracelet.

35

Venetia
Sunday

VENETIA HUNCHES OVER HER phone late Sunday night, shoulders tight. Twenty-four hours have passed since Felipe told her about the results of his Google search. About the wrong house. About Savannah Holmes and the other 26 Oakpark. The woman who is not – *was* not – Susan O'Donnell. Venetia's blocking it out. She's scrolling, searching for more information on Susan O'Donnell. Susan who sent the message. Susan who has two sisters. Susan who has a baby. Venetia has no sisters now, because Aimee is dead. And there's no baby, because Aimee's baby died with her. The size of a bean, and no chance to grow. But Susan's baby grew, and Susan's sisters are fine. Greta and Leesa. All happy in their nice houses with their nice lives. Venetia flings the phone on the floor. It skitters across the carpet, slowing when it hits the rug in front of the fireplace. She gets up to retrieve it and keeps reading.

Felipe is at her side in seconds, hunkering down.

'I'm not sure this is helping . . .' he says, trying to soothe the phone from her hands.

'Of course it's not helping,' she snaps, 'but I need to know everything about her. She's the reason Aimee is dead.'

Felipe rubs his beard and briefly closes his eyes. 'We don't know that for sure.'

She stares at him. 'We absolutely do. That message is what killed Aimee. And Aimee's baby.' Her voice cracks. 'And Susan has a baby who is fine.'

He sits beside her, leaning in to look at her phone.

'I searched for her online, and nothing. How did you find out about her baby?'

'Facebook.'

'You found her on Facebook? I didn't see her there.' He says it in a neutral, almost chatty way and she knows he's trying to humour her, to keep things calm, while secretly worried this will send her back to heroin. And Felipe doesn't know what she has in the shoebox in the bottom of her wardrobe.

She humours him back. 'Susan O'Donnell has an old Facebook account she doesn't use, but her sister, Leesa, tags her anyway. I found pictures of the baby on Leesa's Instagram.'

He's still leaning, looking at her phone.

'What's MumsIRL?' he asks, pointing at a logo on her screen.

'It's—' She stops. She's told Felipe enough. He's not going to be on board with what she's doing. 'It's an ad I clicked on by accident.'

'Ah. Will I make another pot of tea?' He gestures towards the mugs on the coffee table.

She nods.

'Oh, by the way,' he continues, with false nonchalance, 'where did you go, this afternoon, when you went out?'

'For a walk.' It's the same answer she'd given him earlier.

'Not to Oakpark, right?'

She looks him in the eye. 'I was at the supermarket, that's all.'

'Good. Good. I think it's better if we stay away from Susan O'Donnell and all the rest of it. The police will be doing investigations and . . . OK, I'll make the tea.'

She waits till he leaves the room and clicks in again. It's so much easier to find people online than anyone ever realizes, especially if you have their phone number. WhatsApp, for example – in any group you join, you have access to every single phone number. Snapchat also uses phone numbers to suggest connections, and this has been extremely useful in the last twenty-four hours.

It started late last night, when Venetia took Susan's number from the screenshot shared in the Buy and Sell group and saved it into her contacts. She tried X, WhatsApp, then Snapchat. On the Quick Add tab on Snapchat, Venetia clicked into All Contacts, where her phone contacts were crossmatched with Snapchat users. She scrolled to Susan O'Donnell. And at midnight last night, as Saturday ticked over into Sunday, she struck gold. Susan was there as 'DaisyJones6'. Anonymous on Snapchat but not for anyone with her number in their phone. Not for Venetia. That's when Venetia's heart rate began to speed up. On X, she found nothing, but on Facebook she found a newish profile with the name DasiyJones6 and a daisy avatar. Venetia clicked in to see the Friends list; to check if they had anyone in common, or if Daisy was connected to Susan's sister Leesa, but there were no friends at all. That in itself was interesting. Then she checked the Facebook pages that Daisy had liked. There were just four, and they were exclusively parenting sites – Mumsnet, Netmums, MumsIRL and Rollercoaster. She tried the first two but found nothing. Then she got to MumsIRL. She typed 'DaisyJones' into the search bar and, finally, there it was. Dated three months ago, a post by DaisyJones6:

Hi, first-time poster, please be gentle . . . I'm scared of thoughts I've been having about my newborn. I keep thinking I'm going to hurt her. I'm really not coping. She cries all the time. I think about walking away and leaving her and then I feel horrible, but it

happens again and again and again. When I'm rocking her to get her to stop, I can imagine rocking her harder to try to stop her and I can understand (please, please, don't judge me) why people could end up doing that. I wouldn't do it, I know I wouldn't, but I can't make the thoughts stop. And what if I'm wrong? I can't tell anyone in case she's taken off me. I know she's not in danger. But also, I'm scared.

Well. Venetia sat back. Here was something she could work with. A woman afraid she'd hurt her baby. A mother afraid of being judged. Fearful that her baby would be taken from her if anyone knew she was having these thoughts. Venetia reread the post on Facebook, thinking.

Wouldn't it be interesting if people found out that Susan O'Donnell was afraid she'd deliberately hurt her baby . . .? Then she shook her head. That wasn't enough. She thought some more. What if Susan came to believe that something bad might happen to her baby while in her care? She thought about Aimee's unborn baby, inside Aimee's body, cold and dead in a morgue. A knot of rage uncurled again inside Venetia. She worked to tamp it down. This wasn't the time for spending energy on anger. She thought some more. And then it came to her. It would certainly be interesting if Susan thought something bad would happen to her baby. Venetia sat up straight. But wouldn't it be even better if, ultimately, something bad *did* happen to her baby?

36

Venetia
Five days earlier

'CLOSE YOUR EYES!'

Aimee was brimming with excitement. Venetia, sitting opposite her on the L-shaped couch, closed her eyes briefly. Wary; just as she always was in her sister's house. Scrutinizing her face for bruises. Listening for the key in the door. Rory didn't like Venetia to visit, so she always called when he was at work. But once, he'd come home early and she'd seen it in his expression as soon as he walked through the door. Oh, he was polite. Perfectly cordial. But cold. And Venetia could see Aimee tense, deflate, curl in on herself. All too aware that she'd be the one to pay. Later. When no one could see. Venetia had begged her to leave, so many times, and sometimes Aimee came close. But she was always too scared. Knowing he'd come after her. Afraid it would make things worse.

'OK, open your eyes!'

Venetia looked. Aimee was holding up a piece of paper. It took her a moment to absorb what it was. A scan. A baby scan. Oh god.

Aimee's eyes brimmed with tears. 'Isn't it great?'

Venetia stared. No words formed.

'Oh, Vee, please say you're happy for me?' The tears spilled over. Not happy tears, Venetia thought; desperate tears.

She took her sister's hands in hers, the scan clasped between them.

'How far along?'

'I'm – oh, hang on.' Her phone vibrated beside her on the couch. 'Let me just check this message.' Aimee dislodged her hands to pick up her phone. Venetia watched as she read, watched as Aimee's expression changed.

'That's Rory, he's left work early. He'll be back in ten.' Aimee moved to the edge of the couch. 'I should probably check on dinner. We can catch up again, I'll fill you in properly . . .'

'Hold on, take a second.' Venetia grabbed Aimee's hand again, kept her seated. 'How far along are you?'

'Eight weeks.' She laid the sonograph image on the coffee table. 'I went for an early scan because of . . .'

Venetia nodded. Because of the baby she'd lost when Rory pushed her down the stairs. Right here in their house, because she was moving too slowly. A terrible accident, they both said after. She'd tripped on a corner of loose carpet. There was no loose carpet. And then there was no baby.

'Aimee. Listen to me. You can't stay. You have to leave him.'

'But he's been so good since he heard the news.' Aimee smiled through her tears. 'He's being so gentle.'

'Of course he is. Until the next time you make the wrong dinner or wear the wrong top. Then what?'

Aimee glanced towards the bifold doors to the kitchen. 'Vee, he'll be home any minute and I need to check on the shepherd's pie. I don't want it to dry out. And look, I really think he's changed. He . . . he's minding me, telling me to put my feet up.' A small hesitation. 'He even wants me to give up my job, so I can rest more. We'll be tight for money, but he says he only cares about me and the baby.'

'Oh my god, Aimee, you can't give up your job, it's your only bit of independence. He's cut you off from all your friends. He's tried to cut you off from me. The job is all you've got.'

Aimee looked towards the front window, then checked her phone. 'It's not exactly a great job though, when you're pregnant. All the night-time events.'

'He just doesn't want you working in such a social setting, meeting other people.'

'That's not it. He's been so different, so soft since the baby news.' Aimee's eyes went to her phone. Rory would be here any moment now. Venetia knew she didn't have much time.

'Aimee, he literally pushed you down the stairs when you were pregnant with the last baby. Nobody changes that much. He will hurt you again.'

Aimee shook her head but didn't speak.

'You have to protect yourself and you have to protect *this* baby.'

This baby. Venetia didn't mean to put the emphasis so baldly. Aimee flinched at her words.

'I know that sounds harsh, and I know it's not your fault what happened the last time – it's his fault – but you have to do this now for the new baby. You have to leave. Come stay with me. I'll mind you. And I'll mind the baby. We can do it together.'

Aimee eyed her. Venetia knew what the look meant.

'I've been clean for over a year, you know that.' This is almost but not quite true.

Aimee's glance goes to Venetia's arms, looking for evidence that her sister is telling the truth. But Venetia's wearing a long-sleeved T-shirt.

'Trust me. Even at my worst, I'm a safer bet than he is.'

'But what about when you're at work?'

Good, Venetia thought, she's wavering.

'Felipe is always there when I'm at work, and I'm there when he's at work – I'm still doing mostly closing shifts at Bar Four. We're like ships passing in the night.' A smile. 'You'd have on-tap babysitters.'

Aimee was quiet for a time. Venetia picked the scan from the coffee table and held it up.

'Aimee, do it for this little one.'

More silence. Venetia didn't push her. Time ticked by, but she didn't say a word. Aimee had always been like this, even when they were tiny. She needed to process, to decide in her own head.

Eventually, she spoke, her voice small. 'OK.'

'OK? Really? I mean, OK, let's do it. Let's get you packed.' Venetia was off the couch and heading for the living-room door before Aimee could change her mind. 'Where can I find a bag to pack your stuff?'

'No, no, no.' Aimee stood, waving her hands. 'He's due in' – she looked at her watch – 'three minutes. If I start packing now, he'll see the bag. Even if I hide it, he'll know. He'll find it.' Her voice quivers. 'He can find anything.'

'Please, Aimee. I'll stay here, I'll look after you while you pack.'

'Tomorrow. As soon as he leaves for work in the morning. You come over, we'll pack up everything I own. Bring your big suitcase.' A watery smile. 'I'm not leaving without every single pair of heels. And you're due in work soon, anyway, aren't you?'

Her phone beeped and she glanced down.

'He's sent another text.' Her brow furrowed and her mouth moved in silent words as she kept reading. She looked up. 'He's asking me something about a screenshot, some message that's doing the rounds.' She shook her head. 'God only knows what he's on about, but you'd better go.'

'Aimee, please.'

The sound of a car door outside stopped her. Shit. Rory.

Venetia looked at Aimee. Panic slipped over her sister's face.

'Vee, please, you have to go. He's . . . he'll . . . just go out the back. Go!'

Venetia stood in the living room. Not moving. She should grab Aimee now. Stand up to Rory, tell him what's happening, march Aimee out the door.

She looked at her sister's imploring face.

'Please, just let me do it my way. This is better, I promise.'

The sound of the key in the door.

'Please!'

Venetia slipped soundlessly through the bifold doors to the kitchen as Rory walked into the hall. She turned the handle of the back door as Rory arrived in the living room. She pulled it quietly behind her and crept around to the side passage. Letting herself out through the side gate, she stopped only to sneak a look through the living-room window. Rory had his back to her; Aimee was on the couch.

'See you tomorrow,' Venetia whispered, before slipping down the drive.

But she never saw Aimee again.

37

Susan
Monday

As soon as Jon leaves for work on Monday morning, I start to dig, with a visceral need to know who he's seeing. It's like pressing a bruise, but I need to know everything about her. Opening our joint credit card account on my phone, I scroll to the drinks from the Marker Hotel, the charge I spotted on Friday. The next few transactions are all mine. Then another charge at the Marker Hotel, one I missed on Friday, this time from two weeks ago. Again, about the price of two drinks. Which doesn't tell me anything concrete and doesn't tell me who she is, but still. It's nowhere near his office so it probably wasn't work drinks, and surely he'd have mentioned if he was going there with someone else? Apart from an occasional night out with his friends, Jon does three things: works, runs, hangs out here with Bella and me. I'd remember if he said he was going to a bar, wouldn't I? This day two weeks ago. Monday. I try to work out what we did that evening, to hook on to any memory, but I can't. Every day is the same. Every evening's the same. Bella's bedtime routine, then collapse in front of the TV. I keep looking. But there's nothing else. And it's not surprising – the Marker Hotel charges are blips, no doubt. Jon would use his own credit card for anything he doesn't want me to see. His statements are all online, his access via the app on his phone. Is there any way to get into his account? Do I know his passcode? Did I ever? I remember he used to keep a spreadsheet with all his bank account details and codes . . . would he still have that? We each have our own laptops, and he brings his in and out of work, but there's also the shared computer, the one Jon used to use for personal admin. I don't know if it will even function, but it's worth a try.

Bella's getting heavy in my arms now so I pop her in the sling and go through to the den. The PC sits on top of a tall stack of Ikea bookshelves. It's heavy to lift, especially with Bella in tow, but I manage to get it down and on to the floor, then the monitor too. The power button is dusty but depresses easily.

Five minutes later, I'm in a folder marked 'Taxes and Finances' – one of Jon's. There are dozens of spreadsheets here, dating back years. I can't remember the name of the one where he kept track of his account details, but I've seen it before, back when we pored over finances, applying for a mortgage. Bella stirs and I kiss her head. The noise of an engine pulls my attention to the window. Jon couldn't be home, could he? But there's no one there. Back to the files. And there it is. Fin17.xls. I click in. Worksheets for every bank account, diligent notes on what each one was for. And on the final worksheet, his list of codes, including his eight-digit Bank of Ireland login and his six-digit PIN. I sit back for a moment. If I do this, it's crossing a line I can't uncross. But then Jon's the one who crossed a line first. My phone is in my hand before I can think too much more, and I'm entering the numbers. Will it send him a message to say a new device has logged in? I don't know. But he won't know it's me, so what's the worst that can happen? Ten seconds later, I'm in. And then I'm in his credit card, and it's all laid bare.

38

Susan
Monday

HUNDREDS OF EUROS. LUNCHES in One Pico and Chapter
One. Places we never go. Not big expense-account work
meals but intimate lunches for two. Drinks after work in dimly
lit wine bars. Dinner in Susie's, a tiny Michelin-star restaurant off Grafton Street. We'd gone there on our first wedding
anniversary, and swore we'd go every year, because, as Jon
said, it was named for me. We never went back. But now, it
seems, he has. Tickets for Cineworld in the city centre and the
Lighthouse Cinema in Smithfield, two places I've never been.
Morning purchases from Vanilla Pod – coffees and pastries?
They certainly weren't for me. I'd remember. I sit for what feels
like hours, scrolling through his credit card statements. More
drinks, more dinners. Chez Max. Trocadero. L'Gueuleton. All
city-centre restaurants, none close to here. None close to people
we know. Then a charge to Boodles. Not a restaurant, a jewellery store. Of course. The bracelet. The fucker. Bella whimpers
in the sling and I kiss her head and keep scrolling. None of this
tells me *who* he's seeing, and I'm hungry now for information,
desperate to know more. Could I cross-check his nights out
with messages on my phone, photos in my gallery, my online

calendar, to jog my memory? I pick the Marker night, this day two weeks ago, and check my messages. A long thread with one of my teacher friends about TV recommendations. Both of us sitting in, comparing notes on *Ripley* and *The Bear*. Jon was working late, according to one message from me, time-stamped 9.05 p.m. God, it's so obvious now. Nobody works that late – people come home and log back in if needed. How could I have missed all this? Because nobody believes their own spouse will cheat, that's how. In my gallery, there are photos of Bella. I can see that I sent a picture of Bella to Jon at ten and told him I was going to bed. His reply was 'night night, love you x and kisses to Bella'. Was he with someone else when he wrote that? That level of betrayal makes me feel sick.

Numb now, I cross-check another credit card entry – a coffee-shop debit on a Saturday at the end of June. I have no idea what I was doing that day and my messages give me nothing useful either. Then I remember Google Timeline and the email I ignore every month, telling me where I've been. Clicking into my June email, I scroll to the last Saturday of the month and see that I drove from home to the supermarket, and home again. Exciting times. Then it strikes me – if Jon gets a similar email, won't I be able to see where he's been going? That would involve somehow getting into his email, which is pretty indefensible. Then again, I'm already looking at his credit card, having broken into his online banking, so . . . I don't, however, know his email password. And I don't know if he has Google Timeline, if his location is being tracked. That gives me another idea – Greta has been telling Jon to download an app called Strava, to track his runs. Maybe I can see his runs on her phone? She'd let me look, I think, without it raising suspicion. Which begs the question, why don't I just tell Greta and Leesa what's going on? But the thought turns my stomach. If I tell them, it

sets things in motion . . . Another thought keeps nudging in –
what if we split and Jon tells people I used to be afraid I'd hurt
Bella? Would he get full custody? Even if my counsellor and GP
spoke up, explained that I was never a threat, it would look bad.
And my sisters would be horrified. Would other people find
out too? Would Bella find out when she's older? Shame floods
my body. *Slow down. Deep breaths.* I shut down the catastrophiz-
ing part of my brain and get back to investigating. My mind is
whirring now, thinking about location tracking. Google Timeline, Strava, Snapmaps, Find My Phone. And the Airtag on Jon's
keys. I can almost see the lightbulb going on above my head. I
don't need to break into his email, I can just check his Airtag. It
doesn't show historical data, but it does show current location.
It's not linked to my phone right now, but I'm pretty sure I can
set that up as long as I have his keys. I check my watch. Only
nine hours to go till he's home.

It's Monday afternoon when it happens. I'm upstairs, staring
at Jon's side of the wardrobe, contemplating going through his
pockets. Bella is downstairs, asleep in her Moses basket. Suddenly, she bursts into a loud cry. Not the whimpering awake
she usually does. A loud cry of shock. I'm down the stairs in
seconds and in the living room, scooping her up. Her face is
red and creased with rage and, even when I hold her close,
rocking and shushing, she howls. What on earth could have
caused this? Can babies have nightmares? Tummy pain? She's
never had colic, she's not teething yet – or maybe she is? God,
there's nothing like new motherhood to make you feel lost. I
sit and lay her down on my lap to check her forehead – warm
but not hot – and her tummy – rounded but soft to touch.
Just as it always is. Not that I'm any kind of expert, but it feels
normal? Then I notice her arm. Four bright red marks on her

skin. Four bright red marks that look like fingerprints. I stare. They can't be. Yet now that I've seen them, I can't unsee them, and they look very much like someone has gripped her arm and squeezed. My head snaps up, scanning the living room. Jon's not here, is he? And even if he was, he'd never grab her arm like that. Then . . . what caused the marks? Surely I didn't do it when I was trying to comfort her? Gently, I rub her arm. The marks look less angry now. Fading into her skin. I stare, waiting for them to disappear. Willing them to disappear. It couldn't have been me. Could it?

Bella is calm now, and I place her gently back in her crib. The marks have all but gone. It *was* me, wasn't it . . . Trying to comfort her, I managed to hurt her. My own baby. Christ, I'm a useless mother. I put my head in my hands and stand there, rocking for a moment, trying not to cry. It was an accident. But do other people do this? Hurt their babies? I need to book another appointment with my counsellor. I need to sort my thoughts, sort what's real from what's not. I need to— The doorbell rings, startling me, stopping my spiral.

On my way out to answer, I ready my stock 'we're fine, thanks' response for the power-supply reps who regularly call. But the man on my doorstep isn't trying to sell me anything – it's Felipe, Venetia's husband.

39

Susan
Monday

FELIPE STEPS BACK FROM the door when I open it, giving me space. He looks uneasy.

'Susan, hi, I hope you don't mind me calling to you like this, but I wanted to apologize for the way Venetia spoke to you when you visited on Saturday and to check you're doing OK.' It comes out in a rush.

'Oh. Gosh, no need to apologize. She's grieving. I understand.' Something strikes me then. 'Wait, how did you know where I live?'

'Ah. Your address is online. People shared it, I'm afraid. You didn't know?' He looks anxious now.

'Oh, I knew,' I tell him with a sigh.

'Could I . . . could I come in for a minute?'

Still on edge, I want to say no and I grapple unsuccessfully for a polite way to do it. *Politeness gets women killed*, I hear Greta's voice in my head, and my brain clicks into gear.

'The baby's just nodded off, so we might talk here, if that's OK.'

It's perfectly reasonable but still makes me squirm. To be fair, Felipe is the opposite of intimidating. Wearing a loose linen shirt and board shorts, he reminds me of a cute surfer I met on my gap year in Australia.

'Of course,' he says, running his hand through his hair. 'I wanted to explain Venetia's reaction. She's very emotional right now.'

'I think emotional is allowed under the circumstances . . .'

'Absolutely. But when she told you to leave, I imagine you weren't sure what to think, so I wanted to explain . . .' The hands are back in the pockets and he's looking at his shoes. Flip-flops. I find myself wondering what his job is. 'She struggles to manage her emotions at times – loses her temper, shouts, then feels bad after.'

I lean against the doorjamb. 'Honestly, she doesn't need to feel bad. I'd be the same if something happened to one of my sisters.'

He nods and grimaces.

'And it's me who should be apologizing,' I continue. 'I should never have written that message about Aimee. I'm truly sorry.'

'Did you really see her with that man Warren?' he asks.

'Yes.'

He looks baffled. 'What was she thinking?'

'I guess she wasn't thinking.'

'No, but—' He stops himself.

I'm curious now.

'What is it?'

'She's normally . . . a careful person.'

'You mean she had lots of affairs but never got caught?'

A soft, sad laugh. 'No, quite the opposite. Her husband, he was . . . well, he was her only boyfriend ever. They'd been together a long time. They married young. She knew him very well.'

There's something in the halting way he says all of this, something he's not saying. I wait.

'She certainly knew him much better than I did,' he adds with a sad smile. 'Anyway, that is all. I'm sorry about Venetia, but she is upset, so I think perhaps don't call to the house again . . .' He looks down, embarrassed maybe at asking me to stay away. 'Best you avoid her.'

Again, there's something he's not saying. Something between the gaps in his words but, whatever it is, it's not forthcoming.

'Absolutely,' I tell him. 'I'll leave you guys in peace.'

That evening, Jon arrives home from work at six thirty on the dot for the first time in weeks, and this gives me pause. Is he trying to divert suspicion? Does he know I know? Is that why he's been so on edge? But how would he guess? Could he have discovered that I have the bracelet? I should have left it where I found it . . . but then what's the point of that? I'm not the bad guy here. I haven't done anything wrong. When he goes upstairs to change, I grab his keys and connect his Airtag to my phone. Now. Let's see where he goes when he's not with me.

40

Nika
Monday

THE DIARY IS ON Nika's bedside locker, dusty after almost five years under her bed. What would Maeve think if she knew Nika had it? She'd be fucking terrified. Nika remembers when it went missing. ('Missing'.) Maeve frantically checking all over her bedroom, asking Nika if she'd seen it. Nika putting on a worried face and helping her search, the diary buried at the bottom of her bag. Why she took it, she's not sure. An impulse. Curiosity. The knowledge that someday it might come in useful. She'd seen Maeve writing in it from time to time, her hand crabbed around the page, shielding it from anyone who might walk into her bedroom. Nika was newly thirteen then and Maeve was still twelve, the two of them fresh to secondary school, holding on to their primary-school friendship. Or at least, Maeve was. Nika was ready to meet new people, and Maeve was . . . well, kind of basic. A try-hard. Always trying to walk home with Nika, tagging along with Nika's new friends. And by October, just two months into their secondary-school life, Nika was over it.

It was Halloween, and Maeve wanted to go trick-or-treating together, then have Nika stay over. Nika wanted to go to a party in Ariana's house. So she compromised – which, if you think about it, was actually really nice of her – and got Maeve invited to Ariana's party too. But it annoyed her all the same. This dragging feeling, being held back by Maeve. It bugged her that she had to call by Maeve's house on the way to Ariana's. And walking into Maeve's room, finding her hunched over her diary, not yet ready to go, annoyed her even more. Maeve shoved her diary under her pillow and went out to the bathroom to change. Nika sat on her bed and pulled the diary back out, one eye on the bedroom door. What would Maeve write about? Wishing she had more friends, maybe, wishing she looked more like everyone else? Her curly hair didn't fit with the straightened look everyone else went for and her clothes were just kind of . . . well, still a bit primary school. The first pages were exactly as Nika expected – boring nonsense about the new school, and witterings about her sister coming into her room uninvited. ('AOIFE IF YOU'RE READING THIS YOU'RE DEAD.') Then Nika turned a page and found something else entirely. Her eyes widened and her jaw dropped and, just then, the bathroom door unlocked. She needed more time. She hesitated for a second, then slipped the diary into her backpack and got up from the bed as Maeve came back – to Nika's horror – dressed as a Minion. She was twelve, not three, for god's sake. Nika had put huge effort into her outfit – strappy black dress, black boots, cute black button nose, smoky eyes. ('What are you?' her dad had asked. 'A cat, Dad, obviously?') And now she'd have to walk into Ariana's party with a Minion.

That was the end of it, really.

Nika did her best at the party to steer clear of Maeve, leaving the room each time Maeve came in. It would be mortifying if the others thought she was friends with the Minion. She heard them laughing about Maeve's costume and slid over to join in. She thought of the diary. Imagine what they'd think if they knew what was in that.

When Maeve's dad arrived to pick them up, Nika said she was staying on at the party. Mr Khoury insisted on texting Celeste to make sure that was OK. It was, of course. Celeste didn't mind what Nika did; she trusted her. Nika had discovered early on that if she confessed and confided small indiscretions to her mother, Celeste believed her daughter was the kind of child who told her 'everything'. Which is why she believed she hadn't been involved in the drama with Maeve in fourth year ('Mum, I left her on Delivered for, like, a day? And she called it bullying?') and why she believed Nika didn't drink ('I tried a small bit of vodka and Coke, but I hated it. I don't know why people drink') and why she believed Nika had had her first kiss at sixteen (ha).

Nika went back to Maeve's the following morning to get her backpack, watching while Maeve searched for her diary, apologizing for not staying over the night before – vague excuses about her mother needing her home to keep an eye on Cody. She left saying she'd call her later. But she didn't. The next day, when Maeve snapped Nika, she ignored it. The end of a forty-day Snap streak and the end of an eight-year friendship.

And now, it's time to use the diary.

41

Nika
Monday

NIKA LICKS HER FINGER and thumbs through to 29 September. She reads the entry one more time, pushing down the small knot of something she can't quite place.

Dear Diary,

I know the 'dear diary' sounds very formal (and silly? Wait, are you judging me, diary?), but this is a big deal. Today I'm going to tell you something I haven't told you before. I'm in love. OK, not in love. I do know the difference between love and crush. I have read many, many books, as you know. So here goes, I'm in crush with Ariana. Not Grande (though, yes, wow, love her obvs) but Ariana Webb from school. I know. Insane. And probably just a phase. But I can't stop thinking about her. I don't know what it is. But when I'm near her, I feel tingly. Self-conscious. Trying to impress her. As if she'd even notice I'm there. But actually she did. And that's when it started. It was in French class. She sat next to me and asked if she could copy my homework, and then she said she liked my ring. The one with the skull. And that's when the tingling started, and now it's every time I see her. And then I had a dream that she kissed me. I know. I'm so embarrassed writing that, but, hey, you won't tell anyone.

Nika sets the diary aside and picks up her phone. The new Snapchat account she set up last night has only six connections so far, but that's going to blow up soon. AWGoss is the username and there's nothing at all to link it to her. Meanwhile, there are dozens and dozens of new messages in the xNGx group. Hurtful, hateful comments, daring her to reply. Daring her to show her face. And still nothing from Ariana.

Nika angles her camera directly above the diary entry, making sure the shot is perfectly framed to capture every single word. Ariana will go nuts. Maeve will die of embarrassment. And Nika will finally be left alone.

42

Jon
Monday

ON MONDAY EVENING, after a solo dinner (Susan had eaten earlier, something she never does) Jon pauses outside the living-room door, bracing himself. He has no idea what to say to her. The bracelet in her night-stand drawer and what that means haunt every minute of his day. Everything else is on autopilot. Should he say something? Just get it out and over with? But what exactly can he say? And if he asks her anything about it, he can't take it back. And if he's wrong . . . there's no talking his way out of it afterwards. Greta hasn't been quite as much help as he'd hoped. The stupid bracelet. He grimaces. Even Jon knows it's not the stupid bracelet's fault. This all started with him and his wandering eye, the oldest story in the book. He just never meant for it to go this far or for Susan to find out . . . It was fun, but he certainly didn't intend risking his marriage. And yet, once he strayed, of course that's exactly what he'd done.

Deep breath. He opens the door. Susan is curled on the couch, a book on her lap. Deeply engrossed, not looking up. He can't help thinking this is for show.

'Tea?' he offers.

A glance up. 'I'm fine.' Back to the book.

God. This is excruciating. Should he go in and sit beside her, just as he normally does?

As though reading his mind, she uncurls and stretches her legs, taking up the length of the couch. Even Jon, not known for his ability to read between the lines, can pick up on that signal.

'I might head out for some air. Make the most of the long evenings.'

'Do,' she says, reaching for her phone. She meets his gaze. 'Take your time.'

43

Susan
Monday

AS SOON AS JON closes the living-room door I sit up straight and click into the app. The front door shuts, I hear him lock it from outside, and, moments later, the Airtag shows that he turns left at the end of our driveway, walking past Juliette Sullivan's house and up through Oakpark towards the main road. So, whoever she is, he can get there on foot, he hasn't taken the car.

After a few minutes, it gets boring watching him and I go online to see if there's anything more on the Cherrywood murders or Savannah Holmes. The newspapers have nothing new, but on a whim, I go to MessageBoards.ie, to the subforum where my Google Alert led me last Wednesday. There, opinions and speculation are rife.

Poor Savannah, RIP. She was an inspiration. HannahBan95

Lock ur doors guys, I heard it's a serial killer. She shd never have answered the door MaryAnnOBrienGargan82

She was a bit of a show-off. The pix of the shoes and stuff. And a lot of photos of drinks, glasses of champagne. A bit of a lush? Probably fell over and hit her head when she'd had too much to drink ☺ Ellengr8Santana

I feel really sorry for Savannah Holmes. But it's a lesson to us

all. If you put stuff about yourself online, you're asking for trouble. Anyone following her Instagram would have known what kind of car she drives and where she lives – she was always putting up selfies at her front door and at her hallway mirror. You could see the front driveway in the reflection and her car reg. LarOToole

Kinda showing yourself there, Lar, aren't you? With enough victim-blaming to keep me going for a lifetime, I scroll to the comments on the Cherrywood murders. There's a bit of chatter about Rory Quinlan in particular – popular guy, it seems, with lots of friends and contacts through a gym he owned. Aimee seems to have been less well known. There are a few posts about the night of the murders – someone knows the neighbour, the woman who raised the alarm, and apparently she'd heard a door slam on Tuesday night. There'd been a car outside, but nobody knew what colour. And there'd been a car outside Savannah's house on Wednesday morning. So . . . some caller who'd killed her, they speculated, and maybe the same car had been outside Aimee and Rory's? Did anyone know what kind of car? Blue, black, dark grey came the answers. I scroll back up to the Savannah comments.

Imagine opening your door, not knowing the person is going to kill you someone had typed in the last few minutes.

My throat tightens with guilt and sadness. I look around. It's quiet and growing dark and, suddenly, I don't want to be alone. The app shows me Jon is almost here. I've discovered nothing about who he's seeing, but then again, he hasn't been gone long enough to meet with anyone. So maybe it really was just a walk. I watch on the app as he comes up the driveway and into the house. Except there's no sound of the front door. No attempt to open it, no turn of the key. Online, he's in the house; in real life, he's not. Is the app glitching? I zoom in, confused. Then I realize what's going on. He's not here. But I do know exactly whose house he's in.

44

Maeve
Monday

MAEVE IS LYING ON her bed, scrolling. From downstairs, she can hear her mother talking to Aoife. The best thing about summer nights is that her mother is not on her case to get her stuff organized for school. Nothing to get up for tomorrow morning, nothing to go to bed for tonight. She's just thinking about putting a film on her laptop when a Snapchat notification from an unfamiliar account pops up. The account is called AWGoss. She clicks in and sees a photo that's confusing because it's familiar, but from long ago, and it takes a moment to work it all out, to realize that it's her diary. At least, it looks like her diary. It must be just the same cover as hers – the white background and the pink flamingos; hers disappeared years ago. But then why is she being tagged in the post? A video appears now. A video that begins with the same diary. Then an unseen hand opens the cover and the camera zooms in on the writing on the first page. She knows this writing. She knows this inscription.

Property of Maeve Khoury
Address: 42 Rowanpark Drive, Blackrock, Co. Dublin
Age: Almost 13

And in block capitals: AOIFE IF YOU'RE READING THIS YOU'RE DEAD

No, no, no.

She sits bolt upright, cold and sick, staring in horror. *How . . .?* The unseen hand turns the page. There it is: her writing, her diary entries. *No . . .* She closes her eyes, trying to make it stop, to make it disappear. The audio – Katy Perry's 'I Kissed a Girl' – is still playing. The video is still playing. She forces herself to open her eyes. The pages are flipping forward. She knows why. This is the boring stuff, the what-I-did-in-school-today stuff. The other stuff is further along. And she knows what it is. She remembers writing it. Her face grows hot, her stomach cold. How can she stop this? Panic surges up inside. Who can see it? Everyone. Everyone can see it. Whoever is behind the account AWGoss has tagged everyone in their year. The pages keep flipping. She knows what's coming. The distant memory is now clear, burnt on to her brain. And there it is, on her screen.

. . . So here goes, I'm in crush with Ariana . . .

Maeve makes it to the bathroom just in time to throw up.

45

Susan
Monday

I'M STARING AT MY phone, at the Airtag location, trying to make sense of it. Why is Jon in Greta's house? Then again, why not? They've always got on well. They're both practical, long-term-goal-focused people. Both career-oriented and a bit less into the fun side of life than Leesa and Samir. We all balance each other out, I suppose. Jon tends to gravitate towards Greta when we all get together – two like-minded people who'll happily discuss politics and mortgage interest rates while Leesa and Samir will tell you about the new season of *The Boys* or how to make a strawberry daiquiri in a Nutribullet. I'm somewhere in the middle, happy in both camps. I know Jon and Greta message each other occasionally and have done for years. But I can't think of a time when he called into her socially, without me.

I know how it looks. That it's right there in giant neon letters. That I'm literally here tracking him on my phone to find out who he's seeing, and he's in her house.

But that's not what this is. I appreciate that it sounds like I'm deluded, but you couldn't imagine a more platonic friendship if you tried for a hundred years.

Maybe I'm wrong about where Jon is; maybe the Airtag is glitching. One time Leesa told me she checked Find My Phone to see where Maeve was and it looked like she was in the sea. Leesa had a moment of panic, before the little arrow jumped back on to dry land. Maybe that's what this is. But nothing has changed: it still looks like he's there.

I type a message to Greta.

Did Jon call into you?

Greta is typing. Then nothing. Then Greta is typing again, this time for what seems like an age. Stopping and starting.

I check the Airtag. No change.

Then finally, a reply:

No, he's not here.

Only I'm absolutely certain he is.

46

Maeve
Monday

THE KNOCK ON MAEVE's bedroom door sounds quiet and unsure, which means her mum has heard her being sick and is probably worrying she has an eating disorder. If only it was an eating disorder and not the end of her life as she knows it. Maeve sits on her bed, staring at her phone, at the notifications lighting up as more and more people see the video. What is she going to do?

Another knock. 'Maeve? Are you OK?'

'I'm fine!' *Go away. Please.*

The door is opening.

'Mum, don't come in without asking.' She flops back on the bed, shoving the phone under her pillow.

'I thought I heard someone being sick?' Leesa steps forward. 'You're very pale. Are you OK?'

'It wasn't me. Maybe Aoife?'

A voice comes from behind Leesa. 'Nope, wasn't me.'

Jesus Christ, why is Aoife always hovering? Listening. Creeping.

'Are you sure? Sit up so I can see you properly.' Leesa is moving towards her, hand outstretched to feel her forehead. Maeve pushes up on one elbow.

'You're quite clammy.' Leesa keeps her hand on her forehead.

It's cool against Maeve's skin and suddenly this is all she wants. Her mum's hand on her head, her mum's arms around her. But then she imagines telling her. Imagines showing her the video of the diary. Those words. Her face burns.

'I'm fine, I told you. God, Mum, you never listen.'

Leesa steps back, hurt washing over her face, then a forced smile as she tries to hide it. And now Maeve feels bad and, also, more annoyed than ever.

A creak from outside. Aoife is still hovering. God, Aoife is going to see the video. Everyone is going to see the video.

'Can you both leave me in peace, please?' Maeve snaps.

Leesa holds up her hands. 'I'm going. But if you need anything or you feel sick, tell me. OK?'

'OK.'

Leesa leaves and closes the bedroom door.

Maeve lies back then turns on her side and curls into a ball, shoulders shaking, tears streaming. What is she going to do?

47

Susan
Tuesday

LEESA CALLS IN ON Tuesday morning, just as I finish tracking Jon's route to work on my phone. Leesa's the loud one of the three of us. Loud in a good way. Effusive, chatty, mile-a-minute, warm. When we were small, it drove me mad – constant questions and chatter. Now that we're adults and our entire social existence centres around conversation, I like her high energy. Life is never boring when you meet Leesa for tea or wine or a walk in the park. But she's quiet as we sit in my kitchen this morning and I'm so lost in my own worries it takes me a while to notice.

'What's up with you?' I ask her.

A worried sigh. 'Maeve. There's something wrong, and I don't know what. I'm pretty sure she was sick last night, but she wouldn't admit it. And her eyes were red and I heard her crying when I was going to bed, but when I stuck my head in, she said she was fine.'

'Friend stuff?'

Leesa holds up her hands. 'I don't know. I'm scared though. After what happened over the last two years with Nika and Ariana and those other girls. What if it's happening again?'

I want to make her feel better and worry less, but I honestly don't know how to reassure her. Teaching at a secondary school has taught me that anything is possible with those not fully developed brains.

'I can't believe we're still dealing with bullying, generation after generation. How have we not evolved as a society?'

'I know.' Leesa sighs. 'When they're small, you worry about what you might do to them or what someone else might do to them. When they're teens, you worry about what they might do to themselves or to each other.'

What you might do to them. There's a huge part of me wants to ask her more. Maybe I'm not the only one who worries about hurting my baby. But instead I go for a platitude.

'You're doing your best. You can only bring them up as well as you can and keep lines of communication open.'

She smiles. 'And mostly cross your fingers.' A pause. 'I'm thinking of getting Aoife on board. She's the one who told me what was happening before . . . I could get her to kind of . . . take a look?'

'Take a look?' I push back my chair. 'Here, let's walk and talk. I think I heard Bella.'

Together we go upstairs to bring Bella down to the kitchen, and Leesa explains her thinking.

'I could get Aoife to look around Maeve's social media, her friends' accounts. Listen for gossip, you know?'

'The word I think you're looking for is "snoop".'

She bites her lip. 'Am I a bad person?'

'Not at all – I would absolutely do it too. You're trying to protect your child.' I look down at Bella in my arms. 'Jesus, I'd do anything to protect this one. Whatever it takes.'

We decide to take fresh coffees to the back garden. It's 17 degrees already, not hot by Mediterranean standards or even anywhere-but-here standards, but for Ireland, this is enticingly pleasant for ten o'clock in the morning. I set up a parasol to shade Bella and lay her on her back on a playmat. Leesa and I sit on loungers, faces to the sun. Unlike Greta, who is milk-white all year round and never lets a UV ray touch her skin, Leesa is a sun-worshipper and ardent tan-seeker. She closes her eyes, and I do the same, trying to stem my racing thoughts. It's quiet at this time of morning. No lawnmowers yet, no paddling-pool shrieks. Just birds, and the distant hum of an occasional passing car. I'm starting to feel sleepy when Leesa asks after Greta and Jon.

No news from either of them, I tell her, the lie like a lead stone in the pit of my stomach. She chats on then about Greta's Long Covid, Aoife's aversion to sport, what she'll wear to the Oakpark street party on Thursday, a documentary about diving, and whether or not she needs another pair of sunglasses. She already has eighteen pairs, I reckon, but that's never stopped our Leesa. The nice thing is, she just sort of talks to herself, and as long as I hmm every now and then, it's quite soothing.

After a while, the creak of her lounger tells me she's on the move and I open my eyes. She's sitting up straight, finishing her coffee, and says she'd better get home to log on for her shift.

It happens when I walk her to the door. We stand there chatting for a minute about Celeste's family and friends, and who of them might have broken our window. It's when I think of this, and Bella in her cot beneath the window last Tuesday night, that I start to feel uncomfortable. I shouldn't have left her out the back on her own. Even if it's only for a minute. I say a hurried goodbye to Leesa and run back through the house and out to the garden.

And Bella is there, of course she is, kicking on her playmat, exactly where I left her.

Only . . . I realize now, not exactly where I left her.

She's not under the shade of the umbrella any more.

I'm confused for a moment, staring, then I stoop to pick her up. Her cheeks are red, her forehead too. She's hardly got sunburnt in a few short minutes? Surely she's flushed, not burnt . . . But how could she have moved? She's not able to roll over yet. Has the sun moved? It makes no sense. If the sun didn't move, then Bella did. But she can't. Which would mean what . . . someone moved her? I look around, holding her close, shielding her from the sunlight. Tall hedges line both sides of the garden, hiding high walls that divide our property from Greta's on one side and Juliette's on the other. At the back, giant evergreens give us privacy. There's nobody here; of course there isn't. This is not like the supermarket, where someone could have accidentally or deliberately moved her. This is our garden, enclosed by a gate on one side and going right up to the garden wall on the other. Nobody came in. This is on me, misjudging how quickly the sun moves. I kiss her forehead, and she starts to cry. Her skin is still red. Flushed or burnt? Either way, common sense kicks in and I take her inside. Jesus Christ, I am the worst mother in the world.

48

Venetia
Tuesday

VENETIA PUTS HER KEY in the lock but doesn't turn it. She leans her forehead against the front door, spent. Her elation, so high, so brief, has flattened, and grief has taken over. What did she expect? Nothing can bring Aimee back. But god, for a moment, it felt good to do something. To give Susan O'Donnell a shake. To poke her where it hurts. She thinks about the surprised look on the baby's face when she pulled it by the ankles into the sun. Just a few inches, that's all it took. A little burn for baby, a little worry for Susan.

Venetia turns now, sagging against the door, and stares down the front path towards the small gate and beyond to the street. People walk by, getting on with their days as though nothing has happened. As though her life hasn't come to an end. She hates those people. She hates everyone.

The door behind her is pulled open and she stumbles back before righting herself. Felipe's arm goes around her shoulder, steering her gently into the kitchen.

'Where were you?' He propels her into a chair.

She shakes her head.

The high cupboard above the fridge hangs open, the dark

green paint chipped on the inside. A carton of juice sits on the countertop, its lid missing. Below the washing machine, a pile of laundry sits unwashed. All things that would have annoyed her before. *Before.*

Felipe follows her gaze.

'The washing machine stopped working again. A guy is coming to look, but not until next week.'

'I'll take the washing to the laundrette,' she says dully. 'Put it in my brown holdall and leave it in my car. I'll do it tomorrow.'

Felipe nods emphatically, pleased, no doubt, that she's talking about normal things like chores. He fills a glass with water and places it in front of her.

'Where were you?' he tries again.

'Out for a walk.'

'You didn't answer my messages . . . I was worried.'

She turns to look at him. 'What, that I'd do something to myself?'

He shakes his head. And she gets it now. 'That I'd do something to her?'

A nod. There's a look in his eyes that she hasn't seen since her worst days as an addict. It's not just worry. It's fear.

'Promise me you'll stay away from her.'

She thinks about the house. The side gate with the sliding bolt. The ease with which anyone – *anyone* – could slip a hand through the slats and slip the bolt across. The baby, lying on the playmat. The sisters, chatting in the garden like one of them didn't just kill someone. Chatting about a documentary on diving and buying sunglasses.

Then the unexpected opportunity. The irresistible chance when they went inside. Venetia quite liked the sense that the baby had no idea what she was doing. Squinting at the sudden sunlight, unaware of burning skin. Unable to understand the change of circumstance, unable to move itself back under the shade. Confused, not fearful. Babies are very trusting. She imagines Susan's reaction on finding she's somehow left her own baby out in the sun, and a shiver of pleasure runs through her.

49

Celeste
Tuesday

CELESTE SLIDES A BOTTLE of Albariño from the wine fridge and pours herself a glass. Then 180ml into a jug – is that the correct amount? She re-checks her cookbook. Yes, 180ml for the white wine cream sauce. She's heard on the grapevine that she supposedly has a personal chef. As if anyone has a personal chef. It's South Dublin, not LA. She doesn't do anything to disabuse people of the idea. It amuses her. But the truth is, she likes cooking. It's therapy after a long day at work. Relaxing. Or at least, as relaxing as anything that's not alcohol or prescription medication can be. And she *likes* to spend time in her kitchen, contrary to what people might expect. After all, she spent enough time and money designing it and arranging the renovation. She sits on a high-backed chair at the island to sip her wine and admire her work – the navy cupboards, the oak floors, the gold-leaf lamps hanging from the ceiling. The marble island and the Stanley range. She had visualized it and she had made it happen. Because that's the kind of person Celeste Geary is. The sauce bubbles on the stove top and she slips off the chair to go to the pantry for garlic. Back at the kitchen counter, she peels off two cloves, then reaches to the knife block for her sharpest vegetable knife, but it's not there. It's not in the drawer, it's not on the draining board and it's not in the dishwasher. There are a million explanations for the missing knife, but Celeste's mind goes to just one.

Upstairs, Nika is in her bedroom, brushing her hair at her dressing table. Celeste knocks on the open door and steps inside, eyes scanning surfaces quickly but discreetly. In the mirror, Nika watches. 'Are you looking for something?'

'The lint roller,' Celeste says smoothly. 'It's not in the drawer in the kitchen.'

'I've got my own one, I don't use the one in the kitchen.' A shrug and a smile. 'Want me to help you look?'

'No, it's fine.' Celeste hovers by the bed, then smooths a patch of duvet and sits.

Nika's eyebrows arch. 'Are you OK, Mum?'

On some level, Celeste knows that this isn't right. That other mothers and daughters must sit on each other's beds and chat. But she doesn't dwell on that now; there are more urgent concerns. She's read enough about self-harm to know that missing knives are a red flag, and she's not going to relax till she finds it.

'I'm fine. Are *you* OK?'

She notices again the dark circles under Nika's eyes. 'Are you sleeping all right?'

Nika opens her mouth then closes it again. She tilts her head. Is she surprised, confused? Or hiding something?

'You know you can always talk to me.'

A small smile now. A smile that might mean *we both know that's not true.*

Celeste tries again. 'I know you've always been very . . . well adjusted and haven't needed my guidance, but if ever there is something, do let me know, won't you?'

Nika nods. Celeste's eyes go to her daughter's arms, taking in the long-sleeved hoodie she's wearing, despite the warm July weather.

'Aren't you too hot?'

Nika folds her arms across her body. Has she got thin, Celeste wonders now? She's always been slim. Celeste knows you're not supposed to care about your children's weight as long as they're heathy and happy, but she's always been secretly glad Nika is slim. Her friends go on and on about body positivity but, honestly, if people just . . . she stops the thought before it takes off. That's not why she's here. She scans the room again, taking in the make-up and the skincare that costs almost as much as her own. The handbags hanging inside the open wardrobe door. The vast array of trainers, neatly boxed below rails of dresses. The schoolbooks on her desk, ready for September. All the hallmarks of a perfectly well-adjusted teen. Maybe the knife's just gone, the way of odd socks, never to be adequately explained. And Nika would tell her if anything was wrong. They're not the most chatty mother and daughter, but they don't fight. Yes, Celeste thinks as she stands and walks to the door, Nika would tell her.

Out on the landing, she pauses at Cody's open door and glances in. He's in his gaming chair, his back to her, engrossed in some online thing, his hand moving a joystick at speeds she'll never understand. Imagine if he applied the same focus to school. Something grabs her attention then. Something about his hand. His knuckles. Bruised purple. What on earth has he been up to now? She takes one step into the room and falters. This would be better dealt with by Warren. She steps back out and quietly closes the door.

50

Maeve
Tuesday

ON TUESDAY EVENING, MAEVE is curled on her bed, eyes closed, when her mother knocks, comes in without waiting for a response and sits down beside her.

'Can I get you anything?' Leesa asks, brushing a hair from Maeve's clammy forehead.

A headshake.

'I . . . I heard about . . .'

'No.'

'What?'

'Don't say it. Don't say anything, Mum. I just want to be left alone.' *I want to die.*

'OK. I could go to Nika's parents?'

Nika? Oh god, of *course* it's Nika behind the diary video. Maeve realizes now she probably knew it was Nika but hadn't quite believed her former best friend would go this far. That she'd use something from a time when they'd lived in each other's pockets. Abuse her trust. Throw away a childhood friendship so completely.

How does her mother know it was Nika? Maeve wants to ask but also doesn't want to talk, not now, not ever.

Leesa reads her mind or sees something on her face.

'It was Nika behind the account. Aoife found out. She did some digging and careful asking, and you know her friend whose brother is pals with Cody Geary?'

A tiny nod.

'That's how she found out for sure, but she'd already guessed because the anonymous account is online whenever Nika is online and she could see on Snap Maps that they're in the same location at all times.'

Oh my god, only Nika could be stupid enough to have Snap Maps on for a troll account, Maeve thinks.

Her mother rubs her back. 'Want to talk?'

'No.'

'OK, I'm going to bring you something to eat.'

'I don't want anything.'

'I'll bring it anyway, and you can eat it or leave it. I love you.'

She bends and kisses the top of Maeve's head. 'Greta is downstairs. She called in on the way home from hockey camp. She wants to come up and see you.'

Maeve shakes her head, but Leesa is already up and out the door.

As soon as Leesa's gone, Maeve sits up, opens her laptop and clicks into Google. She stares into space for a moment, then starts hammering keys.

How to kill your friend. How to murder a bully. How to get the best revenge on the worst person in the world.

She won't do any of it, obviously, but it feels better to look it up than to sit here crying. Fucking Nika Geary. How could she do this? A flashback now, to another July day, five or six years earlier. Lying on their stomachs in Nika's garden, baby oil on their backs like Maeve's mum used to do when she was their age. Listening to Spotify on Maeve's phone. Licking Magnums before they melted. Sharing gossip, sharing secrets, sharing everything. How could Nika do this to her? She types again:

How to kill your best friend without being caught.

The first search results bring up a novel, something called *How to Kill Friends and Get Away with It.*

She types again.

How do you kill someone who has a tree-nut allergy? If you stuff nuts in her lunch, will she die? Will the fucking bitch die?

She lets out a breath that turns into a sob just as Greta sticks her head around the door.

'Can I come in?'

A nod. Maeve has never said no to her aunt and she doesn't now either. She adores Greta, but she's a tiny bit . . . intimidated by her. Leesa is much softer, and Susan, bless her, mostly hasn't a clue. But Greta is strict. She still remembers her mother up at the till in the bookshop in Blackrock a few years ago, about to buy her a copy of Colleen Hoover's *Verity*, until Greta tapped Leesa on the shoulder and said it wasn't suitable for thirteen-year-olds. Of course Leesa put it back on the shelf. Leesa and Susan did everything Greta said, like they were all still kids. It was Greta who talked Leesa out of letting her go to Tribe, the local disco, when she was twelve, and Greta who suggested Snapchat could wait until secondary school, that it only ever led to tears. Now *there's* an I-told-you-so moment if ever there was one, Maeve thinks, rubbing her eyes.

Greta takes the laptop from Maeve's hands and sets it aside, then sits on the bed.

'Maybe give yourself a breather from screens?'

Maeve's shoulders hunch lower.

'It's not the screen causing the problem, it's the people behind the screens.'

Greta gives a non-committal nod and Maeve waits for the 'back in our day' speech. But she goes a different route.

'That little weapon, Nika, is in my hockey camp. Want me to stick my leg out and trip her up?'

Maeve laughs in spite of herself. 'Yes, please.' Then in a quiet voice, 'I hate her.'

Greta pats her knee. 'I know. Me too.'

Maeve eyes her. 'I thought you and Mum always said we should never hate anyone?' She mimics her mum. '"Hate" is too strong a word, just say "dislike".'

'I'm making an exception for Nika.' Her voice softens. 'Maeve, this will pass. I know it doesn't feel like it now, but something new will come along and they'll all forget it. And, just to say, having a crush—'

Maeve shoots her hand up. 'Stop, no. Please.'

Oh god, if Greta starts telling her about her own schoolgirl crushes she will literally climb out of bed, walk over to her window and throw herself out.

'OK. Your mum is worried about you.'

'What am I supposed to do? I'm sorry Mum is worrying, but there's only so much I can handle right now.'

'I know, I know.' She looks around the room with what appears to be fake nonchalance. Then she pats the pocket of her hoodie. 'Damn, I left my tablets downstairs. Maeve, will you be an absolute doll and get them for me?'

Maeve stares at her. Why is Greta making her go when she could get them herself? It's either to get Maeve to go downstairs so Leesa can trap her into eating, or it's so Greta can have a proper snoop in her room, making sure she doesn't have seventeen packets of paracetamol stashed under her pillow. She wants to say no. If it was her mother, she'd say no. But she's never talked back to Greta in her life, and today is not that day, apparently. Politeness wins, and she swings her legs out of bed.

'What are the tablets called and where are they?' she asks, injecting negative levels of enthusiasm into her voice.

'Naltrexone, in my bag, hanging on a kitchen chair. Thanks, Maeve.'

Maeve backs out of the room, bumping straight into Aoife, who is hovering right outside her door, listening in.

'Go away,' Maeve says under her breath, unable to muster any feeling in it.

Aoife grimaces and pats her sister's shoulder and, to her surprise, Maeve feels tears well up again.

51

Susan
Tuesday

To MY RELIEF, BELLA'S already in bed when Jon finally gets home from work on Tuesday evening, so I don't have to explain the redness. I feel sick every time I think about it – there aren't many hallmarks of negligent parenting worse than a sunburnt baby. I stayed indoors all afternoon, watching and waiting for the redness to fade, googling solutions. Cold compresses, the internet advised, and pain relief if she's in pain. She didn't seem to be in pain, she was in reassuringly good form, but I need air after a long afternoon fretting indoors, so as soon as Jon arrives into the hall I leave for a walk. A *long* walk. *Don't wait up*, I tell him, putting my earbuds in and pulling the door after me.

It's a beautiful sunny evening and Dún Laoghaire pier is full of walkers enjoying the weather, but nothing can lift my mood; not the sea view, not the Oreo-dipped ice cream, not the promise of a glorious orange sunset. My eventual walk home takes me past Bar Four, its beer garden full of Tuesday-night drinkers enjoying the unusually warm weather. People without a care in the world. I slow, looking in, envying them in their carefree lives.

'Thinking of going inside?' says a familiar voice from behind me.

I turn to find Felipe, Venetia's husband. Tonight he's in a bright tropical-print shirt, the kind you can only get away with if you're under thirty-five and good-looking (he is both). I wonder what age he is. Thirty-one or -two, I reckon. Venetia is slightly older, closer to my age, I'd say. It would be interesting to know what brought them together – this soft-at-the-edges guy and his sharp-angled partner.

'Oh, no, I wasn't going to the pub. I'm just on my way home from a walk on the pier.'

'I'm going in for a quick glass of wine. Will you join me?'

I should say no. But something – the open look on his face, the knowledge that Jon probably wasn't really 'working late' all those nights in recent weeks – makes me say yes.

We grab a small wrought-iron table near the main door to the pub, and Felipe is back from the bar two minutes later with a bottle of Pinot Grigio in an ice bucket and two glasses. I'm not convinced this will be the 'quick' drink Felipe suggested, and I'll be later home than Jon expects, but actually, I don't care.

'So, I was wondering,' Felipe says as he pours a glass for me, 'have you seen Venetia?'

He doesn't look at me as he asks and there's a forced casualness about his tone, his entire demeanour.

'Gosh, no, of course not. I said I won't call again, and I won't.'

'Good . . . good. Well, *salud*. Cheers.' He clinks my glass with his, looking a little less than cheerful.

'It must be hard at home right now,' I say gently, wondering if that's why he's here.

'Yes.' A heavy sigh. 'Venetia doesn't want to talk, and I respect that. Personally, I think it would help to open up, to talk about

Aimee, but—' He lifts his hands, his deep brown eyes huge and sad.

He's clearly desperate for someone to talk to; it's emanating from every pore.

'Well,' I say, 'why don't you tell me about Aimee?'

That does the trick. He tells me about meeting her for the first time, how vivacious she was, how close the sisters were. How in love Aimee was. Her perfect wedding. Her busy career. Her energy. Her love of life. His voice cracks with emotion once or twice, though he doesn't seem self-conscious. He pours more wine, and I drink more wine, wondering if this is a terrible idea. But my heart goes out to this almost-stranger and his bottled-up grief.

'You obviously knew her very well,' I say.

He shakes his head. 'That's the problem. I realize now I didn't.'

'What do you mean?'

'This thing with Warren Geary. It's not like her. And—' He shakes his head.

'Go on?'

'Nothing, it's nothing.' He takes a deep swallow of wine, and we sit in silence for a bit.

'Felipe, the thing with Aimee and Warren – look, even the most unlikely people will stray. These things happen more often than you'd think.' *Don't I know . . .*

He twists the wine glass between his fingers, studying it. 'Yes, but to be quite honest, if you knew Aimee, knew what her marriage was like, I . . . I don't know why she did it.'

'And I guess that's adding to Venetia's grief and shock? She's lost her sister but feels like she didn't know her as well as she thought she did?'

'Yes,' he says, but I get the distinct impression that's not it at all.

Felipe stands and says he'll get another bottle. I gesture for him to sit and say I'll go, it's my round. There's no way I'm getting us another whole bottle though.

I return with two glasses and we talk about other things for a while: his childhood in Bolivia and his move to Ireland – more of a backpacking stop-off that became a permanent home than any long-held plan to live here.

'I stayed for the weather. I could not resist your very attractive grey skies,' he says, and I laugh.

'In defence of my country, we're sitting outside at ten at night in short sleeves,' I point out. It's true. It's unnaturally warm for this time of evening and the beer garden is thronged with midweek drinkers making the most of it. The heatwave has a way of dissolving any thoughts of early mornings and alarm clocks. I wonder if Felipe has an early start and ask about his job. He's a software engineer for HP, he says, doing contract work, though he's taken leave this week to be there for Venetia. It was through work that he met her, he tells me, taking another swallow of wine. He'd gone to a wedding as a colleague's plus one and gone home with Venetia. He never really left, it turns out. He moved in permanently to the cottage in Coal Place soon after. 'As a paying tenant of Venetia and Aimee,' he adds with a grin, 'in case you think I'm a kind of gold-digger.'

The sisters co-owned the cottage, he explained, having inherited it from their grandmother. They'd grown up there. Their grandmother had raised them since their mother walked out when they were eight and six. *Jesus. Poor Venetia and Aimee.*

'And when did you get married?' I ask.

A sheepish look crosses his face. 'Soon after we moved in together.' He looks at me under hangdog lashes. 'Don't judge me, but Venetia suggested we marry so I could stay here. My holiday working visa had run out.' A shrug and a grin. 'I am

Gérard Depardieu in this story. You know, from the movie *Green Card*?'

My eyes widen. 'Wait, a sham marriage?'

'Oh, we were really dating. But we would not have married if not for the visa problem.'

Were dating. *And now?*

'Wow,' I say, instead of asking the questions that are in my head.

'Yes. She needed someone who could pay her good rent for the house – her wages bartending are not as much as she would like.' He clears his throat. 'She doesn't settle easily in jobs; she moves a lot. She's had some problems . . . And I try to look out for her, to take care of her. I was grateful to her for the visa, but also, she reminds me of someone who used to—'

He stops. 'Anyway, I wanted to stay here in your beautiful grey-sky country. So, it was convenient, a win–win for both of us. But also good,' he adds. 'We did get on well.'

That seems a muted way to put it, but who am I to judge, all things considered?

'We still do, mostly,' he continues. 'The version of Venetia you met on Saturday, she's not always like that. Though it's true she can be difficult, she is not so . . . soft.'

I think of the person I met at the bar, however briefly. Cool, terse, spiky in her body language, and I nod.

He takes a sip of wine then sets his glass carefully back on the table, using both hands to line it up perfectly in the centre of his beer mat. It's as though he's using the glass to steady himself.

'But she can be kind too. Especially with Aimee.' His eyes brim. 'It was Aimee's wedding. That's where we met.'

Instinctively, I reach for his hand.

'Oh, Felipe, I'm so sorry.'

He whispers something then, something I can't hear.

'What was that?' I ask.

He looks up, eyes damp.

'It's my fault. I can't tell you why, but it's my fault Aimee's dead.'

52

Susan
Wednesday

ON WEDNESDAY MORNING, I pretend to be asleep when Jon leaves for work. It's not difficult; I'm shattered and headachy from the wine with Felipe last night. My dreams were a montage of the three murder victims, the inscription on the bangle and Felipe's statement that Aimee's death was his fault. He had rushed to reassure me that he wasn't saying he'd actually killed her, but that something he'd done had triggered a chain of events. I nudged a little to find out more, but he just shook his head and said it didn't matter. We'd parted ways soon after. Instinctively, at the entrance to Bar Four, I hugged him goodbye. His arms closed around me and we stood there for a moment, locked in a strange, unspoken connection, my face buried in his collar. His skin was warm, his smell old tobacco and fresh laundry. The hug, different from Jon's, comforted and saddened me both at once, reminding me of everything I was losing. We pulled apart, promising to stay in touch.

Bella, who was up three times overnight, is snoozing peacefully in her crib. I pad over to peek at her skin and a huge weight lifts – she's back to her pale-as-milk little self. And realistically, she couldn't have burnt in that short space of time. But I still can't believe I left her so close to the edge of the umbrella or how quickly the shade moved. If anyone knew – especially after the supermarket drama and the baby-monitor mix-up – they'd think I'm losing it. I flop back on the bed, staring at the ceiling, trying to order my thoughts. Am I losing it? Am I imagining things? The murders were real. The texts were real. The broken window was real. And Jon's affair is real . . .

Before I know what I'm doing, I'm over the other side of the bed, pulling open Jon's night-stand drawers. The gloves are off. There are too many elements of my life out of my control right now – at the very least, I need to know who he's seeing. There's nothing in his night-stand, so I try his wardrobe next, going through his suit pockets once more. Nothing. I'm down on the floor now, running my hand across the bottom of the wardrobe where he keeps his shoes. My fingers close around a coin, a paper clip, and then a crumpled piece of paper. I pull out the paper and smooth it on my lap. A receipt.

Dinner in Peronique in early July. French onion soup and mussels to start. Fish special and fillet steak for main. Pepper sauce on the side. That's Jon. The fish, needless to say, is not me. Nothing against fish, just that I'd remember if I'd had a date night with my husband any time in the last four months. Dessert – one chocolate bomb. Two spoons, no doubt. I feel like throwing up. A bottle of Croatian rosé, organic. Two espresso martinis. And then something that stops me cold.

Now I know who she is.

53

Nika
Wednesday

NIKA WALKS INTO THE clubhouse, wiping sweat from her brow. Jess, breathless from the morning session, follows close behind. Jess is a good player, but not quite as fit as Nika, which is why they can be such good friends. Jess is also one of the few people who didn't join the Ariana-gate pile-on. Nika takes a slug of water from her bottle, pushes open the changing-room door and makes her way past the first bank of lockers. It's quiet this morning: only she and Jess have come in during break; the others are still on the pitch. She turns the corner to the second bank of lockers and stops. There's someone there, crouching on the floor. Nika freezes, startled. Then confused, as the person on the floor looks up.

It's Greta O'Donnell. And she looks . . . panicked?

At first, Nika can't make out what she's doing on the ground. Then she spots something familiar. Her hockey bag – bright pink and brand new – open on the changing-room floor. And her lunchbox, also open, beside it. *What the—* Inside the lunchbox, Nika can see the granola bar and the brownie she packed for herself this morning. The brownie looks different though, like there's brown sugar or . . . sand on it? She steps forward to take a closer look, but Ms O'Donnell slams the lid back on and gets to her feet, clutching Nika's lunchbox.

Confused and indignant, Nika reaches to take it.

'Leave it.' Ms O'Donnell's face is bright red.

'What are you doing?'

'Just . . . leave it.'

Jess is shoulder to shoulder with Nika now, still breathless.

Nika reaches again to take the lunchbox, and Ms O'Donnell takes a step back.

'Why can't I have my lunch?' This is *bizarre*.

'It . . . it might be dangerous for you. Your nut allergy.'

It dawns on Nika now. A familiar grainy flour she's seen inside packets in the baking aisle. *Not brown sugar, not sand.* 'It was ground almonds.' Nika's eyes widen. 'You put ground almonds on my lunch?' She turns to Jess, then back to Ms O'Donnell, mouth open. Nika enjoys a drama and is very happy to ramp up the theatrics when needed. But there's no ramping up needed now. She's genuinely shocked. 'Oh my god, Ms O'Donnell, are you literally trying to kill me? I need to phone my mum.'

54

Celeste
Wednesday

CELESTE HAD MISSED FOUR calls from Nika on Wednesday morning before phoning her daughter back and, at first, she couldn't make any sense of what Nika was saying. Now, standing in the changing room of Whiterock Hockey Club, missing an important meeting, she still can't make sense of it.

Greta O'Donnell, who runs the summer hockey camp, is standing by the wall, arms folded, doing her very best to look calm and firm, but Celeste can tell she's worried.

Nika is sitting on a bench, crying. Her friend Jess is rubbing her back.

'Mum!' Nika gulps a sob. 'We need to call the police. Ms O'Donnell tried to kill me!'

A sigh from Greta. 'Nika, I didn't. This has all gone too far. I think we need to calm d—'

Celeste holds up her hand. 'Could someone please explain what's going on?'

Jess stands and talks Celeste through a rather bizarre story of food tampering, pointing at a lunchbox – Nika's lunchbox, Celeste realizes – in Greta's hands.

'We shouldn't take the lid off now because it might actually *kill* her,' Jess adds with a final flourish to her story.

Celeste stares. This is not what she was expecting. Calls like this – teachers searching bags – are usually about vodka or vapes.

'Ms O'Donnell was trying to kill me,' Nika hiccups between sobs, 'for what I did to Maeve.'

Jess nudges Nika's foot with her toe in what looks like a warning. Celeste registers it but doesn't dwell – there are more urgent questions.

She takes the lunchbox from Greta's hands and steps a little away from her daughter to open it. Inside, there's a brownie in one compartment and a granola bar in the other. On the brownie, Celeste can see something that looks like sand liberally sprinkled on top. Ground almonds. Not something she buys any more, for obvious reasons. She turns.

'Greta, what's going on?'

'Needless to say, I didn't put anything on her food and I'm not trying to kill her,' Greta says with what is clearly forced calm.

'Then why did you take her lunch out of her bag?'

'I . . . I had an inkling something was wrong.'

Celeste stares at her. She has no idea what's happening here, but she is sure of one thing, and that's that Greta is lying.

'An inkling? I'm going to need more than that, Greta.'

'She's lying, Mum. She did it,' Nika sobs.

Greta's eyes narrow. 'And why would I do that? Why would I want to hurt you?'

Celeste can hear the challenge in Greta's voice.

'I don't know, because you're a psychopath? Mum, we need to call the police.'

Jess nudges Nika again, wedging the toe of her trainer under Nika's foot.

'*What?*' Nika glares at her friend.

Jess makes a face at her and Celeste catches it. *What are they trying to hide?* There's one way to find out.

'I think you're right, Nika,' Celeste says. 'We need to contact the authorities.'

Now all three – Nika, Jess and Greta – baulk. Nika catches Jess's eye then looks at Celeste.

'I . . . I might have made a mistake.' Nika swipes at her tears with the heel of her hand. 'Maybe . . . maybe Ms O'Donnell was trying to help me, like she says.'

'Well, *someone* put the ground almonds in there – this is very serious,' Celeste says, arms folded. 'You could have *died.*'

Greta gives her a strange look, and it takes a moment for Celeste to work it out. She stoops belatedly to give her daughter's back a comforting pat.

Jess clears her throat. 'There was a kid in our class who posted something on Snapchat about nuts recently – he's a bit, um, dim? So he might not have realized how dangerous it is.'

'You think he did it? Came into the girls' changing room and tampered with Nika's lunch?' Celeste doesn't bother to keep the incredulity from her voice. 'Is he *at* the hockey camp?'

Jess shrugs. 'I think I saw him earlier . . .'

Celeste waits for more – something from Nika or Greta to confirm or deny the hypothesis – but neither says a word.

'This is not the end,' Celeste says, pulling her daughter up from the bench. 'You'll be hearing from me, Greta.' And a swipe at Greta is a swipe at Susan O'Donnell, she thinks, quietly pleased. She propels her daughter out of the changing room. 'I'm sure I can leave you to dispose of the lunchbox.'

55

Susan
Wednesday

I FEEL SICK. I'M going to throw up. The receipt shakes in my hand. Two espresso martinis, a bottle of rosé, and a note about a customer.

Tree-nut allergy

And the pieces fall into place. Savannah Holmes.

Jesus Christ, I've been tracking him on my phone for the last two days for no reason. He's not seeing her any more because she's gone. Lying in a morgue. And now it dawns on me. Is Savannah dead because someone thought she was me, or is Savannah dead because she was seeing my husband? And there's only one place that thought leads . . . No. I put my head in my hands to stop it. Jon's a lot of things, but he's not a killer. Then again, I didn't think he was a cheat either.

OK. Stop. Take a breath.

It might not be her.

It is her.

I try to reason with myself. Lots of people have tree-nut allergies. Nika Geary in my tutor class does. And no, Jon isn't seeing a seventeen-year-old; I know that better than I know he's not a killer. But . . . there are too many coincidences. Links that can't be

203

ignored. I sent him to her . . . a package that came here, back when Bella was tiny. I hadn't the bandwidth to contact the courier company, so he said he'd drop it to her. He told me he'd left it on her porch. But what if he called in and they hit it off, and what if she was far more interesting than the post-partum baby-blues sobfest that was waiting for him at home? OK, OK. Another breath. This still doesn't mean I'm right. I need to think this through rationally. All I know for sure is that Jon is cheating – the bracelet tells me that. His credit card statement backs it up. This receipt in my hand tells me that someone he had dinner with has a tree-nut allergy. And this is not a work dinner. This is not dinner with his dad. This is dinner for two in the oldest story in the book.

I need to go through everything, sort the facts from the guesses. More deep breaths.

1. Savannah had a tree-nut allergy. It's something she talked about on her Instagram, I know it for sure, and it's one of the reasons I followed her account in the first place.
2. Savannah had a link with me. We lived at the same street number and street name and our packages got mixed up.
3. Jon has been to her house, re-delivering a package.
4. Jon has been cheating on me; the bracelet is proof of that.
5. Jon has been weird for the last few days: wary, hovering, on edge. I thought it was because I was being distant with him. But is it because his girlfriend was murdered?

On shaky legs, I get up and go to my night-stand. The bangle is still inside. I take it out now and run my thumb across the inscription. 'Happy one-month anniversary, all my love, Jon.'

I really am going to throw up.

How the bracelet got here is a mystery, but the rest of it makes sense. Jon is cheating on me with Savannah Holmes. Correction, Jon *was* cheating on me with Savannah Holmes, but not any more because she is dead. Which brings me right back to my earlier question. Why is she dead, and is it somehow down to me?

56

Savannah
Last week

AT EIGHT O'CLOCK LAST Tuesday evening, Savannah cycled home from the gym in glorious amber sunlight. It was wasted on her though; she was wrecked. Wrecked from the long day of work, the stint on the XSGym machines, and OK, the two glasses of white in the afternoon. She was ready to collapse on the couch. Braking at her front porch, she slipped off the bike and considered for a moment. She *should* wheel it around to the back garden, but the side gate was locked. And the effort to go through the house, out the back and around to unlock the bolt, was too much. Anyway, Oakpark was a safe neighbourhood. Nobody was going to come in and steal her bike. She left it propped against the front wall of the house and made her way inside.

From her kitchen, after her third shower of the day, she texted Jon to see if he was calling over after work. They always came here or went to hotels. Jon lived in Maynooth, which was miles away, and there was no chance Savannah was bothered travelling all the way there when they could as easily come here. Jon had a brother living in Blackrock, and he sometimes stayed there if it was too late to go home. She'd stayed there once, when

Jon was housesitting for his brother and sister-in-law. It was an OK house, as far as she remembered, though her recollection of that night was hazy. They'd had a *lot* of wine, first in Peronique, then in Goggins. She *did* remember that the house was a little shabby, but deliberately so, the way people do when they want to invest in home decor but don't like anyone to know they care. People could be such weirdos. She remembered a hideous yellow couch that they sat on for all of five minutes before moving upstairs, and the rest was a blur. The only other thing she recalled was dropping Jon's sister-in-law's retinol serum on the en suite tiles the following morning when she was rushing to get out to work. Luckily, she'd cleared it up before Jon noticed. She'd actually felt a smidgeon of guilt – it was an expensive brand, one she used herself. But hey, these things happen, and Jon's sister-in-law probably didn't even notice.

Jon texted back – he was working late and heading home to Maynooth. Savannah sighed and leaned against the kitchen counter. A long evening alone stretched ahead. She had never minded being on her own . . . but suddenly, she did. Was she falling for Jon? Until now, she'd seen it as a casual fling. But maybe that was changing? Her bracelet glinted in the evening sunlight and she ran her fingers over the inscription. It had seemed too much at the time. But now . . . maybe she could see herself with Jon long term? Her gaze fell on her wedding photo. The photo that made her mother sniff in disappointment every time she called by. Savannah knew it was probably time to take it down, but also, she had never, ever looked as good as she did in that photograph. Her beautiful cream taffeta dress, and Albie so smart in his tux. She'd thought they'd be together for ever, that he was the one. But maybe Jon was the one? Maybe it was time to take down the photo . . .

Not today, but soon.

57

Susan
Wednesday

I'm sitting on my bedroom floor, Peronique receipt in my hand, when my phone beeps with a notification. I ignore it. Six more beeps follow. It's Leesa, messaging in our sister group, asking 'what the hell is going on?' It takes me a moment to read back, to piece it together, but it's about something Celeste has just sent in the Oakpark group. Leesa sends a screenshot.

Just a note to any parents considering the Whiterock Hockey camp run by Greta O'Donnell. My daughter was in the camp, but we've had to take her out due to a serious and possibly life-threatening incident. Details are not yet clear but, at best, there is negligence at play and, at worst, the incident may have been deliberate. I don't want to name names, but I'd be very wary of anything being run by Greta O'Donnell.

I type a reply to our group:

'Don't want to name names' . . . Jesus, she's some wagon. What is she on about?

Leesa replies:

I have no idea. @Greta, what's happening? Can we help?

Blue ticks tell me Greta has read my message, but from Greta herself, there's nothing. We usually stick to texting, but this is too important. I hit the call button and Greta answers with a heavy sigh.

'What's happened?'

She tells me the whole story. Or not the whole story, because there's something missing.

'OK, Celeste is a lunatic, we all know it wasn't you, but how did you know to check the lunchbox?'

Silence.

'Greta?'

This really isn't like her.

'I mean, it wasn't you, was it?'

More silence.

'Greta, what's going on? I know you wouldn't do something like this.'

'I'd better go.'

'Hang on.' I look down at the receipt on the carpet in front of me. Jesus, I'm being haunted by nut allergies. 'Have you seen Jon in the last few days?'

A beat. 'No. Why?'

'Not at all?'

'Not since your house on Saturday.'

This is a lie. My sister is lying to me, and I don't know why. And I can't say it to her. I should. I should just ask her. We're close. We always have been. But I can't make myself say it.

Instead, I say goodbye, and sit on my bedroom floor staring at the receipt.

58

Jon
Wednesday

IT'S WEDNESDAY EVENING AND Jon is sitting in the car in the driveway, unable to summon the will to go into the house. His mind goes back to this morning, leaving for work – Susan pretending to be asleep and him pretending he believed her. Is this how it will end, he wonders? Avoiding each other until one of them finally calls time on the marriage?

You already called time on the marriage, says a voice in his head, *or what else would you consider an affair?*

He hadn't considered it at all, that was the problem. He is a horrific cliché, and he knows it. Post-partum wife, newborn baby, and he's off finding himself a girlfriend. If he *had* to explain, he'd call it a panicked response to fatherhood. A reaction to the baby-shaped permanent seal on his relationship. You can leave a marriage, but it's a lot harder to leave a child. And the stupid thing is, he never *wanted* to leave the marriage. He loved Susan and still does, and if he could turn back time and never meet Savannah, he would. Right now, he can't think of a single thing he regrets more than the affair, something that was little more than a knee-jerk response to Bella's arrival; a need to prove to himself that he was still young and still had it.

God, he makes himself sick. *Not sick enough to stop though, was it?* Nope. That's the harsh reality. If Savannah was alive, he'd still be sleeping with her. But Savannah is dead and the police are investigating and his wife is caught up in it too. How much longer until she knows it was Savannah he was seeing? And how long before the gardaí come knocking on his door?

On autopilot, as he's done a hundred times since last week, he retrieves his second phone from under the driver's seat and reads Savannah's final text.

I've had it up to here with ALL of you. My ex-husband is being a PRICK, turning up at my house because I'm with someone new, then I find out you're MARRIED. Then you leave me with that bitch in my own home, jesus christ you have literally driven me to drink. She's gone btw and if she ever comes back or you ever come back, I'm calling the police. I'm deleting your number. DO NOT EVER CONTACT ME AGAIN, YOU PRICK.

He wonders again about his anonymous call to the guards – why hadn't they acted on it? Why was Albie Byrne, Savannah's ex, giving newspaper interviews instead of garda interviews? Maybe because Jon called anonymously. Or maybe because he didn't give Albie's name? He hadn't known Albie's name at the time, in fairness. He'd seen Savannah's wedding photo, but never noticed that the husband was the same guy as the one on election posters – now ten years older and twenty pounds heavier. Maybe it's worth trying the guards again, but this time giving Albie's name, he decides, hitting the number for Blackrock garda station on the pay-as-you-go phone he'd used to text Savannah.

'I have information about the Savannah Holmes murder,' he says as soon as the call is answered. 'I can't say who I am, but I know for a fact that her ex-husband, Albie Byrne, was harassing her right before her death. You need to question him.'

The garda tries to say something, but Jon keeps talking. 'I called about this already last Wednesday, but I didn't know who her ex was, so I didn't give his name. I've since found out it was Albie Byrne, the politician. You have to question him; he was harassing her because she was—' He stops himself, and disconnects.

That should do it.

Outside, as he opens the car door, he spots Leesa walking up their driveway. Leesa is his least favourite of the three O'Donnell sisters and he suspects she knows it, though he works hard to disguise it. He wonders if he can slip back into the car and hide, before she launches into one of her streams of consciousness about a film he must see or a wine he must try or a thing she saw on Facebook. But no, she's level with the car now and he's not escaping without a chat.

'Hey, Jon, just popping in to see how Susan's doing.' Leesa smiles warmly. She has no idea what he really thinks . . . She's actually the best-looking of the three sisters – more athletic than Susan but curvier than Greta, and her golden hair gives her a fun, sunshiny look. If she talked a bit less . . . Jon shakes himself. This is exactly how it started with Savannah and he needs to cop on. He tunes in again to what Leesa is saying.

'. . . she was really stressed about the sunburn. Has it gone down? I told her it would. It's not the end of the world. When we were kids, nobody knew about sun damage. We used to slather ourselves in baby oil, for god's sake!'

Sunburn? Jon has no idea what she's talking about, but then he didn't see Susan last night, not properly. She went for a three-hour walk and crept into bed smelling of wine. She could have been burnt head to toe and he wouldn't have known.

'Yeah,' he says. 'It's fine now.'

'Good. Poor little mite. Sure she won't remember a thing anyway.'

Leesa isn't making a whole lot of sense, but she rarely does. He smiles agreement rather than asking questions; it's quicker that way.

'When I had her last week, I didn't even think to put sun cream on her, though I didn't have her out in the garden, so I suppose that's fine. And it wasn't that hot on Wednesday anyway, was it?'

Is she waiting for a reply? Jon nods, feeling lost. 'I'd better head inside.' Something stops him then. 'Wait, Leesa, do you mean Bella? You were minding Bella on Wednesday?'

'Yeah, while Susan was at physio. Don't tell her what I said about forgetting sun cream.'

Physio. That stops him cold.

'Are you sure she said "physio"?'

'Yeah, she said she thought she was all done but the pain flared up again. I remember when Aoife was born—'

Jon cuts her off. 'And did you say Wednesday? You're sure?'

She looks at him quizzically. 'I'm sure. But just ask her yourself. Why?'

'No reason. Maybe don't say anything to her. She'll kill me if I keep forgetting her appointments.'

'OK.' She looks expectantly at him.

A brief silence.

Then she gestures towards the door. 'Aren't you going in?'

'Oh, right – I just remembered I was supposed to get milk on the way home. You go in. I'll be back in a bit.'

She nods, and he slides into the car. *Physio.* There is no physio. He knows that. Susan knows that. 'Physio' is code for marriage counselling. But *he* wasn't at marriage counselling last Wednesday. And Susan was hardly there on her own. So where was she? There could be any number of answers to that question. But one stands out. And the idea of it, the very idea, makes his blood run cold. He needs to speak to Greta.

59

Venetia
Wednesday

JUST AFTER SIX ON Wednesday evening, Garda Orla Connolly, the guard who broke the news of Aimee's death last week, turns up at Venetia's cottage. Her fourth visit now, and this time she's with a woman she introduces as Detective Kellerman. Venetia leads them through to the kitchen and gestures for them to sit. Felipe is at the hob, stirring Bolognese. He greets them and begins filling glasses with water by unspoken agreement; it's too hot for tea or coffee.

Venetia faces Orla. 'You have news?'

Orla's expression is hard to read. Sympathy? She nods towards Kellerman, who is doing the talking this time, it seems.

'I'd like to ask you about your sister's relationship with her husband.'

So they know. Venetia lowers herself into a chair.

'It was good,' she says. 'They were together since they were teenagers. They had ups and downs like anyone, but they were good. Solid.'

Kellerman says nothing for a moment. Her eyes roam Venetia's face. Doesn't she believe her? This woman is not as nice as Orla.

'Have you found something?' Venetia asks.

'The woman who lives next door to Aimee gave us some new information.' Kellerman's gaze never leaves Venetia's face. 'She's the person who called us on Wednesday morning. She'd heard a door bang late Tuesday night, and texted Aimee Wednesday morning to see if everything was OK.'

'I see.'

'Does that strike you as unusual?'

'No?'

'OK.' Kellerman writes something in her notebook. 'She got no reply from Aimee but saw that both cars were in the driveway and got worried. We wondered why that had made her worry – maybe Aimee was having a lie-in or had switched off her phone – and she said she'd heard shouting and banging from time to time. The walls are thin. She worried that all was not well in their relationship. Does that tally with your opinion on their marriage?'

'No, not at all. I mean, everyone shouts a bit, don't they?' Venetia glances at Felipe. Felipe never shouts.

'I see.' Another note. Orla says nothing, but she's watching Venetia throughout.

'Do you think murder-suicide?' Venetia whispers.

'No. We're certain both Aimee and Rory were murdered.' A pause. A million unspoken words slip into that pause.

'One more question and then I'll leave you in peace. Did either of you know a woman called Savannah Holmes?'

Evening sunlight slips through the slats of the blind, momentarily dazzling Venetia as she sits on the couch pulling on her boots.

'Where are you going?' Felipe asks, and Venetia startles. She hadn't heard him coming into the room.

'Just out.' She goes through to the hall, and he follows.

'I'll come with you. A walk will be good.'

'No. I'd rather go alone.' She needs a break from Felipe minding her, watching her.

He opens his mouth, as though searching for something to say. A way to insist.

'I won't be long,' she tells him before he finds the words, and she opens the front door. There's no need to worry.'

'I can't help worrying,' he says miserably. 'After everything we did . . .'

'Nobody knows. We're safe.'

'The detective today. Kellerman. She knows something.'

'She's just doing her job. It doesn't mean anything. You were there, you heard me – I told her Aimee and Rory were good, and that we didn't know Savannah Holmes.'

'Why tell them Aimee and Rory were good, I don't understand.'

'Because the less we knew, the better. Think about it.' She throws up her hands. 'This is all so messed up. We're being visited by the guards and worrying about questions and grieving my sister, and who's interrogating Susan O'Donnell? Nobody. She's just living her life, not a care in the world, and she killed my sister.'

'Rory killed your sister.'

'Yes, but if it wasn't for Susan O'Donnell's message, she'd still be alive.' She sighs, exhaustion and grief briefly replacing anger. Her voice cracks. 'And I still don't get *how* he saw it. He isn't even on Facebook. Stupid, ignorant people sharing screenshots without thinking of the consequences.' She moves out to the front step. 'Anyway. Stop worrying, we're safe, nobody knows.'

'But what if the detective asks where we were on Tuesday night last week?'

She stares at him. 'We were here. Together. As long as neither of us says anything different, we're OK. And neither of us will say anything different, will we, Felipe?'

He dips his head, but in resignation not agreement. She'll need to keep an eye on Felipe.

60

Venetia
Last week

VENETIA, TIRED FROM HER short but draining evening shift at Bar Four and still mulling over her visit to Aimee, slipped out of the pub and began her walk home. The idea that she'd had to escape out the back door of Aimee's house to avoid Rory . . . if that didn't hammer the message home, nothing would. Aimee *had* to see that wasn't normal? Tomorrow. Tomorrow everything would change. Aimee would leave and Venetia would take care of her and they'd never see Rory again. Venetia yawned. Tuesday nights weren't usually busy, but there'd been a football-club table quiz and she was exhausted – exhausted pulling pints and looking at happy, healthy, club-joining types. Crossing the road, she pulled out her phone to check her messages. A text from Felipe asking what time she'd be done. Same time as every night, she replied in her head as she swiped it away. A bunch of Facebook notifications, mostly from Freecycle, Buy-And-Sell and local area groups posting about lost dogs and traffic problems. Nothing from Aimee. Tomorrow though. Tomorrow Aimee would escape.

Another text from Felipe, checking she was OK. It was endearing at first, the way he looked out for her. But over time, it had become cloying. Was it still worth the rent he paid, the tea he made, the company? It had been on her mind more and more this year. They'd be married three years in December, and after that, if they split, he could still hold on to his visa. And with Aimee moving in now, space would be tight. Maybe it was time for a conversation.

Lighting a cigarette as she walked towards Coal Place, she scrolled through Facebook. A post in Blackrock Locals caught her attention, a screenshot of a WhatsApp message. There's always something open-the-popcorn about a WhatsApp screenshot.

Those were the words going through her mind as she read the message. Her eyes focused on one sentence.

her husband wrapped around the PR girl at the opening party for Bar Four.

Bar Four. The PR girl. Aimee. A husband wrapped around Aimee. Venetia dropped her cigarette on the ground, re-reading. Who . . . what? Rory, Aimee's husband? But no. That's not what the screenshot meant. It was a message about someone called Celeste, according to the caption. A message about Celeste's husband and Aimee. In the comments, the husband was identified as Warren Geary. Aimee and Warren Geary. And the message had gone viral. More than six hundred likes, and eighty-four shares. Venetia began to run.

61

Celeste
Wednesday

CELESTE STIRS THE DAL makhani and sips her wine, watching out of the corner of her eye as Warren sidles into the kitchen. She can already guess what he's going to say.

'Hey.' He clears his throat. 'So, I saw your message about Greta O'Donnell in the Oakpark group and I asked Nika about it and she said the almonds thing was a misunderstanding?'

She shrugs, to annoy him. He tries again.

'I know the O'Donnells aren't our favourite people right now, but if it's not true, maybe we shouldn't say it . . .'

'So someone tries to harm your child and this is your response?'

'Celeste, a rational person knows you can't just accuse people like that.'

'Oh, a rational person knows, do they? And would a rational person do what you did?'

'Is this about . . . the Bar Four girl?'

'Yes, Warren, the girl who happens to be dead.'

She carefully places her wine glass on the counter and leaves the room before he can reply.

*

Halfway up the stairs, she passes Cody, on his way down. His bruised knuckles have healed a little, but they're still swollen. She needs to ask him what happened, but part of her doesn't want to know. Sometimes it's easier to say nothing. The missing knife pops into her head then. But Cody wouldn't do anything with a knife, would he? She thinks again about the injured hand. About the message from Susan that lost him the work placement. The incident that started all of it, with Moira Fitzpatrick's son. Cody is not . . . right. There's something damaged about him. The realization hits her like a slap. On some level, she's always known it, but she's pushed it so far down, it was easy to ignore. Warren was trouble as a child too, she knows that from his mother. Not the pull-wings-off-flies kind of trouble, but she has the sense that his mother was always trying to cover for him. Celeste realizes that's what she's been doing too. She never asks Cody what he's been up to because she doesn't want to know. When he was small, she avoided playdates in case he'd hurt the other kids. When he was older, she let him out on his own and asked no questions. But she can't keep her head in the sand any more. The sound of the TV wafts up from the den. Cody's put something on. He'll be flopped on the couch, zoned out.

Quietly, she pushes open his door.

62

Jon
Wednesday

JON PULLS UP OUTSIDE Super Valu but doesn't get out. His brain hurts. He needs to order his thoughts, to buy the milk, to go home. *OK. OK.*

He is almost certain Susan knows what he's been up to: the way she's acting, the bangle in her drawer. But the new news from Leesa just now – that Susan went out somewhere last Wednesday morning – that's freaking him out. The morning Savannah's body was found.

So where was Susan? And crucially, does she know where *he* was on Wednesday morning?

Something niggles now. Something about the bangle. Something about the last time he was with Savannah. Cold dread trickles its way through his stomach. It can't be. Can it? He casts his mind back. Sun streaming in through Savannah's front door, dappling light across the hall floor, across his back and his damp work shirt, over her face and shoulders. Savannah in a loose-fitting pale pink tank top and green khaki shorts. A work-from-home outfit. Or work from the garden, as she liked to do on hot, sunny days. Her tanned shoulders. Her toned arms. Her slim wrists. The bangle, glinting in the morning sunlight. Sitting on her left forearm, twisting under her fingers as they argued. He blinks, as though to refresh the memory. To be sure. But he is sure. Savannah was wearing the bangle just before she died. And now, it's in Susan's night-stand drawer.

Needing space, needing to think, he pushes back the driver's seat, ignoring a woman in a Jeep who's gesturing to ask if he's about to leave the parking spot. Something dislodges as he does so, jangling to the footwell. He reaches down. As his fingers close around the metal and plastic, it comes back to him. The keys. Savannah's car keys. Shit. Why does he still have them? And what should he do with them now? The guards will be looking for them. This is not good. Not good at all. Almost subconsciously, he pulls the tail of his shirt from his waistband and begins to polish the keys, the fob, the XSGym keyring. Sunlight beams through the windscreen of the car and sweat trickles down the back of his neck on to his collar. A quick glance across the car park tells him there's a bin just beside the entrance to Super Valu. OK. This could be a mistake, but the sooner the keys are out of his possession, the better. He gets out of the car. The woman in the Jeep is still looking for a car space. Evening sun hits him square in the eyes, but his sunglasses are missing. Not missing, he remembers now, but in Savannah's house, on her kitchen shelf. She sent him a picture. Eight days ago but somehow also a lifetime ago. Will it matter if the police find them? He's not sure, but right now, he needs to focus on the keys.

With the cuff of his work shirt pulled down over his hand, he strides across to the bin and tips Savannah's keys inside. Then follows them with the burner phone. Gone for good. He hopes.

63

Celeste
Wednesday

CELESTE STEPS INTO CODY'S room. It's not dark yet, but the curtains are closed already. Actually, she realizes, they've probably been closed all day. When he was small, she used to come in and open his curtains, but in recent years, he just closes them again, so she's stopped bothering. She's stopped going into his room at all. She's not one of those mothers who picks up after her children. If they have laundry or used glasses, they can bring them down themselves. She hears other mothers talking about picking through their teens' bedrooms for PE gear to wash and she quietly eyerolls. Children need to learn independence. And she doesn't spend all day at work to come home and do her children's laundry.

Where did she go wrong, she wonders, gazing around the room. Posters she doesn't understand on the walls. Not music posters like Nika's nice Harry Styles ones. Dark images that look sinister. Skulls and devils and death. Posters of games or comics, maybe? Not very suitable ones, in her opinion. On the desk, Cody's gaming monitor blinks, the screensaver swirling and dipping. His Xbox and laptop sit side by side. She opens the laptop, but it's password protected. Even if she knew the password, she probably wouldn't look. Snooping on her children's devices has never been her thing. She tells her friends it's because she trusts them. But in truth, she doesn't want to know. If Celeste can't see it, she can't worry about it. And Celeste has enough to worry about already.

She steps away from the desk to examine his bookshelves. Mostly true crime, she sees now. She hadn't known Cody was into that. Some graphic novels. Some dog-eared *Horrorland* books, but mostly true crime. She slips a hand behind the top row of books and finds nothing but dust. She'll have to have a word with the cleaner. Behind the next row of books, her fingers wrap around something. She pulls it out. A vape. Even though he'd promised after the last call from the school that he'd stop. *For goodness' sake.* She knows it's not the worst thing he could be doing. In fact, it probably *isn't* the worst thing he's doing. But it annoys her that he's been expressly forbidden and yet he keeps going. Why don't children today do what their parents tell them? She'd have been given a whack of a ruler if she'd been caught smoking as a child. And of course, now you're not allowed to do *that* any more either. She did when they were small. A light smack on the legs or the behind if they were misbehaving. And surely everyone did. People just don't admit it because it's not politically correct.

She slips the vape in her trouser pocket and tries the third shelf. Nothing there but dust and some other residue . . . she pulls her hand out and sniffs. It's barely there, but she can just about pick up a herbal smell she recognizes from her own college years and one particular housemate's room. *Oh, Cody.* It's like he's set out to be the stereotypical troublesome teen, just to get on her last nerve.

She turns to his bed, a mess of balled-up duvet and discarded clothes. How can anyone leave a bed unmade? She reaches to straighten the duvet but stops. There it is, glinting in the thin stream of sunlight that's slipped through the crack in the curtains. Its tip protruding from under his pillow. Her missing knife. Now, what on earth is Cody doing with a knife in his bedroom?

A sound from downstairs stops her – the click of a door. Cody? Maybe he won't come upstairs. She holds her breath, listening. At first, it's quiet. Then comes the unmistakeable creak of the third-last step at the top of the stairs. Too late.

The door opens and there's Cody, glaring at her.

'What are you doing in my room?'

His tone is angry but, beneath the anger, Celeste hears the worry.

'I have every right to come in here. It's my name on the deeds of this house, last time I checked.' She pulls the vape from her pocket. 'What's *this* doing here, more importantly?'

'I'm minding it for a friend.'

'Of course you are. Well, you can tell your friend I'm minding it now.'

'For god's sake, I'm fifteen, not five. You are unbelievable.'

'Oh, you're not *five*. So what happened to your knuckles? Am I going to get a call from someone's mother?'

A strange expression crosses his face. 'I hit my hand off a wall.'

'Sure. If I get a call about this, you're out on your own. I'm not going to spend the rest of my life bailing you out of trouble.' She reaches to pick up the knife from under his pillow. 'Why do you have this?'

His face changes again. The belligerence is entirely gone and there's something hooded, dark and secret in his eyes. He doesn't speak.

'I'm waiting.' As she says it, she wonders why she's doing this.

What does she want him to say? What if he's planning to hurt someone? Good god, she's not equipped for this. They'll have to bring him to a therapist, they'll have to—

'I needed to cut an apple.'

Relief floods her body. OK. An apple. That makes sense.

There are no apples here. There are no plates. No apple pips or cores. But it doesn't matter. Because Cody has explained, and they don't need a therapist.

'No food upstairs,' she says crisply.

'Whatever.'

Good god, he's so annoying. 'And stop sulking. You brought all this on yourself, you know. If you hadn't locked that child out, you wouldn't have lost the internship. The flap of the butterfly's wings.'

'The message would have gone out anyway. I just wouldn't have been mentioned,' he mutters under his breath.

Is he trying to blame *her*?

'Take some responsibility,' she snaps. 'You locked that child out and these are the consequences.'

'I was fourteen, Mum. I had no idea what I was doing.' There's something so plaintive in his eyes right now it stops her for a moment. Somewhere deep in there is the small boy she once held in her arms. She steps forward.

He steps back. 'You shouldn't have let me do the babysitting.' He's sulky again, and she sees red.

'Oh, so that's my fault too? You need to *grow up*, Cody. Why can't you be more like your sister?'

'More like Nika? Ha. You'll see. And when it's over, don't say I didn't warn you.'

64

Susan
Wednesday

'Jon said not to bring this up, but sisters before misters, obviously.' Leesa's at the sink, filling the kettle, and turns now to look at me. 'About your physio last Wednesday – I mentioned I'd been minding Bella when you went and he seemed . . . taken aback?'

Shit. Of course he was. Now he thinks I was up to something. Why didn't I think of that and tell Leesa I was going to, like, I don't know, the dentist? The appointment was a just-in-case one, to nip any downward spiral in the bud. And the only reason I didn't tell Jon was so he wouldn't worry. Except now that I know we're potentially destined for divorce, the last thing I need is for him to know I had to go back to my counsellor. And that I let our daughter get sunburnt. *Fuck.*

Leesa walks over and touches my arm.

'What's up? Are you guys OK? Is it the stuff that's been going on with the message and all that?'

I nod. If only that's all it was.

She scrutinizes me; sympathetic, I think, but also not quite buying it.

*

I can't believe I'm doing this, but Leesa's just gone and Jon is upstairs with Bella, and I'm texting Felipe to see if he wants to meet again tonight. It's a little bit to talk, a little bit to escape, and a little bit because, well, I like him. Not in *that* way. Not that I'm trying to have my own affair to get back at Jon, but it's nice being in the company of someone who isn't my cheating husband. And sometimes it's easier to talk to strangers.

We agree to meet in Conways this time, a cosy pub with low lighting and a flagstone floor. Despite the warm atmosphere, I'm on edge. All the way through my walk here I felt like someone was watching me, and I try to push it away now as I greet Felipe. I'm just being paranoid. There's one table free at the back, with two small wooden stools – I grab it while Felipe goes to the bar. I don't have the chance or, to be honest, the inclination, to tell him not to buy a whole bottle this time, and he arrives back with just that. I ask about Venetia. She's struggling still, he says, and changes the subject then, asking me what it's like teaching maths. He had a brilliant maths teacher in school, he tells me; she's the reason he became a software engineer. His parents, an artist and a musician, were surprised at his choice of career, as were his brothers. They're all big personalities, he explains, larger than life. He lights up when he talks about his family, becoming animated. 'They think a software engineer is the most boring job in the world and I am the most boring man in the world, and they are probably correct,' he says with a grin. 'I am the quiet one.'

'Well, you know what they say.' I clink my glass to his. 'It's always the quiet ones.'

He asks me about my family then, and I find I can talk in a way that I usually don't.

I tell him about my useless dad and my beautiful mother. About my serious sister and my fun sister. How close we are. He talks a little then about Venetia and Aimee and their closeness: messaging every day, borrowing each other's clothes, watching the same TV shows, texting throughout. They'd both been through tough times, he says, then, with a tell-tale glisten in his eyes, he tells me about his cousin back home who died from a drug overdose. I can't work out how we jumped from Aimee and Venetia's 'tough times' to his cousin's tragedy, exactly, but I don't ask.

Eventually, as we near the end of the bottle, I take a big gulp of wine and bring up the elephant in the room.

'Felipe, I didn't mention this last night or when I called to your house on Saturday, but . . . you don't think there's any link, do you, between my message and what happened to Aimee and Rory? Like, it's such a huge coincidence,' I rush on. 'Three people died and I'm the common link. I'm just worried . . .' I trail off.

He stares at me, his expression hard to read, then shakes his head. 'It's not your fault. If anything, it's mine.'

'What do you mean?' I ask softly.

He raises a hand to wave it away, but his expression belies his gesture – he's desperate to let this out, whatever it is.

'What is it, Felipe?'

A pause. 'It was me. I forwarded a screenshot of your message to Rory. He was not on Facebook. He would not have seen it if it wasn't for me.'

'OK . . .' I'm not entirely sure where this is going, but there's a curl of anxiety twisting through me. Does he mean Rory *did* do something to Aimee? I mean, otherwise, surely it doesn't matter that Felipe sent the screenshot? My heart rate quickens. This is bad.

Felipe continues, staring into his glass. 'Rory was always mocking Venetia – to her face and behind her back. Suggesting that fidelity isn't her thing.'

'Oh.'

'All disguised as a joke, of course.' He looks up at me. 'Have you noticed that people can say anything they like if they say "It's a *joke*" after?'

I nod.

'Anyway, it became too much. He was, excuse me, sometimes a very annoying asshole. So when I saw your message shared on Facebook, I sent a screenshot to Rory. So stupid.' He shakes his head. 'I was tired of the way he spoke about Venetia, but I should never have done it.' His shoulders slump. 'And look what has happened.'

I'm listening, but I'm also panicking. 'What are you saying? Did Rory . . . but the police said he was murdered?'

He blinks. 'He was murdered, yes.'

Oh, thank god. 'Not a murder-suicide.'

'Not a murder-suicide.'

Relief washes over me. But confusion too.

'Then the fact that you forwarded the screenshot to Rory didn't really cause anything?'

'Absolutely. But I feel very bad.'

OK . . . that doesn't quite tally with 'it's my fault', but he's grieving and has had quite a bit of wine . . .

'So, the theory is still that a stranger murdered them? And it had nothing to do with my message about Aimee and Warren?' Yes, I am absolutely putting words in his mouth now, but I also need this to be true.

'That's it: it has nothing to do with you.' He reaches across the table and rests his fingers on mine, then pulls away as though he's remembered that we don't know one another very well.

But the gesture is touching. And an hour later, when I slip into bed, I can still feel the imprint.

·65

Venetia
Thursday

THERE ARE MANY WAYS you can get at people who've done you wrong, Venetia knows.

You can spread rumours about them.

You can target them online.

If they have a business, give them a one-star review. Make up a whole host of accounts and give them lots of one-star reviews.

You can send an anonymous note to their boss or their boyfriend.

You can smile at them when you see them, then for your own quiet satisfaction whisper 'bitch' as they go past.

Venetia has done all these things. The girl who made her life a misery in sixth year is baffled by the negative reviews for her yoga studio. The man who fired her from her last bar job doesn't know where the rumours of rodent infestation started. The customer who was rude last week is trying to convince his wife that he knows nothing about the woman on Facebook who keeps asking to meet again.

But all of that was before this. All of that was when Aimee was here and life was good. Now it seems petty and trite. Now her rage is directed at one person only.

She makes her way up Susan O'Donnell's driveway and slides a leaflet from her satchel into the letter box, pulling her baseball cap low over her face. Nobody ever questions leaflet drops. She's often thought that, as she watches them make their way in and out of residential spaces, unopposed and undisturbed.

Once the leaflet is in the letter box, she moves away from the porch as though going back down the driveway. But she slips to the side, past the corrugated door of the garage and around to the side gate. She sticks her hand through the slats and slides the bolt. One of these days they'll surely padlock it, but they haven't yet. It's Thursday morning and the husband has gone to work, even earlier than usual. There's a man not interested in spending time with his wife and child, she thinks.

So it's just Susan and the baby in the house.

The back garden is swathed in sunlight and the patio doors to the huge kitchen-dining space are closed this time, but unlocked. Nothing stirs from inside. Susan might be upstairs or in the living room, Venetia supposes. She steps into the kitchen. What will she do if Susan suddenly appears? She doesn't know. But she also doesn't care. She stands still to listen. From upstairs comes a sound. The hum of a vacuum cleaner. She pads quietly into the living room, her rubber-soled boots making no sound. And there it is. In a Moses basket, wide awake and babbling. Venetia steps closer and stares down. The baby coos and smiles at her.

Oh, you can smile, she thinks. You don't know what I can do to you. You don't know who I am.

Venetia reaches into the crib and lifts up the baby. She holds it at arm's length. It's still smiling. She squeezes it. Just a little. Not quite as much as she did on Monday, when her finger-marks branded its arm. Its face changes. Confusion. Like it doesn't know humans can hurt it.

Venetia carries the baby to the kitchen and outside, then through the side passage to the front garden, keeping well out of sight of the doorbell camera.

Yes, she thinks, the baby hasn't yet learned to fear humans.

That's about to change.

66

Venetia
Last week

'JUST GO THROUGH THE red light, for god's sake, Felipe. It's eleven o'clock at night, there's nobody around.'

Felipe did as he was told. Venetia gripped the seatbelt with one hand and kept trying and retrying Aimee's number with the other. No answer. Please let her be asleep. Please let her be OK. The last words Aimee had said kept coming back.

He's on his way. And asking me something about a screenshot, some message that's doing the rounds.

Venetia would give anything, anything in the world, to be wrong. But her gut is telling her she's right to be scared.

Felipe had been waiting up for her and had offered to drive when he saw her getting in her car. He still didn't get what was going on, though she'd explained it twice now. He ran another red light. Almost there.

Venetia had the passenger door open before Felipe put on the handbrake. She made her way past Aimee and Rory's cars, deciding not to ring the bell. Instead she used the spare key from their lockbox. If it was all a mistake, there was no point in waking them. And no need to explain to Rory what had gone through her head. Not when they're this close to Aimee leaving. And if it wasn't a mistake . . .

Venetia ran down the hall and into the kitchen, but it was dark and empty. The living room too. Felipe stepped inside and opened his mouth to speak. She shushed him with a finger to her lips, then pointed up the stairs. The carpet, new and deep pile, muffled any noise as she went up towards the landing, with Felipe following. Straight ahead was the bathroom. To her right, the spare room, and then Aimee and Rory's bedroom. Aimee had been so proud when they got the keys to their smart, new-build townhouse. A pretty two-storey in show-house neutrals. Rory would be easier now, she'd said. Calmer, less stressed, once out of the tiny flat they'd been renting until then. And he had. For a week or two. Then he'd realized that parents from a local school were parking outside their house every morning, and he'd taken it out on Aimee.

Venetia swallowed, digging her nails into her palms. Felipe was right behind her, still confused, but knowing better than to speak.

She stepped forward and touched the bedroom door. For a moment, she couldn't move. Afraid of what she might find, afraid it would be too late. Then a sound caught her attention. The sound of sleep. The sound of snoring. Relief swept over her. Briefly, she closed her eyes. It was going to be OK. They were asleep, he hadn't seen the message, and Aimee would leave him tomorrow.

She pushed the door of Aimee's bedroom.

And that's when she saw it all laid bare. Red sheets where there should be white. Dark stains on the carpet. A metal bar with something heavy on the end. A barbell. One of Rory's barbells. And Aimee. Her beautiful, perfect, innocent sister lying across the bed. Her head lolling, hanging down over the side.

Arms by her ears. Eyes open. But gone. So gone. And as Venetia stepped forward, to do the impossible, to will her sister back to life, a noise caught her attention.

There he was. In his chair, head thrown back. The sound of snoring, the rattle of sleep. He'd killed her sister and taken a nap. Rage and grief and horror surged inside Venetia and rose like a volcano spilling out in a roar as she picked the barbell off the floor, raised it waist high and slammed the weight against Rory's head. And again. And again. Then arms were around her as Felipe pulled her away. And Rory slumped sideways on to the floor.

Venetia had two regrets. Not making Aimee leave earlier that day. And not making Rory suffer for what he'd done. He never knew what hit him.

67

Maeve
Thursday

MAEVE KHOURY STARES AT her bedroom ceiling, willing herself to get up, to take a shower. To change out of the track-suit bottoms and T-shirt she's been wearing day and night. A shower might be too much; maybe she could just wash her face and brush her teeth. But despite her mother's pleas and her own best efforts, she can't make herself move.

It's Thursday morning, and Maeve hasn't left her house in three days, not since the diary video on Monday. She's barely left her room. But she knows exactly what's going on in the world, through the window of her phone. She knows it was Nika who shared the diary video, and she knows people have completely forgotten about Nika seeing Ariana's boyfriend, which was presumably what Nika intended. Word is going around that Greta tried to hurt Nika. It's only a rumour, and Nika is keeping quiet. Probably because she knows she'll be in trouble for the AWGoss Snapchat account otherwise. Online harassment is against the law in Ireland; they've been told that in CSPE class at school. She turns on her side, curls her knees to her chest, throws her phone down towards the end of the bed and sighs. From downstairs comes the click of the front door, then Greta's voice. She sounds stressed. Guilt and worry curl through Maeve.

Celeste's message about Greta has led to people pulling out of hockey camp, apparently, and Maeve isn't sure what to think of any of it. Surely Greta didn't do it? She's not shy about confrontation or speaking up when something isn't right. But would she hurt someone? She couldn't have.

Then again, if it's a coincidence, it's a fairly massive one: Maeve googling what happens if you put nuts in someone's lunch and then someone puts nuts in Nika's lunch? Greta was alone in Maeve's room on Tuesday when she asked Maeve to get her naltrexone, and the laptop was open. She could have seen it . . . and she wouldn't have known that Maeve didn't really mean it. Or maybe she *did* know and that's why she did it. To follow through where Maeve wouldn't. And Greta knows Nika would have an epi pen on her, and maybe there's one in the first-aid box too. Greta would have been on hand to make sure it was nothing more than a scare.

Maeve waits for some kind of response to kick in. Shouldn't she feel glad that her aunt tried to avenge her? Some kind of satisfaction? But all she feels is scared.

68

Susan
Thursday

GOD, HOW AM I hoovering when my life is falling apart? Like some kind of 1950s housewife, just getting on with things. My husband has been cheating on me with a woman who was murdered last week, my sister is lying to me, my niece hasn't left her room in three days, and I'm hoovering.

My mind wanders back to last night, to the conversation with Felipe in the pub. His reassurance that Aimee and Rory's deaths had nothing to do with me. The warm touch of his hand. His guilt over sending the screenshot to Rory. Rory's 'jokes' about Venetia's fidelity or lack thereof.

Something strikes me now. I stop in the middle of the landing and switch off the hoover. Venetia's supposed infidelities. Felipe's claim that cheating wasn't in Aimee's nature. Felipe's account of Aimee and Venetia's closeness – daily texts and swapping clothes. The silver jacket that night in Bar Four.

Oh my god. Did I get it wrong? After all this fuss and drama, was I mistaken? Was it Venetia I saw with Warren? And if so, having spread it far and wide with my message, do I set the record straight? Or with Aimee and Rory both dead, does it matter at all? Felipe certainly doesn't need to know that his

240

wife may have been cheating on him, marriage of convenience or not. Warren obviously *does* know who he was kissing but isn't going to say. Nobody benefits from any kind of clarification, I realize.

It's too little, too late, but this time I'll keep my mouth shut.

Still thinking about it, I head downstairs to check on Bella and make a coffee. The only good thing that's happened in the last week is that Bella has started to nap properly mid-morning and, even when your world is falling apart, a sleeping baby can feel like a miracle. I go to the kitchen first to power up the coffee machine, then into the living room, oh so quietly, to check on Bella. I tiptoe, listening for those deeper, quieter breaths I don't want to disturb. She's sleeping so deeply there's no sound at all. I move closer and peer in.

Only the crib is empty. Bella is gone.

Jesus Christ. My throat seizes up and blood pounds in my ears.

Oh Jesus, oh Jesus, oh Jesus. I spin in a circle, looking around the living room – could she have fallen out? She's too small; she can't even roll yet. *Oh my god.* Did I leave her in another room and forget? I didn't. I'm sure I didn't.

'Bella!' I'm shouting now, shouting and running. She's not in the kitchen. I race to the hall and stand frozen for a moment. Did I leave her upstairs? Am I losing it? No, she was definitely downstairs. Oh my god, I'm going to be sick. I check the den: she's not there – how would she be there? Where is she? Upstairs or . . . or . . . I look at the front door. She can't be gone. But where else can she be? Has someone been in the house? Has someone taken her? It's not possible. I locked the back patio door last night myself and I haven't been out there this morning. Christ. I unlock the front door and run outside. There's nobody in the driveway. I run towards the gateway, panting and crying, and look both ways. A car passes by at the intersection with the main road, a man walks his dog. There's nobody else. I need to call the police. I don't know where my phone is. I don't know what to do. I need Greta to help me, and Jon, and I need to phone the police. I turn to run back up the driveway, and then I see her.

In the front garden, lying on the grass. Bella. Oh my god. I'm with her in three quick strides, scooping her up, holding her to me, checking, checking, but she's alive and awake and looking at me. How did she get out here? This makes no sense. Someone came into our house while I was upstairs and took her outside? Who, and why? And how? The door was locked. I'm almost certain. How could this happen?

Juliette Sullivan's voice pulls me back to real life. She's by her car, a box of what looks like plastic wine glasses in her arms.

'All set for the summer party tonight?' she calls, then squints at me and walks towards our dividing wall. 'Susan, are you all right?'

'No.' I'm crying, I realize now. 'Someone . . . someone put Bella in the front garden. They took her out of her crib and laid her on the grass.'

Juliette tilts her head. 'That sounds distressing. Far too hot for a little one to be out in the sun. I saw she was a bit red earlier in the week – did she get sunburnt? You might be better to keep her indoors during the hot spell.'

'It wasn't me! I didn't put her here.'

'Absolutely. But best take her in now?'

'I need to call the guards.'

'Of course you do,' she says in an over-the-top soothing tone. 'But bring her inside first, won't you? And have a cup of tea. And if you still feel you need to call the police, you could do it then.'

She thinks I did this myself. And bloody hell, the guards are going to think the same. I'm still reporting it. Let them believe what they want about me; they need to look into it. Juliette is still talking.

'You might just want to be careful they don't get on to Tusla, or whatever the child welfare people are called.'

Oh god.

'Between the sunburn and this today,' she continues, 'they might have some . . . concerns about Bella's welfare?'

Blood pounds in my ears. I hate her so much right now, but what I hate even more is that she's right.

'Not me, obviously. I have no concerns,' she adds smoothly. 'And I'm sure your husband would vouch for you. But people who don't know you might think there are some . . . problems with Bella's care?'

'I . . . I don't know what happened, but yeah, I need to get her inside.'

Juliette purses her lips and nods. She'll be straight on to her crony, Celeste, to tell her Susan O'Donnell has lost the plot and is harming her baby. Fuck.

69

Venetia
Thursday

VENETIA IS ON A high. That felt good. Laying the baby on the grass. The confused look on its face. The sun in its eyes. Squinting. Too small to do anything else. It couldn't roll or move or protect itself in any way. Just like Aimee couldn't, once Rory saw that message. Venetia makes her way through Oakpark, passing a big, leafy green. Two women are setting up trestle tables, covering them in white cloths. A tall stack of crates sits nearby – plastic glasses glinting in the sun. Venetia's been at parties like this, but only ever filling, serving, cleaning, gathering. Will Susan be at this party? Venetia smiles to herself. After what she's just been through, probably not. She keeps going, taking a shortcut through the trees, towards the road home, imagining Susan's panic. Imagining her shock at the empty crib. Her frantic search. Her confusion at finding the baby lying on the lawn. She might think she did it herself. She might think someone is coming to get her. Someone *is* coming to get her. It's been cathartic, toying with her. Enough though. It's time.

70

Jon
Thursday

JON PACES HIS OFFICE floor. In the conference room down the corridor, the Thursday-morning Heads of Department meeting rumbles on without him. He'd said he had a conflict. His door is closed and his blinds are drawn and he just needs peace and quiet to think. He can't get Leesa's revelation out of his head. Susan went somewhere the morning Savannah's body was found, and she lied about it. Where was she, and why lie? There could be any number of reasons, realistically – maybe she just needed some time on her own. A coffee, a massage, a trip to the shops. But he can't get away from one possible reason that terrifies him. And one cold, hard fact: Savannah was wearing the bracelet last week. And Susan has that bracelet now. What did Susan see? He needs to talk to someone. And there's only one person who can help.

Greta picks up, sounding snappish.

'What is it, Jon? I'm having a nightmare day so please don't make it worse.'

'Do you know where Susan was last week when . . . when Savannah . . .'

'What? At home with Bella, I assume. Why?'

'She wasn't. I found out she asked Leesa to babysit. She said she had physio.'

A sigh. 'So presumably she had physio. Look, Jon, I'm dealing with a complete shitshow here. My hockey camp has lost half its members and people want their money back and there's talk of calling the police and I really don't need an extra headache.'

'Greta, there *is* no physio. It's just something we said when we needed a babysitter for . . . well, we were going to marriage counselling.'

Silence.

'Greta?'

'You really are some fucker, aren't you? You were cheating on Susan while going to marriage counselling? Is this all one big joke to you?'

'I thought maybe the counselling would help . . .'

'I think maybe breaking up the affair would have helped more,' Greta says dryly.

'I know, I know . . . but Susan suggested counselling and I had no good reason to refuse. She knew there was a distance between us, but she thought it was the pregnancy and the baby.'

'And you let her think that. You're a monumental dick, Jon, you know that?'

'Absolutely,' Jon says. 'But we are where we are, and Susan lied to Leesa about where she was on the morning Savannah . . .'

Greta barks a laugh. 'Oh my god. Next thing you're going to say is that Susan went to Savannah's that morning.'

Jon doesn't laugh.

'Jon, come on. Pull yourself together and think straight. If you fall apart now, we're both going to be in trouble. You told me you called the gardaí yesterday and gave them Albie Byrne's name, right?'

'Yes.'

'So they're probably questioning him as we speak. Anyway, why on earth would you think Susan was anywhere near Savannah?'

'Because Savannah was wearing a bracelet that morning, one I gave her. And now Susan has it.'

'Maybe it's just a similar bracelet.'

'No, it has an engraving.'

Silence.

'What if Susan was there that morning, Greta?'

'She wasn't. You'd have seen her. So stop thinking it, and for god's sake stop saying it out loud. Get back to fixing your marriage, and I'll get back to fixing my business.'

'What if the police—'

But she's hung up.

71

Susan
Thursday

BACK INSIDE THE HOUSE, away from Juliette Sullivan's prying eyes and false concern, I hug Bella close and make my way to the patio door. It's not locked. Despite what Jon and I agreed, it's not locked. It was definitely locked last night, and I haven't been out the back this morning, so how is it unlocked? A movement catches my attention. The robot lawnmower Jon bought himself at the start of the summer is making its way across the lawn, manicuring the grass in neat lanes. Jon sometimes goes out to set it on its course when it stalls on a tree root or a rock. Maybe he was out this morning before work? I try ringing him, but he doesn't answer. I text him to ask. But even if the patio door was left unlocked by Jon, how would someone get into the garden? On one side, the house goes all the way to the dividing wall with Greta's. And on the other, the side gate is kept locked. I go there now to have a look, Bella still in my arms. The bolt is drawn across, as it should be. But not padlocked. We only padlock it when we're going on holidays. And it strikes me now that someone with sufficiently small hands could probably slide the bolt open from the outside. I try it now, slipping my hand through the slats of wood, and it's doable. Shit. I can't stay here. Even if I lock it now, whoever is doing this will find another way. It's probably the same person who smashed the window that first night. Meaning it's all linked to the stupid message. But what could be so bad in that message to warrant this kind of response? *Nobody died* pops into my head before I can stop it. *People did die.* I go inside to call Jon again, to tell him I'm going to stay somewhere else with Bella. I stop before hitting the call button. Could any of this be down to Jon? Did he leave the door unlocked on purpose? Is he gaslighting me, making me feel like a bad mother? Is this somehow linked to his affair with Savannah? Or . . . or her murder? Another question hits – where was he last Wednesday morning when Savannah was killed? God, I hope he was at work. I put down the phone. That's something I need to find out.

72

Susan
Thursday

JON WORKS FOR GS, a French bank, based in Dublin's financial
services centre, having moved strategically between various big
European banks over the last fifteen years. He's now head of
Corporate Trust, which means a car space, his own office and
a personal assistant. When I need to call Jon, I usually ring his
mobile, so I don't know Benedict, his assistant, at all, and as I
look up Jon's work number I'm crossing everything that Benedict will give me the information I need.

My call is answered promptly by a man who sounds reasonably young and very English. 'Jon Mullane's office. How may I
help?'

'Oh, hi. My name is' – *why don't I have a name ready?* – 'Jenny
Jones, and I'm calling to see if I left my wallet in Jon Mullane's
office last week. I met with him on Wednesday morning at . . .
at ten.'

'Hmm, no wallet was handed in and . . . I don't see any meetings last Wednesday morning in his diary. He wasn't actually
here at that time – could it have been another day last week?'

He wasn't in his office the morning Savannah was killed.

I swallow. *Keep it together.* I need more information. I really want to ask where he was, but that would sound weird. Maybe I can find out what time he came into the office.

'Oh wait, I think it was later on Wednesday. He was in later that day, right?' Bella gurgles in my arms and I bounce her gently as Benedict checks.

'He was, but again, I'm not seeing any in-person meetings scheduled, just a conference call at two . . .'

'It wasn't scheduled. I was just passing and stopped in.' I have absolutely no idea if this is likely or at all believable. 'I'm a friend.'

'Ah! You're the lady with the red hair! It's me you met when you were here. Sorry, I didn't make the connection, I misheard your name at the start of the call.'

Lady with the red hair.

'OK, so let me just check what time it was' – he makes a clicking noise with his tongue as I wait – 'ah, there you are, Greta, you signed the visitors' book at 11.04 a.m. Now, I don't think this is going to help much, since no wallet was handed in . . . I can ask Jon though.'

'No, that's OK – you've jogged my memory and I know where I left it. Thanks so much!'

'Not at all. Hope you find it. Bye now.'

What the actual fuck?

73

Susan
Thursday

MY PHONE IS STILL in my hand when it rings, startling me.
'Garda Station' flashes up on screen and, for a second, I think,
this is it. They're taking Bella away. I'm an unfit mother, Juliette has reported me, and it's over. It wouldn't be the guards
though, it would be social services, right? So that's not what
this is. *Calm down, Susan.*

Even with a few deep breaths, it takes me a moment to find
my voice when I answer, anxiety drying my throat.

'Hello?'

'Ms O'Donnell?'

'Yes.' It comes out in a croak.

'This is Detective Kellerman in Blackrock garda station. We
have a few more questions about Savannah Holmes – could we
ask you to come down this morning?'

'I . . . I have my baby. I wouldn't have anyone to mind
her . . .'

'Right, no worries, we'll go to you. Are you at home now?'

God. Why am I so anxious? There's nothing to hide. Still.

'Ms O'Donnell?'

'Yes. I'm here. It's fine.'

It doesn't feel fine. It feels the opposite of fine.

Detective Kellerman and the young garda from last week are in my kitchen, sitting at my table. Bella is in my arms, anchoring me, giving me something to do with my hands. They'd said no to coffee. They won't be long, apparently. Just a few questions about the morning Savannah Holmes died. I swallow and nod. For a fleeting moment, I consider telling them about Bella, that someone was here, that someone took her and put her outside. But Juliette's voice rings in my ears. *They might have some concerns about Bella's care.* I clamp my mouth shut.

'We have reports of a caller to Ms Holmes that morning,' Detective Kellerman says, 'and we wanted to check if you were anywhere near her house?'

'Me? Of course not. I didn't know her. We'd never met.'

'You didn't call there that morning to drop off a package or collect one?'

'No, definitely not.'

'Could you let us know where you were on Wednesday morning last week?'

Jesus. Is this really happening?

'Here. I'm always here.' I dip my chin towards Bella and force a laugh. 'She keeps me tied to the house.'

'Is there anyone who was here with you at the time who can confirm that?'

'I don't – oh, yes! My sister Greta was here.' I'm inordinately pleased to remember this.

'Great, what time was that?'

'From about eight till nine, or nine thirty maybe.'

'And after that? Was there anyone else here with you?'

'No . . .' My face heats up as I realize I'm lying by omission now. I *was* here early in the morning, and Greta was here, and there was nobody else here after – all of that is true. But of course I did leave then, to drop Bella to Leesa's and see my counsellor. I should tell them that. Or maybe I don't since they didn't ask?

Kellerman is eyeing me, noting the colour in my cheeks, I imagine. 'What kind of car do you drive?' she says.

This catches me off guard. 'Um, it's a dark blue Ford Mondeo.'

'I see. A dark blue Ford Mondeo was seen parked outside Ms Holmes's house on Wednesday morning. Does that ring any bells?'

My face is on fire now. *Christ. Answer them.*

'I . . . I can tell you with absolute certainty that I didn't go to Savannah Holmes's house last Wednesday morning.'

The rest of their questions barely register. My mind is on only one thing. I didn't have the car on Wednesday morning, Jon did.

74

Nika
Thursday

NIKA WAKES VERY LATE on Thursday – it's almost lunchtime – and at first, she doesn't remember what happened yesterday afternoon. Then it all slams back – finding Ms O'Donnell going through her bag, realizing what she'd done to her lunch, processing the fact that this grown adult – this *coach* – had tried to kill her. Maybe she wouldn't have died, but Greta O'Donnell couldn't have known that for sure. What kind of person does this? Adults are supposed to be the calm ones, while teens are 'impulsive'. It doesn't make sense. And on top of everything else, they can't go to the police because Greta will no doubt tell them that Nika's behind the online stuff with Maeve's diary. Nika wasn't convinced at first that it's really against the law, but Jess has been sending her links to the Harassment and Harmful Communications Act and, by the looks of it, she could actually be in trouble for the AWGoss account. Jess says she should delete it, but she hasn't yet. If Maeve Khoury put her aunt up to trying to hurt Nika, she deserves to have that diary video up there for the rest of her life. She slides up in bed so she's half sitting and asks her Alexa to open her blind. Bright sunlight dazzles her and she shields her eyes, groping for her phone. Fucking Maeve. She always was a loser. Nika is not one bit surprised she tried to get at her. But Greta O'Donnell? It's not the kind of thing adults do.

Nika sits up straighter.

Of course it's not the kind of thing adults do.

It's the kind of thing a teenager would do. Someone like Maeve, out for revenge. So does that mean . . . Greta was telling the truth? She was genuinely trying to stop Nika eating the food? And that it was *Maeve* who actually put the ground almonds on the brownie? Oh my god. That makes so much more sense. Of course Greta O'Donnell, grown adult woman, head of PE, responsible citizen, did not try to send her into anaphylactic shock. She was trying to stop *Maeve*. Trying to prevent Nika from getting sick and Maeve from getting caught.

Jesus Christ.

Maeve tried to kill her. For a bit of fucking online banter. She tried to actually *kill* her. Her chest tightens and her heart is beating faster now. Maeve Khoury tried to kill her. How dare she? Her breath quickens and blood pounds in her ears. That *bitch*. If she was here right now, Nika would grab her by her stupid throat and smash her head against a wall. She's shaking, shaking with rage.

One thing's for sure.

She's not going to get away with it.

75

Venetia

Last week

SHE'S NOT GOING TO *get away with it.*

Those words kept swirling in Venetia's mind as she hovered by the wall of her sister's bedroom, ignoring the pulpy, bloody mess of Rory's head. Felipe was standing in the open doorway to the en suite, face in hands, almost catatonic. Above him, just inside the en suite, the open skylight window showed a slice of navy sky and let in the sounds of the neighbourhood – a car door closing, a front door opening.

How long had they been there? Why wasn't she crying? Maybe she was still in shock, or maybe she was too filled with rage to let the grief in yet. She looked at her phone again. At the glib, throwaway message that had ended her sister's life. *The glib, throwaway, factually incorrect message*, said a little voice in her head. Venetia ignored it, still looking at her phone.

As she glanced up again, she saw her sister's lifeless body on the bed and rage fired up inside her, propelling her away from the bedroom wall.

'Where are you going? We should . . . we should call the police.' Felipe sounded broken. They were both broken. They'd never be the same again.

'I'm going to see her. The woman who sent the message.'

'We need to call the police.'

They stared at each other for a beat, Felipe still in the en suite doorway, her car keys in his hand. Venetia looked over at Rory.

'I'm not going to prison for him.' She shook her head. 'Not after what he did tonight and how he treated her all these years. No way.'

'What do you mean, "treated her"?'

She looked over at her sister. 'He'd been hurting her. She was going to leave.'

'*What?* Rory?'

'Yes, Rory.' She glanced at the bloodied mess of her brother-in-law's body. Like someone had put his head in a food processor.

'But he was so . . . are you sure?'

'Were you going to say "nice"? Or "normal"? Of course he seemed normal to you. But you don't know what was going on behind closed doors.'

Felipe looked utterly horror-struck.

'Venetia, why didn't you tell me?'

'It's private. Family stuff.' Suddenly clear-headed, she pulled the thin nylon scarf from around her neck and reached for the barbell.

'But they're my family too. I could have helped!'

'No.' The barbell didn't even feel that heavy in her hands now. How was there so much blood? 'You couldn't help, Felipe. I tried to. She was going to leave. Tomorrow. And look what happened.' As she spoke, she used her scarf to wipe the bar. The whole length of it, not just where she'd gripped it. Her finger-prints wouldn't be in any database, but still. *What about DNA? Can you really wipe away DNA?*

'That message. All because of one stupid screenshot. And now she's dead.' Still she polished. 'We need to go, Felipe. We need to be gone before they're found.'

He ran his hand through his hair. 'Venetia, I don't know.'

'Do you want me to go to jail for this?'

'No . . . but you'll be running for the rest of your life. Scared to be caught.'

She took his hand. 'I'm not scared. I'm fucking furious. I want to burn the whole world down. And I want to see the woman who sent the message. I'm going to her house.' She held up her phone, showing Felipe the Facebook page with the screenshot and the doxing: SO'D aka Susan O'Donnell, 26 Oakpark.

'It's just across the road. A two-minute drive. I'm going there now.'

'Venetia, you cannot go to that woman's house.'

'Don't tell me what to do.'

'I'm trying to help. I can't let you do this.'

Still holding his hand, she twisted the car keys from it and, before he could process what she'd done, she was running down the stairs and out to the car.

76

Venetia
Last week

THE HOMES IN OAKPARK were mostly in darkness, but in number 26, the living-room light was on. Venetia stood at the porch, not yet sure what she wanted to say or how to get Susan to answer her knock. She could see into the hall through the tall glass panels either side of the front door. A black-and-white tiled floor. A slim glass table beneath a huge silver-edged mirror. A lamp emitting amber light. A coatstand with no coats. And a package, just inside the door. Venetia knelt to read the name on the label. Susan O'Donnell. Venetia's anger swelled. To her right, just beyond the porch, a bicycle leaned against the wall. Would that make her come out? Venetia pushed the bike, knocking it flat. The crash jarred with the night-time silence. Loud enough for Susan to hear. Not loud enough for neighbours to notice. At least, she hoped. She glanced back towards the end of the driveway, where she'd left the car.

From inside the house came the sound of footsteps. Venetia slipped into the shadows and waited. The door opened and a head peered out. A dark-haired woman with an unfocused expression and a drink in her hand. Venetia rushed forward, pushing the door, shoving the woman backwards. The drink flew out of her hand, its contents spilling on the hall floor. The woman stumbled backwards, shock all over her face. Venetia stepped inside and closed the door.

77

Savannah
Last week

SAVANNAH STARED AT THE woman, her mind scrambling to understand. On some level, there was tiny relief. *It's a woman.* A woman in a black T-shirt and black jeans and heavy Dr Marten boots. No mask hiding her face. Whatever this person wanted, at least it was a woman. Women didn't hurt people, right? She took in the wild hair, the angry, red-rimmed eyes. Someone having a psychotic episode? A neighbour, maybe? Someone who'd been drinking? She couldn't smell drink. It didn't seem like a drink thing. A burglary? Did women burgle?

Savannah opened her mouth to tell her to leave, to ask what was happening, but couldn't find the words. Her throat seemed to have closed over. The woman stepped forward, towering over her. Savannah shrank against the wall.

'I . . . I have jewellery. It's upstairs. Take it all. I don't have cash. But take the laptop, my phone, whatever you want.' She swallowed, her voice gone again.

The woman stepped closer.

'I don't need your jewellery, Susan,' the woman hissed. 'I need you to take responsibility for what you've done.'

Susan?

'I'm not Su—' A hand shot out and grabbed the front of her T-shirt, twisting the fabric, pulling her close. Hot breath on her skin. The stale smell of cigarettes and coffee. And eyes flashing with white-hot rage.

78

Susan
Thursday

WHEN THE GARDAÍ LEAVE, I sit with my head in my hands. I should have told them I was out on Wednesday. And what about this car they mentioned? A dark blue Ford Mondeo, one that looks like Jon's – well, ours, but I know it wasn't me – outside Savannah's house the morning she was murdered. And according to Jon's assistant, Jon wasn't in his office at the time. It might mean nothing. There are lots of blue Ford Mondeos around. But realistically, it can't be a coincidence, can it? And yet, I didn't say any of this to the guards just now. I don't know why. Some kind of self-preservation, making me slow down and think before blurting it out? Protecting Jon to protect Bella, at least until I think things through? Or the fear that if I go up against Jon, he might have Bella taken off me . . .

And then there's Greta. Greta lied about seeing Jon on Monday night. And she couldn't babysit last Wednesday but didn't say why. And now I know she met with Jon in his office that morning. I can't think of a single reason Greta would do that. I mean, OK, if it wasn't for the cheating, I'd think *maybe* Jon was organizing a surprise party and getting help from my sisters. Leesa and I surprised Greta with a trip to Paris for her fortieth, and then Greta and I surprised Leesa with a weekend in Monart after all the stuff she went through with Maeve. I keep telling them it's my turn for a surprise. I *do* have a birthday next month, but . . . it's not a milestone one, and my husband cares so little about me he's been having an affair while I'm at home with our newborn baby. So no. I don't know why Greta was in Jon's office and there's a horrible, sick feeling in my gut telling me this is all linked to Savannah Holmes.

A noise from the garden catches my attention and, for a moment, I freeze. The doors are locked, the side gate's pad-locked now too: nobody can come in. But still. The idea that there's someone out there, someone trying to get at me or trying to hurt Bella, or maybe . . . maybe deliberately making me look like an unfit mother? I pull Bella close and stand, craning my neck to look out the window. A squirrel darts across the lawn and up an apple tree. That's all it was. But it's enough. I can't live like this. I'm not staying here.

And although she's the obvious choice, I don't want to go to Greta's. I hate admitting it to myself, but I don't fully trust her. Leesa's house is not ideal – it's smaller than ours, and two extra people is a lot – but I don't know what else I can do. I pick up the phone.

I give Leesa an abbreviated version. Someone tried to get into the house while I was upstairs. This is true. I don't tell her the person actually did get in and took Bella and put her out-side in the front garden, because the last thing I need is my own sister thinking I've lost it and my child isn't safe with me. She says we're welcome for as long as we want to stay and, within an hour, I'm unpacking in her spare bedroom as she sets up the Moses basket beside the bed.

'Sorry, it'll be a bit cramped for the three of you,' Leesa says, eyeing up the double bed. 'I could see if Aoife would swap with you guys, but then you'd have to live with her dark purple walls . . .'

Oh. Shit. Now I have to tell her Jon isn't coming.

'It's just Bella and me for now. Jon is OK staying in our house; he's only there at night after work, so . . .' I trail into a shrug that's supposed to explain everything.

Leesa frowns. 'Oh. Won't he miss Bella? And if you're worried about whoever tried to get in coming back, he'd be as well off here. Do you think it's the same person who broke the window?'

'Yes.' That part is true. It has to be the same person.

'Which is also the person who sent the death threat, I guess? Can I read it again?'

She points at my phone, but I know it off by heart.

'"You got away lightly last night. You deserve to die for that message and what it's done."'

'Nice. So, it's either Warren losing face, Nika losing friends, Cody losing his work placement, or Celeste . . . losing her mind.' Leesa smiles, delighted with her play on words. 'OK, on a serious note, if Jon wants to stay here, we'll make room. He's your husband, he's family.'

My husband who doesn't know I've moved out. God, I'd better tell him.

'I'll think about it, and thanks a mill for everything, but you probably need to log on to work.'

She glances at her watch and hurries from the room as I hit Jon's number on my phone.

'Hey.'

There's that wariness. I feel sick.

'Hi. I wanted to let you know that I'm staying in Leesa's for a bit. Something happened this morning at the house and—' I stop. I'm about to tell him the whole thing – but what if we separate? What if he wants custody? Imagine his case. My wife let our daughter get sunburnt. My wife put her out in the garden and forgot. It doesn't sound great. And right now, apart from everything else, I don't trust him.

'What happened?'

'I think someone tried to break in. Everything's fine, Bella's fine, but I don't feel safe.'

'OK. I'll pack some things and come over after work.'

'There isn't room here for three of us, really. And I think once Bella's safely out of our house, that's the main thing. I think you'll be fine.' Much as I hate him right now, much as I don't trust him, the conversation makes me sad.

'Oh.'

Silence then, and there's so much in that silence. An entire marriage. Eventually, I whisper 'bye' and disconnect.

Now, there's one more call I have to make.

79

Maeve
Thursday

MAEVE IS STILL IN bed when her mum sticks her head around
the door to tell her that Susan and Bella have moved in. Just
like that.

Maeve likes Susan and the baby, but this is a lot on top of
everything that's going on. And – the realization dawns now –
it's going to pull her mother away from her. Her mother, who's
been trying to talk to her for days now, is going to be distracted
by Susan. And even though Maeve hasn't responded to any of
her mother's attempts to talk, she still wants her to try. One
of these days, she's going to let her sit on the bed and she's
going to collapse in her arms and feel the hug and speak the
words, but now it's too late because Susan is here. She knows
she's not being rational, but that doesn't change a thing. Now
her mother has left the room again, rebuffed by an only half-
intentioned scowl, and Maeve is lying on her back, staring at
the ceiling, wondering if she'll ever get out of bed again.

Susan's voice wafts in from the spare room next door. She's
on the phone to Jon, telling him she's going to be staying here.
Which is weird, because Maeve is almost certain she just heard
Susan tell Leesa that she and Jon had agreed the plan together.

Maeve sits up in bed. What is going on with Susan and Jon?

Susan's making another call now. Maeve doesn't mean to eavesdrop, but her mother has left the door ajar and Susan's speaking as though she doesn't know there's anyone else upstairs. She probably doesn't.

'Hi, my daughter did a trial run at your hockey camp last Wednesday and mentioned a coach who was very good, someone who also does one-on-one coaching. She thinks the name was Greta, but she wanted to check for sure? Last Wednesday morning?'

Maeve is alert now. *What is Susan up to?* Is she trying to help clear Greta's name for the thing with Nika? The tinny sound of someone else's voice on the other end of the line is just about audible, but the words are not. Maeve waits.

'Oh, you're sure Greta wasn't there last Wednesday morning?' Another wait.

'Ah, OK. My daughter probably mixed up the names. I'll check again. Thanks, bye now.'

Maeve is perplexed. Why the sudden interest in what Greta was doing last Wednesday morning? She casts her mind back. The morning after Susan sent her message. The morning everything came tumbling down.

Suddenly, more than anything, Maeve needs her mother. She's the only one who still makes sense, who hasn't changed. She's just as annoying and safe and stable and warm and frustrating and cloying and comforting as she's always been. Maeve swings her legs out of bed, pulls on a hoodie and heads downstairs.

Leesa is in her office, at her desk, headset on. Maeve slips in behind her and sits on her mother's reading chair. Forest green with a teal cushion, it's Maeve's favourite spot in the house, at least if she *must* leave her bedroom. Her mother turns, eyebrows raised in an 'All OK?' question.

Maeve nods, and her mother indicates with a rotating finger that her call is about to wrap up. Maeve stares out the window as she waits, at the poplars swaying against the backdrop of a cloudless sky. She can't imagine going out there. Seeing people. People staring, talking, pointing. The girl with a crush on Ariana Webb. She can never go back to that school. She can never see those people. She can never leave the house again.

Her mother has finished her call and swivels in her huge office chair.

'Hey!' Leesa says. Maeve can tell she wants to add 'good to see you out of your room' but holds herself back.

'Hi.' Silence.

'Can I get you something to eat?'

'No, thanks. Mum, is everything OK with Susan and Jon and Greta?'

Her mother tilts her head, confused, and Maeve can see immediately that it's real. She's not covering anything up.

'You mean because Susan is staying with us? She's worried someone tried to break in.' Leesa grimaces. 'And what do you mean about Greta – the whole thing with Nika?'

'Yeah. But also because Susan just called the hockey camp about a made-up daughter who was supposedly there last Wednesday, basically so she could find out if Greta was there, I think.'

Leesa frowns. 'OK, that's odd – could you have misheard?'

'Nope.'

'Maybe she's trying to help fix this thing with Nika . . .'

'How would her fake daughter help?'

'I have no idea. But I do need to get on another call. It's good to see you looking brighter. You won't forget babysitting tonight, will you?'

'What?'

'For Moira Fitzpatrick. I won't be able to collect you after –
I'll be at the Oakpark party too, but you'll be OK to walk home,
won't you?'

'Oh god, Mum, I can't babysit. I'm not leaving the house.'

'You can't let Moira down, love. That's not fair. She's part of
the organizing committee. I saw on her Instagram earlier she's
got fireworks and wine and about five thousand burger buns
ready to go.'

'Can't Aoife do it?'

A wry look. 'Remember what happened when the Fitzpatricks had a fourteen-year-old babysit? I don't think they're
ready for a thirteen-year-old.'

'Can't you tell her I'm sick?'

Leesa slides off the chair and hunkers down by Maeve.

'Love, I know it's hard. But in a way, something like this –
a night of babysitting, where there's nobody from school,
nobody your age – is a perfect way to dip your toe back in the
world. You're going to have to go out there eventually . . .'

'Urgh. Fine. I hate this.'

'I know. If you want to talk about the—'

'Don't. Please.'

'OK. But if you change your mind, I'm here.' Leesa looks at
her screen behind her. 'Right, gotta do this call, and it's video,
so . . .' She nods at the door.

Maeve heaves herself off the chair and slopes out. Aoife is
standing in the hall, supposedly gazing at some family photos
that have been there for a decade.

'God, you're so nosy.'

Aoife turns to look at her. 'Yeah, well, sometimes it pays
off.' She tosses her hair and gives Maeve a knowing look, then
swishes back to the kitchen.

80

Venetia

Last week

VENETIA HAD NEVER FELT rage like it. Or power. This woman –
this Susan, cowering in front of her. Not so glib now. Not so
brave. Blood roared in her ears as she thought about slamming
Susan's head against the wall, how it would feel, what it would
do, and it took her a second to realize she was being jerked
back. Pulled away, pulled backwards, stumbling, towards the
front door. Felipe. *How is he here?* She struggled against him,
but he was stronger than expected. Quiet, gentle Felipe, now
dragging her out of Susan O'Donnell's house.

She lashed out an arm to grab the doorjamb and held firm.

'I'm coming,' she hissed back to Felipe.

She turned to face Susan, who was slumped against the wall,
a look of horror on her face. It gave Venetia only the smallest amount of satisfaction before Aimee's body filled her mind
again.

'I know where you live, Susan. And if you call the police, I'll
slit your throat. You know I mean it, don't you?'

A terrified nod. No words.

Venetia jabbed a finger towards her. 'I know you, but you
don't know me. If you tell the guards, they have nothing to go

on. While they're trying to work out who I am, where I am – I'll be back here, this time with a very sharp blade. Got it?'

Another nod.

Felipe yanked her back and pulled the front door shut. He began to steer her down the drive but stopped after a few steps, turned and peered in the window beside the front door. Then he was back, propelling her to the car, into the passenger seat before getting into the driver's seat himself. Wordlessly, she handed him the keys. The engine stuttered when he started the ignition and he tried again, cursing under his breath. This time it took, and he pulled quickly on to the road. Streetlights illuminated beads of sweat on his forehead and his breathing was ragged. He must have run here. She shouldn't have told him the address. And what was he doing looking in the window afterwards?

'Were you checking if she was OK? My sister's lying dead in her house, and that's what you're worried about?'

His knuckles whitened on the steering wheel. 'It's you I'm worried about. Venetia, my god, what were you thinking? You will go to prison if you're caught threatening people like this.'

'I don't care.'

'You will care if you are arrested. Whatever self-defence kind of thing we can say about Rory's death, it gets complicated if you are threatening this woman. She is going to tell the police. You know that, right?'

'No, she's not. You heard what I said. She's fucking terrified. And she doesn't know who I am.'

'It won't take her long to figure it out. How many other people did she mention in a message tonight who worked as PR for Bar Four?'

'I didn't say anything about the message or Aimee or any of

273

it. She has no idea who I am. I'm the monster who came to get her. The monster who'll come back if she tells a soul.'

'Venetia, you cannot go back there. You will be caught.'

'I don't care if I get caught. Aimee's gone. I have nothing left.'

She glanced over just in time to see the flash of sadness.

And then she turned away.

81

Savannah
Last week

THE RINGING IN SAVANNAH'S ears continued long after the door shut. Long after the man looked back in the window. Long after the couple had driven away. *What the hell was that all about?* She slid down the wall to sit on the hall floor, head in hands. Where was her phone? She had to call the guards. Whatever that woman had said, Savannah couldn't let this go. What if they came back? But that was precisely the problem . . . *what if they came back?* The woman had put it so succinctly. She knew where Savannah lived. And Savannah had no idea who she was at all. On shaky legs, she stood and double-locked the front door, then pulled down the blind with a chain that was dusty from lack of use. This was a nice neighbourhood. Smart, clean, landscaped space. Newly built luxury homes. Privacy and driveways and hedges. No need for blinds. No need until now. And this woman, this crazed woman, knew where she lived.

But – she realized – she didn't actually know who Savannah was.

She had called her 'Susan'.

Why had she called her Susan? Savannah's eyes went to the package by the door. A parcel for Susan O'Donnell. Had the woman seen the label and assumed that was Savannah's name? But why? A thought struck then. They were living at the same address, she and Susan. Was it possible the woman thought Savannah was Susan? Was she at the right address but the wrong house?

Savannah needed a drink. Her rum had spilled on the hall floor when the woman barged in, but the glass – a heavy Norlan Rauk tumbler – was intact. She picked it up now, poured a double, sat back on the bottom step of the stairs and typed 'Susan O'Donnell' into Google. She'd never thought to do it before. To her, Susan was just someone who ordered (quite boring) baby clothes and (even more boring) women's clothes. Brands Savannah wouldn't be caught dead in. Not that she'd been opening the packages, apart from a few hasty mistakes over the years and – she glanced at the taped-up package by the door – this morning's retinol.

But the branding on the outside of the parcels told of a woman stuck in a Zara and H&M rut while her baby lived in Next and Gap. Savannah didn't want kids – that was one thing she loved about being with Jon; he didn't want kids either – but if she ever did change her mind, she'd dress them a lot better than Susan O'Donnell did.

Google returned the usual results – multiple Facebook and Instagram profiles of various Susan O'Donnells with no way to know which was the right one. She scrolled down past LinkedIn, a set of images of many more women all called Susan O'Donnell, a few MessageBoards.ie links, and on to a variety of workplaces and universities. Since she had no idea what Susan looked like or where she worked, none of this was of any use. Next up, a corporate awards ceremony and a charity auction. Then she spotted something familiar on screen. Or rather, some*one*. And it stopped her cold.

82

Savannah

Last week

JON. *HER* JON. IN a social diary photograph from *Image* magazine. A gala dinner for a children's charity. Her Jon, in a tux,
presenting a cheque to another man in a tux. The caption identified him incorrectly as Jon 'Mullane' instead of Jon McIlroy,
but it was definitely him. Why had Jon's photo come up in a
search for Susan O'Donnell? A creeping unease set in while her
eyes skimmed the text of the article. Jon Mullane, head of Corporate Trust at GS Bank . . . at the dinner accompanied by his
wife, Susan O'Donnell.

His *wife*.

Frantically, words swimming on the screen now, she scanned
further, searching for an image of Susan. There was none. But
the words were there in black and white. And the words said
enough. His *wife*.

That prick. She dialled his number and let it ring until it rang
out, then tried again. She tried a third time, checking her watch.
After midnight already. He was possibly asleep, though he didn't
usually sleep this early. They often texted until much later than
this. Was he avoiding her calls? No, because he couldn't know
she'd just found out he was married. Maybe he was with his

wife. She should have guessed he was married. When they always went to hotels or her house, she should have guessed. He said he lived in Maynooth in Co Kildare and commuted to Dublin. Only, she realized now, he didn't live in Maynooth at all. She picked up the package. He lived in 26 Oakpark, with Susan O'Donnell. The other Oakpark. Which was no more than a ten-minute drive away. She picked up her car keys, pulled on her Uggs and slammed the door behind her.

Eight minutes later, she pulled up outside the other 26 Oakpark. His so-called brother's house, she realized now. She didn't remember much about the outside of the house that night, but of course this was it. Her stomach hurt as she took it in. So suburban. So neat. A couple home. And, oh god, the realization hit her – those packages of baby clothes – a family home. Jon and Susan had a baby. All those lies. *God.* She texted him now.

I know about your wife. I'm outside your house. Unless you want me to come in and announce myself, I suggest you come out to see me.

Two blue ticks. He'd read it. She waited, drumming her fingers on the steering wheel, staring out her car window at Jon's well-kept lawn.

A reply pinged through:

I can't come out. I'll explain tomorrow. Go home and get some sleep.

Furious now, she hammered out another text.

I swear to god, come out now or I'm coming in, you PRICK.

A new reply:

Calm down. I said I'd talk to you tomorrow.

Calm down? Did he actually just say that? Savannah yanked open the car door and ran into the driveway, fury roiling at the sight of the house in front of her. All the lights were off: he must be in bed. *They* must be in bed. She couldn't remember which was the main bedroom but guessed it might be the big picture window on the left, upstairs. She glanced around and spotted loose bricks on a section of the garden wall. She picked one up, flung it hard and high. The sound of cracking glass surprised her. She hadn't really expected to hit the window, let alone break it. But that's exactly what she'd done. *That'll show him.* On reflection though, as lights went on in Jon's house and in a house two doors up, she decided against staying around to see the aftermath. She jumped back in the car and sped out to the main road. She'd deal with Jon tomorrow.

At home, back inside the questionable safety of her house, she double-locked the front door again and checked every other opening in the house, then poured herself a treble Captain Morgan's rum. Had all of that just happened? Jon had given her a fake name. Jon was married. And not to just anyone, to Susan O'Donnell, the woman whose packages had been arriving here on and off for the last three years. So was that the connection? Had Jon called by to leave one of the misdelivered parcels and stayed to ask her out? He'd never handed her a package, she was certain of that. But the first time they met was outside her house . . . He was getting into his car at her gate as she arrived home from the gym. He'd stopped, midway into the driver's seat, and smiled at her. Was it someone she knew, she'd wondered, someone from work whose face she'd misplaced? She slowed and asked if he was OK. He said he was good, just doing Saturday-morning errands. He pointed at her gym bag with the XSGym logo and asked about it, said he'd been thinking of joining. At first it sounded like a line, but as he kept talking, he seemed genuinely interested in the gym. He'd done a couple of trial visits there and was thinking about signing up but worried about how busy it might get on weekday mornings. They ended up in a long conversation about gym equipment that evolved into a longer conversation about restaurants they both liked and a film they both hated. They wondered if a just-released film from the same director would be any better. And then, as he left, he asked for her number. Suggested they try the new film together; it was showing in the Lighthouse cinema. She glanced at his ring finger. Nothing there. And he was certainly attractive. Not that she had any shortage of attractive men asking her out. But it was more than that. There was, if it didn't sound too romance-novel-ish, a spark.

So was it all a lie, she wondered now, sipping her rum, back on the bottom step of the stairs. Or at least, a lie by omission? Was his 'errand' a parcel drop to her house? She tried to think back, but she couldn't be sure. Couriers delivered stuff every day, mostly leaving it outside her door. There was no way to remember if there had been one there the day Jon came into her life.

It made sense though. And it certainly couldn't be coincidence that he was married to Susan O'Donnell.

But none of it explained the woman who'd burst into her house earlier calling her Susan. Unless . . . could that have been someone else Jon was seeing? A third woman? Who thought she was Jon's wife and wanted to hurt her? That was hardly fair, Savannah thought. She had no care or concern for Susan O'Donnell in all this, but she didn't feel inclined to beat her up, for goodness' sake. Who does that?

Either way, Jon was going to have a lot of explaining to do tomorrow. She finished her rum, left the glass on the floor and went to bed.

83

Celeste
Thursday

CELESTE PASSES HER ANGRY, sulking son on the stairs. He's still not talking to her since the vape argument yesterday evening.

His parting words ring in her ears as she crosses the landing to Nika's room.

More like Nika? Ha. You'll see. And when it's over, don't say I didn't warn you.

What does that even mean? Good lord. She can't wait till the teenage years are done.

She knocks on Nika's open door and steps in. Nika's lying on her bed, scrolling. On her laptop, *Gossip Girl* plays, subtitles on, sound down. There are dresses strewn across the chair at her desk and some have slipped to the floor. The normal disarray of a teenage girl.

Nika sits up straight, cross-legged now on her bed.

'Oh, hi, Mum. Did you finish work early?'

'No, I'm not done, I have a call with the US at seven, but I'll do it from home. Are you feeling better after all that drama with Greta O'Donnell yesterday?'

'A little,' Nika says, summoning a small smile. 'I'll be fine, Mum, don't worry.'

'Well, how about some shopping to help cheer you up?'

The smile widens, becomes more real. 'I'd love that! I was thinking, could we go to Kildare Village? Jessica went with her mum last week and they got gorgeous stuff and had lunch and it sounded—'

'I was thinking more about online shopping. It's easier than going in person, isn't it? I can give you my credit card and you put yourself together a nice haul from Brandy Melville?'

'Oh. Sure. That would be great.'

Is Celeste imagining it, or is there something flat in Nika's response? She usually loves an opportunity to shop. Maybe this thing with Greta hit her harder than Celeste realized.

'How about you order that Chanel bronzer you were hinting about the other day and pop a few more things in a Cult Beauty basket for yourself?'

'Great. Thanks. Actually' – Nika sits up straighter – 'could I take your car tonight?'

'Ah, I'll need it after my work call. I have pilates at eight.'

'You could use Dad's car.'

'He's at the golf club.'

A petulant pout. Celeste had always thought it was cute. Maybe less so now that Nika is almost eighteen.

'Aw, Mum, come on. I told Jess I'd call over, and there's no way to get there without a car.'

Celeste thinks back to her own teenage years – she got buses and walked everywhere. Different times, she supposes.

'All right, I'll skip pilates – my call will probably go on past eight anyway. But drive carefully.'

'Always. And thanks for the offer of the bronzer. Will I get something for you too?'

'Do, surprise me.' Celeste smiles at her daughter and leaves the room.

If only Cody was as easy as Nika.

84

Jon
Thursday

JON HAD SKIPPED ALL his meetings on Thursday afternoon and now he's leaving work at four, telling his PA he has a headache. It's not a lie; he really does have the mother of all headaches. His wife has moved out – not officially, not formally, but that's what this is, right? – and taken his baby with her. He believes Susan when she says she's staying in Leesa's to keep Bella safe, but he also knows it's to escape him and the unbearable distance that's developed between them. Jon stops himself there, sufficiently self-aware to admit that using the passive tense is not valid or fair. The distance did not develop of its own accord. He caused it by having an affair. And maybe there's more to it. Does Susan think he did something to Savannah? Where was *she* last Wednesday morning, and how does she have Savannah's bracelet? He's going around in circles, and his brain is about to explode.

The house is eerie in its emptiness. It hits him now that he's rarely been here alone since Bella was born. He comes home to find both of them here every evening, and sometimes he wishes he could arrive to solitude, throw off his suit jacket, collapse on the couch and crack open a beer. He knows that's not fair, and that's why he'd never say it out loud – he's not an imbecile – he knows that Susan's the one at home all day with the baby. He knows it's his turn after work and he absolutely accepts that. But it doesn't stop him wishing every now and then that he could come back to quiet emptiness.

And now that he's home alone, throwing off his suit jacket, collapsing on the couch, it's not so appealing. In fact, it's not what he wants at all.

Within three minutes of arriving, he's leaving again. Down his own driveway and into Greta's. Her car is there, gleaming under late-afternoon sun. On the porch, three planters of blue flowers wilt in the heat. A full watering can sits by their side and Jon picks it up now to give the soil some much-needed water. That's not like Greta. She's usually religious about her plants. Before he can hit the bell, the door opens. Greta's face furrows into a frown.

'What do you want, Jon?'

'I thought we should chat.'

She pulls the door wide to let him into the hall.

'I don't have long.'

Jon suspects she's not going anywhere, but Greta is good at that – marking her boundaries without apology.

'Susan's moved out.'

'*What?* Where?' She looks around her hall, as though Susan might appear.

'To Leesa's.'

A hurt expression crosses her face, but she covers it quickly. 'Why?'

He tells her about the noises Susan heard, and Greta clicks her tongue dismissively.

'Though, obviously,' Jon continues, 'as I told you, I think she knows about the affair, so maybe . . .'

'Maybe indeed. OK, I'll call her.' She starts to reach for the door handle to see him out. 'I need to get on with things, Jon.'

'I'm worried. I'm afraid she went to Savannah's, the bracelet . . .'

'OK, and what do you want me to do? Why are you telling me this?'

'Because . . .' Because a problem shared is a problem halved? *Because she was there too.*

'Jesus, Jon, pull yourself together and stop being such a baby. I take that back – that's an insult to babies. You made your bed, now lie in it.'

'But you were there—'

'Stop! I'm stressed to the hilt – I'm about to lose my business. You need to handle this yourself.'

He folds his arms, straightens his shoulders. 'Greta, you know as well as I do, we're in this together.'

'And you know as well as I do, this is all down to you. Now get out of my house before I tell Susan what really happened last Wednesday morning.'

Fuming, Jon marches back down Greta's driveway but stops short when a garda car pulls up outside his own house. A sick feeling takes hold. *Calm down.* They probably want to speak to Susan again. And knowing that Savannah's keys are lying at the bottom of a public litter bin gives him some solace. He swallows and pastes on a smile.

As he approaches his gateway he spots Juliette Sullivan walking down her driveway, a box of paper cups in her arms. She slows her step and cranes her neck. *Shit. This is the last thing he needs.*

A woman in uniform gets out of the garda car and steps towards him.

'Mr Mullane?'

'Yes. Susan's not here, unfortunately. She's at her—'

'It's you we'd like to speak to.' She nods towards his car. 'Is that your vehicle?'

'Yes . . .'

'Right. Could you come down to the station to answer a few questions?'

'Uh . . . sure.' Jon takes his car keys from his pocket.

'We'll bring you in our car. We may need to take yours in for forensic examination.'

Jon swallows, discreetly sliding his keys back into his pocket. The garda smiles.

'Don't worry, we use a tow-truck.'

His throat bone dry now, all he can do is nod.

85

Susan

Thursday

THURSDAY AFTERNOON AND EARLY evening go by in a haze. Sitting at Leesa's dinner table, smiling and passing dishes, is excruciating, but just about doable when Leesa doesn't know the whole truth. Imagine the questions. Jon was having an affair? With the dead girl? He might have been there that morning? Is he a murderer?

I mean, is he?

'Come on, smile!' Leesa's voice pulls me out of my thoughts. She's standing, phone aloft, taking a photo of all of us around the table. Reverse camera so she can be in it too. This is very Leesa: no family gathering slips by without photos and no good outfit goes undocumented – she's in a gorgeous Whistles dress, ready for the Oakpark summer party.

Maeve rolls her eyes. 'Do *not* put that on Instagram.'

'I'll crop you out.'

'You're not really putting that up, are you?' I ask.

'Oh, you know Mum, she puts everything on Insta.' Aoife clutches her hands to her heart and mimics her mother. 'So blessed!'

Leesa swipes at her daughter. 'Well, we *are* blessed. And we're all here for one another.' A meaningful glance at me. 'And it's good to show that to everyone out there too.'

This makes me well up. It doesn't seem quite the time for social media, but her heart is in the right place.

She's typing on her phone now. 'Don't worry, Bella's face isn't in shot, and Maeve, I've cropped you out.' She looks at her watch. 'Don't forget you're babysitting in an hour. You're OK to walk over to the Fitzpatricks?'

A heavy sigh from Maeve makes it clear just how much she's looking forward to that.

As soon as we're done cleaning up, I feign a headache and go to the guest room. My phone sits silently on the night-stand, daring me to try calling Jon. To say what? *You absolute fucker, how could you cheat on me? And where were you last Wednesday morning?*

And I keep wondering, should I be phoning the guards to tell them Jon had our car that morning? But I can't bring myself to do that any more than I can imagine confronting Jon. So, for now, I do nothing but worry.

It's only when I start to get Bella ready for bed that I realize I've forgotten to bring her sleep suit and her soother. I've also forgotten to bring spare socks, my book, and my vitamin C serum, all of which I can do without, but I don't want to put Bella to bed in the milk-stained dress she's been wearing all day and Leesa's house is a little chilly for sleeping in a vest. Much more crucial is the soother – there's no way she'll sleep without it. But I'm not brave enough to go home to pick up what I need – I don't want to see Jon. Bella is lying on the guest-room bed, kicking her legs and gurgling.

'Oh, you look so happy now, but just wait until we try to get you to sleep without your dodie . . .' I stoop to kiss her, resigned to what's ahead – I'm going to have to walk up to Dunnes to buy replacements.

I pop Bella on to my shoulder and go downstairs. The house is quiet, apart from the low hum of the TV. Leesa has gone to the Oakpark summer party, and Maeve has left for babysitting. My options are either bring Bella with me to the shops or ask Aoife to mind her. I peep in the living-room door, eyeing up Aoife as she lies on the couch looking at her phone. I love her. She's great. She's quirky and funny and interesting. But in terms of leaving my only child with her, I'm not convinced. Quietly, I close the door.

As I'm easing Bella into her pram, my phone dings with a text from Juliette Sullivan.

Saw Jon being picked up by the police – very stressful for you all, I'm sure. I'm busy with the Oakpark summer party right now, but if I can help in any way, let me know. I could call in to keep you company in the morning?

Oh god. What does this mean? Was he at Savannah's on Wednesday? Or is it simply procedure; question him and rule him out? God, I hope so. The entire situation is hideous . . . and now Juliette Sullivan is dying to get in on the action.

It does, however, mean that Jon is out of the house and I can go there to pick up the sleepsuit and soother instead of walking all the way up to Dunnes Stores, which, to my everlasting regret, is what I decide to do.

86

Susan
Thursday

IT'S WARM AND BRIGHT outside, the kind of July evening you'd have on tap if you could, but none of it lifts my spirits as I push the pram down Leesa's driveway. I stop at the gate, thinking. My gut is telling me I'd feel better with company on my return trip to our house. But with Leesa at the Oakpark party, I'm not sure who else to ask. My friends are great, but none of them live so near that I can text at nine on a Thursday night to ask them to keep me company going to my own house . . . then Felipe pops into my head. Sweet, funny Felipe, who is easier to talk to than anyone else right now. Could I ask him? Would it be weird? I'm past caring about weird. I scroll to his number and hit call, but it rings out. I text instead of leaving a voicemail:

Staying with my sister Leesa for a bit but have to head home to pick up some things. If you're around, company would be great!

I start walking, pushing the pram along the footpath. On the green, a group of kids kick a ball, their shrieks reminding me of my own childhood summers. A dog barks somewhere ahead and a car engine revs somewhere behind. I check my phone. No blue ticks, no reply from Felipe. That leaves Greta. And I don't know how I feel about her right now, which is giving me a pain in my heart. She definitely lied to me on Monday night when she said Jon wasn't in her house. And for as long as I've known her – my whole life – she's never lied to me. I mean, sure, she's told me I look good when I don't look good, and she's told me I wasn't that drunk when I really was that drunk. But an outright lie? Then again, it's Greta. There must be a good reason. Also, I'm out of options. So I message to ask if she'll come with me to pick up stuff from the house, and she says to call in to her when I get to Oakpark.

As I walk towards her house, the sound of the summer party wafts through the evening air. Chatter and peals of laughter and Pharrell Williams's 'Happy' on the speakers. The Oakpark partygoers are down on the green, too far away to see me, but I turn my face away anyway. It'll be a long time before I can hold my head up at any social gathering in our neighbourhood.

When Greta answers her door, she looks the same as she always does – dressed in leggings and an oversized hoodie, hair in a pony-tail and a no-nonsense expression on her face. She's just made a cup of decaf tea and she makes one for me too. For the first time in forever, I feel lost for words. I don't want to tell her I might have left Jon or that he's been taken in for questioning. My 'someone put Bella out in the garden' story is sounding increasingly batshit. And I can't bring myself to ask her why she lied about Jon on Monday night. So we talk about my upcoming birthday and she asks me if I'm free on the twentieth because she's booked a sister-dinner in our favourite restaurant in Dún Laoghaire. She tells me I should dress up, and a funny look crosses her face, like she's trying not to smile.

And suddenly a piece of the jigsaw slips into place. I dismissed it so quickly earlier, but oh my god, it *is* a surprise party. I let out a silent breath. This doesn't change the fact that Jon has been sleeping with Savannah Holmes, but it does explain why

Greta and he have been conspiring. My sister is not lying to me for any terrifying reasons, she's just being her usual slightly prickly but secretly lovely self.

Buoyed by this realization, I feel lighter. Not because of a surprise birthday celebration (certainly not one organized by my husband) but because my sister, one of the three most important people in my world, is still the person I thought she was.

I'm still feeling lighter when we walk up my driveway. Jon's car isn't here – maybe he drove himself to the station, which is at odds with Juliette's dramatic 'picked up by police' text. This makes me feel better again – it can't be that serious if he drove himself. We let ourselves in the front door. There's no way to know how long Jon will be in the garda station; I guess he could arrive back any minute. I leave Greta holding Bella in the kitchen and dash up to our bedroom to grab what I need. But before I do anything else, I check my night-stand drawer for the bracelet. Did Savannah want to be caught, I wonder now? Or did she simply lose the bracelet when she was here? And how did she die? And does her death have anything to do with Jon or with me? This brings me back to Greta. Would she really go into Jon's office to talk about a surprise party, something they could easily discuss over text? Or was it something more urgent, something she didn't want to discuss by phone? My earlier elation feels false and flat now. Maybe I need to bite the bullet and ask Greta outright. As the first fireworks go off outside, I pocket the bracelet and go downstairs.

And what I find stops me cold.

87

Savannah
Last week

SAVANNAH ROLLED OVER IN her bed, groaning at the slant of morning sunlight that pierced her too-much-rum headache. At first she was confused. Something had happened. Then it filtered back. The woman who'd burst into her house last night. Her discovery of Jon's marriage. Jon's utter indifference to her calls and texts. She grabbed her phone and checked the time. Just before eight. She'd be late for work. She wasn't going to work, she decided. She had more important things to do. She texted Jon. He'd call by on his way to the office, he replied, but couldn't stay long.

He arrived fifteen minutes later. Dishevelled, bleary-eyed, contrite. She slapped him. Right there on the doorstep. Stunned, he stepped back, his hand to his cheek.

'You'd better come in,' she muttered, surprised at herself for the slap. 'I don't want the neighbours seeing this.' The neighbours wouldn't see anything; the driveway was too long, the hedges too high. But she wanted an explanation. His attention. His apology. He stepped past her, eyeing her warily, and she closed the front door.

In the hall, she asked her questions. Under the stream of early-morning sun, she heard all about Susan O'Donnell, teacher of maths. Susan O'Donnell, wife of Jon. Susan O'Donnell, mother of one. That part stung more than she'd expected. Jon had always said he didn't want kids. Just like she didn't. And all of it was a lie. Of course he didn't want kids with *her*, he already had a kid. In his real life, with his very real wife. Her hand itched to slap him again, but she forced herself to stay calm, conscious too that she'd smashed his window last night, which wasn't a great move. Though, strangely, he didn't bring that up.

She gestured for him to follow her through to the kitchen and take a seat at the table, and she set about making coffee, autopiloting into the routine they'd had a dozen times before.

'What about the other woman?' she asked, sitting down opposite him as the coffee percolated in the cafetière.

'What other woman?'

'She came here last night, barged in. Thought I was your wife. I don't know her name. Tall. Brown hair, kind of a rocker look. Jesus, Jon, how many women are you seeing that you don't know which one this is?'

'I have absolutely no idea who you're talking about. What did the police say?'

'I didn't call them. Not yet, anyway. She said she'd come back if I did.'

'Christ . . . look, I don't think I should get caught up . . . I don't want to get dragged into anything.'

Don't want to get dragged into anything? Savannah had often heard the phrase 'she saw red', but now, for the first time in her life, it really did feel as though she was literally seeing a red mist in front of her eyes. It was blood pressure rising, no doubt, or blood in her ears, but suddenly she wanted to punch Jon in the face and then keep punching and punching.

'Jesus Christ, Jon. You don't want to get dragged into anything? Because of you and your wife, *I'm* the one who got dragged in. Are you actually serious?'

He stood and held up his hands in a dismissive gesture that made her blood boil even more.

She stood too and grabbed her car keys from the shelf behind her.

'Right. Let's see how your wife feels about all this.'

'What?'

'I'm going to 26 Oakpark – the *other* 26 Oakpark – to let Susan know what's been going on.'

He stared at her for a moment then stepped towards her and took the keys from her hand.

'I'm sorry, Savannah, but I can't let you do that.'

88

Maeve
Thursday

MAEVE HAD NEVER BEEN less enthusiastic about anything
than she had been earlier this evening walking over to Moira
Fitzpatrick, trudging one foot in front of the other, chin dipped,
shoulders down. Her beanie hid half her face, or at least, she
hoped it did. Snap Maps told her there was nobody from
school in the vicinity – nobody she'd bump into between her
house and Moira Fitzpatrick's over in Oakpark. But still, someone might have had Maps switched off . . . If she had to walk
past anyone, she would die. Her mum would say she was being
dramatic, but her mum doesn't get it. For all her talk of remembering what it was like being a teen, she obviously didn't if
she was insisting Maeve go ahead with the babysitting. Maeve
zoned in on Nika on Snap Maps. She was down in Blackrock,
probably in Jessica's house. And Ariana was on Westminster
Road, in her own house. God, if she ever saw Ariana again.
Maeve's cheeks flamed at the thought.

Moira Fitzpatrick beamed when she opened the door, tucking a
blonde strand behind her ear. She was all dressed up in a 70s-print
jumpsuit, gold hoop earrings and metallic strappy heels.

'You look lovely,' Maeve said politely.

'Oh, thank you!' Moira rewarded her with an even wider smile.

'My mum has the same jumpsuit,' Maeve added.

Moira's smile thinned, and Maeve remembered that her mum was a little older and Moira might not see herself in the same fashion demographic.

'Anyway, how are *you*? Enjoying summer?' Moira asked, fixing her hair in the living-room mirror as Maeve followed her in.

'I'm good, it's great,' Maeve said in the way of teenagers everywhere since time began whose lives are falling apart.

Senan is a devil child, Maeve decided, just twenty minutes after the Fitzpatricks left. Good god, no wonder Cody Geary put him in the back garden, she thought, as he tore around the living room, jumping from couch to chair to couch, shrieking at the top of his voice. His sister stood beside Maeve, arms folded, foot tapping, saying, 'You know he's not allowed to do that?' over and over.

Maeve reached for him as he raced past and grabbed him around his middle. His shrieks got louder and he wriggled out of her arms, elbowing her in the eye in the process. It hurt far more than a five-year-old's elbow should and tears sprang to her eyes and, suddenly, all Maeve wanted to do was sit on the floor and cry.

It was early – half ten – when the Fitzpatricks got back, though Maeve had only just got the kids to sleep. The first six times she put Senan up, he came back down. In the end, she sat on the floor outside his room, to steer him into his bed each time he emerged. This seemed to tire him out eventually and, close to tears again, Maeve made her way downstairs and on to the couch just as the key turned in the front door.

'Hello!' Moira stage-whispered, peeping into the living room. 'We didn't stay long – work in the morning. All good?'

'Yes, all great,' Maeve said, through gritted teeth.

'Fab.' Moira slipped into the room, wobbling a little in her silver heels as she rummaged in her bag. 'I'm delighted.' She pulled out a rolled-up fifty-euro note and pressed it into Maeve's hand. 'Sometimes Senan can get a bit . . . excitable. He's a great kid, but not everyone is as capable as you.' She pursed her lips.

Maeve smiled, feeling a new solidarity with Cody Geary.

'Senan's a sweetheart,' she said, and picked up her bag.

And now, at the end of the Fitzpatricks' driveway, Maeve stops to put the cash inside her phone cover. It's actually two fifties. *Wow*. Moira's never paid her this much before. Maybe she's desperate to hold on to anyone who'll put up with the devil child. Maeve checks Snap Maps to see who's around. Ariana is still in her own house. And Jessica is in hers. Nika, however, is on the main road, near the turn for Oakpark. Shit. Though according to the app, she's in a car, so maybe she won't notice Maeve. She switches off her own location and starts her walk home.

89

Nika
Thursday

Nika swings the steering wheel hard to turn into Oakpark. She's going faster than she should, she knows that, but she doesn't care. She's fuming. More than yesterday, more than this morning. She's just spent three hours in Jessica's room, talking it over, and she's more riled up than ever.

'It was definitely Maeve who did it, by the way,' Jess had said, as if Nika needed any convincing. 'Ruby and Alison think they actually saw her near the clubhouse, skulking in her stupid purple beanie. She's so embarrassing.'

'Enough to tell the police?'

'They weren't *that* sure but, like, almost.'

Nika sighed. 'Fucking Maeve Khoury.'

'You can't let her get away with it,' Jessica said. 'She literally tried to kill you. And she's just getting on with her life.'

'I know.' Nika stood at Jessica's wardrobe, riffling through her dresses. She was there to pick out something to wear to a party next weekend, but the whole Maeve thing was making it hard to focus.

Jess frowned. 'Like, if it wasn't for the AWGoss account, we could get her arrested. I hope she knows that.'

'Annoyingly, she probably doesn't.' Nika sighed. 'God, I wish there was a way to tell the guards without getting in trouble.'

'Well, you can't, but there has to be a way to get your own back.' Jess was sitting on her bed, painting her nails. 'Honestly, you can't just let her off. Like, we can't change the law, but all you did was put a video online that was actually true? You didn't make anything up. Doesn't matter what any stupid law says, what she did was way worse.'

'I know. I'm fucking furious.' Nika held a short pink Oh Polly dress against her and checked the full-length mirror. 'I actually can't believe she's getting away with it. I just feel so . . . powerless?'

'You *are* powerless when it comes to the laws and stuff. But you can take *back* some power and sort it out yourself, you know?' Jess had warmed to her theme. 'Like in the TV show, *The Power*?'

Nika had seen the show too. It was about the patriarchy, not about teen girls fighting among themselves, but this wasn't the time to correct Jessica.

'I should. I will.' She put the pink dress back in the wardrobe, too distracted to think about clothes. 'So what will we do?'

'We'll think of something,' Jessica said darkly.

But now, two hours later, and on her way home, she still hasn't settled on a plan. Jessica had wanted to go online again. Fake some diary entries in Maeve's handwriting, stuff that would be way, way worse than her crush on Ariana (because, for god's sake, let's face it, Jessica said, everyone had a crush on Ariana at some point). Nika is nervous of the online route though. There's always a way to track people down, as far as she knows, through IP addresses and so on. She'd asked Jessica if she wanted to set up the anonymous account this time, but she didn't, it needed to come from Nika, to get 'closure' Jessica had said.

There has to be a way to get at her, Nika thinks now, as she speeds through Oakpark. But there has to be a way she can do it without getting caught. That's when she sees the figure ahead. Someone walking along the path by the green. She squints. Someone in a distinctive Ed Hardy hoodie, lit up now as she walks under a streetlight. It couldn't be, could it? It is. It's her. This is too much. Maeve Khoury. Out walking as though everything is fine. As though she hasn't just tried to kill Nika. Getting away with it, no consequences. Thinking she's untouchable because her aunts are teachers. Thinking she's great. Nika's not thinking she's great. Nika's not thinking at all when she jams her foot down on the accelerator. The car revs and speeds forward. She turns the wheel without a plan, fuelled by adrenaline and white-hot rage. The car mounts the footpath just as Maeve turns her face to see what's coming. And then Maeve is gone, knocked to the ground. Motionless. And Nika keeps driving.

90

Jon
Last week

'I'm sorry, Savannah, but I can't let you do that.'

Jon put Savannah's car keys in his pocket, his heart hammering in his chest. He absolutely couldn't allow her to turn up at his house and tell Susan what's been going on. His marriage would be over. Susan would take Bella. How had he got himself into this? Before he could figure out next steps, Savannah lunged forward, reaching for the keys from his pocket. He grabbed her wrist to stop her and it took a moment to register what she was saying.

'Jon, stop! You're hurting me!'

He unwrapped his fingers from her wrist and, with a jolt, took in the angry red imprints he'd left on her skin. The rose-gold bracelet slid down her forearm, the inscription mocking him.

'Shit. Sorry. Savannah, I didn't mean to hurt you . . .'

'Then give me my fucking keys,' she hissed.

He held up his hands and stepped backwards. 'Look, can we talk first?' He swallowed.

'No. Susan deserves to know what kind of prick she's married to.'

How could he get out of this? *Think, Jon, think.*

'We're pretty much separated.'

'Oh sure. How convenient.' Savannah rolls her eyes.

'Honestly, we sleep in separate rooms most of the time, we both see other people. We're just keeping up appearances.'

'Jon, I didn't come down in the last shower. This is an attempt to save your own skin. My god, I thought we were getting serious.' She glanced over at her wedding photo. 'I'd even started to think you were the *one*. I can't believe you've done this to me.'

'Savannah . . .' He stepped towards her again.

'No! You've hurt me. You've *humiliated* me. And I'm not going down lightly. Fuck you.' She reached again for the keys in his pocket and he jumped back.

'What are you going to do, Jon, stay here for ever holding my keys? I'll get a cab, you fuckwit. I'll walk. Whatever.' She turned to move towards the doorway to the hall and Jon reached for her arm. She shook him off. 'And I'm calling the police, by the way. You can't just take my keys, you'll be done for attempted car theft.'

'Savannah—'

His phone interrupted him, buzzing on Savannah's kitchen table. He craned to see the screen. Greta. What did Greta want?

'Let me guess, your wife.' Savannah stood in the doorway, arms folded. 'Well, aren't you going to pick up? Since you're supposedly separated and she won't mind that you're here?'

As his brain whirred ahead, trying to come up with a plan, he answered the call.

'Jon, listen,' Greta said, without any greeting, 'I was thinking we should scale down the plan for Susan's surprise party, in light of her message about Celeste last night. We'd need to take Juliette Sullivan off the guest list; she's good friends with Celeste. And there's a few others to consider . . . Anyway, look,

I've just left your house. I told her to switch off her phone, but it's a bit of a shitshow overall, and since Susan doesn't know about the party anyway, I wonder should we just cancel?'

Jon glanced at Savannah. She met his eyes and tilted her head. 'Why don't you pass the phone to me, Jon,' she said sweetly. 'Let me talk to your wife?'

Jon swallowed. There was one way out of this. It might not work, but Savannah was handing it to him on a plate. It was worth a try.

'Susan . . . there's something I have to tell you,' he said into the phone, skirting around Savannah and moving out to the hall.

'What? This is Greta.'

Jon glanced back at Savannah through the open kitchen doorway. He was nearly sure she couldn't hear Greta's side of the conversation, only his.

'Susan, I've been seeing someone else, and . . . and I know we said we'd keep it discreet if we did, but she wants me to tell you.'

'Jon, are you drunk?'

He keeps going. *This won't work. It has to work.* 'Her name is Savannah, she lives at the other 26 Oakpark, where your internet shopping sometimes goes.'

Silence now.

'Savannah's just found out we're married and she insisted I tell you, or she would. I'm here with her now in her house in Oakpark.' He darted a look at Savannah, who was still standing in the kitchen, arms folded, glowering at him. 'I've tried to explain that we're pretty much living separate lives and that you're OK with me seeing other people . . .'

When Greta spoke, she was incredulous and furious all at once.

'Jon, you absolute fucker. You've been cheating on Susan?'

'Yes, unfortunately.'

'Unfortunately.' She snorted. 'And this woman is threatening to tell her?'

'Yes.'

'It will break her.'

'I know. That's why I'm telling you now.'

'She thinks I'm Susan? That you're confessing on the phone?'

'Yes, she wanted to go to see you right now at our house.'

'OK. And why hasn't she?'

'Because I'm telling you now on the phone. And I've explained that we pretty much have an open marriage.' He lowered his voice. 'And I have her keys.'

'Jesus. Jon. What have you got yourself into?'

'I know.' He raised his voice slightly again. 'Susan, I'm sorry for the early-morning drama, I'll see you at home later.'

He disconnected the call.

Leaning against the kitchen doorjamb, Savannah held up an index finger.

'No way. You don't get off that easily. For all I know, you disconnected that call before you said the "seeing someone else" part. Here, give me the phone. I'll call her back.'

She held out her hand. Jon shoved the phone in his pocket and backed towards the front door.

'*Fine.*' A furious look. 'Then I'm still going over there. Susan and I can compare notes.'

Oh god. Why wasn't she listening to reason? If only he'd never met her. If only he hadn't been so stupid. If Susan found out . . . it didn't bear thinking about. He still had Savannah's keys, but she could get a taxi, like she said. Or go tomorrow if she didn't go today. What was he going to do, keep her prisoner here for ever? No, he needed to calm her down, make her see sense, buy himself some time . . . an idea struck. Would it work? Probably not. But he was desperate.

He pulled the phone out again and hit Greta's number.

The call was answered, but she didn't speak. Jon could feel the silent fury coming down the phone line.

'Um, hi, I wonder if you could come over here to the other 26 Oakpark to help me out. Savannah wants to see you in person.'

In the kitchen doorway, Savannah looked confused, and slightly alarmed.

On the phone, Greta cleared her throat.

'Jon, what the actual – are you asking me to come over and pretend to be Susan?'

'Exactly.' Anything to keep Savannah away from Susan, away from their home. Maybe there was still a chance he could walk out of this house today, marriage intact, and never see Savannah again.

'For fuck's sake.'

'I know. I'm sorry.'

Silence. He willed her to do it. Even if it just bought him some time to plan, it would be worth it. Anything to stop Savannah going to see Susan right now.

'*Fine*,' Greta said eventually, 'but this is a temporary fix while Susan's dealing with the fallout from the message. Once that blows over, you confess. She is *not* to hear it from that woman. You'll tell her everything yourself.'

'Sure, I absolutely will.' He absolutely *wouldn't*. He wanted to magic Savannah and the entire affair out of existence. But he'd worry about that later. For now, he just needed to keep Savannah away from Susan.

'And just to be clear,' Greta added, 'I'm doing this for Susan. Not for you.'

'Understood. Just please, hurry.'

91

Savannah
Last week

SAVANNAH STARED AT JON as he stood in her hallway, talking to his wife about their affair. She hadn't expected that. She was furious and desperate to punish him, but now it was all feeling a bit . . . too real? And now he was telling his wife to come here, to Savannah's house. Why would he do that? It would be horrifically awkward. In Savannah's version, she would call at Susan's door, tell her who she was and what he'd done, then flounce off to leave them to it. She didn't actually want Jon's wife in her house or in any kind of in-depth conversation. What was he thinking?

Jon had ended the call but was still in the hall, looking at something on his phone. Or pretending to, at least.

'Why the hell is she coming here? I don't want to see your wife!'

'You said you wanted to talk to her?'

The puzzled frown was both fake and infuriating. The dynamic had shifted and Savannah didn't like it.

'That doesn't mean I want her in my house.'

'Fine, she can stay on the doorstep. It's not a big deal, to be honest. We live quite separate lives, as I said. But if you insist

on talking to her . . .' He finishes the sentence with an infuriating shrug.

'If the marriage is "all but over", why wouldn't you come out
to see me last night when I was outside your house?'

'Because it was after midnight. The baby was asleep.'

There was something in the way he said that – as though his
and Susan's needs trumped hers, just because they had a baby.
Like a baby-on-board sign personified. Fury surged again.

'Then why did you take my car keys?'

'Christ, Savannah, do you think I want this drama on my
doorstep? The other Oakpark isn't quite as private as this one –
the hedges aren't so high and the driveways aren't so long. The
entire neighbourhood would witness it.' He muttered something then under his breath, and she was almost sure she heard
the words 'broken window'.

'What was that?'

'Nothing.' He heaved a sigh. 'We have a lot going on at the
moment.'

We. She couldn't help feeling he and Susan were still very
much a family. A trio. And Savannah was the bit on the side.
Disposable.

'So what happens now? Your wife gives us her blessing and
we carry on seeing each other? I don't think so, Jon.'

He held up his hands. 'No argument from me. Best we end it.'

How magnanimous. She launched into another series of 'how
could you?'s while he stood there, head down, taking it all,
saying nothing. Just as she was about to take off her bracelet
and fling it at his stupid head, a figure appeared at the front
door, visible fleetingly through the glass at the side.

Jon opened the door. And Savannah came face to face with
Susan.

She wasn't what she'd expected, but then again, she'd only

known of her existence for about twelve hours and she hadn't found any photos online. Susan was tall, taller than Savannah by a good six inches, and had long, curly auburn hair framing a porcelain-skinned face devoid of make-up. No jewellery, no adornments of any kind. Without thinking about it too much, Savannah had assumed subconsciously, she realized now, that Susan would look like her, but an older, more matronly, more mediocre version. She took in Susan's clothes – navy tracksuit and Asics trainers, the kind of clothes Savannah wouldn't be caught dead in. But somehow they suited Susan.

'Savannah, this is Susan.'

Still on the doorstep, Susan threw Jon a dagger look, and Savannah caught it. *Interesting.* However this woman felt about her husband's affair and whatever truth there may or may not be to the open-marriage story, she clearly wasn't happy to be there.

Jon was speaking again. 'Susan, I've told Savannah that you don't mind me seeing other people. Understandably, of course, Savannah didn't believe me, so I thought it would make sense if you came and explained and we could all move on.'

Savannah shook her head. God. He was talking about it like it was a minor workplace dispute over unwashed cups in the kitchenette.

Susan stepped forward. 'Savannah, I'm sorry you got caught up in all this and had to find out this way. In all honesty, Jon is a complete fuckwit.'

In spite of herself, Savannah grinned.

Jon looked like he wanted to argue, but clamped his mouth shut.

Susan kept talking. 'I don't care what he gets up to away from home, but we have a small baby, we live in a very nosy neighbourhood, and I work in the local school, so I absolutely cannot have this brought to my door.' She stepped forward again. Savannah stopped grinning. Susan was kind of scary. 'Do you understand?'

Savannah nodded, feeling like a naughty child being chastised by a teacher.

Susan tilted her head, as though appraising her. Then she turned to Jon. 'Jon, why don't you head into work? You're going to be late. I'll have a coffee with Savannah here to make sure we're definitely on the same page.'

Jon hesitated, looking as though he wanted to speak. Then something else crossed his face. Relief maybe? He was dying to get out of there, Savannah realized, happy to leave Susan to deal with her. What a coward. What had she ever seen in him?

Jon hesitated for just a second more, then nodded and turned to walk out the front door.

Leaving Savannah alone with his wife.

92

Venetia
Last week

VENETIA HADN'T SLEPT TUESDAY night. And now, at ten o'clock on Wednesday morning, she was still upright on the living-room couch, events of the last twelve hours playing on a constant loop. Aimee's death mask. Rory's pulped head. And that woman, Susan O'Donnell, cowering in her hall as Felipe pulled Venetia away. The gurgle of pipes told her Felipe was in the shower. His third shower since they'd come home. Horrified at what she'd done to Rory, terrified they'd be caught. More worried about her than about himself, she conceded, but when did that ever get anyone anywhere? And Susan O'Donnell was just getting away with it. Felipe had told her to steer clear now. But Aimee wasn't *his* sister. He didn't get it. She picked up Felipe's old phone, the cheap pay-as-you-go he'd bought when he first moved to Ireland, and copied Susan's number from the WhatsApp screenshot. Then typed out a text:

You got away lightly last night. You deserve to die for that message and what it's done.

Whatever Felipe thought, this wasn't the end of it. Susan

O'Donnell would be seeing her again. And again and again and again.

At lunchtime, the guards arrived. One of the hardest things Venetia ever had to do was feign surprise when they knocked on the door. She forced a smile, before remembering nobody smiles when the police arrive, and adjusted her expression accordingly.

'Could we come in?' the younger of the two gardaí asked, after introducing herself and her colleague. Orla was the speaker's name, that's all Venetia could remember. A garda who looked to be no more than thirty, with the kind of perfect make-up and glossy pony-tail Venetia didn't associate with gardaí.

Venetia ushered them into the living room, frowning a warning at Felipe as he padded down the stairs. Felipe was a loose cannon.

'What can I help you with?' she asked, as she imagined some-one might.

'We're very sorry to tell you,' Orla said, 'but we believe your sister, Aimee, has been the victim of an attack.' A pause. To let the first part sink in, Venetia guessed. To nudge her, to pre-pare her for what was to come. And then it came, when Orla continued, her voice low and soft and kind and sad. 'Unfortu-nately, a body we believe to be Aimee's was found at her house this morning, along with a body we believe to be that of her husband, Rory Quinlan.'

The rest of it went by in a blur and, in the end, no further acting was required. Hearing the formal news of her sister's death was like experiencing it all over again. For Felipe too, it seemed. He stood in the corner of the room, still as a statue, face ashen. Neither of them spoke for a long time after Orla stopped. She'd said something about identifying Aimee, Vene-tia realized now, replaying the last few words.

Venetia nodded agreement, then asked what had happened. She didn't want to hear what had happened, she'd been reliving the discovery over and over since last night, but it's what anyone would ask in the circumstances.

'We believe both Aimee and Rory were attacked with a plate from a barbell.' Orla's voice cracked a little here.

Venetia slumped back on the couch. Knowing it already didn't make it any easier to hear.

'I'm very sorry.' Orla's voice was still low, apologetic.

'Rory owns a gym,' Felipe offered from his stance by the fireplace. 'I think he keeps some extra weights in the house. I guess it was one of his.'

Venetia couldn't tell if Felipe was acting a part or thinking aloud or trying to help. Probably all of the above.

Orla looked over at him. 'As far as we know, yes. The murder weapon was still at the scene.'

Venetia asked then if they knew who did it, because that seemed like something a person would ask.

'It's very early in the investigation,' Orla told her, 'and we're still taking fingerprints and DNA from the scene. We hope that will tell us something.'

'DNA?' Felipe asked. 'What kind of DNA?'

Shut up Felipe, Venetia shouted at him in her head.

'Hair follicles, skin particles, saliva . . .'

'Saliva?' Felipe looked puzzled.

'When people shout or even talk, they often expel tiny bits of saliva. Spittle, basically. Especially someone in a rage.'

Felipe nodded dutifully.

'And we know the perpetrator would have been very close to the victims during the attack, the weight is only eight inches in diameter. So we're confident we'll find DNA on the victims.'

Venetia processed this information, puzzled. The bar attached to the weight meant she'd been at least – what, four feet? – away from Rory. Were they keeping that information back on purpose? Or maybe Orla wasn't there and was passing on second-hand information?

Silence now and, against her better judgement, she filled it.

'Won't there be lots of DNA and prints all over the house, from Rory and Aimee and us and their friends?' she asked.

Orla nodded. 'Absolutely. And when you're ready, we'll need to take samples from both of you, and anyone else who might have called regularly to the house, so we can exclude you and see if we have DNA from unknown sources.'

'And how can you discover who they are, if they're unknown?' Felipe asked.

'With a bit of luck, it'll be someone we already have on file. If not, we'll continue the investigation the old-fashioned way – asking neighbours for doorbell-camera footage, anything they might have seen. And we'll need to speak to you too, to find out more about Aimee and Rory, people in their lives, any habits they might have had that could get them in trouble. Anything about their relationship, and so on.'

Felipe's eyes widened. Worried.

Venetia nodded, keeping her expression neutral, willing him to do the same. She needed the police to leave.

'Maybe you're OK to chat about that now?' the garda tried.

'I . . . I need to lie down,' Venetia whispered. 'I feel sick. I really want to help, but I think I'm going to throw up.'

Orla and her colleague stood, readied to leave. They understood, they'd be in touch, they were very sorry for her loss. And finally, after what felt like forever, they were gone.

Venetia really did feel sick, she realized, making her way to her room, Felipe hovering behind her. The bedroom was in darkness, her grandmother's heavy, lined curtains shutting out July sunlight. Good. Venetia never wanted to see day again.

Felipe pulled back the duvet for her and she curled on to the bed, still in her clothes. He pulled the covers up to her shoulders and sat on the bed beside her.

Something niggled as she closed her eyes.

'Why do they think it was just the disc, the weight at the end of the barbell, I mean? What she said – that the person was right up close to Rory?'

The person. Her.

Felipe tucked the covers closer around her. 'That is not a thing you need to worry about.'

What does that mean? But Venetia was too tired to ask. Finally, mercifully, sleep took over.

93

Nika
Thursday

NIKA'S HEART IS HAMMERING in her chest as she speeds out of Oakpark. Blood pounds in her ears. She can't believe what she just did. Did she mean to do it? She's not sure. Rage just seemed to take over. Her hands were definitely not fully in her control when she steered the wheel towards Maeve. Not *fully*. But . . . a little. And it felt good. Exciting. In that moment, satisfying. Now, driving back towards Jessica's house, she feels sick. What if she gets caught? What if Maeve dies and she gets done for murder? She won't. Nobody saw. That stretch of road is bordered by two greens, both lined with oak trees. No houses overlooking. She just needs to get back to Jessica's and act as though she never left. Jessica can say Nika was in her room the whole time. She pulls in to the side of the road and shares a photo on her Snapchat Story, one from her Gallery, taken in Jessica's bedroom about half an hour ago. Would the police be able to tell it was a Gallery photo and not a live Snap? The police probably don't know much about how Snapchat works. She shares one more, turns off her location and sets off for Jessica's house.

*

But Jessica isn't answering. She's either asleep or taking a shower. She's not replying to Nika's messages and she's not coming to her window. Nika can't call at the door; then Jessica's parents will know that she left and came back. But she needs to be somewhere: she needs an alibi. She can't be anywhere near Oakpark, so she can't go home. The only other person who lives nearby is Ariana, on Westminster Road. They haven't spoken in the last few days and Ariana probably didn't *love* the diary pages Nika had shared, but they'd been friends for five years; that had to count for something. She reverses out of Jessica's driveway and heads for Westminster Road.

Driving back up Carysfort Avenue, she hears sirens. As she passes the turnoff for Oakpark, the sound grows louder. Ambulance? Police cars? Scared now, she puts her foot down on the accelerator.

94

Savannah

Last week

JON HAD GONE, LEAVING his wife to do the talking. And, Savannah realized now, that spoke volumes. Slinking away at the first sign of trouble. When someone shows you who they are, believe them.

With a shake of her head, she stepped towards the kettle. She was having more coffee. Whether or not Susan wanted to join her was up to her. She had to admit, though, she was curious. What kind of person agrees to an open marriage? Especially with a newborn baby in the mix? Unless . . . Maybe the baby wasn't Jon's?

She turned and inclined her head to invite Susan into the kitchen for what was surely to be the strangest conversation of her life.

'Coffee?' That seemed like a reasonable start.

Susan, looking grim and irritated, stepped into the kitchen and nodded. 'Sure.'

She nodded towards Savannah's wedding photo on the shelf by the back door.

'You're married too, I see?'

'Divorced. Your . . . arrangement is not for everyone. Is

Jon telling the truth? You really don't mind him seeing other people?'

Susan exhaled heavily. 'It's not an ideal marriage,' she said dryly, 'but we make it work.'

'Why not divorce?'

She rolled her eyes. 'We get on well as friends, we both like our house and neither of us wants to move out. And we have Bella to think of.' Another grimace. 'The baby.'

'So you . . .' Savannah tried to think of a way to ask her next question.

'Yes, we occasionally still sleep together, and Bella was the unplanned outcome of one such occasion.' Susan looked deeply uncomfortable now. Perhaps this was the first time she'd come face to face with one of Jon's girlfriends. Assuming there were others and this had been going on for a while.

'Has it always been like this? Or is it a new arrangement?'

Susan paused, as if trying to remember. 'A few years now.'

'I think he's seeing someone else too,' Savannah said as she washed out the cafetière and Jon's abandoned coffee cup. 'A woman called here last night and confronted me. Really aggressively.'

Susan looked taken aback.

'You didn't know he was seeing other people as well as me?'

'I . . . no. But nothing would surprise me about Jon this morning. Absolutely nothing.'

Savannah added two heaped spoons of ground coffee to the cafetière and filled it halfway with boiling water.

'God, I can't believe he didn't just tell me. Why lie, if you knew anyway?' Savannah carried the cafetière and two clean mugs to the table, nodding for Susan to sit.

'Would you have agreed to go out with him if you'd known he was married, open marriage or not?' Susan asked.

'Probably not. Yeah, I see how it could be a mood killer.'

'Jon is a man-baby,' Susan said. 'He's weak. He's needy. He wants to have his cake and eat it. He's an all-round useless specimen of a human.'

Savannah poured coffee. 'That doesn't sound like "we get on well as friends".'

Susan seemed to shake herself. 'It doesn't, does it? Maybe I'm getting too old for this.'

'How, um, old . . .'

'How old am I? Really, that's what you want to know?' Susan looked amused. 'I'm forty-six.'

'Wow, and you just had a baby. That's amazing!'

'Yes. Not what I expected.'

'How old is the baby?'

'She's four months.'

'And will you tell her when she's older?'

'We . . . we haven't thought that far ahead. Look, thanks for the coffee, but I'd better get going.' Susan pushed back her chair, leaving the coffee untouched. 'I run a hockey camp and I need to check in.'

Savannah eyed her curiously. Wasn't she a maths teacher? Maybe this was a summer gig.

'Oh, of course. Who minds the baby?'

'What?' Susan looked suddenly flustered. 'My . . . my sister.'

Savannah examined the visitor's face. Why the fluster over a straightforward question? She couldn't help pushing for more.

'Oh, cool, does your sister live nearby?'

'Next door.'

Savannah knew she was on to something. Susan definitely looked uncomfortable now, far more so than when talking about her open marriage.

'That's handy. What's her name?'

'It doesn't matter what her name is. I really have to go.'

Savannah looked at her quizzically. 'Why aren't you on maternity leave?'

'What?'

'You said you have to go to work – why aren't you on maternity leave?'

'Because I, well, the hockey camp is my own business and—'
Susan was really floundering now.

Savannah's eyes went to her hand, to her left ring finger.

And suddenly it all made sense.

'You're not Susan, are you?'

And the woman with the red hair sat back down.

95

Maeve
Thursday

THE GROUND IS WARM beneath Maeve's cheek, but she can't feel it. She can't feel anything. She's lost consciousness from the impact. Not from the impact of the car, but because her head hit concrete when she landed, six feet away from where Nika mounted the footpath and hit her. Maeve doesn't know that she's been knocked down. She doesn't know she's unconscious, that if someone doesn't get her to a hospital, her chances of survival will dwindle to nothing. She'll die. Maeve's mother thinks she's still babysitting. Moira Fitzpatrick had told her to text when she's home, but in the way of people since texts were invented, Moira forgets to look out for the message. Aoife is wondering if Maeve will be home soon and checks Snap Maps, but Maeve's got her location switched off. Nobody knows where she is. And in the shadow of a tall oak, Maeve doesn't know that she's dying.

96

Savannah

Last week

'YOU'RE NOT HIS WIFE.' Savannah shook her head, surprised that she hadn't copped sooner. 'Who are you?'

'Oh, for god's sake.' The red-haired woman clicked her tongue. 'This was the most stupid idea ever.'

'I knew it. This is all to stop me telling his real wife. There's no open marriage, is there?'

Silence.

'I actually can't believe he did this. Well, that's it – I'm going to the other 26 Oakpark.'

The red-haired woman shook her head. 'You can't.'

'Just watch me.' Savannah stood and slipped on her newly purchased silver ballet pumps that were ridiculous with her shorts and tank top, but she was way past caring. She walked towards the hall then stopped and turned. 'Who are you, anyway? Another girlfriend of Jon's?'

The woman rose from the table now too. 'I'm Greta, Susan's sister. And furious as I am with Jon right now, none of this is Susan's fault. She's going through enough already.'

'Oh, poor Susan,' Savannah said in a mock-pitying tone, very aware how childish she sounded. 'What is *poor Susan* going through?' She walked towards the front door. The woman followed.

'She's dealing with a pile-on because of a stupid message . . . well, it doesn't matter, but someone smashed their window last night, because of it.'

Savannah started to laugh.

'What's so funny?'

'That was me. I smashed the window. What message did she think it was linked to?'

'Forget the message – what the hell were you doing, throwing a brick at their window? Bella's cot is right there – she could have been badly hurt!'

'Not my baby, not my problem.'

The woman – Greta – inhaled sharply. Then suddenly she raised her hand and slapped Savannah, right across the cheek, just like Savannah had slapped Jon earlier.

'What the— how dare you?'

'How dare *you*. It's one thing to want to punish Jon. And I get why you want to tell Susan. But "not my baby, not my problem"? What kind of person says that?'

Savannah understood the point. On a rational, objective level, she absolutely knew it was an awful thing to say. But the rage was so strong in that moment, she couldn't and wouldn't backtrack. Jon had lied about being married, then made a fool of her by asking this woman to turn up and play at being his wife. And now this woman had slapped her, in her own home. She'd had enough.

'Get out.'

Greta didn't move.

'Get out of my house or I'm calling the police.'

Greta raised her hands in a gesture of surrender, skirted around Savannah and opened the front door.

'Don't you dare go near Susan or Bella. If you do, I'll be back, and it'll be more than a slap.'

Greta slammed the door after her, leaving Savannah breathless and numb in the hall. How was this happening? In less than twenty-four hours, she'd been threatened by two unhinged strangers, despite having done nothing at all to warrant it. Slowly, she moved back into the kitchen.

In a daze, she searched for her phone. Fuck that woman and fuck Jon. They had no right to tell her what she could and couldn't do. She was going to tell Susan. Where were her car keys? Oh, for god's sake, Jon still had them. What an absolute tool. When she gets her hands on him—

That's when she heard someone at the front door.

97

Venetia
Thursday

VENETIA'S HEART HAD BEGUN to race as soon as she saw
the Instagram post on Thursday evening. She stared at her
phone, blood rushing to her ears. There she was, Susan
O'Donnell, smiling brightly for the camera. No more than
a few hours since Venetia had taken her baby and lain it out
in the garden. No more than a week since Aimee's death. A
group shot of a family meal. Not a care in the world. Her
baby in her arms. Her family flocked around her. Her sister's
words in the caption:

**So blessed to have my sisters in my life. I don't know where I'd
be without this lot. Not pictured, Greta, who is here most of the
rest of the time. Pictured: Susan, my favourite younger sister,
the baby of the family. Love is . . . people you care about most in
the world, gathered together to eat and laugh.**

Rage bubbled up inside Venetia. Aimee was dead, and this
was what Susan and Leesa were doing. Jesus Christ. They didn't
care. They didn't care one bit about Aimee, about Venetia, about
Aimee's unborn baby. Susan O'Donnell had broken Venetia's
life, shattered it to unmendable pieces, and she didn't care.

The high she'd experienced earlier, leaving Susan's baby on

the lawn, had gone now. Dissolved by grief and a call with a funeral director, and now this. This happy-family photo.

Felipe had arrived at her shoulder, reading then wincing at the Instagram post. He followed her when she grabbed her car keys, asking her where she was going, begging her to stay put, to calm down. *Calm down.* What person alive has ever responded well to *calm down*?

As she pulled on her boots, he pleaded some more. Claimed she was getting obsessed, that she'd end up back on heroin. That stopped her for a moment. A half-formed idea struck and she ran upstairs to the shoebox in her wardrobe, the one Felipe didn't know she had. With a syringe in her pocket, she ran back downstairs and grabbed her jacket from the hall closet.

'Please, Venetia,' Felipe tried one more time.

'This is my problem, Felipe!' she hissed. 'It has nothing to do with you!'

'It does. Apart from the fact that I care about you, I'm implicated. I was there. And I . . . helped.'

'You didn't. You stood there with your hands over your eyes.'

'I . . . I helped cover up.'

'*What?*'

A sigh. 'I'm the reason they think it was just the weight from the barbell that was used, why they're not looking for the murder weapon and won't find your DNA.'

'What did you do?'

'It was when you left in the car for Oakpark. Before I could think too much, I unscrewed the bar from the weight. I know you wiped it, but it wasn't enough. They'd have found something. Skin particles, I don't know.'

'But where is it?'

'I went into their en suite and climbed up to the skylight window and I rolled the bar down to the gutter at the bottom of the roof. It's still there. Maybe someday someone will find it, but not yet.'

'Christ.' Felipe was the last person she'd expect to get involved with hiding evidence. 'But won't *your* DNA be on it now too? Fingerprints? When they eventually do find it, I mean?'

'I put a pair of Rory's socks over my hands and I brought those home with me. But I don't know if they'll ever find it.'

'Jesus . . .'

As she processed this, Felipe moved to take a position in front of their hall door, arms folded, a determined expression on his face.

She shook her head and stepped forward, but he stood his ground, physically blocking her from leaving. Her hackles rose. He was as bad as Rory. Trying to control her, like Rory had tried to control Aimee. Had successfully controlled Aimee. Had *killed* Aimee. Was Felipe going to do the same? This new version of Felipe, this person who would hide evidence and cover up crimes and stand in her way? She'd never let that happen. She'd get there first if she had to. He looked so resolute, standing there, dead set on stopping her. What had she ever seen in him, she wondered? *His kindness*, said a distant voice in her head. His evenness. His stability. She waved it away. He was an obstacle. A man trying to control her.

'Venetia, if you go now, it's over between us. I can't keep going like this, I can't keep protecting you, trying to help you, when you won't help yourself.'

'Then I guess it's over.' She said it so quietly, then, like lightning, almost enjoying the shock in his eyes as she did it, she grabbed his right arm with both her hands and with all her strength she yanked him away from the door. He stumbled, falling sideways against the living-room door, landing on the floor. Venetia had pulled the front door open and run to her car. She was blazing down Stradbrook Road before he'd even picked himself up off the floor.

And now she's standing in Susan's kitchen. With Susan's baby in her hands.

98

Maeve
Thursday

MAEVE FEELS THE FAINTEST sense of breath on her face. A looming presence. Someone leaning over her. She tries to move and pain sears through her shoulder, her left leg. She bites down on her lip, tasting blood, then forces her eyes open. Where is she? It takes another moment for her eyes to focus. The face swims in front of her then firms into shape.

Cody Geary.

What is he doing and why is she here? The car. It comes back. The sound of a car. An engine revving. Speeding up. And then shock and pain and darkness. Cody is saying her name, and now he's saying something else. He's speaking to someone on his phone, calling an ambulance. That's good. That's a good thing to do. She lets out a slow breath. A hand on hers. Cody's hand. Something else. Something glinting in the streetlight's glow, a few feet away. It looks like a silver cat . . . a silver jaguar. Cody is murmuring. Was Cody driving the car? Now another voice. A woman's voice. Shouting.

'Get away from her!'

Cody is yanked back, and someone else is hunkering down. Familiar scent. Bright print. Moira Fitzpatrick.

'Oh, Maeve, my god, what did he do to you? I'll stay with you, don't worry. I'll call the guards and an ambulance and your mum.'

Cody's voice. Distant. Telling her he's already called an ambulance.

'A bit late for good deeds now,' she hisses. 'Maeve, I've got you. And he won't get away with it this time.'

Maeve registers the sound of a siren and drifts off to black.

99

Nika
Thursday

NIKA FEELS LIKE SHE'S in an American teen movie, throwing pebbles at Ariana's bedroom window, but she's running low on options. She's messaged her six times in the last four minutes, and Ariana's left her on Delivered. Eventually, there's a twitch in the bedroom curtains, then moments later, Ariana opens the front door.

'Hey,' Nika says, eyes downcast like she does when she's in trouble with her dad. 'I wanted to apologize properly for seeing Zach behind your back. I should never have done it. I'm so sorry.' She looks up now, under her lashes. This has to work, it always works. And Ariana didn't even really like Zach; she'd said so. She'd said Nika was welcome to him.

Ariana stares at her.

'Could I come in, so we can talk properly?' She just needs to get into the house. To snap some pics, to be there for a while. To see Ariana's parents, ideally. Someone who can vouch for her if this ever comes back on her. She's fairly sure Maeve couldn't have recognized her – the headlights would have blinded her – but still . . .

Ariana says nothing.

'You'd gone off Zach, you said. So I thought it was OK . . .'

Ariana sighs. 'You're right. I had gone off him. To be honest, I didn't really mind that you were seeing him and I did try to stop the pile-on. But you know what people are like . . .'

Nika smiles and shakes her head ruefully. 'I know. Unreal. But I'm OK, and it's not your fault. Maybe I can come in and we can chat?'

'Sure thing.' Ariana pulls the door wide.

Nika steps forward, but Ariana holds up a hand.

'It's just . . . there's one other tiny thing.'

'Oh?'

'Yeah. The diary pages you put online.'

'Sorry about that. I *know*. Maeve Khoury is the most cringe person ever. She's like . . . anyway, sorry you got caught up in it. It's kind of a compliment though, when you think about it?'

'I'm not worried about me being *caught up in it*.' Ariana makes air quotes and mimics Nika in a way that leaves Nika feeling less sure of herself. 'I just can't believe you'd do that to some-one? Especially someone who used to be your best friend. Her diary? Her most private thoughts? You stole it and then put it on the internet?' Her upturned nose crinkles in distaste. 'What is *wrong* with you?'

Nika's face heats up and an unfamiliar feeling rises in her gut. She's not used to being chastised or confronted or criti-cized and . . . and who does Ariana think she is, to call her out like this? But this is not the time for arguments . . . she needs to get inside the house.

'Could I come in to talk about it?' Nika steps forward.

'That'd be a no.' Ariana tilts her head and smiles. 'Off you go now.' She makes a shooing motion, steps into her hallway and shuts the door in Nika's face.

It's only when she's getting back into the car outside Ariana's that she notices the little silver jaguar from the front of her mum's car is gone. Shit. Did it come off when she . . . when she . . . she can't think the words now. It seems too crazy. Did she really do that? In a daze, she slips into the driver's seat, just as Celeste phones to ask her where she is. It's time to come home, her mother says. Nika heads for her house, feeling sicker by the minute. What was she thinking? Why had she driven at Maeve like that? Not that Maeve didn't deserve consequences for the attempted poisoning, which is *literally* murder, but Nika should have come up with something that wouldn't land her in some kind of prison for juveniles. Or adults? She'll be eighteen next month – would that make her an adult if she's caught and it goes to court after that date? She has no idea. This is not a problem she's ever encountered before. *Shit.*

At home, she darts in through the back door, then up to her bedroom, without calling in to the living room to see her mum, or the den to see her dad. She's only just flopped on her bed when she hears Cody's footsteps thundering up the stairs and the slam of his bedroom door. Then, a moment later, the door-bell rings. Shit. Is it the police? She cracks her door to listen. It's not. It's a woman's voice. Nika creeps out on to the landing and peers through the banisters at the top of the stairs. She can see now, the woman at the door is Moira Fitzpatrick. What is she doing here at this time of night? Nika strains to listen. She's saying . . . oh crap, she's saying Maeve's in hospital. But why is Moira here? Even if she knows about the accident, what would bring her to their house? *Oh god.* Realization hits. Nika sits on the top step of the stairs, weak and sick. Maeve must have seen Nika after all. What is she going to do? Should she confess now, get ahead of it? Make sure they know it was an accident?

Then she hears something else that stops her in her tracks.

100

Celeste
Thursday

CELESTE STARES AT MOIRA Fitzpatrick. She can't have heard her correctly.

'What . . . what did you just say?'

'I said Maeve Khoury's in hospital and, I'm sorry to tell you, Cody seems to have attacked her.'

'Wait, stop for a second. Is Maeve OK?'

'I think so. She was conscious in the ambulance, and I phoned Leesa; she's on her way to the hospital. But unfortunately, it appears Cody was responsible.'

Celeste feels her jaw clench. She will *kill* him. She will absolutely kill him. How has it come to this? She knows how. Ignoring the signs, not getting him assessed, putting her head in the sand. Ignoring the knife and the bruised knuckles. The babysitting incident with Moira Fitzpatrick's child. Oh god, Moira in her ridiculous gaudy jumpsuit is loving this. Revenge.

'I've contacted the guards, but I wanted to do you the courtesy of letting you know before they arrive.'

The courtesy. *You wanted to gloat, that's what this is.* But Jesus Christ, she is going to murder Cody. She's going to throw him out, that's what she's going to do. There is only so much her mental health can take. She hears a noise from the landing and glances up to see her daughter's face peering between the banisters. All of this is so unfair on Nika . . . She straightens her shoulders. Celeste is in no mood to defend Cody, but she can't lose face.

'I'm sure there's been a misunderstanding.'

Moira is shaking her head. 'No misunderstanding. I went out after Maeve because I accidentally gave her two fifties for the babysitting.' Her cheeks colour slightly at the admission. 'I didn't know what I was seeing at first – one figure leaning over another. When I got closer, I realized it was Cody and that Maeve was semiconscious on the ground. Maybe from one of those drugs people put in drinks . . .'

Celeste suppresses an eyeroll. This woman is an idiot. 'Moira, Maeve was babysitting in your house, not out having her drink spiked. And Cody was here most of tonight; he wasn't out putting drugs in anyone's drink. He's fifteen – he'd hardly be in a pub.'

'Here *most* of tonight, but out for a while, you mean?'

Who does she think she is – Columbo? 'I'd better go and find out what's going on. Thanks for letting me know.' A tight smile.

'No problem.' Moira's smile is wider. She turns. 'Oh, here are the guards now.'

Celeste's heart thumps as headlights beam from the end of the driveway, momentarily blinding her. Two car doors open and close.

Moira steps back to make room at the porch but doesn't leave.

Two gardaí loom out of the darkness, both in uniform. The taller one speaks.

'Mrs Geary?'

'Yes?' Celeste keeps her face neutral. Inside, she feels sick.

They introduce themselves, but Celeste is numb, taking none of it in. Nothing until one of them says something about a car.

'I'm sorry, I missed that, could you repeat it?'

'I said, we'd like to take a look at your car.'

'My car?' The fear starts to lift. This must be some kind of misunderstanding. Cody doesn't drive. This has nothing to do with him after all.

'Yes, we're investigating a hit and run. A young woman in a vehicular incident here in Oakpark.'

Moira's hand goes to her mouth. 'Oh my god, he knocked her down!'

'Don't be ridiculous, Moira,' Celeste snaps. 'Cody is fifteen. He's never driven a car in his life. And anyway, Nika had the car tonight.'

Oh.

Oh god.

101

Susan
Thursday

I'M STANDING IN MY kitchen, shaking, light-headed, struggling
to process what I'm seeing. The woman – Venetia – the woman
I met in the cottage, is here. Felipe's wife. Aimee's sister. She's
here in my kitchen, and she's holding Bella. Why is she in my
kitchen and why is she holding Bella, and why isn't she holding
her properly, like you're supposed to hold a baby? She's holding her by her arm, one arm, and Bella's just dangling. Like a
ragdoll. Is she . . . she's not . . . but Bella's eyes are open, wide
and puzzled. She's OK. But she's not OK – what is this woman
doing in my kitchen? Where's Greta? I look about wildly. Greta
is here. She's on my kitchen floor, in a crumpled heap. My eyes
dart from my daughter to my sister and I move towards my
daughter.

Venetia catches Bella around the waist with one arm then
holds up her other hand.

'No you don't. Stay put or I'll show you what would happen
if I hold her by the legs and slam her head against a wall.'

I stop still. 'Please,' I whisper, 'what . . . what do you want?'

In my peripheral vision, I see Greta move. Then a small
groan.

'Greta, are you OK?' My eyes don't leave Bella.

'She'll be fine. It's only a whack on the head.' Venetia nods towards a heavy metal rod on the worktop, about a foot long with a crook at one end. A tyre iron, I think. Not mine . . . So she brought it with her? To hurt us. *Oh god.*

Bella's face begins to crumple.

'Please, let me take her. She's scared.' I reach for Bella.

Venetia whisks her to her side, tucking her under her arm, and waves me away.

'Ah, ah. No. You'll get her back in due course, if that's what you choose.'

'I do, that's what I choose, please!'

'You haven't heard the other option yet.'

What other option could there possibly be? *Of course I want Bella back.*

Greta pulls herself to a kneeling position, rubbing her head. She looks over at me, then at Venetia, her face creasing in confusion.

'This is Venetia,' I say, as calmly as I can. 'Her sister, Aimee, was one of two people murdered last week in Cherrywood.'

Venetia shakes her head. 'Interesting use of the passive tense there, Susan. As if it had nothing to do with you.' She turns to Greta. 'I'll explain. Your sister here sent a message to hundreds of people last week, with a reference to Warren Geary and the PR girl from Bar Four. That PR girl was my sister Aimee. And Aimee's husband, Rory, was not a nice man. He didn't like Aimee going out or having friends and wasn't mad on her having a job either, but tolerated it for the extra cash it brought in. Then he saw that message and it tipped him over the edge.'

Oh god, no.

Venetia leans against the counter, still holding Bella at her side. With her other hand, she picks up the tyre iron and slides one end of it into the back pocket of her jeans. Then she pulls a knife from the knife block.

'Rory came home that night, and do you know what he did? He beat my sister to death.'

Blood roars in my ears. *This can't be happening.*

Greta stares at Venetia. 'That's a horrific thing to happen.' Calming. Soothing. 'For your poor sister, and for you. But it was Rory who killed Aimee, not Susan. Susan couldn't have known what would happen.'

'That's not going to bring my sister back, is it? Excuses and not-my-faults?'

Greta touches the back of her head and winces. 'I understand, but whatever about Susan, it's definitely not Bella's fault.'

Venetia looks at Bella, then at me. 'That's why I'm giving you the choice.' She pauses. 'You can choose your baby or your sister.'

'*What?*'

'I lost my sister. Now you pay with yours. Unless you don't want to, in which case, you get to save your sister and we sacrifice the baby instead.' She holds the tip of the knife against Bella's neck. Bella is crying now.

'Please don't do this. I'm so sorry about your sister—'

'Say her name.'

'I'm so sorry about Aimee.' I take a tiny step forward. 'But you must know that I couldn't have predicted this. I never meant it. I'm not the first person in the world to send a message to the wrong group. We've all done it.'

Venetia shakes her head. 'See, you're doing it again. Making excuses. Deflecting blame.'

Deflecting blame. I think about my theory – that it wasn't Aimee with Warren, but Venetia. Is that part of this? Putting the entire blame on me to deflect her own guilt, her own part in this mess?

341

'I know it wasn't Aimee,' I say softly. I take another tiny, tiny step forward. 'With Warren.'

Her eyes narrow. She wasn't expecting this.

'You're still doing it, still trying to blame other people,' she says, recovering quickly. 'It doesn't matter whether or not Aimee was really with Warren Geary, what matters is she's dead, and that's down to you. So now we're going to even things up.'

She moves the tip of the knife so it indents the skin on Bella's neck. I jump forward and, this time, she swipes the knife against Bella's arm and draws blood. Bella lets out a loud, shocked cry.

'Susan, stop, stay back! She'll hurt her again!' Greta croaks. She has hauled herself on to a kitchen chair.

Venetia smirks. 'So who will it be? Your sister or your baby?'

I stand open-mouthed, staring at her, willing Bella away from her, unable to take any of this in.

Greta speaks, quietly and calmly. 'She chooses me. She saves Bella.'

I turn to her. 'No!'

'Cool, that's agreed then, you choose to kill the baby.' Venetia brings the knife to the side of Bella's neck, then pulls it away, as though ready to stab.

'Stop!' I yell.

'Which is it to be?'

'She chooses for me to die and Bella to live,' Greta repeats.

Venetia smiles and looks at me. 'I need Susan to say it.'

Oh god. But there's no option. No choice, not really. I say the only thing I can. My eyes fill with tears. I look at my sister.

'I . . . I choose for Greta to . . . to die and for Bella to live.'

Venetia nods. She tilts her head towards something on the counter. I can make out a syringe with a liquid inside, and what looks like a small leather belt.

'She'll go out on a high, literally,' Venetia says with a grim smile.

'What . . . what is it?'

'Liquid heroin,' she says matter-of-factly. 'Let's be honest, even with your baby's life at stake, someone like *you* won't be able to stab your sister or beat her over the head. So tie the strap around her upper arm, get yourself a good vein, and off she goes. And don't even think about coming near me with it because I'll get to this one before you get to me. There are a hundred ways to kill a baby this small. I can literally strangle her with one hand.'

'I . . . I can't do this.'

'Then we sacrifice the baby.'

'No!'

'So take the syringe.'

Greta calls my name softly. 'Susan. You can do this. It'll be painless. And it will save Bella.'

'I . . . I . . .'

Greta pulls her hoodie over her head. Underneath, she's wearing a sleeveless running top. She holds out her hand. 'Pass me the strap.'

'Greta.'

'You do have a choice, Susan,' Venetia says in a sing-song voice. She lets Bella slip, as though dropping her to the floor.

'No!'

But she's still holding Bella, clutching her to her hip. Bella's wails get louder, filling the room as, outside, fireworks pop.

'Your choice.'

Greta stands to walk over to the counter, to take the strap.

Venetia holds up a hand. 'Susan has to do it. This is not a suicide. It's a murder. She needs to live with this for the rest of her life. She needs to know she caused it.'

There's something in the way Venetia says it, a crack in her voice. This is all a pretence, I realize. She knows she bears some responsibility for what happened. But it's irrelevant; she's not going to listen to reason. She's way beyond reason.

Greta is buckling the strap around her upper arm.

'I'll do this part, and Susan can do the injection,' she says calmly. My big sister. My rock. Giving her life for Bella. And I've spent the last five days thinking all kinds of things about her.

Greta sits back down. Her bag is hanging off the back of the chair and it slips to the floor now with a thud. She picks it up and puts it on her lap. She looks at me. Her eyes are trying to tell me something, but I don't know what. Am I supposed to do it a certain way? Not do it? Fake do it? Is that even possible? Not with Venetia watching us. What is she trying to say? I stare back. Maybe she's just saying goodbye.

Greta coughs, a heavy, chesty cough, covering her mouth, closing her eyes.

'Take the syringe now, Susan, and off you go.' There is glee in Venetia's voice.

Greta opens her eyes again and nods at me. This can't be happening. I meet her eyes. They bloom with tears. In all my life, even when our mother died, I've never seen Greta cry.

One last time, I try Venetia. 'Please?'

'No. An eye for an eye.' In her arms, Bella whimpers.

I pick up the syringe.

102

Susan
Thursday

THE SYRINGE FEELS LIKE nothing. It should feel cold or hot or heavy, something to signify the power it holds, but it doesn't. It's light and nothingy. My hand shakes as I inch the tip of the needle towards my sister's vein. She closes her eyes.

'I'm sorry,' I say, and push the syringe, flooding her blood with poison.

To my horror, it's instantaneous. She slips sideways on the chair, then down. Her prone figure on my kitchen floor. In seconds, it's over. And all because of a text.

'It's done,' I sob, turning to Venetia, willing myself to stay upright, to hold myself together. 'Give me Bella.'

She smirks. 'You know, I don't think I will.'

She's high on power, deranged. The most dangerous kind of anger, and it's terrifying.

'Please.' I reach for Bella, but she jerks her out of the way. She still has the knife in her other hand. With her elbow, she pushes down the handle of the back door.

'I'll keep her until I get bored.' She says it nonchalantly. Then her voice hardens. 'Follow me and I'll cut her.'

'Venetia, the police will come. I know where you live, who you are.'

'You think I'm going back there?'

And then she's gone.

Frozen for a second, I stand in my kitchen. Bella or Greta? I shout at Greta's prone body to wake up, to find my phone, to call the police, but even as I shout I'm already running out the back door, away from her. Towards Bella. Letting Greta down again, leaving her dying on the floor. But I know who she'd want me to choose.

I race around the side passage to the front of the house. No movement, no sound. Where has she gone? Then out on the street, an engine revs. Lights. A car screeching away from the kerb.

Venetia. She has Bella, and she's driving away.

Panicked, sick, not stopping to think, I start to run. She's driving down Oakpark, weaving between parked cars, and I'm running, panting, crying, screaming Bella's name. Blinded by tears, I keep running, following her tail lights. I have to get her. I have to get Bella. I need the police. Why isn't anyone helping? Why can't my neighbours see me running, screaming, past their houses? They're not here, I remember now, as music from a distant speaker wafts up from the green. My neighbours are at the summer party and Venetia is heading for the main road, and Bella, oh my god, I have to do something. That's when I hear it. A bang. A crunch of metal on metal. The tail lights have stopped moving. Did she crash into something? I keep running. My ankle goes from under me, pain rips through me. I'm limping, slower, but I can't stop. Closer now, and hard to see in the falling dusk, but there's another car. Blocking her way. The bang. Did she drive into the other car? Bella. Oh my god. I keep running.

103

Venetia
Thursday

Dazed, Venetia lifts her head from the airbag. Someone's just swerved in front of her car and she's gone into the side of theirs. What the . . . the baby is wailing from the back. Still in the footwell, inside a bag of laundry. She yanks open her door and stumbles into the dusk. That's when she recognizes the other car. Felipe's. Realization dawns. He did it on purpose. Pulled in front of her to stop her. She truly didn't know he had it in him. She grabs the tyre iron and the knife from the passenger seat then yanks open the back door and scoops the crying baby out of the holdall. The car isn't going anywhere. But Venetia is.

This does not end here.

Felipe is out of his car, stumbling towards her, hand on the back of his head. There's blood. His own fault. He's calling her name. And from behind, another faraway shout. Venetia swivels her head. Susan O'Donnell in the distance, limping, shrieking. For fuck's sake. She turns back. Felipe is close now, blood on his hand as he reaches for her. No, not for her, for the baby. That's what he wants. To save Susan O'Donnell's baby. Rage fills her. With the baby under her right arm, she raises the tyre iron high. Felipe doesn't see it coming. She gets him across the temple and he drops like a stone. She turns back. Susan is closer now. And other people. People not far behind, running. Fuck. Fuck it. Maybe this does end here. For Susan O'Donnell, for the baby.

She lays the baby on the ground and kneels beside it, sitting back on her heels. Its cry has reduced to a whimpering sob, exhausted now.

'It's nearly over,' she whispers. 'You're too small to understand. And it's not your fault, it's your mother's fault.' She pauses, staring at its confused face. It really isn't the baby's fault. But then, it wasn't Aimee's either. Resolute again. 'You won't suffer. It will be quick. But Susan will suffer, and that's what counts. This is for Aimee's lost baby.'

She kneels upright now, stretching. The baby laid out in front of her, like a sacrifice on an altar. She takes one look at Susan. Takes in the horror on her face as she limps towards them as fast as she can, but not fast enough. There's still enough space between them. Venetia smiles at Susan. Raises the knife high over the baby. Exalted. Adrenaline coursing through her. For Susan and Susan's baby, this ends here.

104

Susan
Thursday

LIKE THE WORST NIGHTMARE, it unfolds in front of my eyes, so near but so far. I'm screaming, hobbling, running through pain. Venetia is demonic now, lit by a streetlight, a smile on her face, knife in both hands, high above Bella. Felipe is on the ground beside them, unconscious maybe.

If I can just . . . but I can't, I'm too far and she's lowering the knife now, and I can't . . . I can't make it, I have to but I can't and then oh my god, Felipe . . . he's there, still on the ground, but he's shoved himself somehow, thrown himself on top of Bella, and I'm still running and the knife comes down and makes contact but . . . but it's in Felipe's back, oh god, she's stabbed Felipe, and he's on Bella, lying across Bella, and I keep running. Venetia is . . . she's trying to pull the knife out of his back. It's not over. But I'm here now and I can help . . . the tyre iron, on the ground. I grab it and, with no warning, no mercy, no room for error, I smash it across the side of her head and she goes down sideways and she's . . . she's not moving. Out cold, slumped on the ground.

I turn to Felipe, drop to my knees. He rolls to the side and shows me Bella, beneath him, not stabbed, not dead, alive.

Dazed, silent, but alive. I pull her into my arms. I'm never letting her go. Beside me, Felipe lies on his side, pale and sweating.

'She's OK,' he whispers.

I swallow, my throat tight, and nod. 'She's OK, she's OK. Oh my god. Felipe.' My whole body is shaking. I hold Bella close, trying to stop the quiver, but I can't. 'You saved Bella, but we . . . we need to get you to a hospital.' I look up. People are coming, people are here. Neighbours running, phones out. Already I can hear the distant sound of a siren. I look back at Felipe, take his hand in mine, rubbing it, kneading it. 'Help is coming, you'll be OK.'

His eyes flicker closed. This is not good. I need to keep him awake, keep him talking.

'Stay with me, talk to me . . . tell me what happened . . . how did you know where Venetia would be?'

His eyes open again, and he smiles a faint smile, his face pale in the streetlight. 'I got it wrong first.' It comes in a whisper. 'Venetia, she was furious, in a rage . . . I thought she would come here, to your house, but . . . but no. I arrived and there was nobody here. Then I saw your text.' Two shallow exhales. 'And wondered if she'd . . . she'd gone to your sister Leesa's house. The Instagram post.'

I nod, teeth chattering. People are here now, hunkered, blurred, but I focus only on Bella and Felipe. 'Keep going. Tell me the rest.'

'Venetia wasn't at Leesa's either, so I came back here. I saw her driving, I saw someone running, I didn't know for sure if it was you, but somehow I did. So I swerved to stop her . . .'

People are saying things. *Help them. Don't touch them. Take the baby. No, leave the baby. Wait for the ambulance. Pull out the knife. Don't go near the knife. Anyone else hurt?*

At that, I remember. Oh my god, *Greta*.

I have to get to Greta. I scan the faces around me, still holding Bella to my chest, still holding Felipe's hand. I spot Juliette Sullivan.

'Juliette!' I scream. 'Go to Greta, get to my house, she's in the kitchen, unconscious or . . . or—' *Or dead.* A sob. What if it's too late? Was it already too late when I left her? 'Call another ambulance. Tell them it's a heroin overdose.'

Juliette's jaw drops, but to her eternal credit, she doesn't ask questions. Her phone at her ear, she begins to run back towards my house.

Someone else, Juliette's husband I think, puts a blanket over my shoulders, whispering that the ambulance is coming.

I turn back to Felipe. His eyes are closed again.

'You're going to be OK. You saved Bella. You . . . you . . .' I'm sobbing. 'You need to stay awake, stay with us.' Sobbing and laughing. 'It's a rule, I'm sure of it. If you save someone. You have to be, like, a life-long guardian.' Whispering now. 'She needs you. I need you.'

'She's going to be OK.' Staccato, hushed words. 'She has a great mother . . .'

Blood soaks his T-shirt and voices around us grow louder, more anxious, as his eyelids flutter open and closed.

'*Felipe!* Stay with us. Please.' Sirens. 'The ambulance. It's nearly here.' I squeeze his hand. 'Please stay with me.'

'Don't let go,' he says softly, a whisper of fear. 'I don't want to . . . die on my own.'

'Felipe,' I whimper. 'I won't let go.'

Felipe closes his eyes and takes a final breath.

105

Susan
Friday

IT'S JUST AFTER 3 a.m. when Jon finds me in the hospital, in the room they've given Bella and me. She's being kept overnight for observation, though she's been given the all-clear. Despite everything Venetia did, Bella has escaped with just one cut from the knife in my kitchen and a small amount of bruising from the car crash. The guards think she was inside a bag of laundry. It's hard to process this – Venetia shoving her into a bag of soiled clothing, but knowing too that this was what protected her.

The gardaí have finished questioning Jon, for now, about where he was the morning Savannah died, partly because he's been able to show them a text he got from Savannah after he arrived in work that morning, with his assistant and colleagues vouching for his presence. We do not talk about the elephant in the room, the question of why he was at Savannah's house at all that morning, why he has a text from her. We both know we have to talk about his affair, but Bella's hospital bedside is not the place for that. Greta will be able to vouch for him too, he says, once she's well enough for questions, because she called by his office that same morning, saw him there.

Greta. I close my eyes and give silent thanks yet again that she's alive. That I didn't kill her. That the ambulance arrived in time.

It wasn't just the ambulance that saved her, it was Greta herself. An extraordinarily kind doctor came to find me in Paediatrics to reassure me that Greta was going to be OK, mostly because she'd taken a handful of naltrexone just before I injected her. I remember it now: the bag on her lap, the look in her eye as she tried to tell me something, the cough into her hand. Not a cough, a swallow. She took more naltrexone later, helped by Juliette, while they waited for the ambulance.

This left me baffled. How could her Long Covid medicine help with a heroin overdose? Because that's what it does, Dr Fitzgerald explained. Reduces the impact of alcohol and opiates. The tablets Greta took protected her somewhat when I injected her, and the extra she took with Juliette saved her.

I tell Jon about Maeve being knocked down, that Leesa is with her, that she'll be OK, that Samir is flying home. Then I stop. The effort of speaking is too much. I don't know what I'm feeling. Mostly, I'm numb. Or in shock? Bella is safe. Greta is alive. Maeve is recovering. Felipe is dead. *Felipe.* Tears flow again. Jon and I don't speak. He grips my hand and we sit and watch our daughter.

106

Celeste
Friday

IT'S FOUR IN THE morning when Celeste, Warren and Nika get back from the garda station. It's no longer Thursday night – Friday is dawning, the sky pinkening in the east as they step inside the house.

Quiet, withdrawn, defeated, Nika goes straight to her room. Celeste does not go after her.

Cody, to her surprise, is in the living room, curled on the couch, watching YouTube on the TV. He turns it off when they come into the room, and in a whisper, asks about Nika, what will happen.

'She's been charged with a section 3 assault,' Warren says, his voice breaking, and Celeste feels herself crumble all over again. Her daughter, her own flesh and blood, the child she created and raised, appears to have deliberately knocked down another child. Celeste sits beside Cody. She is broken. Warren sits on an armchair opposite, glazed with exhaustion.

'Will she be OK?' Cody asks in a small voice. 'Will she go to prison?'

'I don't know. We've been told the courts will do whatever they can to keep a young person out of jail, but it's pretty serious . . .' *Christ*. Nika probably *should* go to prison. But no matter what she's done, Celeste doesn't actually want that for her. She hates Nika right now, but she loves her too. She wants to slap her, to shake her. But she wants to hug her too. She's seventeen, but she's a child. How much of who she's turned out to be is down to Nika? And how much is her parents' fault?

'I don't want her to go to prison,' Cody whispers. He lays his head on his mother's shoulder. She takes his hand. 'Me neither.' She rubs his red-raw knuckles. 'Cody, what really happened?'

'I told you, I punched a wall.'

'Why?'

'Because . . . I don't know.'

'Please, Cody. I'm worried about you. Why did you punch a wall?'

'Because . . . I . . . because I'm dumb. I'm bad at everything. I'm always in trouble. No matter what I do, I don't get things right. This was something I *could* do . . . and I guess it made me feel better. For a minute, anyway.'

'Oh, Cody.' *Oh, Celeste*. All those red flags for self-harm, and she'd been looking in the wrong direction. She'd even read about it – read that boys hurt themselves differently to girls – punching walls, taking drugs. Busy reading, but not seeing.

'And the knife?'

He pushes his head closer into her, nestling like the baby he once was.

'I thought about it, but I didn't do anything.'

'I'm so sorry.' A sob escapes. 'I've let you down, Cody, and I'm sorry. I've let both of you down.'

'It's OK, Mum.' He hugs in closer again and a small cry shudders out.

'I'm here now,' she whispers, kissing the top of his head. 'I'm here now.'

107

Susan
Sunday

GRETA IS MORE THAN likely being discharged just as soon as her doctor does her rounds this afternoon. She's still in a hospital gown, but I've brought in a sweatshirt and leggings for her. It'll make her feel more normal, she says, while she's waiting for the green light to go home. Leesa and I are sitting on hard plastic chairs either side of Greta's bed. I've been here for an hour already, whereas Leesa has just arrived, having spent all night and all morning with Maeve. Bella is at home with Jon, so I'm free to stay here as long as they need me.

Venetia is somewhere here too, in the same hospital, and much as she terrifies me, I'm relieved I didn't kill her. I don't know if I could handle that on top of everything else.

Maeve, thank goodness, is going to be fine. Concussion and a broken leg, but nothing more serious. Not that that's any small thing, but compared to what might have happened . . . Leesa is pale, her eyes red-rimmed and dark-circled, but she's managing a watery smile for Greta.

'Samir is with Maeve, and she's chatting away now, back to herself, so I said I'd pop over to you,' she says. 'Handy you're both in the same hospital. Thanks for that.' A grin.

Greta grins back. 'I aim to please.' For all her attempts at normality, she's still deathly pale and her voice is hoarse.

They banter back and forth to avoid talking about the tough stuff: the fact that four people are dead, that three are in hospital, that two will face charges. I can't join in. I can't stop thinking about all of them, but most of all, Felipe. Felipe, who died saving Bella. Kind, good, well-meaning Felipe. Now I understand his guilt, why he felt so bad about sending my screenshot to Rory, triggering what Rory did to Aimee. But he never meant for any of it to happen – he was one small cog in a machine of actions and consequences. Aimee's death is on me more than it's on Felipe. But Felipe has paid with his life.

Leesa is standing now, saying goodbye, returning to Maeve, and once the curtain falls back into place, I tune in to Greta, who is saying something in a low voice to me.

'Sorry, what was that?'

'I didn't want to say this in front of Leesa, but I think it was Maeve who put the almonds in Nika's lunch.'

'Oh my god, stop. She wouldn't.'

'I know, but I saw something on her laptop about spiking food . . . I didn't think it was serious – obviously, I'd have said something if I did. But then, the next day, Juliette Sullivan was dropping off her daughter's gum shield and told me she thought she'd seen Maeve go into the changing room, and I got a bit worried.' Greta bites her lip.

'Wait, Juliette was accusing Maeve?'

'No, not at all – it was just an opportunity for Juliette to get a little dig in, having a go at Maeve for wearing a hoodie and woolly hat in the warm weather. She did that little laugh she does to show she's just joking, you know?'

'Oh, I *know*.'

'But it stopped me cold,' Greta continues. 'Maeve, as we're

both well aware, does not play hockey and had no reason to be in the changing room.'

'Oh shit.'

'Yeah. So that's why I checked the bag and the lunchbox.'

'And then you got caught and couldn't admit you were afraid Maeve had done it.'

'Exactly.'

'Even though it meant taking the blame yourself and losing business?'

A hapless shrug. 'We're family. She's a kid. Kids do stupid things.'

I think about Bella at home with Jon. What would I do if she did something stupid? Anything, I realize. I'd take the blame, go to prison, whatever it took. I think of Celeste now, and what she faces with Nika, and for the first time since all this happened, I feel for her. We're all trying our best, and none of us can predict how this parenting roller coaster will go. When Celeste first looked at baby Nika in her arms, there's no way she could have known it would come to this. God, there's no way for any of us to know what our kids will do, what will be done to them.

I clear my throat. 'Speaking of stupid things . . . I can't believe I got us into a situation like this. I can't believe I injected you with heroin.' My voice breaks. 'Greta, I'm so, so sorry.'

She holds up a hand. 'Stop! I insist you do exactly the same thing if a crazed psycho ever comes after us again. I'm bullet-proof on naltrexone.'

'Did you know the tablets would stop the heroin from, you know . . .'

'Killing me?'

'Yeah . . .'

A headshake. 'Not really, but I do know it's given as an

antidote for overdoses and that it reduces the effects of opi-oids.' She crosses her fingers on both hands and holds them up. 'So I hoped. When you injected it, I reacted like I'd seen people do on TV. Who knows if it's real or not, but you'd assume if we see it that way onscreen often enough, it must be reasonably realistic?' A smile.

'I thought you were dead.' A sob escapes now.

She reaches across the bed cover and squeezes my hand.

'I know. I'm sorry. But I had to make sure she believed it. And it did have a huge effect – I was fairly out of it. I knew the daily dose I take would have some antidote impact, but maybe not enough, and I was terrified I wouldn't be able to get the box out of my bag.'

I wince at the thought of this, the terror she must have felt.

Another squeeze. 'Susan, go easy on yourself. What hap-pened is horrific, but you didn't intend any of it.'

And that's the thing. None of us intended any of it. Is that enough, though, for absolution? I'm not sure I'll ever be able to say.

108

Susan
Sunday

I'm still at the hospital, but with Maeve now, keeping her company while Leesa and Samir get something to eat. Her face changes as soon as her parents leave, and she grabs my hand.

'Susan.' She says my name in an urgent whisper. 'They're saying Nika drove at me because she thinks I spiked her lunch with nuts. That I tried to kill her.' Her eyes tear up. 'I hate her, but I'd never do that, no way. She was my best friend once. Like, I'd never do that to anyone, even my worst enemy.' A sad smile. 'Which she also is, of course. But I'm really scared Greta did it.'

'What do you mean?' I'm stalling now, trying to work out what to say.

'She saw my laptop.' She reddens. 'I was googling, stupid stuff. I'd never have done it. But I'm scared it gave her the idea . . .'

'She didn't.' Relief floods through me. I know it wasn't Greta, and now I know it wasn't Maeve. 'I swear to you, she didn't. We've talked about it. It might have been a kid in the class . . . I heard some guy posted on Snapchat about putting nuts in someone's lunch.'

Maeve lets out a breath. 'Are you sure it wasn't Greta?'

I reach and gently push her hair out of her eyes. 'Maeve, I'm certain. I've known Greta all my life, and you couldn't find a better person. She wouldn't hurt a fly.'

Her eyes bloom with tears. 'OK. OK. I feel better.' She smiles and gulps a sob. 'Please promise me you'll never tell her I thought that about her?'

'I promise.'

One more secret, but one worth keeping.

Maeve falls asleep and I slip outside to call Jon and check in on Bella. A figure by the corridor entrance catches my attention. Celeste. Tall, imposing as ever, her red hair gleaming in the evening sunlight. But on closer inspection, her structured navy dress looks crinkled and there are purple shadows visible under her eyes, despite carefully applied concealer. My mind goes back to our phone conversation last week. Her anger, my embarrassment, her request for a public apology. Our eyes meet, just briefly, then she looks down. I take a step towards her.

She clears her throat and looks up again. There's nothing imposing about her, I see now. She looks . . . broken.

'Is . . . is Maeve doing . . . Is she OK?' It all spins across her face – horror, sadness, regret, resignation.

'She's fine. A broken leg, but she's doing OK.'

Her shoulders sag. A sob shudders out. 'Oh, thank god.'

I take another step towards her. 'Is Nika OK?'

Her face crumples as she shakes her head.

'I'm so sorry. Susan, I'm so, so sorry for what she did.'

On impulse and to my surprise, I find myself holding out my arms to her, pulling her into a hug.

Another sob escapes Celeste's throat and now I'm crying too. For all of us. For the children, trying to fit in, trying to navigate, trying to survive. For the adults, trying our best.

Celeste pulls away, her face streaked with tears.

'And Bella? Is Bella OK?'

'Bella's perfect. She's safe at home with Jon.'

Bella *is* perfect, despite what she's been through. Jon and me, though, our marriage – I guess that's over. We both know; we just haven't said it. Whatever thoughts I had of not confronting it, it's clear now that there's no coming back from his affair. There's an irony there somewhere, and it strikes me as I stand here hugging Celeste in the hospital corridor. He'll finally be free to see his mistress – only his mistress, of course, is dead. And still, nobody knows who killed her.

109

Savannah
Last week

SAVANNAH LOOKED DOWN AT her phone, then up at the front door as the bell rang a second time. Who on earth was calling now? Someone else ready to attack her for no good reason? Once bitten, twice shy: she wasn't going to open the door so easily again. She moved quietly further into the hall and craned her neck, but she couldn't see much now that she'd closed the blind on the hall window, leaving only a slice of daylight down near the floor. Silently, she slipped upstairs to look down from her bedroom window.

A man this time, someone she'd never seen before, though it was hard to tell from up high. Then she noticed he was carrying a Brown Thomas bag. Had she ordered anything from Brown Thomas? She didn't think so, but she didn't always keep track of what she ordered online, especially after a few glasses of wine. The sequinned leggings she'd bought during the first lockdown Christmas sprang to mind. A little fizz of excitement bubbled up now – the same fizz she always felt when packages arrived. Even – it turns out – on days when she's been slapped by strangers and discovered her boyfriend is married.

As she dropped the blind, the rose-gold bangle clinked against her watch and, on autopilot, she pushed it up her forearm. Then caught herself. What was she doing? That meaningless inscription. The effort she'd gone to, replacing it when she'd lost it. Getting the same words inscribed, so Jon would never know. And what did he care? She wasn't the love of his life; she was the bit on the side. As she passed the bathroom to go downstairs, she flung the bangle into the bin. Time to move on.

She skipped back down the stairs, happier now with the dopamine hit an impending delivery always brought. At the bottom of the stairs, she stepped towards the front door, not noticing the puddle of rum still on the floor since last night. Her silver ballet pumps – new, not yet broken in, smooth and slippy – slid out from under her, and she landed flat on her back, her head cracking against the corner of the radiator on the way down.

Outside, the man waited, then rang the doorbell a third time. Still no answer. He checked his phone, clicking into the Adverts app. That's when he realized his mistake. The person taking his bag of old CDs was at 36 Oakpark, not 26. He was at the wrong house. He turned and walked away.

110

Greta

THAT STORY – SAVANNAH SLIPPING – is entirely fictitious. The
kind of thing anyone might imagine upon reading in the newspaper about the inquest findings. Only one person in the world
knows what really happened that morning, and that's Greta
O'Donnell.

Greta reads through the inquest findings a second time,
folds the newspaper and nods to herself. The dash downstairs
to answer the door, the slip on the puddle of rum, the new
ballet flats. All perfectly valid assumptions, really. Accidental
death. No foul play after all.

But that's not how it happened.

As soon as she walked into Savannah's house that Wednesday morning, after Jon's ludicrous phone call pretending she
was Susan, Greta knew for sure who Savannah was. She had
looked Savannah up on Instagram that morning in Susan's kitchen, when Susan first told her about the mixed-up packages
and her 'alter ego', Savannah Holmes. The name rang a not-
too-distant bell. Yes, it's South Dublin, with its fair share of
Nikas and Arianas among the teens and kids, but not so many
Savannahs among the adults. Back when she crossed Greta's

path (literally, as it happened), she was Savannah Byrne, married to Albie Byrne. A footnote in the story of the car accident that gave Greta her limp and ended her hockey career. The passenger who escaped uninjured while her husband broke his ankle and Greta ended up with six months of physio. But was Savannah a footnote? That's the part Greta wondered about, especially after she met Albie's sister, Phoebe.

Phoebe joined Greta's hiking club, and they hit it off immediately. They did that thing everyone in South Dublin does – did you grow up around here, what school did you go to, who do we know in common? And their common denominator, they soon realized, was Albie, Phoebe's brother. At first Phoebe was horrified; she knew what had happened, the outcome for Greta. But Greta didn't hold any grudge against Albie, she told Phoebe. The road was icy that night, visibility poor, it wasn't his fault, and it wasn't Greta's. They chatted on, sometimes on hikes, sometimes in pubs, and then Phoebe mentioned her love of skiing and, in due course, the ski trip she'd taken with her brother and his ex-wife Savannah. The trip on which Albie broke his ankle. The trip that took place a week before Greta's accident. So how, Greta wondered later that night, at home in her house, had Albie driven the car?

Her mind whirred over the facts. Albie had a broken ankle before the accident, so must have lied about injuring it *in* the accident. Albie surely couldn't have been driving the car. Meaning Savannah was driving. Meaning they lied.

Greta had never known who was in the driver's seat: she was unconscious. So why did they lie? There were only a few reasons she could think of – no insurance, no licence, drugs, or drink. So she started to dig some more, gently questioning Phoebe. Why had Albie and Savannah divorced? What was Savannah like? And the picture became clearer. Self-absorbed, flaky, shallow and vain, according to Phoebe. That didn't really help though. Greta pushed a bit more. A bit of a drink problem, Phoebe confided one night in the pub. Not the kind that'd put you in rehab, she clarified. But Albie had told her Savannah was opening wine before he got home from work most evenings, and often drinking with lunch. He'd had a gentle word with her and she'd said she'd stop. But what if she didn't? What if she'd been drinking the night of the accident? What if he'd asked her to drive him somewhere? Would she have done so, rather than admit to Albie that she'd been drinking?

Greta reached out to Albie but got no reply. Not surprising. If he had lied to the gardaí for Savannah, he'd be in almost as much trouble as her. And now that he was a politician, well, he'd blocked Greta everywhere he could. So she let it lie for a while, trying to make peace with not knowing.

But the universe (if you believe in that kind of thing) had other ideas for Greta. Suddenly there she was in Susan's kitchen, hearing how Susan's packages went to one Savannah Holmes. Greta didn't know what Savannah looked like – they'd had no contact back when the accident happened – so the Instagram account didn't help per se, but as she scrolled, she spotted a comment from Phoebe Byrne. It had to be the same Savannah, right?

When she phoned Jon to cancel Susan's surprise party, inadvertently interrupting his showdown with his mistress, the opportunity to see Savannah in person was too good to resist. And god, Jon was so pathetically grateful. Of course Greta wanted to protect Susan, prevent her sister from finding out about the affair right in the middle of the shitshow with the Oakpark text. But a huge part of her just wanted to see for herself – was this *the* Savannah Byrne?

The clincher was the wedding photo. Sitting proudly on Savannah's kitchen shelf, because she was too vain to take it down. There was Albie, on Savannah's arm. And then there was Savannah, right in front of Greta. The woman who drove drunk and gave Greta her limp? She still wasn't sure.

Greta slapped her, but that was truly for her 'not my baby, not my problem' retort. She left, seething, and sat in her car, around the corner from Savannah's house. White knuckles wrapped around the steering wheel, thinking. She was *this* close. She needed to know. She really needed to know.

Greta watched as a courier van drove slowly by. Another package for Savannah, perhaps, living her happy life in her lovely house with her very nice things and other people's husbands.

Greta just needed to know.

So she walked back around to the house, up the driveway, and rang the bell. Savannah opened the door, a furious look on her face.

'What the fuck do you want now? If you don't leave me alone, I'm calling the police.' She put a hand to her cheek. 'If people hear you slapped me, it won't look good for your hockey camp, will it, especially with all the trouble you're already in. I googled.' A smirk.

'I don't care about that. There's something else I need to know. That's you and your ex-husband in the photo in the kitchen, isn't it – the wedding photo?'

A frown. 'Yeah, so? We're divorced now.' A shrug.

'Albie Byrne, right?'

'Yes, why?' She was curious, Greta reckoned, to see what this was about. Looking for gossip, almost.

'You were driving that night, weren't you? The accident? When Albie supposedly broke his ankle? Only I know for certain he injured it skiing a week earlier and couldn't have been driving.'

Savannah's face was a picture. How they'd gone from Jon

and Susan to this left her scrambling to catch up. But she recovered quickly.

'What are you . . . why are you asking me this?'

'What was it – drink? You'd had a couple of glasses of wine and didn't want to admit it to Albie?' Greta nodded towards the bottle of Captain Morgan's at the end of the stairs. 'Maybe a morning rum and Coke?'

Her cheeks coloured. 'That bottle is there since last night.'

'Whatever. But I'm right, aren't I – you were drinking that night, and you were driving, and Albie covered for you? I have proof that he hurt his ankle on the ski trip, and I'm going to the guards with it.' Greta didn't have proof, only Phoebe's recollection, and Albie wasn't likely to admit anything now, but it was worth a shot.

'I don't know or care where you got your information or why it's any of your business, but it's a moot point. There's a statute of limitations on personal injury claims and drink driving accidents so' – she threw Greta an in-your-face smile – 'there's nothing anyone can do.'

'It was me in that car, I was the other driver. I have a life-long injury as a result.'

Savannah pursed her lips, taken aback again but trying to hide it.

'Well,' she said finally, 'after the way you came into my house this morning, lying about who you were, helping Jon with his charade, and then *slapping* me in my own hallway, I'm delighted you have your life-long injury. Couldn't have happened to a nicer person.'

It was the sanctimonious tone that got Greta. It's not an excuse, she knows that, but it just got under her skin. Savannah was so delighted with herself, so glad to have got away with it, and no ounce of empathy for Greta, no regret for what she'd caused. Rage surged up inside Greta and, without thinking, she stepped forward and pushed her. There's no sugarcoating it – she pushed her hard. Savannah stumbled backwards, hit her head on the radiator, and that was that.

Greta checked, but she knew even before she went near that Savannah was dead.

Practical, pragmatic Greta kicked in then. The serious sister. The solver of problems. The eldest. The protector. Only this time, she was protecting herself. And honestly, she thinks often, if Savannah hadn't been dead, she'd have called an ambulance. She's not a psychopath. But she *was* dead. And Greta wasn't prepared to go to prison for Savannah Holmes.

Savannah's phone had fallen when she fell, and Greta eyed it, thinking. Nobody knew she was there. Well, nobody except Jon. And Greta really didn't need Jon believing she had something to do with Savannah's death. Even if he didn't go to the guards, he'd fall to pieces and get Greta caught one way or another. As long as Jon believed Savannah was alive when Greta left, and that someone else was in the frame for her death, Greta would be OK.

She thought for a moment, choosing her words carefully, then texted Jon from her own phone.

I've left, on way to your office, are you there?

The reply comes quickly.

Yes, in office, all OK?

OK, good. Greta nodded to herself. If Jon was already in his office, he wouldn't be in the frame for Savannah's death. Not that he deserved protecting, but Susan did.

And if Jon was to get a text from Savannah right now, at a time he was in his office, that would nudge things a little closer to airtight.

She picked up Savannah's phone, covering her fingers with

her T-shirt. Jon was saved in Savannah's phone as 'Jon♥' and the thread of WhatsApps was predictable: arrangements to meet up, late-night chats, declarations of almost-love. Nothing with any mention of Jon's work, none that even mentioned his name. Then two texts from last night:

I know about your wife. I'm outside your house. Unless you want me to come in and announce myself, I suggest you come out to see me.

I swear to god, come out now or I'm coming in, you PRICK.

Greta thought for a moment, glanced over at the photo of Savannah and Albie, then typed one final message from Savannah to Jon:

I've had it up to here with ALL of you. My ex-husband is being a PRICK, turning up at my house because I'm with someone new, then I find out you're MARRIED. Then you leave me with that bitch in my own home, jesus christ you have literally driven me to drink. She's gone btw and if she ever comes back or you ever come back, I'm calling the police. I'm deleting your number. DO NOT EVER CONTACT ME AGAIN, YOU PRICK.

No doubt Albie was somewhere suitably public and politician-y and wouldn't actually be in the frame for murder, but the idea that he might be questioned or suspected of harassment at least gave her quiet joy. And, more importantly, it would misdirect Jon. She absolutely couldn't have Jon thinking she'd done this.

She went back to contacts, poised to delete Jon's name, along with the entire thread of messages. But the guards would find them, she was pretty sure. Nothing is ever really deleted. And that would create huge suspicion – if someone deleted a contact and messages. That suggested murder. She thought for a another second, then quickly changed how Jon was saved in Savannah's contacts from 'Jon♥' to 'Sam♥'.

She checked Instagram, but they hadn't DM'd there. Jon

rarely used it. If they'd been messaging anywhere else, there was no quick way to find out, but she suspected it was just WhatsApp.

Then, with her sleeve over her hand, she spilled more rum on the floor. They might question Albie, they might look for 'Sam', but ultimately, she hoped, it would appear to be an accident.

Jon confirmed they'd only ever used WhatsApp and only ever on his pay-as-you-go phone when Greta went into his office to update him in person. She told him she'd calmed Savannah down. That she had ended up feeling sorry for Savannah – she hadn't known he was married, after all, and on top of everything, her ex-husband had been harassing her. Greta didn't say who her ex-husband was, of course, not then. In the fictional version of events, Greta didn't know at that point that Savannah had ever been married to Albie Byrne.

And then Jon showed Greta Savannah's final text. The one that had arrived just after the message from Greta to say she was on her way to his office. That sealed the deal. The end of the affair.

When Savannah's death was reported on Wednesday evening's news, Jon was genuinely horrified – he had really liked her, it turned out. And obviously, Greta acknowledges, it's shocking when anyone you know dies, break-ups and fights notwithstanding. Jon heard it on the radio on his way home from work and arrived distraught. Greta was in their house minding Bella when he came in – Susan and Leesa had gone to the garda station to report their concern that Savannah's murder was a case of mistaken identity. Greta and Jon sat together, wringing their hands, trying to make sense of it. Could it have been her ex-husband, Jon wondered? Indeed, it may have been, Greta agreed. And they decided Jon would make an anonymous call to the guards about it. No need for anyone to know either Jon or Greta was there the morning she died, or that Jon was sleeping with her. Her ex, whoever he was, would be questioned, and all would be right in the world. And luckily, Jon pointed out, Savannah had said she was deleting his number. Indeed, Greta said.

What about fingerprints and DNA, Jon wondered, looking worried again.

Greta had cleaned her prints from the doorbell, the inside latch of the front door and the back of the kitchen chair. She hadn't touched anything else, as far as she remembered, though she didn't mention this to Jon. Jon had, of course, touched many things many times, but the gardaí wouldn't have his fingerprints or DNA in their database, she reassured him.

And they'd be looking for a boyfriend called 'Sam', though she didn't tell him that. She needed a boyfriend in the frame to misdirect gardaí, and she needed them to see that final text. Just not a boyfriend called Jon.

'Thank god you left when you did,' he said as Greta was leaving, 'or you might have been hurt too.' He didn't for a second think she'd done it. She's just not that kind of person. His practical and no-nonsense sister-in-law, yes; a murderer, no.

Greta's one big worry was the Albie Byrne connection. She knew it would come out in the media that he was Savannah's ex, and she knew that Susan might wonder about that . . . So she got ahead of it. She set a Google Alert for Albie Byrne's name and as soon as it popped up, on the Saturday after the murders, she 'happened across' the article in front of Susan. She sat in Susan and Jon's kitchen, shocked and dazed to discover that the man involved in her accident had once been married to murder victim Savannah Holmes.

Of course, Savannah's not really a murder victim when you think about it, more of an accident victim – a lot like Greta herself.

111

Susan
One year later

JULY ROLLS AROUND AGAIN, and it's the week of the Oakpark summer party. Celeste isn't going, she tells me over a glass of wine in Conways. She'll be collecting Nika from Clonakilty, leaving very early Friday morning. Nika's been staying with Celeste's cousin in West Cork since last September and completed sixth year in a small school hundreds of miles away from Rathwood Park, while awaiting her next court appearance. The judge had adjourned her case after receiving her probation report, to see how she behaves. According to Celeste, he'd said he was taking the charge very seriously and considering a custodial sentence, but their barrister had told them that in light of Nika's age, her guilty plea, the fact that it was her first offence, the compensation the Gearys paid, and Nika's remorse, there was a good chance she'd avoid detention. Nika's changed, Celeste says, and I listen and nod encouragingly as she says it, though I'm not entirely convinced anyone can change that much. The jury's out, no pun intended.

Cody's changed too, Celeste says. Less sullen, less time in his room. He and Celeste watch *Stranger Things* together – his fourth time, her first, so that's what she'll do tomorrow night instead of going to the party.

I'm not so sure Cody's the one who's changed; I think maybe he was always in there. A little lost, a little different, struggling to navigate, lacking attention. He hasn't changed so much as emerged and become himself. Celeste is the one who's different; softer at the edges now that she's no longer trying to keep up a pretence of perfection. Broken but somehow fixed.

'Anyway, Warren might go to the summer party with his new girlfriend,' Celeste says, raising her glass to clink against mine. 'So *there's* a good reason to stay home.'

'I'm so sorry, Celeste, if I hadn't sent—'

She cuts me off with a raised index finger.

'It's one small silver lining in all this, Susan. We should have broken up long before. Life is better now, without the pretence.'

One *tiny* silver lining. The rest . . . Well, I'm still struggling to get past what happened – the repercussions of my message. A minor slip with terrible consequences, my sisters tell me over and over; you couldn't have known, you have to forgive yourself and move on. Easier said than done.

Warren and Celeste aren't the only ones to split – Jon and I have separated too. We keep things amicable, and Bella is thriving with two besotted parents in two happy homes. Jon buys a house in Blackrock and, to my surprise, I decide to stay in 26 Oakpark. People, it turns out, have short memories. There are new open-the-popcorn moments in the Oakpark WhatsApp group, and people get on with real life too. Nobody, I finally realize, is judging me. Nobody except me.

I'm still seeing my counsellor, trying to come to terms with what my message did. Felipe's death has hit me hardest. On TV, the bad people get comeuppance; the innocent are saved. But in real life, sometimes the good guys die too.

'You are not the only one who made a mistake in all this,' my therapist reminds me. 'Jon had an affair. Warren and Venetia cheated on their spouses. Felipe sent the screenshot to Rory. And ultimately, Rory killed Aimee – he's the only person who can be held responsible for her murder. Guilt can eat you up – it's time to forgive yourself.'

It's true that guilt can eat you up, but sometimes, you have to let it take those bites. And we all feel bad about something – Leesa berates herself for making Maeve babysit that night, no matter how often I remind her it was Nika behind the wheel. Jon hates that he took a sledgehammer to our marriage the day he asked Savannah out. Celeste will never stop blaming herself for all those red flags she missed. Warren – well, I don't know – maybe he just feels bad that he got caught.

The only person not mired in self-flagellation is Greta, but that's very her. Resilient, self-assured, not an ounce of neurosis. Also, I remind myself, thinking of Nika and the brownies, the needle in my kitchen, the car accident – Greta is the one person in the story who spent all her time trying to help other people and didn't do anything wrong.

We still don't know who put the ground almonds on the brownie, though this is one topic Celeste and I don't cover during our glass of wine in Conways. I'm certain neither Maeve nor Greta did it, and I'm sure Celeste thinks one of them did, but there's nothing to be gained by raking over it now. Instead, we finish our wine and stroll back to Oakpark, enjoying the warm July evening. At the entrance to my driveway, we stand for another minute talking, and on a whim, I invite Celeste in for one more glass of wine. She smiles a yes, and in the glow of the streetlight, her eyes seem to glisten.

Aoife's in the sitting room, watching *Outer Banks*, and she pauses it when I peek in the door.

'All OK with Bella?' I whisper.

'Yep, fast asleep. I went up to check on her a few minutes ago.'

'Thanks, Aoife.' For better or for worse, I got rid of the video monitor.

'I'll message Mum to pick me up,' she says, standing and pulling on a purple beanie, though it's a balmy summer night.

'Nice hat,' I say, with a grin.

'Stop teasing,' she grins back. 'And don't tell Maeve. She goes mad that I keep taking it without asking.'

'I'm not teasing! It's lovely and bright – it stands out.' I step into the sitting room, and Celeste follows me. 'Nice to see a bit of colour in a world of neutrals.'

Aoife's eyes flick to Celeste and, for a moment, she looks stunned. Her grin disappears. She yanks off the hat.

'It's a bit much, too bright.' She stuffs it in her bag. Again her eyes go to Celeste, and her expression's unreadable. Maybe this is the first time she's seen her, since what happened to Maeve.

'Right,' I say. 'I'll grab a bottle from the fridge.'

'How is Maeve?' Celeste asks Aoife as I walk through to the kitchen.

I don't hear Aoife's answer, but Maeve is great, by all accounts. School is easier without Nika, though I don't say that to Celeste. A bit like the brownies, some things are better left unsaid.

Leesa collects Aoife and, after a glass of rosé, Celeste leaves too, keen to get home to see Cody. Bella wakes when I check on her, and I bring her downstairs to let her sleep in my arms while I finish the last of my wine and read a few pages of my book. I'm distracted though, thinking over the evening with Celeste and all that's happened. I won't go to the summer party either, I decide. Not because I'm embarrassed any more – it just doesn't feel right, after what happened last year. But that's OK. I'll hang out at home with Bella, and Greta and Leesa might call in.

Someone else who hasn't forgotten what happened last year is Juliette Sullivan . . . I'm just finishing my wine, contemplating transferring Bella upstairs to her cot, when the message arrives in the Oakpark WhatsApp group.

Final reminder, the annual Oakpark Summer Party takes place tomorrow night at 8 sharp on the big green. Let's have a big turn-out, please, and here's hoping it will be lit by just fireworks this year, not ambulance lights;)

Livid, I take a screenshot and type a message to Greta and Leesa.

Have you seen this? How can she be so insensitive? Felipe died that night, that's why the ambulance was there. And you nearly died, Greta. She's such a

I stop. Close my eyes. Take a deep breath. Then I carefully delete the message and delete the screenshot. I put down my phone, kiss Bella's head and pick up my book.

Acknowledgements

THIS IS A BOOK about a neighbourhood WhatsApp group, part-inspired by my own neighbourhood WhatsApp group which has very few open–the–popcorn moments, but hundreds of people being kind. As I type these acknowledgements, there's a power outage in one area of where we live, and people in the group are messaging to offer gas stoves to anyone who wants to borrow one and to help if anyone needs to warm baby bottles. That probably sums up the group – kind, generous, fun, a bit like our fearless leader and group admin, Olive. Of course in fiction, it's a little boring if everyone is kind and generous and fun, therefore that's not the route I've taken in *It Should Have Been You*. So thank you to my neighbourhood WhatsApp group for the hockey stick, the uniform skirt, the number for the plumber, and the inspiration for the book.

This is also a book about sisters, and I'm lucky to have three such people in my life – Nicola, Elaine and Deirdre. They're my first readers and my best friends. (This book is not about them, but they don't believe me.) Handily, Deirdre (Dr Fitzgerald, who gets a cameo) is also very useful for the medical bits that come up in each book – thanks!

It takes many, many people to get a book from first draft on to shelves, and I'm lucky to have brilliant people in my corner: thank you to my amazing editors, Finn Cotton in the

ACKNOWLEDGEMENTS

UK, Jeramie Orton in the US and Bhavna Chauhan in Canada, who were so easy to work with and so patient while waiting for me to see they were right!

Thank you to all at Transworld, Penguin UK, Penguin Ireland, Penguin US, and Doubleday Canada for your support with *It Should Have Been You*: Kim Young, Bill Scott-Kerr, Tom Chicken, Deirdre O'Connell, Rhian Steer, Phoebe Llanwarne, Cara Conquest, Kristina Werner, Catherine Wood, Lucy Beresford-Knox, Becky Short, Jennifer Porter, Vivien Thompson, Sarah Day, Rachel Cross, Sophie Dwyer, Kate Gunn, Leonor Araujo, Brian Tart, Andrea Schulz, Patrick Nolan, Kate Stark, Natalie Grant, Tricia Conley, Tess Espinoza, Nick Michal, Diandra Alvarado, Nicole Celli, Jason Ramirez, Julianna Lee, Claire Vaccaro, Mary Stone, Rebecca Marsh, Andy Dudley, Rachel Obenschain, and the rest of the PRH US sales team, also, Amy Black, Val Gow, Kaitlin Smith, Chalista Andadari, Megan Kwan, Keara Campos and Taylor Rice.

Special thanks to Richard Shailer for the cover design on *It Should Have Been You* and its predecessors – you know you're doing something right when you inadvertently start a new cover trend!

Special thanks too to Jessica Regan, audiobook narrator and all round amazing person, who I got to meet not just once but twice this year.

Thank you to my superstar literary agent, Diana Beaumont – you have changed my life, and thank you to my TV and film agent, Leah Middleton – it has been a wow factor year!

Thank you too to John S and Anne Marie W for the garda information and huge thanks to Cathy C for taking the time to meet me and talk through questions about DNA and crime scenes. Thank you solicitor, crime writer and all round brilliant person Catherine Kirwan (and Catherine's friend) for the legal

ACKNOWLEDGEMENTS

information. Thank you Abina, for the real-life baby monitor story, long ago!

On the personal side, thanks to all the people who are willing to have nights out with me to distract me from edits – Dad, Eithne, my Sion Hill girls, Eithne McGrath, my hp gang, my salon gang, and the brilliant Irish writing community.

Thank you to the wonderful readers and reviewers on Instagram for your incredible support, especially Sinéad Cuddihy and everyone in the Tired Mammy Book Club. Thank you too to the members of BookPunk for all your kindness.

Lots and lots of love as always to Damien, Elissa, Nia, Matthew, and, of course, Lola.

And thank you, dear reader, for reading this book.

Andrea Mara is a No.1 *Sunday Times, Irish Times* and Kindle best-selling author. Her books have sold more than 500,000 copies worldwide, and five of them have been shortlisted for Irish Crime Novel of the Year. *No One Saw a Thing* was a Richard and Judy Bookclub Pick, sold more than 100,000 copies in thirteen weeks, and was No.1 in the UK, Irish and Kindle charts. She lives in Dublin, Ireland, with her husband and three children. You can find Andrea on Instagram @andreamaraauthor or on her website AndreaMara.ie